JUMPING OFF PLACES

JUMPING OFF PLACES

LAURA STRATTON FRIEL

12/04

Cheryl ~
* Please enjoy Nell. If she*
does anything amiss, blame
her, not me.
*   Best wishes, Laura S Friel*

COUNCIL·PRESS™
Springville, Utah

ISBN: 1-55517-832-4
e.2

Published by Council Press
Imprint of Cedar Fort Inc.
www.cedarfort.com

Distributed by:

Typeset by Nicole Williams
Cover design by Nicole Williams
Cover design © 2004 by Lyle Mortimer

Printed in the United States of America

10 9 8 7 6 5 4 3 2 1

Printed on acid-free paper

Library of Congress Number: 2004114873

DEDICATION

To Don Friel, the love of my life.
You believed in me.

TABLE OF CONTENTS

PROLOGUE

Over the years, I occasionally drove by an old pioneer home at the side of a country road in Utah. Never mind where, exactly. Like a crumbling skeleton, it had lost its roof, and nothing but the broken sandstone walls remained. Around the picturesque relic, the trunks of a few dead cottonwood trees leaned against one another, and an old mottled mule barely sustained itself on a large, red-dirt acreage. Each time I passed by, I had the urge to investigate inside what had once been someone's home, but I never took the time.

Then, one day everything changed. The mule was gone, the wire gate lay on the ground, leaving the pasture open, and a cottonwood trunk had collapsed over one of the structure's fragile walls. This time, I stopped. Inside the old ruin, I stood on what once had been a floor with all sorts of barely recognizable debris lying about—a crushed, rusty piece of metal, which wasn't a wash tub anymore, a pile of worm-eaten boards that may have been a table, and a piece of rotten wood, which a hundred years ago, had rocked a chair. Who had lived here? Perhaps, a woman, much like me, one who cooked, rocked children, washed clothing, and cleaned this tiny space. I stood silently in respect for a life that was no more.

I wondered—would a woman one day, enter the broken remains of my home?

Leaving by way of the crumbled wall, something within the debris and fallen stones caught my eye. A tin box! Inside it, I discovered a parched, little book with "Diary" written across the front. Opening it, I barely made out the name: "Nelly Baker Mortenson." On the brittle pages that followed were the entries, the words—all of the words—left to represent a breathing, struggling, loving, dreaming, flesh and blood human being.

"Write me," they begged. "Give me life." Once I had removed the ancient manuscript from the wall, once I carried it away with me, there was nothing else to do *but* to write.

The words entered my mind where they incubated and hatched. I fed and nurtured them. I gave them a pen to scratch in for the day and a roosting place for the night. As nature is prone to do, the words matured and laid other words; they produced and reproduced until thousands upon thousands of black scribbles clucked about on my white pages. They kept coming until I had enough. Then, my conscience urging me to do so, I carried the diary back to the beautiful structure. I dropped it down into one of the standing walls where other warm hands had hidden it. For what purpose, I'll never know. It's not for me to say.

To the best of my ability, here is Nell's story.

PROPOSAL DAY

(Diary)   *May 30, 1844*

Is my fate sealed? Like dear Mama, shall I spend my life working cotton all the way from bale to blouse? Spinning it, dying it, weaving it, cutting it, and stitching it . . . I ask myself, can a woman seek adventure and still make her life a success?

Today, Arthur and I were to be engaged. I could not do it.

Father invited Tom Mortenson to Sunday dinner. He is a gentleman of many qualities.

It was the dawn of a bright new day. Tossing on her pillow and tired from a fitful night, Nell Baker heard a commotion outside. Curious, she stumbled to her second-story window and opened it. Below, the clang and clatter of a rickety wagon startled her awakening senses. In the dim light she made out three young men. One held the reins of an unmatched team, a snorting work plug and a braying old mule, while another scrambled nearby to recover a cage full of squawking chickens which had tumbled off a poorly stacked load, and still another, his legs spread apart, peed against the trunk of a tree. Lightheartedly, they called out to one another.

Nell loved their reckless abandonment. Leaning out the window, she yelled, "Where are you going?"

"Oregon Territory!" bellowed the one who had finished his business at the tree. "Jump down. Come along!" The scoundrel adjusted his trousers. Then, he blew her a kiss.

Playfully, Nell reached out, caught it and placed it at her neck. "Can't," she hollered down to him.

"Won't," he bellowed back. He sprinted after the wagon, holding his misshapen straw hat.

"I'd love to go," said Nell to herself. But, jumping off at this fearful height would be unreasonable. If she left, it would be by way of her own room with all her lovely possessions, past her family, out the front door of her childhood home, and down the streets of Quincy, the only city she had ever known. That would take some doing! Wondering what it was that allowed the young fellows to take a leap of faith into the unknown, to abandon home and security, Nell watched them bump and rumble toward a ferry, which docked on the eastern bank of the Mississippi River. It teamed with excitement.

Everybody in the world seemed to be going somewhere. They paddled canoes, drove timber, fired the engines of riverboats and moved cargo. A few floated leisurely downstream while fishing from tiny tented rafts. In the distance, on the west side of the Mississippi, the sunlight raced across a vast expanse, beckoning anyone who dared to follow it into a new world of possibilities. Out there, somewhere, was, she did not dare to think it, …adventure and freedom. By the thousands, men rushed across the river and over the vast continent to claim the new land that waited for the work of their hands. How she envied them!

Nell closed the window. Suddenly struck with the realization that this was her proposal day, she moaned. The clock in the hall struck seven. Though it was the family custom to rise at eight on a Sunday morning, Nell heard Ruby stir in the attic room above hers. She listened for the slave's light, unobtrusive movements. She waited to hear the strange, mournful tune that Ruby hummed every morning while dressing, and she could almost smell the luscious ham, biscuits and strawberry preserves, which had drifted into her room only yesterday. Ruby's feet crashed down onto the floorboards. First one, then the other, they stomped into their heavy shoes. Then, as if the house were on fire, they clonked across Nell's ceiling when the black woman rushed about to dress. They rumbled down every stair and stumbled over the poker at the hearth, where Ruby noisily struck the flint. Mama called out, "Everybody up! It's Nell's day of proposal."

Why the fuss? Wasn't it all part of the plan? For years now, hadn't she and Arthur told everyone in Quincy, Illinois, that they would marry in June of 1844. Everyone. Ten years ago, when Arthur's family moved next door, she had made the childish mistake of asking him to marry her, all because he pushed her in a swing! Then, he could be as playful and carefree as any child, springing out from a giant pile of autumn leaves to frighten her or pulling shoal fish from the Mississippi while straining at his pole as if he had caught a whale; but, now he had become so starched that if he were a shirt he would stand alone. Since she had reached her nineteenth birthday, the time of accepting was long overdue. Their parents had discussed their "eventual union" for three years now, and Arthur, who worked in her father's bank, saved every penny he had earned to begin the foundation for their home. He "could now afford to keep her in her accustomed manner." "Financially, the time has come," he agreed with Nell's father. So, today Arthur would not ask her *if*, but *when*, they would marry.

Nell scowled at Arthur's likeness on her dressing table. Though he was well-featured and in his prime, having recently celebrated his twenty-third birthday, he acted and groomed himself as if he were of her father's generation. His thin lips pinched together under a mustache, which mirrored her father's; his eyes gazed out from the paper like two flat, cool nickels, and the hair on his head lay rigidly in its proper place. Nell leveled the picture to fling her hair-curling rags onto it.

Like always, Ruby clonked upstairs to open Nell's door and to say, "Wake up, Mary sunshine." But, this time it was, "When yo' married, yo' best don't drop no rags on dat picture, Honey. Yo' need beatin', that's what yo' needs."

"Oh, Ruby, I can't abide the thought of sitting in church this morning. Look outside." She flew to her window. "Let's smell the blossoms on my cherry tree. It's the warmest day yet. Couldn't you just tell them I'm sick? Then, when they're off for church, we can drive down to the river for a picnic." Ruby adored picnics. "Please, Ruby. I'll read *Frankenstein* to you all afternoon." Nell crossed her heart. Mama had forbidden her to read the sinful novel, but Nell, while reading parts of it to Ruby, had gone through Mary Shelly's book three times already.

"Honey, I done tol' yo' a hundred time, I can' lie for yo', 'specially on de Lord's day."

"Oh, crumb, Lord's day's the same as any other. I hate church."

"How you talk! Don' let yo' daddy hear, now," Ruby snapped while closing the door behind her. Again, she opened it. "Proposal day's what got yo'," she whispered. "Quick, now, Arthur goin' be here early, an dat boy don' like waiten."

A half hour later, Nell had pinned her thick golden tresses into a curly ball on top of her head, a bit high for the convention of the day. Her arms ached, but the mirror reflected elegance beyond her years, she thought. She slipped into her new frock of a blue calico fabric, which Mama had commissioned a Mormon seamstress to sew, especially fashioned from a picture in a French magazine for this day. "Something youthful, but for a grown woman," her mama told the seamstress. Mama didn't protest, too much, when Nell suggested a lower neckline, but she refused to permit it until her daughter agreed to wear a large, white bow at the bosom and to take it off only after a secure marriage. All the way from England to Quincy, a lace parasol arrived, with gloves to match. Then, from a bolt of white cotton, all the women in the family stitched a petticoat with such a yardage of graduated ruffles that it took Mama a week to crochet a trim around the bottom. After they stiffened it with sugar, it rustled with every step. When Nell tried on the dress and petticoat for the first time, Christina giggled the whole afternoon. Nell finally pulled her naughty sister's hair when she asked, "Are you going to have babies?"

Her toilette complete, Nell rushed to the parlor for breakfast. As Ruby had warned, Arthur drove up the circular drive in his carriage, before expected, and knocked at the door. Greeting him, Nell chewed her last bite of ham. He paced and glanced at his pocket watch while she scrubbed her teeth and adjusted her new, straw hat.

Once in the carriage, Nell smiled sweetly at Arthur. This, being their special day, she hoped he might admire her outfit or say, like Mama and Ruby had, that her new dress intensified the blue of her eyes. Instead, he fixed his gaze on the road, and when he turned the corner onto Franklin Street, he said what he said every Sunday when he turned the corner onto Franklin Street. "When are you going to marry me, Miss Nellie Baker?"

"Soon," she answered, like always.

"Well, your father and I have decided it's time." He glanced at his watch.

Not now, she thought. Not in the morning while in the dither. She had hoped he would ask when they rocked in the moonlight on the porch swing after supper. The spring air would chill her, then, and he would have to protect her like Major Heyward protected little Alice whose cheeks "flushed more bright and delicate than the western sky" in *The Last of the Mohicans.*

"He wants a grandson and I, myself, am ready for a son."

Nell met his glance with a frown. Men never talked of having daughters. How disgusting for him to speak of babies, anyway, before marriage.

"Oh, I know you've thought of teaching," he imagined he read her thoughts. "But, no respectable woman should bend so low. I'd rather you teach our own children than every runny-nosed brat along the river. At any rate, your working would humiliate your entire family, and me. A wife's place is in the home."

"Please, Arthur. Be patient. I've just begun to wear a hoop." The thought of having babies with him caused her to cringe. Why, she remembered when Arthur wouldn't push her from the front side of a swing for fear of spying upon her pantaloons, and, even now, he refused to do anything with her that he "couldn't do in church." Arthur slept in church, sometimes with his mouth open. Anyway, she dared not express her thoughts on the matter, or even validate her own feelings to herself. As with her mother, her future would be determined by a husband.

"I want to, at least, set a date, announce it tonight at supper," he said as if the thought had, only now, come to him. Customarily, he supped each Sunday at the Baker household.

"Try to understand, Arthur," she touched his shoulder, feeling panicked like the hen she and Christina cornered for today's meal. Why couldn't she set a date? She had intended to. Before, this moment seemed as natural as the sunrise. Now, her heart pounded as if she'd seen the sun rise for the first time. The words she so desperately needed to express spilled over into her mind. "I would like to have my own pupils, to teach what I have studied, at least for a year or two. Miss Griffin has asked me to apprentice with her next fall, and it's an opportunity to make my own money, to decide for myself and to be beholding to no one. I'd like the children to call me 'Miss Baker.' I've been the banker's daughter all my life, and when I marry you, I'll be the banker's wife for the rest of it."

They bumped along, and with the church in sight, Nell found the courage to blurt out, "I want to teach."

Arthur threw back his head and laughed. "If you want to be 'The Old Maid School Marm,' that's what you'll be." When she scowled at him, he patted her gloved hand. "Nell, I'll take care of you. You needn't concern yourself with business." He spoke as one would to a child. "Now, now, be realistic. You've already passed the age when a woman should marry, and when you're twenty, chances are you won't be asked again." He wanted to humiliate her, and did, terribly so. In the words he spoke, Nell recognized her destiny. Her life would mirror her mother's life. Leaning her head to the side, she watched the carriage wheel turn round and round, sometimes escaping the rut, which they followed every Sunday on their way to service, but, inevitably, sliding back into it. Arthur interrupted her reverie. "In a river town, rough characters roam the streets, my girl, and an unmarried woman is not safe. People will talk."

"Oh, let their tongues wag," Nell finally exploded. "I wouldn't give a pickle for what people think of me, Arthur. And, I don't want to discuss..."

"Do try to cooperate, Nell. Aren't you feeling well? Leave off this pretending with me. You know, as well as I do, that it's time to set a date. Why must I..."

A commotion at a hitching post on the side of the church attracted their attention. Churchgoers scurried to the scene. Even before Arthur brought his new carriage to a full stop, Nell jumped down and rushed to discover what was amiss. She pushed through the crowd to the front where she discovered Mr. Hardman's mare off her feet. Somehow, a front and a back leg had become entangled in her grazing rope. When she kicked, the rope tightened on her neck, and the more she fought for her life, the closer to death she came. Her eyes bulged, her mouth foamed, and she flailed about with such fury that no one dared go near to help her.

"What happened?" Nell asked Bobby, Mr. Hardman's young son.

"It's all my fault. Father said to tie her so she could feed," he sniffled. "I gave her too much rope, I reckon. She got all messed up in it."

"Let me knock her on the head," Mr. Hunt, the barber, yelled. "Conk her out, then, loosen the rope."

Miss Griffin, the schoolmarm, clutched Nell's arm. "Oh, tell them not to club her. Tell them. Give the poor creature time to come into her head. When she stops fighting, the rope will slacken. Then, she can free her own legs."

"She won't do that," Nell answered. Most people can't stop what they're doing, let alone a dumb animal."

"Get the owner, before you knock her," somebody yelled. "Where is he?"

"Mr. Hardman's in the building. Meeting with the preacher."

"What's he got to confess about?" someone shouted, and the whole crowd guffawed.

"There's no time to ask anybody," said Mr. Hunt, who swung a post above his head and paused, ready to bring it down. When he side-glanced at Nell, his little black eyes gleamed with lust, and a button popped from his Sunday shirt to reveal his bulbous, hairy belly. She could have sworn that saliva dribbled from the corner of his mouth.

"Disgusting fellow," Nell whispered to Miss Griffin and both giggled into their handkerchiefs. This man had more than once asked her father for her hand, but Mr. Baker let him know she was promised already.

Little Bobby hid his face in his teacher's skirt. For that familiarity, that bond, Nell envied her mentor. When Arthur grasped her arm by reaching through the crowd, she jumped. Though he tugged hard, she wouldn't budge from her place in front.

"Come back here," he said. "You don't need this."

"Do something, Arthur! Please, do something! Mr. Hunt will kill her, sure." Behind closed eyelids, Nell imagined that Arthur leaped next to the horse. She imagined that he talked to it, gently, and stroked its brown neck so that it ceased kicking. With the rope in a relaxed state, Arthur untied it to set the horse free. In her reverie, everyone, including the preacher, congratulated him for his bravery. He was man of the hour. She fancied herself announcing their engagement after Sunday meeting. "I'll marry you whenever you say," she would whisper to him.

"Risk *my* life for a crow bait?" Arthur's voice interrupted her day-dream. He had moved to her side and gripped her hand so tightly with his long, bony fingers that it ached. "Let's go into the church. This will soon be over. I prefer you do not watch."

"Let go, Arthur." She ground the satin heel of her shoe into his toe. "I'm not going!" He never wanted her to see anything exciting.

The horse, breathing the raspy rattle of death, kicked weakly now. The barber again hoisted the post over his head, where it teetered at the apex. Then, suddenly, he was pushed aside. A knife flashed in the morning sun. Kneeling near the mare's neck, a stranger slipped the knife under the rope, sawed back and forth, and pulled the rope aside. With the agility of a cat, he sprang out of harm's way.

Mr. Hardman's mare quivered, her breathing becoming less and less labored. Presently, she snorted, once, and then several times more. Like a newborn colt, she struggled to stand, and, after several tries, gained her equilibrium and limped weakly away. Bobby sobbed in relief.

The young stranger grinned. White, white were his teeth. He was, however, a comical figure in his undersized suit, probably a Mormon since they were known to dress for cover, not fashion. His smooth, muscular neck had already tanned, and his light brown hair, bleached blond at the ends, hung in a misbehaved fashion on his handsome brow like that of an ancient Greek. More than anything, Nell admired his shoulders, strong and broad as if he, not an ox, had strained at a plow. For one swing of a pendulum, the stranger's eyes moved across Nell's face. To her thinking, his full lips turned upward at one corner, ever so slightly.

Arthur nervously inspected his watch. "It's 9:06. We're late." He led her off to the church like a little girl whose father rushed her along, his stride so lengthy that she took two steps to his one. "One of those peculiar Mormons from over in Nauvoo, no doubt."

"Do you know him, Arthur? Who is he?" She turned to wave at the young man, but he strode off in the opposite direction.

"I think I've seen him before, somewhere," said Arthur. "Probably, at the bank, but if you've seen one Mormon farmer, you've seen them all. Swamp dirty shoes. Did you notice?"

"Not at all," Nell answered, hoping, yet fearing, that the stranger had really noticed her.

"No Methodist would come near the church dressed like a penniless immigrant."

"No," Nell agreed, straining her eyes for a glimpse of the heroic stranger, who had set the horse free. He had disappeared.

"Foolish for him to take the chance of getting his brains kicked out."

"Yes, foolish," Nell parroted.

In church, her father sat proud and tall. His tight bottom lip curved in a contented smile as he winked at his daughter and son-in-law, soon to be. Her mama thoughtfully watched them, as if remembering her own day of proposal. Nell heard Christina giggle and felt the greatest urge to slap her; oh, what her wicked sister must be thinking! Presently, Arthur's jaw dropped. He breathed deeply as in sleep, though his eyes remained open. Nell thought he resembled Slow Joe Rosenberg, who had been kicked in the head by a mule when a boy. She nudged him and he closed his mouth, only to have it drop open again when the preacher offered a long prayer for Mr. Hardman's mare. Nell finally ignored Arthur. During the remainder of the sermon, she gazed through the windowpane at the north road leading to Nauvoo.

2

THE PROPOSAL

Nell dearly loved the five acres that Arthur had purchased for his future home site. With him, she often strolled arm in arm under a canopy of silver leaf maples, hickories, black walnuts and wild crab apples on a floor of wild bloodroot, yellow dogtooth and purple violets. In the undergrowth, they might encounter an occasional elk or deer as well as many squirrels, woodpeckers, robins, and cardinals, and at the edge of it, they could watch steamboats on the Mississippi and wave to loads of emigrants, many of them bound for Nauvoo. "One day," Arthur had promised her, "I will build us a two-story brick home with oak trim in all the rooms and a staircase to match. Our place will surpass that of your parents."

Not a word about the house, or anything else, for that matter, passed between Nell and Arthur while they traveled home from church. Usually, Arthur drove past his land to check for trespassers, but, today, he detoured onto a bumpy, cobblestone street. Jolting over the uneven stones caused the hair, which Nell had so meticulously pinned up, to fall down onto her neck. Aggravated, she kept the silence. However, when Arthur told the horse "get up" and raced past Widow Johnson's creamery, Nell wanted to scream. This was his way of punishing her for not accepting his awkward proposal.

"Arthur Reeves, stop," she said. "Look, the sign says fresh strawberries." She craved them with cream, and Arthur knew it. He also knew sermons made her hungry.

"We're not having anything today," he said, the tight skin on his milky brow shining in the sun. His indefinite-colored hair was beginning to thin in front; at this rate, he'd be bald by thirty.

"Stop. I've got my purse. I'll buy my own and walk home."

"No, you won't," he declared. He cracked his whip over the horse's head. By the time they reached the Baker home, Arthur's gelding glistened with perspiration. They halted suddenly, and all of Nell's thick tresses tumbled down. When he helped her out of the carriage, tiny beads of sweat moistened his brow. "Why do you torture me, Miss Nell Baker? Why won't you set the date?"

"Why didn't you buy me strawberries and cream?" she asked to avoid the question. "You know I haven't had them for a year." Perplexed, Nell turned from him. She liked Arthur, overall. For a long time they had been friends, and he would make a proper husband. She wanted to please him but hated his anxious proposal. It had blown winter into her heart. She mouthed the word "shit"—Mama had trained her with lye soap not to use it.

"What did you say?" Arthur asked.

"Nothing." Hurriedly, Nell turned from him and marched up the hedged walk.

"Listen here," he yelled before driving off, "you've got to grow up. A schoolteacher can't marry. When you're past nineteen, the bloom is off the rose, little Miss Spinster."

Through moistened eyes, Nell perceived the fuzzy figure of a man relaxing on the porch with her father. He appeared to be the one who had saved Mr. Hardman's horse. Embarrassed that he may have heard Arthur yell, she knelt behind the hedge, wiped her eyes, pinched her cheeks, and ran her fingers through her hair until she felt it was worthy of admiration. From behind the foliage, she peered. Sure enough, it was he. Neither the broad shoulders nor the silly trousers could be mistaken. She straightened her bent parasol, held it to frame her face, and imagined that she *glided* to the porch.

"Where's Arthur?" Mr. Baker asked. "Have you insulted him again?"

"A friendly disagreement, that's all," Nell answered. Before stepping forward, she slightly lifted her skirt, to reveal the extravagant ruffles of her petticoat.

"Didn't sound friendly to me." Her father turned to the stranger. "My oldest daughter, Nell."

"Beautiful," said the stranger.

"She's promised."

"That right?"

"That's right."

When the Mormon studied her, Nell's heart beat like the drums of Captain Pitt's Brass Band. When he smiled, goose bumps fluttered over her arms and neck. When he spoke, his mellow voice, touched with a Scottish accent, lodged in her stomach.

"This is Tom Mortenson, a Mormon. He's telling me that Joe Smith's running for President. Of all things!"

Nell nodded, smiled, and fluttered her eyelids. Up close, she admired Tom's straight and manly nose, his broad jaw, his steel-blue eyes. She felt certain, and embarrassed, that he read her thoughts. Tom stood. Nell offered him her gloved hand. To her thinking, it lay in his gentle grip like a white dove on her nest.

"Nell," he said, as if he liked saying the name.

"Sit, now, and listen, Nell," her father pointed to the chair next to him. "Even though you are female and will vote through me, you should be able to discuss political issues of the day."

Because he had taken pride in her intelligence, he had pushed her toward an interest in mathematics and business, but since she had highly favored literature and teaching instead, he usually commented upon her "feminine limitations."

"*Brother* Mortenson here is campaigning in Quincy for his *seer*. He's also trying to push his religion onto us. What do you think of that?" He turned to Tom. "I don't mean to discredit you, Sir. But . . . seems odd to me that a fine-looking, intelligent fellow, such as yourself, should be drawn to that fanatical group." When Tom did not protest, her father continued. "He's paying his own expenses to campaign for Smith. Staying at the widow King's boardinghouse the entire week."

"I come to discuss some issues." Tom said. Nell turned from him to avoid blushing. "You have a slave, I see. Not to offend you, Mr. Baker, but Mayor Smith advocates the abolition of slavery by 1850." He smiled at Nell, who, having been told that her eyes were beautiful, fluttered her eyelids again. "In fact, he believes that if he is elected, he could well prevent a civil war. We, of all people, understand the Negro plight, their persecution. No portion of the government has stepped forward for our relief, or for theirs. But, in the eyes of the Almighty God, no man, or woman, was created to slave for another." Tom agreeably nodded at Nell.

"Absurd!" Her father smashed his fist on the tea table next to his chair. "Under the Constitution, slaves are not citizens, and never can be. They naturally lack powers of intellect. I've never known one of them to make a sound decision."

"Not absurd!" Tom stood his ground. "In the Constitution, *men* means *people*, and people have the right to life, liberty, and the pursuit of happiness."

"They are not *people* in the sense that you and I are. They cannot own property. They cannot stand on their own in society. You know that, Mr. Mortenson."

"We don't know that. I believe they could if given the opportunity to read." He turned to Nell. "I would not find happiness in pursuing my goals through another's bondage. Would you, Miss Baker?"

"Quickly, go inside to your mother," Nell's father told her. "I will not have my family corrupted."

Nell retreated, but the Mormon stayed. Christina, Mama, Ruby and she prepared supper and sometimes watched, through the window, the cantankerous men. Mr. Baker, who preferred nothing more than a spirited round of argument, could easily be heard throughout the household while the pair argued through the campaign issues, an establishment of a federal banking system bringing the hottest debate. Finally, Nell's father agreed with Tom that Texas, Mexico and Canada should be invited to join the Union. Both men concurred that America should assert her claim to the Oregon Territory. At last, their talk became jovial, especially when Tom said that he traveled to Quincy, not only to campaign and proselyte but to make final payment on his loan at her father's bank.

"Congratulations, Son," Mr. Baker said. "That old swamp ground around Nauvoo must be productive for you to repay the entire loan in only three years."

"It is, Sir, now we have drained it. With the help of the Lord and our good yoke of oxen, my brother and me will have near sixty acres of wheat under cultivation this summer."

"Ye gods, this is something to celebrate! Harriet! Harriet! Set another place at the table. Brother Tom is paying off his loan."

Nell, however, set the table with two extra places. Out of respect for Tom's firm belief that "no man, or woman, should slave for another," she set a place for Ruby. The slave usually ate in the keeping room after serving the family. Until now, Nell never considered inviting her to the table. It was comparable to inviting the cat. But, she loved the smooth-skinned woman like she loved Mama. Eating with her, just this once, would do no harm.

Abolition, which the Mormons endorsed, would not suit any of the Bakers. Who would arise early to cook breakfast? Who would carry wood for the fire, wash the dishes, bake the bread, and iron the clothing? The very idea unnerved Nell. A woman with the least amount of self-respect and intelligence would not perform all menial tasks in this modern day. For sure, she desired not to. Such work might kill Mama, with her vapors and overall weakness. Since the Mormon had no slaves, he could not fully appreciate the benefits. Besides that, one must think of the slaves themselves. She agreed with her father. How would they get along with no mistresses and no masters to guide and protect them? How would they function? Ruby, who had never learned to add, would be cheated at every turn.

Arthur arrived by way of the back door. Fragrant shaving soap announced his presence. Nell hoped that his anger had diminished and that he would put his arms around her now. "Sorry, my love," he might whisper. He'd have to do something if he intended to propose tonight on the front porch in the moonlight. Instead, he grabbed a hot bun from the plate she carried to the table.

"Mmm, these smell delicious," he told Ruby. "Oh, for God's sake. Don't tell me the Mormon's here! He certainly gets around. Why, just this morning, while we sat in church, he convinced Mother that Joseph Smith should be our next President. Imagine!" He held Nell at the shoulders, leaning so close to her face she smelled his dough breath. "In these trying times, women need to be taught to listen discriminately. I tell you, Nell, those fanatics are smart, working through our weakest citizens. They're taking Illinois like the smallpox."

"Eat yo' bun," Ruby chided. "Yo' droppin' crumbs all ober de flo."

In the center of the Queen Anne table, Nell placed a platter of golden fried chicken, hot from the pan. She lit two fat candles while Ruby brought steaming whipped potatoes, rich giblet gravy, and boiled carrots. Christina set the table with blue on white English China, warmed at the hearth, and an odd assortment of knives and forks passed down from previous generations. Mama rang the crystal dinner chime. Then, when everyone was seated, Nell led Ruby, who protested all the way, from the keeping room to the chair next to hers.

"Father," she cleared her throat. "I've been thinking. I think Ruby should eat with us today."

Mouths and napkins dropped. Mama flushed and gasped for breath. Both Ruby and Christina hurried to Mama's side and fanned her face. To Nell's thinking, Mama did this to control her husband's anger or to create a diversion. Nell despised the antic. She hoped Mama wasn't going to faint, or pretend to faint, and spoil her gesture to please the Mormon.

Mr. Baker, for once, sat speechless. His desire to honor a guest and his respect for Ruby pitted against his support of slavery. Christina covered her mouth to suppress a giggle, and Ruby glowed red long after Nell's father motioned for her to sit. Nell pulled out Ruby's chair. Ruby seated herself like a duchess, nodding a thank you to everyone. Nell noticed Tom's satisfied grin.

First, Mr. Baker introduced the men. They reached across the table to shake hands, but their grip was too long and too firm for civility. "Arthur Reeves is the neighbor's son, my assistant at the bank."

"He's courting Nell," Mama said, recovering. At least she avoided "They're engaged," or "This is their day of proposal," or "We spent the winter stitching Nell's linens." Father introduced Christina and Mama . . . but not Ruby.

"This is Ruby," Nell told Tom. "Her last name is Washington. She's an exceptional cook and a weaver. Father bought her the day I was born, and she's cared for me all my life." Tom, how white his teeth, listened intently and grinned at Nell.

Arthur wanted to know what brought Tom to Quincy. Tom told him that over 240 men had volunteered to preach and campaign for the Prophet in twenty-seven states. "Since it is essential that I harvest a large crop of grain this fall," Tom said, "I can leave my land for a brief time only. For that reason, I was called to work here."

"Called? Who called you?" Arthur asked.

"God," said the Mormon to Nell, not Arthur. At that moment, Nell recognized a connection between Tom and herself. How had it come about? It had nothing to do with common interests, nothing to do with politics or religion or intellect or even poetry, nothing to do with wealth, or language or learning. It had everything to do with magnetism and chemistry, gravity and universal law. Like his missing link, she felt drawn to him. Between his shoulder and his chest was a comfortable place where she desired to rest her head. No one and nothing, not even her own will, could alter it.

"*Brother* Tom," Father said. He never called anyone *brother*. "I understand that you hold priesthood *keys*."

"Just how many *keys* do you hold?" Arthur snickered.

"I hold the keys of the ministering of angels," Tom answered. "And of the Gospel of repentance and of baptism by immersion for the remission of sins. This is the priesthood of Aaron. I also hold the keys of the Melchizedek Priesthood, which gives me the power to bestow the Holy Ghost by the laying on of hands. What keys do you hold?" he asked Arthur, who didn't even hold the keys to her father's bank.

Arthur shrugged it off.

"Well, could you use one of those *keys* of yours to bless the food?" Father asked.

Tom paused with his head bowed as a signal for everyone to do the same. "Our kind Heavenly Father," he prayed. "We thank thee for the bounty spread before us and for the precious hands that have prepared . . ."

Pleased that everyone's eyes remained closed, Nell read the face of God's servant across the table. The candlelight flickered upon his hair, mustache, and brows, touching them with a reddish glow. A slight dimple in his square chin rendered him an approachable, boyish quality. Like Desdemona, she prayed "that nature had made her such a man."

Christina sputtered from under the hand, which continually covered her mouth. At fifteen, she hadn't the sense to concentrate, but spied on her sister. Even Nell's angry glare failed to quiet her. As sheep will run after one another through a gate, one giggle followed the next. She was sent to the kitchen to wash skillets when the blessing ended.

The head of the family poured a tiny glass of red wine for everyone. "Are you ready, Mother? Arthur, my son, I think you have an announcement to make." He passed the glasses all around.

Arthur disgustedly stared at Nell, who stared disgustedly at her plate. "There is nothing to announce," he said. It served him right. An improper proposal begged for refusal. Mama coughed congestedly; she sighed, "Oh, my," as if that would help.

"Ah hum. Well, then," Father said. "Let's at least drink to the final payment on *Brother* Tom's farm. Some men are persistent; they overcome all odds. Congratulations!"

Arthur whispered in Nell's ear, "That malarial swamp can be had for only two dollars an acre."

"Not anymore," Nell answered.

Before Tom drank, he saluted her with his glass. The red wine shimmered on his full lips. "Congratulations, Mr. Mortenson," she managed to say, her voice strangely soft. She tipped her glass to him, hoping the wine blushed upon her own lips as it had on his. Gathering courage to meet his eyes, she feared he knew what she was thinking. Then, she feared that he did not know. He might leave, never to see her again. When Mama and I traveled to Nauvoo last month," she said to draw his attention, "I was surprised by its size and beauty. Why, you're the envy of every city around."

"*Envy* is the right word, Sister. We've grown to about 15,000. Largest city in the state. When the mobs torched our temple in Kirtland, they believed they could shut us down, but we're rebuilding according to God's plan. People know the truth when they hear it. They rejoice at the words of a living prophet who has the authority to reveal God's promise in this dispensation."

"I hear your *living prophet* has requested the authority to summon units of the national army to assist the Nauvoo Legion in the protection of its citizens," her father challenged. "Now, the man wants control of the United States military. Pass the potatoes, Nell."

"In such a case, your Mecca could legally control the entire nation," Arthur jeered. "You people are downright pushy."

"That's an understatement," Mr. Baker agreed.

Nell took Tom's side. "That power is necessary to allow their citizens the rights of worship guaranteed by the Constitution. This is a natural reaction to the outrageous treatment given them in Missouri." Aware of Tom's admiration, Nell breathed a great sigh. She smiled.

"Nauvoo is already a state within a state, not subject to Illinois courts by its charter," Mr. Baker responded. Nell had already heard, and practically memorized, her father's words because Mormons had been the main topic of discussion since they had *invaded* Illinois. "I think, and I must warn you, that your Mayor Smith has gone too far this time."

"Not far enough," Tom answered, taking a generous bite of chicken. Mama retreated to the keeping room to catch her wind. "At this moment there are factions in Missouri, Iowa and Illinois crusading to exterminate us entirely."

"Yes," said Father. "This is what I am telling you. Illinois is a state of frontiersmen. Too high a spirit of reform or arrogance is not tolerated here. You have to admit that your people are religiously egotistical and vigorously unto yourselves. For that reason, Tom, I urge you to leave them. Be practical. Establish yourself apart. I give you this advice for your own sake. I like your spirit, but you are terribly misled."

For a few awkward moments, everyone chewed their food, wiped their chins and adjusted themselves on their chairs.

"I'm not ungrateful for your advice, Mr. Baker. However, I'm afraid you do not understand. I could never leave my Prophet. His will be done. For the Kingdom of Heaven is at hand. Those who desire to receive the blessings must be tried, even as Abraham, and only the faithful will inherit the promise."

Nell thought that the language of both men reflected a memorized quality, as if they parroted the inflammatory speeches of their leaders.

"I see you're religiously committed to Smith," said Father. "But, what makes you think he's capable of being President, for hell sakes?"

"Leading the country behind a Mormon pulpit, for hell sakes," Arthur snorted. He glanced around to see if anyone noticed his clever remark and snorted again.

"Don't sell him short," Tom answered. True as Lancelot, he would carry out his mission. "As Lieutenant General, he holds the highest rank of any officer in the U. S."

"Who gave him that title?" Arthur roared. "God?"

Tom ignored his ignorance. "In five years, he's built a glorious city, unparalleled in organization, and, yes, he does communicate with God. What better qualifications are there?"

"Not that again," Arthur sighed.

"If you want to talk pure politics, he now controls the vote in this state and has the respect of national leaders. How do you think Nauvoo attained so strong a city charter? Through his great power of persuasion, my friends. The country could do much worse."

Mama returned. To break the intense conversation, she said this might be the warmest day so far. Nell furthered her intent by mentioning that the Widow Johnson had strawberries and cream for sale. Arthur also moved to a new topic by saying the ground had dried and he took out his new carriage without flipping mud all over it. Tom remarked that the plow he recently bought "slipped through the moist ground like a knife through warm butter." But, Ruby said nary a word.

All too soon, the meal ended. Tom asked if anyone would like to hear more about Smith's candidacy or about the Book of Mormon.

"I have heard enough," Father said.

"Enough to last a lifetime," Arthur added.

"Rude," Nell whispered.

Tom, clearly a gentleman, took his cue to leave. He thanked the family for the meal and shook hands all around. Coming to Nell, he gently held hers and would have kissed it if Arthur had not placed his hand in the way. "You must be proud of your bright and beautiful daughter," he said, pushing aside Arthur's fist.

The two bankers stiffened at his words. When Tom Mortenson stepped out into the night, Mr. Baker firmly closed the door and braced himself against it as if someone pushed from the other side. "It is a fine thing that this Mormon paid his debt. Our loans to *those people* have allowed us to prosper while other banks have gone under. But, I shall tolerate no more of his kind in my home. It is true, what people say. They are nothing less than deluded fanatics, tampering with our slaves and sowing dissension among them."

"Taking our land, corrupting our women and children," Arthur added angrily. "Our homes need defending against such men. I have heard that Old Joe Smith has asked another man's wife to marry him—for eternity; after meeting this intruder, I believe it is true."

"That's evil gossip, invented by weak men who wish they were dynamic," Nell refuted.

"See, she's already bewitched," Arthur said.

"Don't you defend them in this house," Father pointed at Nell. "Don't insult the man who will soon provide for you." Now, he turned to Arthur. "We must not go too hard on females. They lack judgment." Her father gripped her arm and moved her to the stairs. "Go to your room, Daughter, and stay there without food or drink until you determine your wedding date. You have insulted us, tipping your glass to a Mormon."

"Inviting Ruby to eat with us, of all things," Arthur added.

On the way up the stairs, Nell heard her father inform Arthur, "Women do not know their own minds; their passions rule, and that one bends toward rebelliousness. I raised her the best I knew how, but, apparently, that wasn't good enough. Harriet!" he called, out of control. "She lacks training the same as that damned mule of hers. I fear I shall be forced to whip them both."

"What is it? What?" Mama rushed to her husband's side and adjusted the ruffled kerchief, which covered her head day and night.

Once in her room, out of the reach of the two bankers, Nell threw Arthur's likeness on the floor, shattering the glass. "I don't like this," she said aloud and hoped someone heard. She would not be manipulated. She would decide if, when, and whom she would marry. Gazing out the window, her thoughts as far from Arthur as Venus from Earth, she planned to set a date, all right, but not the date her father and Arthur pressured her to set. She composed a letter, addressed to "Brother Tom Mortenson." She sprinkled lavender toilet water over it, rolled it, and tied it with a pink ribbon. Tomorrow, she'd convince Ruby to deliver it to Mrs. King's boarding house.

May 30, 1844

My Dear Brother Mortenson,

I have given much thought to our discussion today, and I am convinced that the Holy Ghost prompts me to learn more. Like your prophet, I have long sought the truth, and there are so many sects about, that I wax utterly confused. I pray, with each breath, that you may spare me a little of your time . . . to preach to me, in secret. My family, you realize, are devout Methodists.

I propose that we meet at the old grinding mill just north of Quincy, at 1:00 on Monday. I'm bringing strawberries. With all my heart, I wait to read your Book of Mormon and to see your priesthood keys. Until we meet, I remain strangled by a rope of ignorance.

Sister Nell B

3

STUBBORN AS A MULE

(Diary)   *May 31, 1844*

Today, Tom preached to me. Must remember to whip Blondie on occasion.

"Sour grapes. That's what it is," Nell confided in the mule while driving home from her meeting with Tom. "Worthless afternoon." With the look of perfect understanding, Blondie peered around and blinked. Arthur had purchased her for his *intended*'s seventeenth birthday after Nell had admired the animal's frolicsome antics, her rare coat the color of corn silk, her tiny hooves and her freckled snout. That was two years ago. In the meantime, Nell had spoiled her by allowing her to do practically anything she desired: she walked or trotted, ate along the roadside or meandered according to her whim. Nell had always adored her obstinacy, considered her a pet. Once, after Arthur had whipped "the scuff" on the rump, Nell had shunned him for a week. But, the family despised her. The slaves who had trained her to pull a carriage used to chuckle at the odd sight of her; they tried to avoid being seen with her in public.

"Get up, Blondie," Nell yelled, but her mule sat in the middle of the road, turned a wild eye on her owner, and failed to move a muscle. Tom, who was seeing them off after his preaching, galloped to Blondie on his muscular, well-trained bay. When he yanked on her bit, she lowered her ears, stood and finally lunged forward, avoiding rocks that other draft animals ignored. Knowing that Blondie would meander home, if given her reins, Nell relaxed her grip, waved to Tom, and lost herself in retracing the events of the afternoon. Nothing had gone right, nothing.

First of all, she had arrived at the mill an hour late; if she hadn't, the day might have been profitable. But, having to decide whether to dress for a preacher or a suitor had posed a great problem. When Nell had asked for Ruby's opinion, she had received a strong tongue lashing, which delayed her even longer. "I's asham' I took de note," she had told Nell. "I's goin' get whipped, sho. Yo' got no right seein' dat boy. Yo' be promise'. What yo' doin'?"

"I don't know, Ruby. All I do know is that I've got to see Tom, one more time. Don't ask me why. There's no reason in it."

"I sees," Ruby had said. "Now, I sees. Po' chil'." Without further protest, she had chosen from Nell's wardrobe an unflattering, green work dress with a white apron, trimmed and pocketed in green to match. She had explained to Nell that if a young woman wore a pink party frock most preachers would certainly be frightened away. "If'n yo' wants to snag dem kin', yo' gots to do 'er slow and careful. Dat man's no fool like Arfu'."

"I don't want to *snag* him, Ruby. Holy cow! Whatever put that idea into your head? It may surprise you, and some other folks too. *This woman* may have religious needs."

Ruby had snickered. "Yo' might fool other folk and yo' might be foolin' your own self, but you ain' foolin' Ruby. I knows yo'. Don' you give me no lies 'bout Jesus. Dis got nofin' to do wif de Lord."

All this talk and all this deciding had befuddled Nell to such an extent that she had forgotten the lunch basket Ruby had packed. Causing even worse grief and delay had been Bear's attack. Bear was a big black dog that terrified Nell nearly every time she passed by his property. Blondie, however, seemed to enjoy annoying him. Usually, she snorted or hee-hawed to antagonize the canine, but on this day she had plopped down in the street and had glared at Bear. When Nell had rushed to pull Blondie's bit, Bear had growled ferociously, clamping his jaws onto the fabric of her frock. "Help, somebody. Help!" she had screamed. The dog had let loose and had bitten higher and higher up the dress, tearing it to shreds.

This commotion had unnerved Blondie. Up had gone her delicate hooves, which had struck the dog with an awful thud and had sent him flying. He had landed with a mighty yelp on the side of the road, where he had lain, groaning. After Nell had climbed into the carriage, her pent-up anxiety had escaped in the form of uncontrollable trembling. Thank heaven that Blondie had trudged on without guidance, but several times she had paused to bellow out a sound so hideous that people in one house had scurried outside to see what had been the matter. "Whinee-aw ah aw, whinee-aw ah aw." Though Blondie had quickly recovered, Nell had reached the mill in a ruined state, the color having faded from her cheeks. Though she had tried to appear collected, Tom had wanted to know what happened. Describing the incident in vivid detail, Nell had cried in self-pity, but Tom had held her in his brotherly arms, and that had made the whole incident worthwhile. "I'm at fault for allowing you to come alone," he had said. "What a cowardly decision! From now on, I must fetch you." Since she had brought no food over which to chat and relax, and since the dog had destroyed her appearance, she had nothing to do but listen while the Mormon preached. Definitely, he hadn't shown any awareness of her person.

Nearly within town now, Blondie paused alongside the road to nibble a small tuft of grass. "Get up," Nell lashed her whip above the mule's head. "We're late," she reminded Blondie, who turned to blink an almond-shaped, brown eye and plodded on. "If I remember right, authority was his topic. Tom says his is the only true religion. That is fanatical, but he would change for me, if he loved me. I know it." Tom had told her that Christ's Church was taken from the earth because of wickedness. Then, it was re-established when its Prophet, Joseph Smith, received a visitation from John the Baptist. Of all things! A visit from a ghost! Only *its* elders had the authority to preach the gospel, to perform *its* ordinances, to receive *its* revelations directly from God and to attain the highest degree of glory. And, women? They could not attain any glory without a father or a husband's "priesthood." What nonsense!

None of this suited her. Mormon theory assumed that thousands upon thousands of pious people throughout the ages, all those Catholics, Methodists, Baptists and Calvinists sat piously on hard benches through all the Sundays of their lives for absolutely nothing. So far as she was concerned, the Mormons did too. Like the foolish prophets of Khayyam's *Rubaiyat*, their mouths too would be "stopped with dust." What a self-righteous man! And yet . . .

He had touched her—once. It had happened after she had asked him to fasten a dandelion chain around her neck. She had made it while he preached, one ring for each principle. "You are a most distracting woman," he had said. His fingers had accidentally brushed across her neck, and she had felt her skin reach out to his. Other than that, she had accomplished nothing, except to arrange a second meeting.

Parting, he had wanted to "bare his testimony," a reiteration to which she graciously listened. He had said something about Joseph Smith's acting as God's true prophet and the Book of Mormon's being a true record of the Nephite people. A type of instrument translated it; she had already forgotten its ancient sounding name. Then, he had prayed, and Nell again had an opportunity to admire him, the strong, white teeth covered by full, moist lips, the square cut jaw and the mustache sparked with Scottish fire, which he twitched occasionally.

"Will he ever turn aside his prophet to worship me?" Nell asked Blondie.

Upon parting, Nell had asked that Tom allow her to drive into Quincy ahead of him. "Nothing delights a neighbor more than a good round of gossip," she had told him. "If someone saw us together on the road, news of it would reach home before I did."

"You'll have to tell your parents . . . if you really want to be converted, that is," Tom had told her at last. "I won't preach in secret."

His words had lashed out at her hopes. Nothing could have been more troubling, for she feared her father's authority above any on the earth, or in heaven. She could never muster the courage to tell him she wanted the Mormon to preach to her. Considering the consequences, she shivered.

"Oh, I do intend to tell them," she had assured Tom. But, sensing her answer troubled him, she had added, "I *am* telling them . . . slowly . . . a little at a time . . . preparing them. Wait another day. They're sensitive, a bit put off by your doctrine, like everybody else. It takes time."

These had been her words, not her thoughts. "My parents don't need to know at all," she said aloud to her pet. "If Tom's only interest is to add my name to his list of converts, I'll never tell anyone. If I gain his attention, well, that could be a definite problem, couldn't it, Blondie?" For now, she simply wondered how an unmarried man had sat with her all afternoon without asking one personal question.

"Sour grapes day." When Blondie reached for a clump of grass, Nell cracked her whip and, this time, the tip found a mark on her rump. "Oh, no you don't," Nell yelled. "Get up, this instant." The spiteful animal plunged forward and trotted rapidly along.

Nell looked forward to tomorrow's lesson. It must be fruitful. She determined to learn as much as possible about Tom, to use every charm that would force him to notice her, to make him desire her, worship her, as he did his faith. Precious little time remained. Hadn't he planned to leave Quincy within the week? After that, he would live sixty miles away, totally absorbed in growing grain for the hoards emigrating from Europe, building the temple, and "striving to reach the Celestial Kingdom." He might as well be living on the moon. She would be left to marry Arthur, who would comfort her bed only when he wanted a child, left dreaming of Tom Mortenson's passion, wasted on ideology . . . or relished by some Mormon wench who knew better how to win him. Perish the thought!

"Carpe diem!" she yelled to Blondie. Her mule lacked understanding and discipline, but, like a rare friend, she always listened . . . and never told.

4

THE LESSON

(Diary)   *June 1, 1844*

Tom Mortenson has preached to me, and I shall never again be the same as I was before this day. If he will have me, I am his.

Nell drove her carriage toward the old mill. "I want that Mormon," Nell told Blondie. After sleeping on it, she had strengthened her resolution to lead an uncommon and a daring life. "Today, no blunders, especially from you," she told Blondie, who twisted an ear, as if she understood. Nell unfastened three buttons at her neck and turned under the fabric to reveal cleavage. Then, remembering the high neckline of the modest proposal dress, created by a Mormon seamstress, she refastened one button. "Perfect," she said to the mule. "Cleavage only when I bend forward."

How Nell wished she had been schooled in romantic crafts. Today, she could very well be knitting the stitches that would shape her future life; however, no one had taught her to cast on. Friends had told her about men who kissed them passionately, but she lacked experience, having believed those who said "a woman must save herself for her husband or live forever in shame." How selfish their advice! How might a woman learn? Her parents, never affectionate in her presence, had taught her nothing. She believed they copulated twice in their lifetimes, once for her and once for Christina. Perish the thought! They even whispered about breeding the cow. Arthur was no help either. He stroked nothing but the long nose of his horse. Recently, however, he pecked at her mouth a few times, then wanted to know why she "acted so moody." Oh, if only she had played kiss tag after school or flirted with some handsome river scum, just for practice!

Upon reaching the mill and sighting Tom, who waited beside his big bay, Nell inwardly rejoiced. He lifted her down from the carriage, not by taking her hand, but by firmly grasping her waist, raising her upward, as if he wanted to try his muscles, and setting her lightly down.

"Pretty Sister Baker," he said. "Driving alone again. Surely, your parents do not approve. Evil's in them woods. I don't want you hurt. Indians come right up to the road."

"None ever bothered me."

"A woman, small and beautiful, draws the eye. Why do you chance it?" Tom unhitched Blondie and tied her to a sturdy oak. From his saddlebag, he withdrew two books. "The Book of Mormon supports the Bible; did you know that?"

"No, Brother Tom. I'm Christian, I mean, Methodist."

Hoping he heard the rustle of her petticoat, she carried her lunch basket to a sun-drenched patch of grass behind the mill. She spread a quilt on the moist ground, and, to Nell's thinking, they sat on it like lovers from an English novel. Next to the earth, the sun beat warm on their backs, and the only sounds were the *whoit, whoit, cheer-cheer* of crested red cardinals piping to one another in the thickets and the *swish, swish* of mill paddles against the spring run-off.

Tom placed in her hand a small bag with a drawstring. "Hope you like it," he said.

"More than you know." She answered before peeping inside. "Oh, I love hardtack," she said, even though she did not. "How did you know?"

"Women go for sweets."

"Guess what I brought you?" This time, she had remembered the strawberries and drew one from the basket. "Open." She dropped it into his mouth, examining his teeth, white and healthy all the way back. Then, she watched him eat. Heartily, he chewed on a turkey leg and said "yum" in approval of the cheese and biscuits. He drank deeply from his waterbag and wiped his mouth with the back of his hand. If only men knew how delightful it was to watch them eat. They went about it with the same vigor and energy they used when changing a wheel or building a fence. Unlike women, they concentrated on the food rather than on self-conscious manners. While she had his attention, Nell asked about his past.

He told her that when he was sixteen, his mother had died of smallpox. Grieved to distraction, his father had closed the door behind him one evening, never to return. Tom, left to look after his younger brother, Heber, had survived by taking up his father's trade constructing wagon wheels. "Though I was a master wheelwright at seventeen, I knew little about turning a profit, purchasing iron, locating choice timber, selling. Pointed out every flaw to a buyer," he chuckled, "then, wondered why he didn't buy. Now, I realize we made some mighty sturdy wheels back then, wheels to be proud of.

"We would have starved without Kirk Goodyear, a neighbor and convert. He stuck by us while we worked, advised us daily. A salesman, that man. In our worst wheels he found some good. Me and Heber started making a profit and put by a sizeable savings. It was from Goodyear, we learned the gospel. With him, we moved to Far West, Missouri for the gathering of the Saints." As if to wipe away his emotions, he ran his hand over his face and turned from her. "You know the rest, Sister Baker."

"I don't know, Brother Tom. What befell you?"

Tom's mustache twitched. He picked and piled a little mound of violets beside the blanket. "I didn't want to talk about me, Sister, but about the gospel. Let it suffice to say we restarted our business in Kirtland. Owned productive farmland. Me and Heber worked on masonry for the temple. She was a beauty, alright." He paused again and stared off into the thicket beyond the mill. "Prospered 'til mobs came. They burned our crops . . . shot Brother Goodyear . . . drove us out. If they hadn't outnumbered us ten to one, me and Heber, we would have killed them. As it was, we barely escaped with our hides. I looked back only once. Our house, it was a black skeleton in the flames of hell."

"I'm so sorry," said Nell.

"What happened to Brother Goodyear's body, we never found out." Tom heaved a deep sigh. He said that if it had not been for Heber and the promptings of the Holy Ghost, he would have avenged Goodyear's death a hundred times over. "Even now, I'd like to pump lead into Missouri bellies. The mere sight of one . . . "

"I remember all those Mormons who begged for food one winter in Quincy."

"Well, that be us, starving with only our horses and the clothes on our backs. We did hire out, for room and board. People in Quincy kept the wolves from our doors that winter. Finally, our members gathered again and bought that swampland up in Nauvoo. Your father charged us interest a-plenty, but we're beholding to him for that loan. Heber and me, we build wagons again and raise grain."

"What I don't understand, Brother Tom, is why you Mormons don't give up. How many temples will you see burned before you quit?'

"I'll never give up, Sister Baker, never."

"Why? You just make life hard for yourself."

"Freedom. Freedom. I'd rather die than lose my freedom to worship."

"Well, freedom *is* the story of our country. But, I believed that fight was over after the War of Independence."

"Oh, no, Sister. There's always somebody who wants to dominate somebody else. As long as two people are together, freedom is at risk."

"What?"

"When your freedom is stolen, and only then, you will know. They gave us two choices: to stay and be slaughtered or to leave and survive. We left. If they try to mob us again, we'll give them what for."

"Heaven forbid."

"Yes, heaven forbid."

"Where's Heber?"

"Oh, he's tending our crops, when he isn't courting his girl. Elizabeth's her name. Came from over in New York State. I suspect good ole' Heber has married her by now. Women are partial to him. I do believe we survived last winter on cakes and jellies they brought to our door. Couldn't leave Heber alone." He gave Nell that endearing half smile. "A man never had a better brother. Nursed me through the fever I got from draining our land."

Tom told her about their cleared farm in Nauvoo, their daylight-to-dark labor, their clearing of entangled woodlands, and their draining of mosquito infested swamps. The more he talked, the more Nell admired his stamina and his determination to be free. Who were these people? What cause enabled them to build and rebuild? To withstand hatred and envy, to move on again and again, and to become stronger each time?

"Do you have a house?" Nell wondered.

He told her of their two-story brick home with a proper cooking hearth, a bustle oven with an iron door imported from Massachusetts, a summer kitchen, and an underground springhouse for food storage. To the side, they had constructed a carriage house. A well, directly outside the kitchen entrance, provided all the water they needed for the house. "Sorry," Tom said as if waking from a dream. "How I go on! Talking about myself and forgetting the work of the Lord. You are one distracting woman, Sister Baker."

"Oh, please, don't stop; I adore hearing about your life. It outshines mine by far. Are you in the Nauvoo Legion? Do you go to dances? My land. I hear the Mormons dance until sunup. Do women bring you cakes and jellies?"

"Not so I'd brag about it." His eyes lingered upon Nell's lips, and he opened the Book of Mormon. "I've got to tell you about this book. It's the word of God."

To her disappointment, he preached. He said the book witnessed for Christ. "All prophets before Christ told of His coming and all after witnessed that He did come and is the true Son of the living God."

"I know that," said Nell. She offered him a strawberry and drew a deep breath when her finger touched his lips. Tom said, his authoritative voice like that of her Methodist minister, that nearly 600 years before the Savior, Nephi foresaw His coming and the detailed events of his life."

"Who is Nephi?"

"He's a main character in this book, a chosen man of God." Tom pointed to a section, and she moved close to follow the words. His breath smelled oh so sweet and sensuous when he read 1 Nephi 2:18. "And I, Nephi, saw that he was lifted up upon the cross and slain for the sins of the world."

"Hmm," she sighed, leaning even closer. Her cheek almost brushed his. Tom met her gaze, and she nearly drowned in the liquid luster of his blue-gray eyes. Quickly, he turned back to his reading.

"Look here. 'There is none other name given under heaven save it be this Jesus . . .'"

Nell pulled pins from her hair and leaned forward so that it spilled over her face in long, shimmering waves. "How old is Elizabeth?"

"Elizabeth? Oh, yah, Elizabeth. About your age. Your locks . . ." Under the screen of her hair, Nell watched Tom's hand reach out to touch it. He pulled it away and returned it to rest on the pages of his book. "I didn't realize there was so much shine in it." He cleared his throat. "Listen to this, Sister Baker. Word has it that us Mormons are not Christians, but Nephi says, 'We talk of Christ, we rejoice in Christ, we preach of Christ, we prophesy of Christ . . .' Now, what is more Christian than that?"

"Nothing. Is Elizabeth pretty?"

"Why, yes." After a silence, Tom gently stroked her hair. "Like silk," he said. "Oh, sorry," his hand moved to the book again. "I didn't mean to touch it."

"I don't mind."

Tom moved away from her. "What I want you to realize, Sister, is that Mormon doctrine and Bible doctrine are the same. But the Bible does not contain all doctrines and truths. It has gone through many translations and none is perfect."

Nell did not object, even though every preacher she had ever heard said the Bible was the perfect word of God. This was one of the ideas that raised the hackle on many a Christian neck. It enraged the citizenry of Far West and Quincy. Nell knew that. For them, no prophets existed after the New Testament, and Zion was long ago in Israel, not in Missouri or Illinois today. These Mormons!

"Shut your eyes, now, Sister, and tell me from which book I am reading." Nell almost shut her eyes, but left one open, barely enough to watch him. Leaning her face toward him, she pursed her lips. "Well, if that doesn't beat all," he responded. He shook his head and turned his attention back to his book. "Now, listen to this: 'He shall make intercession for all the children of men; and they that believe in him shall be saved.'"

"That's the Bible, for sure. I've read that before."

"Wrong, Sister. It's from the Book of Mormon. Now, what fault can any right thinking Christian find with the prophecies of this book? It seconds Biblical passages and expands Christianity." He placed the book on her lap. "You open your eyes now. Only fools believe one and not the other."

"I agree completely, Brother Tom. You surely fooled me." She bent forward to reveal her neckline. "You have opened my eyes and I shall be eternally grateful." As a bird passes a window, his eyes passed over her bosom, then to the pile of violets he had picked. He asked her to be still while he pressed them into her hair. When he stood back to admire his work, his lips lost color. Befuddled, he opened the Bible to read the first passage in sight. "'If a man find a virgin, which is not betrothed, and lay hold on her, and lie with her, and they be found; then the man that lay with her . . . shall give unto the damsel's father fifty shekels . . . of silver, and she shall be . . . his wife'?"

"What? That couldn't be from the Bible. It's from your book, obviously," she teased even though the top of the page read Deuteronomy. "And, if it is from the Bible, I'd say there's an error—in translation. Imagine, to be bought like a slave. And you preach abolition. Brother Tom!"

"I apologize," Tom said in a sort of quandary. "I didn't know . . . perhaps, if we read it in context . . . " He set the Bible aside. Taking her hand, he raised her off the quilt. "Come with me. I have made something to show you."

They walked side-by-side, hands occasionally brushing, until they came to a swing. Tom had suspended it from a giant cottonwood. A nicely notched board, upon which he motioned her to sit, fit perfectly. "Hold tight, Sister Baker." He pushed her gently, at first, and then harder and higher until her heart caught in her throat and her skirts flew over her face.

"Stop! Tom!" she screamed.

"Not until you promise to stop teasing me."

"I promise," she giggled.

"Will you listen?"

"I promise!"

He let the swing slow and pushed her gently. When she laughed, his laughter echoed hers. All too soon, he wanted to finish the lesson. "I need to teach you so much in so little time. Your salvation depends upon it, for the end is at hand."

I need to teach *you* so much, Nell thought.

While they strolled back to the lessons, a small yellow butterfly fluttered in front of them. Tom watched it glide from one dandelion to another and turned thoughtfully to his student. "You are like that butterfly, Sister Baker, meant for warm days and soft breezes. You need a secure home, satin gowns, heeled shoes. Never to go hungry, never to be slandered or terrorized. Being a Mormon woman is tough. Do you know what you're doing?"

"Sure."

"Oh, how your parents must love you. And Arthur?"

"Arthur? What about him? He's a friend, that's all, just a friend."

"But, he loves you. I see that."

"Maybe so. But, I don't love him, not to marry, anyway."

Until they reached their place beside the mill, neither spoke. Tom's thoughtful expression deepened into gloom. He gathered his books, the picnic basket and the quilt. "I'm sorry, Sister Baker. I can't, in good conscience, preach to you anymore."

Nell hurried to him and grasped his sleeve so tightly that the worn fabric ripped. He dropped his sacred books into some mud. She would not lose this man who cherished her so dearly that he would let her go.

"Butterflies are stronger than you think. They migrate every fall to distant lands, and they return every spring, don't they? They're tough, and so am I."

He looked up the road toward Quincy. "I need to see you home now."

"My dear Brother Tom. Your thinking is terribly wrinkled. Let me press my iron upon it. If you won't teach me the Gospel, shall I go to hell? Why would you deny me heaven? At first, I thought you were different from other men, that you valued women as equals." Now, she held his attention, she retrieved his books from the mud, wiped them with her pink dress, and handed them to him. "But, I am learning you are like all the rest. To you, I am no more significant than an insect, to be brushed off."

"No, you don't understand," he returned, wide-awake to her beauty. "I don't want you hurt. To be a Mormon, you must possess the forgiveness of Jesus, the patience of Job, the courage of David, and the strength of an ox. Then, you will be tested, even as Abraham. You will surely earn the title of saint."

He told her the story of Abraham, as if only Mormons knew of it. Like her minister, Tom admired Abraham's willingness to sacrifice his son. However, Nell believed God would have respected Abraham if he had refused to harm the child, love being above obedience. Even though Mama said it wasn't proper to argue with a preacher or to belittle a man by superior reasoning, she would think her own thoughts while Tom struggled with his conscience. "Be nice," her Aunt Emily advised. "Leave being clever to men who can."

"I fear for you, Sister. The Lord's chosen people are hunted like deer by the most oppressive generation since the days of our Savior."

"Tom. I need to ask you a favor."

"What would that be?"

"Call me Nell. I am not your sister. I'm a woman. I'm Nell, strong as Tom."

"Believe me, I am aware of your womanhood. Yes, there is strength in you. But, think long and hard about learning more and about knowing me. You will be sorely tested."

"Even as Abraham," she said and quoted the only Biblical passage she had set to memory. "Entreat me not to leave thee or to return from following after thee." She stopped short, remembering Ruby's sound advice, "You gots to do 'er slow and careful." Ruth's famous promise, "For whither thou goest, I will go," was too strong . . . for the moment.

"Wow," said Tom, impressed. He told her the gospel should be shouted from mountaintops, not whispered in shadows behind an abandoned mill. A missionary should be proud of bringing souls into the fold, not ashamed of tearing families apart behind their backs. Nell would have to confront her parents, inform them she wanted to know more about Mormonism.

"I can't do that," she told him, right on. "My father would be angry, and Mama's nerves can't take it. Anyway, it's fun, meeting in secret. Why do you want to spoil your holiday?"

"Holiday?" Tom said incredulously. "I'm not on holiday, woman! I'm working for the Lord."

"Well, call it what you like," she said. "I'm not going home until you catch me." She lifted her dress and ran through the heavy foliage at the edge of the forest until she could scarcely breathe. Spying a thick wild grape, she crawled into it, untangled a strand of hair from a branch and gathered in her skirts. She must slow her pounding heart. The only chance would be to outwit Tom, as rabbits outwit foxes, by freezing.

Robins chirped, squirrels chattered their alarm, bees buzzed, and her breathing quieted, but Tom did not appear. Then, suddenly, a war whoop, louder than the squeal of a stuck pig, shattered the silent woods. A stick pierced the earth where Nell crouched, and feet stomped in circles around her lair. Nell giggled at the sight of Tom's white legs covered with curly golden hairs. Having rolled up his britches, he revealed his misshapen, ancient shoes. What a sight! Even though Nell knew the legs were Tom's, she trembled. "Indians," she called out to please him.

"I'll find you. I'll take you to my tribe for a slave." Nell's pulse quickened with a delicious excitement. Tom stood only feet away, his face painted with mud.

"Heaven help me," Nell cried, and she meant it. Nothing she dreamed compared to this. A grown man, willing to play!

"Come here, Beauty," he pulled her to him with full and manly hands. "I am going to eat you." He nibbled at her neck.

She screamed and struggled from his grip, her heart pounding harder than ever. When she raced through the undergrowth, Tom chased after her, growling like a bear. A heavy limb, which she pushed aside, flipped back to strike across his chest.

"Oh, no. I'm dying," he moaned, falling and tumbling in an exaggerated fashion down a slight incline. Coming to rest, he sprawled over the ground on his back, shut his eyes and lay motionless. Nell laughed.

"Tom, are you hurt?" she asked like an actress in a melodrama. "Answer me, please, answer me."

He lay still as a dead cat. She kneeled, lifted his head to her lap, and dusted his damp forehead with her skirt. Leaning an ear to his chest, she listened for his heart. It pounded wildly, and one leg quivered. Nell pretended to sniffle. "Oh please, God, don't let him die." Tom pulled her face down to his. He kissed her like a bee that steals nectar and pays for it in the same motion. The rightness, the sweetness of it, melted all muscles in her body, in particular, her legs. Trembling, ever so slightly, Tom remembered himself, jumped up and dusted his britches.

"Forgive me, Sister, I mean, *Nell*. Have I misrepresented my church?"

"No. I love you for it," she blurted out.

"I have forgotten myself, and my mission."

"Which is to teach, isn't it? You have taught me that Mormons are much, much more than deluded fanatics." Nell had forgotten herself also. But, before her family began to worry, she must go. She told Mama she'd be working at the schoolhouse with Miss Griffin, and school would be dismissed by now.

They gathered their properties and decided Tom should ride to Quincy behind her to protect her from "ne'er do wells." Tom, having forgotten to bare his testimony, pulled leaves from her hair and tried to brush the mud from her soiled skirt. With ease, he lifted her onto the buggy seat. "What will your folks be thinking? I always manage to send you away in such a mess. Beauty. Think seriously. Think about your way of life. Then, if you are certain you want to go on, make this known. Thereafter, I will teach you of glories you have never dared to dream and blessings above any you've imagined. The second coming is at hand."

As if her heart had not decided for her, she told him she would consider the alternatives and let him know.

"Take this with you," he said, presenting her with the mud-streaked Book of Mormon. "Read it, ponder it, and pray about it with an open mind and a contrite spirit. Remember this scripture from James 1:5. It greatly influenced the Prophet and has often guided me. 'If any of you lack wisdom, let him ask God, that giveth to all men liberally and upbraideth not; and it shall be given unto him.'"

"Thank you," Nell turned her best side to him and smiled her best smile. "I will remember your lesson and apply it to all my reading, of course."

Driving homeward, her cheek a-lump with hardtack, she thought not of the trials of Abraham, but of the curly hairs on Tom's legs, not that the Book of Mormon witnessed for Christ, but that Tom's kiss witnessed for him; he definitely seemed interested. She wondered about the glories and blessings of lessons to come and pondered the day's events until they crystallized in her mind, never to be lost, but to be polished by time.

"RUNNER"

(Diary)   *June 1, 1844*

Tom left for Nauvoo. If he does not return, I shall die.

Before daybreak, Nell tiptoed into Ruby's room. "We have to talk."

"I knows," said Ruby, reading Nell's eyes. "I sees yo' frocks, bof days, soiled an' torn. I knows."

"First, you have to promise not to tell anyone."

"I knows dat too. Go on."

"All I want in this world is to be with the Mormon. I can't help myself. It's hard to explain. He's always on my mind."

"Mmm hmm. Yo' tell me somepun' I don' know." Ruby slipped out of her nightgown. Clear, honey-brown skin covered her legs, which were long and slender like those of a marathon runner. Nell admired her short-cropped hair because it gave emphasis to her elegant neck and circular, ivory earrings. Forty-five years of slavery had not spoiled her exotic beauty.

"Then, I guess you know I've seen him twice, and I guess you know I need to see him again."

"I does," Ruby said. She pulled a clean work dress over her head. "I neve' seed yo' cheeks so pink, yo' eyes so bright. Ruby, she know."

"Well, since you know everything, what am I going to do? I love him. Tom, compared to Arthur is, like Hamlet said, 'Hyperion to a satyr.' I can never marry Arthur now. Never." Nell began to cry. "Tom says he won't see me anymore unless I tell my family the truth. I can't tell them, Ruby. They'd never understand. Father would hire an assassin, and the truth would kill Mama. The only thing I can think of is to run away. And I don't even know if Tom wants to marry me."

While Ruby considered the dilemma, she handed Nell a milking pail and motioned for her to walk with her to the goat shed. Mr. Baker had built it for Ruby after buying her two nannies and a billy. He told Ruby that, as long as it didn't interfere with her household chores, she could earn her own money from their milk. Later, he chastised himself. His gesture had brought trouble into the household, he said. Though his original idea was that a slave who owned property was less tempted to run away, he later wished he hadn't given Ruby the wherewithal to become an uppity slave, a brightly dressed slave, a customers-at-the-front-door and a lean-on-the-fence-talking-to-neighbors slave. Having a full purse gave her power. She acted like a real person, and that reflected poorly on the family. It embarrassed him that she charged "so ghastly a price" for her delicately flavored cheeses. Besides that, two husbands complained to him that the goat milk enabled their scandalous wives to "wrangle out of nursing their babies." Because of the household disruption, he forbade Nell and Christina from milking and from learning the cheese making process, but the idea of having a business served only to pique Nell's interest in independence, and she often helped Ruby in secret.

"Nell, yo' and Christina my babies," Ruby said swinging a pail in each hand on the way to the shed. "I wants de bes' for yo'. Yo' not thinkin'; you feelin'. Listen, an' listen good."

"I'll listen. But, if I decide to run away, you've got to come with me. I need you, Ruby, more than ever. If you come with me, I'll set you free. Nobody will ever again tell us what to do."

"Hmm," Ruby frowned. Her deep brown eyes rolled. I ain' runnin' nowhere. Ain' goin' be no runner. Yo' gots to learn de hard way; no good come from runnin'."

"If you don't come along, who will take care of me? You're mine."

"I ain' goin'," Ruby emphatically said. If her slave said a thing twice, she meant it. "I ain' goin' be no runner, an' yo' ain'. Not a lick-a sense in it." Once in the shed, she led a nanny onto the milking stand and placed its head in a chute to keep it in place. Then, she offered Nell a chance to practice. "Yo' looks pale." She felt Nell's forehead. "Spring chick like yo' gots lots of days lef' to decide. Now, yo' stan' up to dem folks, wif dat boy. Have yo' say."

"I can't. Father would lock me away." Meowing for their drink of goat's milk, two of the family cats rubbed around and around Nell's legs.

"Then, you a slave, jus' like me."

"What do you expect me to do, then? Stay here? Marry Arthur? Spend the rest of my life wondering what would have happened if I had run? Listen to this, Ruby. When I met Tom, I felt as if I'd been half a person all my life."

With her big, white kerchief, Ruby wiped her baby's hands. Replacing Nell at the teats, she squirted the meowing mousers square in the mouth with a spray of warm milk. Their anxious lapping made Nell laugh. "Your pap goin' shoot Tom if he come 'round here. He sho' is. I hear 'im say."

"I knew it! Let's run away . . . later . . . tonight."

"I run once," Ruby explained in the deep, mellow voice that Nell had grown to love and respect. "I ain' goin' run no more. Wif my mammy and pappy. I mus' been a babe 'cause it seem like a dream now. My pappy, I 'members, he be strong wif long legs like a tree trunk and big white teef. I 'members dem teef. An' he sing like de angels. Lord, how he sing. We be beatin' it norf to freedom. Mammy cluckin' me 'long, like a hen. When I wore out, Pappy, he carry me in his strong arm, way up off de groun'. Quick like, we hear de debil' footsteps comin' fo' us, so we run 'til Mama say she can' run no more. She wore out. We lays down on de groun', bushes and leafs coverin' us all ove'. De roun' moon shinin' down like she sayin' we be doin' right. Mammy and Pappy hold me. Dey keep me warm. But, I still scared. I know'd dey scared too." With her eyes closed and a peaceful expression on her face, Ruby squeezed the teats with a steady rhythm that built foam in the pail. Suddenly startled, her eyes flew open. "Dogs!"

"Dogs?"

"Yes, dogs. Dey chases us down. Dem white boys shoots my pappy. He die in Mammy's arms. I 'members how she scream. I scream too. In de moonlight, I see Pappy, red blood pourin' out ove' hi' neck like water spillin' over edge de wash basin." Ruby wiped her eyes, shuddered, and breathed a sigh so deep and hurtful that Nell imagined herself in the slave's situation. Finished milking the first goat, Ruby unhitched it, caught the second and led it onto the stand, where she began with a fresh pail to milk from behind.

"Masa', he don' wan' Mammy no mo'. He done put her on de auction block 'cause she be a runner. She stan' der two day, cryin', her lip crackin', an nobody wantin' 'er. Den, dey buys 'er and hawls 'er off. I 'members her reachin' out wif' 'de arms I loves. I hears her bawlin' out my name. Ruby, Ruby, my baby. But, nobody care. Dey takes my mammy away, like de bitch from de pup. Nobody care."

"You never saw your mama again?"

"No. But I neve' fo'get her sweet smell. Neve'." Ruby explained that soon after the running she worked in the cotton fields. Her master worked her beyond her years until her ribs stood out and her feet bled. She lifted so many bales of cotton that her back ached, even now. "Den, yo' mama, she see me. And yo' daddy, he buy me. Dey be good. I tol' mysel' I ain' neve' goin' be no runner. I too ol' to run. I stay put."

"You're not old, Ruby," said Nell. "You're afraid."

"Dat be right. But, I knows, if I run, my life not gwan be bette'. I neve' gwan' have no man, and I neve' gwan' have no chil'. My family right here." The slave finished milking and drove both goats out of the shed and into their pasture while Nell flicked a struggling fly out of the foam with her finger. Closing the gate, Ruby told Nell not to make quick decisions and never to hurt the people who loved her more than anyone else in the world, the people who gave her life and nurtured it. There was no need to run; if Tom wanted her, sixty miles wouldn't stop him.

"I know I owe them, but it's my life. They'll get over it. It's also your life. You've got this one last chance to come along and take care of me or you'll never be free. Ruby told Nell that she did not know how to be free. They each carried to the house, a pail full of milk, which gave off steam in the early morning air.

Taking Ruby's advice, Nell waited all day for Tom to make an advance. He did not. Then, she cursed a night of tossing on her pillow, pacing the floor, talking to herself, opening and closing the window. She must have gone in the honey bucket three times. Finally, she decided to act. She scribbled a letter, the envelope addressed, "To My Loving Parents."

My dear family,

I am going to Nauvoo to marry Tom. Please tell Arthur I am sorry, but after meeting Tom, I realized I did not love him, and never had, though he is

a dear friend. I pray that he will understand. Knowing that you can't under-
stand, I cannot stay to make a proper goodbye. Please do not try to stop me.
I know what I want. This is my life. Forgive me.

Your loving daughter, Nell

Sleeping deeply until the predawn hours, Nell awoke with a start. For the second morning, she disrupted Ruby's sleep and, before the black woman had time to reason, told her to set the letter on the parlor writing desk *if*, and only *if*, she did not return home by noon. "That way, they'll, at least, know where I am." Nell kissed Ruby's cheek and smiled as sweetly as possible. She hoped Ruby might tell Arthur how pretty she looked the last time she saw her.

"Lord, I's sorry," said Ruby. "I didn't mean to raise no runner."

"I'm sorry you feel that way, Ruby. I'm not a runner. If I had a collar around my neck marked with my owner's name, I suppose I would be, but a person has a choice."

Nell rushed to the stall, saddled Blondie, and trotted (because Blondie wanted to) all the way to the widow's boarding house to be united with her other half. She halted in front of the home; and, watching Tom's shadow move back and forth across his curtained window, she rethought her decision. What if Tom didn't love her? What if he didn't want her to go to Nauvoo with him? Had she assumed incorrectly that he might be easily persuaded to marry her? After all, he never mentioned marriage. If he did, would she rue the day she decided to leave her own society and live with his strange people?

"What am I doing?" she whispered in Blondie's ear. She dropped her carpetbag into the middle of a current bush where Tom wouldn't see it. At least, she ought to wait for him to ask her to go to Nauvoo. Blondie snorted, and Tom's head appeared at the window. The lantern blinked out in his room. After a brief time, he came to her, leading Sergeant, who carried Tom's belongings behind his saddle.

"Nell. What are you doing in the cold air?"

"I—I had a question. I wondered about it all of yesterday." Standing close to him, she felt his warm breath on her face. She moved a half-step closer to him, so that their lips nearly touched. With eyes shut, she hoped he might kiss her. Alas, he did not.

"You might think I'm out of my mind for wondering about this, but it is extremely important to me," she said stepping away from him. She must remember the correct terminology. "Umm, can a woman reach the highest degree of glory in the Celestial Kingdom if she is a—a spinster?"

"No, she cannot. It might seem a bit unfair to you right now, but it is God's law. She must be married and sealed in the temple to one who holds the Melchizedek Priesthood."

"Then, if the end comes soon and I have not completed my temple work and have not married one of His chosen, my soul will be condemned to roam for eternity in hell?"

"Perhaps, the Telestial Kingdom, Tom whispered. "Your heart is in the right place."

"And, if you go to the Celestial Kingdom, how will I see you?"

"Most likely, you will not." Roguishly, he half-smiled. "But I might possibly be obliged to preach to you."

Nell turned from Tom and feigned a sniffle. She reached deep down into the neck of her dress and pulled out a laced handkerchief. "I feared so," she gasped, dabbing at the corners of her dry eyes.

At that, Tom reached out for her. His lips wandered across her forehead, traveled down over the bridge of her nose and rested momentarily against her mouth. They pulled away. Then, like a traveler who has come home at last, they covered her lips and lit a blazing fire in her womb. In Tom's arms, Nell felt the restrained strength of him; her legs weakened, but that was of no consequence: her feet were off the ground. One of Tom's hands found its way to her neckline, but stopped short after a quick brush across her bosom. He pushed her away from him by clutching a handful of hair at the back of her neck.

"Sister!" he spoke louder than he wanted to. "I must leave you now, or else . . . "

"Marry me, Tom," Nell blurted out. "I want to go to the Celestial Kingdom."

"You haven't talked with your parents, have you? Oh, what shall I do with you? I can't have you running away. Please understand. Go home to your family." He stepped away from her, his outstretched arms the weapon with which he held them apart. "Write to me," he said. "I am coming back to help you set things right. You can count on that." He hoisted himself onto his saddle, but, in doing so, his open coat revealed at his waistband the most menacing holster pistol. In the moonlight, Nell also caught sight of a rifle, mounted in his saddle boot.

Her heart took flight. Oh, the mystery of this man, the wildness, the passion. Oh, the excitement of loving a Mormon!

"Go home for now, my beauty. And, don't forget your carpetbag, there in the bushes." He laughed and galloped away like Aramis straight out of *The Three Musketeers*.

6

HOW SHE CAME TO THIS

(Diary)   *September 6, 1845*

Sixth day of September 1845, Jennifer Mortenson berthed

Parents – Tom and Nell Baker Mortenson

Nauvoo, Illinois, United States of America

Mary Ann Harper, Midwife

Over a year later, Nell lay in her bed in Nauvoo having Tom's child. She remembered her aunt's tale of her first delivery, the sensation of being ripped apart and of Cousin Morey's big head that wouldn't slip out until the doctor reached his hand inside her—and pulled! And, Mama's story about Nell's own birth, "twenty-four hours of unbearable pain," terrified her when she heard it for the first time; after she and Christina learned what caused babies, they swore on a Bible that they would never allow themselves to suffer such a fate. However, through the years, Nell had heard the stories with such frequency, each of the old aunts trying to outstrip the other like men showing their battle wounds, that she had concluded these were exaggerated narrations, told for the sole purpose of frightening young women into chastity—and to brag.

Not so!

Quickly and bitterly, Nell realized that *her* pain was real. No matter that Tom kissed her, vowed his love, and promised to cherish the baby and to protect the two of them with his life. No matter that Elizabeth frequently moistened her lips with damp cotton, rubbed her back, and assured her it would soon be over. Neither did it matter that her two midwives, each confident, calm and proud, crowed about bringing "more than a hundred healthy children into the world." Never mind any of them! No matter how hard and long anyone prayed, paced, fasted or deprived themselves of sleep, they could not share in what she alone had to do.

After shooing Tom away, the midwives heated water at the hearth. Elizabeth brought the birthing cloths. With intricate, blocked baby quilts, donated by the good sisters of the Relief Society, she made up the little cradle, which Tom had crafted of river oak and decorated panels. Nell and Elizabeth had also sewn a bundle of tiny dresses, leggings and robes, which lay in a drawer awaiting the new life. For the first five hours, Nell had been able to doze, at least, between each contraction, but they had gradually developed into fierce pains about six minutes apart. "Damn," she heard herself tell Elizabeth. "How did I get myself into this?"

It all started with her refusal to marry Arthur. If she had married him, she speculated, there would not have been any deliveries to bear. "Tom," she murmured under her breath, "if only you had not returned." But, return he did in late June of 1844. Five letters and three weeks after he left her outside of the widow's boarding house, Tom stood on the Baker family porch in a new suit, handsome as a prince, asking her mama if he might speak with her. Mama said she supposed so, as long as she chaperoned, but she wheezed when her daughter burst through the doorway into Tom's arms and kissed him.

Then, Tom introduced Heber, his "brother and bodyguard." Nell remembered being struck by Heber's features, for he resembled Tom, except that he stood a few inches taller, was not so broad in the shoulders and hips, and grew no mustache. Strikingly similar to Tom's were his strong teeth, gray-blue eyes and heavy jaw, but his hair sported more red in it. When Heber hugged Nell, Christina and Ruby covered their mouths in awe, and Mama feigned a dizzy spell. After apologizing for his enthusiasm, Heber said that he had heard so much about Nell that he already considered her a sister. At these words, Mama ran whimpering into the house while the confused Heber sprawled quietly on the porch steps, holding a bouquet of violets, which he had picked for Nell along the way.

Relaxing on the porch swing, Tom asked her to open her mind to him.

"My mind and my heart are open to you," she remembered herself saying. "I can't believe you have come back to me."

"Is it your will to learn the gospel and be baptized into the only true Church of Jesus Christ?"

"Yes." Out of her longing for Tom, she had come to this.

"Well, then, we will preach to you . . . but only after your father has agreed to it."

Mama screamed from behind the parlor window, "Ruby, bring her inside. Christina, run for Charles and Arthur!"

"Kiss again," Christina giggled through the curtained window. Heber blew her a kiss instead, and an embarrassed Christina disappeared.

Tom was an honest, direct man. Wanting Nell to fully comprehend that converting to Mormonism could involve her in the explosive problems of its people, he explained that a new press called the *Nauvoo Expositor* had printed foul lies about the Prophet, namely accusing him of power-abuse and questioning his political revelations. The lies aroused doubts and dissension among certain uncommitted members. So, they signed and printed affidavits stating that they had personally seen a copy of Smith's revelation permitting a faithful saint up to ten wives. Aghast, Nell recalled the virgins in Deuteronomy, sold for fifty shekels.

"Under our Prophet's orders, the Nauvoo Legion destroyed the press. They spoiled the type of the *Expositor*," Heber said. "Though the Prophet's motives were purely to protect God's chosen people, you know how freedom of the press sits in these United States. The incident has been blown out of proportion in Hancock County. It points to slanders and afflictions beyond imagination. We are despised, to the point of slitting our throats—and—raping our wives."

"Could you tolerate being spat upon and called *whore* to your face?" Tom paused for a reply. Nell did not answer. "If your parents don't want you converted, what then? Will you leave them?"

"No," said Ruby, poking her head out the window. "No," she shook her head.

Despite the vigorous protestations of Nell's family, Nell stood her ground, and the handsome Mortenson brothers preached to her on that day and for two days after. On the third day, Ruby secretly informed Nell that they were in grave danger. "De gwan get kilt," she said. "I feels it." Nell convinced them to leave. But, the next time they returned it was to take her with them. In a letter, delivered in secret, Tom had asked Nell to marry him and she replied, "I want to be baptized and I want to be with you for the remainder of my life." Though it wasn't the proposal of her dreams, it would do.

Nell remembered her logic. After marrying Tom, she would change him. Eventually, she would turn him against Mormonism, and they would live happily in Quincy with him working in her father's bank, like Arthur. Or—if he had to—he could build wagon wheels. Even if that meant they would never be rich, she was willing to accept it. These were her thoughts at the time. But, she had not been able to change him—yet. Only once had she dared to mention the topic, shortly after their marriage, on the day the Illinois militiamen murdered Joseph Smith and his brother Hyrum in the Carthage Jail.

"The Church will fall now," she told Tom. "The members will scatter like chaff into the howling wind."

"Deliver me back to Quincy so I can make amends with my parents. Forget this religion, I beg you. It controls your life."

"Never, never again, ask me to leave these people," he warned. Tom looked as if she had slapped him across the face.

Another pain.

"I've had it, Elizabeth. Squeeze my hand. Squeeze hard."

Her sister-in-law rushed to her bedside, petted her and sponged her forehead and neck.

"You're doing good. Five minutes apart," Elizabeth called to the midwives, who had given her charge of their watch. "The Lord revealed in Moses that the purpose of it all is 'to bring to pass the immortality and eternal life of man.'"

"Amen, seconded the midwives in unison. "By bearing children unto the holder of the blessed priesthood, women become helpmates," one continued.

"'Only a woman can bestow upon her man that supernal title of father,'" Elizabeth further quoted the verbiage. "I wish I was having a baby for Heber."

"No, you don't," Nell yelled, her voice that of a prehistoric ancestor. "This is no birthday party. And, all I get out of it is a wailing, hungry mouth to feed. How will I make the trek west?"

"I'll be there for you. 'The Lord works in mysterious ways his wonders to perform.' Hush, now," Elizabeth whispered in Nell's ear. "Don't let the sisters, nor the Lord either, hear you babble like that.

You'll regret it."

"Damned if I care," said Nell. "This is killing me. Mama!" After the pain subsided, she tried to preoccupy herself by remembering what Mama told her on the day she broke and ran with Tom from her childhood home.

"Allow me," Mama glared at Heber and Tom. She pulled Nell into the parlor where Ruby slumped on a side chair, her head in her hands. "Do you know what you are doing?" Mama asked. "Your father will not have this. I know it. Someone's going to be killed. I have the most awful feeling. Last night I dreamed my teeth fell out. You know what that means."

For some unexplainable reason, these dreams invariably portended some traumatic family event, or so Mama wanted everyone to believe. She told her tooth dreams *after*, not before, old Bossy died, *after* the fire burned the hearth rug, and *after* the mysterious cracking of Grandma's antique bowl. Though the superstitious dreams annoyed Nell, she half-believed in their ominous power.

"You go out there and tell those nits to leave at once. How dare you accept a proposal! For shame! We don't need preaching. We don't need to put Papa and Arthur's lives in danger." Mama raised her hand to slap Nell's face, but Ruby, who had aimed to stand aside, caught it.

"What if I want to learn about their church?"

"Church?" Ruby scowled. "Don' you lie."

"Mama, I can't marry Arthur," Nell finally admitted.

"Why not?"

"I don't love him." There was a long silence.

Finally, Mama's eyes sparked with understanding. "Oh, oh, now I know. It's those horrible novels. If I told you once, I told you a hundred times. They're written to delude young ladies. Hear me out. There's no such thing as falling in love. You don't fall in love; you grow in it, silly girl. It takes a lifetime. Raising children, pouring candles, storing food, nursing the sick, making do. It's the family you love. What you're talking about is animal attraction. It will lead you to hell."

"Mama. I love Tom."

"My parents selected Charles for me, and I respected their choice. In our wisdom, we have done the same for you."

"Well, I mean to choose my own husband."

Ruby moaned.

"This is rash, rash," Mama said, clutching at her heart. "Don't do this to me. I am your mother. I gave you life. You know I can't bear this tension."

"Not this time, Mama. Will you hear *me*? I have to have my say."

Ruby nodded. "Have yo' say, chil'."

Mama glared at Nell, her face too close for comfort. "The choices you make now will determine the rest of your life. Don't you see? What hurts *you*, hurts us. If you involve yourself with Mormons, chances are you'll marry one. Then, where will you be? Dead? Driven from pillar to post? Poverty stricken? Oh, I wish I could shake some sense into you."

"That won't happen to me."

"No, not to you. You're one of a kind. Listen! A woman must be practical. We're cursed to follow our emotions, isn't that right, Ruby? This weakness requires us to marry honest and practical men, ruled by reason. Arthur is a kind, clean man, willing and able to provide for you. He will spare you the troubles of the world. What else do you want?"

"I don't want to be spared. I'm not like Ruby, traumatized once and forever after afraid to live."

"You're not a man, Nell. You can't support yourself, that's all there is to it. A married woman can't teach. You can't own land. You can't vote. Can't borrow or sign. What you *can* do is be wise. Use your beauty. Marry someone with power. Marry Arthur."

"Learn yo' place. Stop sewin' wif de wrong side de needle."

"No," she told her mother. "No," she yelled at Ruby. "This is my life." Despair spread its dark cloak over her. Could her mother and Ruby be right? Could being a woman mean being only half a person?

"Please, God, help me," Nell cried at the return of her labor. "I should have listened to Mama. I should never have left home."

"Four minutes apart," Elizabeth called out. When the other women scowled, Elizabeth explained that Nell was "overcome with the delirium."

Elizabeth gave Nell a birthing stick, which she had cut and wrapped in a damp cloth. Firmly, Nell held the twig between her teeth, but the pain rolled over her, too overwhelming for endurance. She spat the stick across the room and screamed. It was not her voice, but that of a mad woman. Her body "tore itself apart" like Old Aunt Emily said.

When the midwife tried to check if the baby's head showed, the misery seemed even more intense, and Nell accidentally kicked her aside. Insulted, the woman packed her birthing bag and made a dramatic exit by slamming the door behind her.

"Look what you've done!" the apprentice midwife yelled. "You're such a lot of trouble, yah."

"Good." Nell scowled. "I hate everyone."

"She's not in her right mind," Elizabeth said.

"Yah," said the apprentice, "I know how to deal vit her kind, I do."

"Yah," mocked Nell. "You get out too, you flee bitten old . . . "

"I fetch her back," the novice told Elizabeth. "I don't haf to put up vit dis."

She left.

"Control yourself." Elizabeth's hands gripped Nell's throat. "We've got to have at least one of them. I never saw a baby born before. If they both drop out, you and I will be left—alone!"

"Help me, Elizabeth," Nell screamed. "Do something!" Through the window, the neighbor's cow bellowed in return.

"Can't you make a better showing than this? For crying out loud! Screaming doesn't help anything. Concentrate, next time, on breathing, on the first time you and Tom was together, anything. Concentrate. Precious Jesus," Elizabeth placed her hands together in prayer. "Heber stopped by to tell me Tom's taking this pretty hard. The last time you cried out, he cut his head on the hearth, he pressed against it so. What are you trying to do?"

"I don't know. I hate this."

"I've got it. Next time, we'll pray."

"Oh sure. I can't pray."

"Why not?"

"Cause I . . . I don't even believe," Nell laughed hysterically. "I'm going to be one of the first ones baptized when the temple's ready, and I don't even believe that bit about the golden plates. I only said I did so Tom would marry me. How do you like that, Elizabeth?"

The pain subsided. Elizabeth lay beside Nell and cried for her sister's everlasting soul.

"Hold your tongue. Now, don't you say another word about not believing the Gospel. It hurts me. If these women pocket that secret, they'll plant it all over Nauvoo before morning."

To steady her nerves, Nell tried to recall when she and Elizabeth first met. She, Tom and Heber, weary from two days of travel from

Quincy, had no sooner rounded the curve, which allowed for Nell's first view of her new home, when Elizabeth sprang through the doorway. Only if she had been keeping watch could she have known of their approach. Arms outstretched, she glided like an angel over the road calling in a voice as clear as an oriole's warble, "Heber, you're home. Tom. Sister Baker."

Even at the distance of two city blocks, Nell sensed Elizabeth's warmth and femininity. She was a lively, striking tow-headed woman with a high, intelligent forehead, a broad face and wide hips, which accentuated a small waist. As the distance closed between them, Nell saw a little bun on top of her head and the fine hairs that framed her face like a wispy, white spider web. Being of the belief that all Mormon women wore stiff, black satin dresses and hid themselves in folds and gathers of fabric, Nell felt relieved that Elizabeth wore a soft yellow calico with short sleeves and a crisp white apron, which spoke for her cleanliness. The fanciful woman embraced and kissed Heber. She locked arms with Tom and quickly moved to peck Nell upon the cheek. "Welcome," she said, her smiling eyes shaped like the crescent moon. "I never had a real sister before."

The two women strolled arm-in-arm toward their home, a reddish-brown brick Colonial with white windowpanes and shudders, two chimneys and a new picket fence. "I've never seen a man so hopeful as your Tom," Elizabeth confided behind her hand. "Directly after stomping for the Prophet in Quincy, he ordered bricks and began expanding the house. Why, he begged off working on the temple," she whispered. "Imagine, Tom doing a thing like that! He was definitely struck!"

Nell wished he were more stricken with her than with God but didn't dare to mention that to Elizabeth. "If he's struck with me, as you say, why does he distance himself so?" Nell asked, free to confide on this. "He kissed me and held me but thrice, the last time in the presence of my mother when he first saw me three days ago. Do you suppose he's sorry he came for me?"

"Sorry?" exclaimed Elizabeth. "Heavens no. The way I see it, he's scared."

"Of what?"

"Of his own emotions. Why, at the very mention of your name, he turns all pale around the mouth. He won't eat. I don't know if you've noticed it, but he's a passionate man. Open your eyes, girl. Don't you see it?" Instantly, Nell felt she had known Elizabeth all her life. Why was it that some people could meet for the first time and feel like old friends? The bond, which usually comes after years of learning to trust, had already sealed.

The apprentice midwife and Nell's next contraction returned. "Look vhat you've done!" the woman scolded. Her thin lips pursed when her button-like eyes narrowed. "She's gone. I could not coax her back. Yah. And, you've upset de men."

"Oh, no, not again," Nell whispered. This time the contraction was a crushing wave.

"Control yourself," said Elizabeth. "Two minutes apart!"

"I can't. This is the worst time of my life."

"You must."

"Why?" Nell moaned.

"Because we know how painful this is, don't you see? Tom and all of us suffer with you, we love you so. After this, all of us will be changed."

"I can't help myself. Wait until you do this. Then, you'll know."

"If you can buck up to this, girl, you can do anything."

Elizabeth's words lay with Nell. Although Elizabeth, newly converted from a revival sect in New York, was very much a zealot, and although she knew the secret of Nell's false conversion, she had stood by her friend like family and had done Nell's chores at the end of her term. Her advice had been sincere and true. Next time, Nell decided, she would spare the men.

"After it's all over," said Elizabeth, "we'll send a messenger to tell your people. They might visit to see their grandchild."

"No, they won't. They don't even want to know. When I told my father I wanted to marry Tom and to have him preach to me, he said, 'Over my dead body.' He raged at Tom and cursed me when I bundled my belongings. 'From this day forth,' he said, 'you are no daughter of mine.' If I left, he never wanted to see me again."

Nell moaned and Elizabeth offered her the twig. "Hold on, dear girl. You can do this. Do you remember when you told me people can't stop doing what they've always done? They can't turn around? Well, can you?"

"Yes," Nell clutched the bed cover. Even if it killed her, she vowed silence. Why cry out? The cavalry wasn't coming. "Alright, here it comes," she warned. "You pray, I'll bite."

"Precious Jesus," Elizabeth chimed. "Have mercy on her soul. Mercy, Jesus." She gently stroked Nell's arm.

That remarkable touch, contrasted with the pain, strengthened Nell's resolve. She tried with all her might to think of something besides the crushing contraction, namely, the Valley of the Great Salt Lake that everyone had been discussing, "nestled on the slopes of the Rocky Mountains, where the Saints would thrive, unmolested, at last." Breathing long and deep, she imagined the home she and Tom would build there.

"She believes. I know she believes," Elizabeth prayed. I ask thee, Lord, that thou might take into account the agony of this dear girl, and, in the name of Jesus Christ, I give her a sister's blessing that she might soon deliver her little child into the world, for it is only through a woman that a man might become the father of fathers, and, therefore, is a woman superior to the man, in that she brings forth life . . . "

Elizabeth prayed without pausing to breath. She sobbed until she trembled; then, she spoke in tongues, better known as "the language of heaven," and flopped upon the bed next to Nell. In falling, she dropped the birthing watch.

"If dat's broke, you pay," the midwife barked. "Yah, you haf to pay."

After a time, whether short or long—Nell did not know—the pressure failed to let up at all. Pulling on the slats of her headboard, she cracked one and threw it, along with the twig, at the wall. She bore down and never as much as sighed, even after Elizabeth come back to herself, mumbled for a time and finally asked what was going on.

"The head, it's the head," Elizabeth finally exclaimed. She clapped and jumped in elation. "It's got hair!"

"Push," commanded the midwife. "Das is goot."

With all the strength that remained in her exhausted body, Nell pushed, and her daughter slipped, snorting and squealing, into the world.

FAMILY

September 7, 1845

*Tom placed our precious child at my breast, and all memory of the birth
vanished. What I thought to be the most horrid experience of my life is now
the richest, most natural and meaningful. I thank God for our perfect little
Jennifer and for my beloved family. My cup runneth over.*

Nell slept. After eleven hours of labor, she did not awake until
the setting sun cast shimmering elm leaves across her pillow. In the
rocker beside her bed slumped Elizabeth, her head drooping so far to
the side that it appeared her neck had been broken. "Elizabeth, you
look awful." When Nell pushed her shoulder, her drowsy head dropped
forward, nearly into her lap.

"Wha. Mmmm. Awful?" She rubbed her swollen eyes, stretched,
and yawned. "Shall I bring the baby?"

"What is it?"

"A girl."

"Good. Healthy?"

"Perfect. Ten fingers, ten toes. Will you nurse her now?"

"I don't know. I don't think I can."

"Nobody knows how the first time. Accept her like a cat accepts
her kittens. Offer the nipple. I'm going to bed, Nell. I'm done for.
You're fine. When the baby cries, Tom will bring it." Elizabeth stumbled out of the room.

At the moment, Nell was not certain she wanted to renew a relationship with Tom or to claim her child. Both represented takers, and,

emotionally, she had nothing left to give. Peering into the hand-mirror on her nightstand, she was surprised that a young woman looked back, for she felt very old. Never in her life had she been so sore. Never had she been so helpless and exhausted. How was she to mend herself? If she hadn't sparked Tom nine months ago, flirted and egged him on, she wouldn't be in this vulnerable state now; she wouldn't be forced to bear up under the awesome weight of taking charge of a new life.

Her thoughts raced back to their wedding night a week after their arrival in Nauvoo, the night when Tom slept beside her on their bed, her under the quilt, him on top of it. He made no move to consummate their marriage. "Goodnight, Nell" was all he said, and he had passed her mouth for a Platonic kiss on the cheek. Clutching her hand, he immediately fell into a contented sleep. Nell concluded that the wedding preparations and dancing to the lively music of Captain Pitt's Brass Band at the recreation hall exhausted both of them, mentally and physically, and that patience and understanding must prevail. Besides, she remembered Cousin Julia's saying that the first time was the worst, and she dreaded it . . . somewhat.

However, after waiting for three full weeks, she felt insulted. Oh, he treated her with all kindness. But, solely in his words did the fire of desire burn. "I love you, my beauty," "we will never again separate," "precious," and "my sweet" dripped daily from his tongue; but each time she drew near him, he turned pale about the mouth, as Elizabeth had observed, and shuffled his feet like a schoolboy.

Nell heard footsteps on the stairs. Was it Tom, bringing Jennifer to nurse? Since her door did not open, she continued her reverie of the events that led up to her present state. She remembered spending many hours each day at her dressing table arranging and re-arranging her hair. To attract Tom, she bathed often—every fourth day, at the least. And, she constantly questioned Elizabeth about her breath, her speech and her clothing. Is this skirt too full? Does this fabric go well with my complexion? What physical characteristic do men most admire in a woman?"

"I have no idea. Well, maybe the breasts. Maybe not. Do I detect lust?" Elizabeth winked. "I could use a little help with the dishes."

"Everyone knows he hasn't touched me. Heber, and everybody else, must think there's something wrong with me."

"I didn't know you cared what others thought. Pride is one of the seven deadly sins, you know."

"Pride? Elizabeth, you don't understand."

"Oh, I do," said Elizabeth. "I have my eyes. Like Heber, Tom's mind is heavy lately; there's the pressure of finishing the temple so we can do our sealings and endowments before traveling as true saints into the wilderness; there are the mobs and spies, the wagon building, the growing of crops and food preservation. Why, don't you see, the man is beside himself with work and worry. He's filled with hatred over the martyrdom of President Smith and Brother Hyrum. And Heber, too. I heard them wishing for a chance to, how shall I say it, 'avenge our beloved prophet's blood.' You've got to be patient."

"How long? Heber has the same work and worry as Tom; so do the other men. But, I don't see them neglecting their wives."

Nell wondered if the baby took after her side of the family or Tom's. Surely, it must have awakened by now. Was there a problem? To while away the time, Nell tried to reinvent Elizabeth's exact words. "Tom is not 'other men.' Heber thinks it has something to do with his being the older brother and having all those responsibilities when their father left. I think different. I think it comes from losing his mother. The brothers loved her so. When she died, Heber said all the sweetness in their lives died with her. Tom took it hard. Losing a mother is a terrible thing." Elizabeth's lower jaw trembled. "She was from Scotland. Jennifer. The boy's father called her *Jenny* when he brought her flowers from the fields."

"So? I had nothing to do with their losses. Why must I suffer?"

"So, I'll speak right out. He's terrified of losing you. He doesn't want you with child during the exodus. This, I know. Don't ask me how. Just take my word on it. Now, you dry and I'll wash."

Nell considered what Elizabeth told her, but it didn't seem logical. Married couples had children. That came with the territory. Finally, after attending church on Sunday, she thought she had stumbled upon the reason Tom kept her at arm's length. The speaker said that without his wife he could not have "the highest and most lasting blessings of the priesthood of the holiest order of God." He quoted from the Doctrine and Covenants: "In order to obtain the highest, a man must enter into this order of the priesthood (meaning marriage); And if he does not, he cannot obtain it." She concluded that Tom had married her, not for herself, but for the purpose of advancing himself in heaven!

While Tom failed to embrace her for another week, Heber continually mauled Elizabeth. Nell, envious of their openness, pointed out that their immodesty offended her. They regularly retired early, murmuring low in their dimly lit room deep into the night, and once Heber chased Elizabeth, her laughter ringing like a bell, into their tall, bountiful corn patch, where they stayed for upwards of an hour. On the contrary, each night long after Nell had climbed into bed and had turned down the lantern's wick, Tom crept into their chamber room. Because she knew he wished it, she pretended to sleep. And, when she studied his peaceful face in the early morning hours and admired his strong bare shoulders, she dreamed of lying in his arms, of feeling his lips on her neck and his hands on her. Then, recalling that lust was another of the seven deadly sins, even worse than pride, she turned away from him on the verge of tears.

Nell's breasts looked and felt enlarged under her quilt. An urgent need to have her child overcame her. "Tom," Nell called out, and her voice sounded strangely weak. "I want my baby." While waiting for an answer, Nell drowsed and continued to reminisce about how she allowed the contrast in relationships to shame her for nearly a month. She remembered her determination to turn matters around, whether or not it meant sinning and whether or not it meant making herself a fool. For sacrament meeting, she decked herself in bright pink party attire, complete with a swooping neckline, a hoop and a great black sash. Her most outlandish bonnet, white with black feathers on the edges, crowned her head, and she painted her lips like a doll's, for good measure, to capture Tom's attention. Because Nell took her time to dress, Heber and Elizabeth decided to go ahead. When they left, she revealed herself to Tom. He stood speechless.

"For you," Nell said. "How do you like it?" She whirled around.

"Well, my dear, I don't . . . um . . . know. He turned his back to conceal a smile. "Most of the women wear black frocks. You know, black with long sleeves. No frills. You might feel a mite out of place." He cleared his throat. "It's not that I don't like ball gowns. It's just that . . . Don't you have something else?"

"Oh," said Nell, innocently. "I do have a black dress. Wait. I'll hurry." She rushed into their room, but left the door sufficiently ajar for Tom to watch her change. Slowly, she undressed. Feeling a twinge of guilt, she wondered what Elizabeth would call *this* sin. She glanced through the slit in their door, uncertain if Tom watched or not. He lounged at the keeping room table, his back to her, watching the last flames die at the hearth. "Who is he?" she wondered. "What have I done to discourage him?" "Shall a woman take the first step? And, if she does, will the man stand even further off?"

To avoid worrying, she undressed as if she were alone. After removing the fanciful gown, she stood in her pantaloons and camisole before the mirror. She pinched her cheeks. Then, surprising herself, she pulled the camisole over her head to reveal her full breasts. Bending, swaying her hips, and stretching as if to yawn, she located another camisole in her bureau. Then, she wiggled into it and leaned forward to tightly draw the string, which lifted her breasts higher than the other had. The dress she slipped into might have been modest on some women, but not on her. Despite its high linen collar and long sleeves with linen cuffs, its snug fit enhanced her petite and full figure to its greatest advantage. Tiny mother of pearl buttons and narrow pleats at the bodice added an elegant touch. Mama once said it bordered on sinful but conceded that her daughter was not to blame.

Now aware of Tom's attention, Nell admired herself in the mirror by running her hands over her neck, breasts, waist and hips. She combed through her hair, turning the stiff ringlets into waves that nearly reached her waist. Securing it back with a black, satin ribbon, she exposed the ears, which she had caught Tom admiring on the journey from Quincy. After securing the genuine, pearl earrings, which Tom had given her on their wedding day, she blotted her flaming lips into a soft pink tone. When she flung open the chamber door, Tom gave her that side smile, which made her yearn for a kiss. "The more modest your dress, the more desirable you become," he smiled. "But, never you mind. You can't help it."

Arm in arm, they sauntered toward the meetinghouse, Tom's leg swishing rhythmically across Nell's crisp silk skirt. Every minute or so, he glanced down at her and then lifted his head high, proud and holy as any bishop. They exchanged greetings with several neighbors, the men obviously unable to conceal their enchantment, the women veiling their envy. Nell recognized it in their eyes when she said, "How do" as artless as a lamb. She saw that Tom was proud that men admired his wife.

Finally, he remarked, "I really do appreciate your changing, Nell, without being offended. You are not aware of our ways, that's all. Time will easily change that."

"Oh, I don't mind, Tom," Nell returned. "The only problem is that in my haste, I forgot my pantaloons." To Nell's disappointment, his only reaction was a tiny twitch at the corner of his eye. Finally, a restrained grin played on one side of his mouth. Several times, he moistened his full, manly lips. Suddenly, at the gate of the church, he stiffened, twitched his mustache, and heaved a great sigh. He gathered Nell into his wondrous arms. This time, their kiss simmered with passion.

"Excuse us, Brother Mortenson," a male voice spoke.

"Really," said a feminine one. Nell's skirt whistled as neighbors passed on the narrow walkway.

Nell took pleasure in remembering the delicious hours that followed. Tom had whisked her off the ground and carried her to Heber's carriage where he leaped up next to her and raced home. They had consummated their marriage. She remembered, and hoped never to forget, her overwhelming feeling of being connected to all the forces of nature. The white around Tom's mouth had disappeared. In the days that followed, it had seemed very sweet when Elizabeth and Heber retired early to whisper in the dark.

These memories were hers and hers alone. Keeping them private would be appropriate because some events in one's life are too sacred for writing or discussion. However, a few months later, Nell had realized she was with child. Because she had committed in that day most every sin known to man, she had become the fountainhead of her own suffering.

A newborn fussed outside her door. Tom's heavy knuckles rapped on the wood.

"Come in," said Nell. The baby, at last!

"Thank you," said Tom. The sweet innocence of his child reflected in his own countenance. His large hands cradling the tiny bundle took Nell's breath away. "How can I repay you for our little girl?" he asked. He pressed Nell's hand to his lips, nibbled it, and brushed hair from her forehead. Then, he placed the new life close to his wife's breast. "She's hungry."

Nell smelled the pink, warm baby. She ran her hand over the fuzzy little head. Instinctively, she licked its cheek. Between them was nothing . . . and everything. When the new life cooed and rooted for nourishment at her neck, Nell offered her engorged breast, and it suckled without being taught.

"I want to call her Jennifer, after your mother . . . Jenny for short."

"That will be just fine," Tom grinned. "How did you know? I love you . . . for thinking of her." He offered a prayer of thanksgiving.

In that moment, Nell forgot all about the delivery, the seven deadly sins, and the hardships of caring for a new life. It was as her mother, her Aunt Emily, and her cousins had said. She knew mother love.

ALL IS WELL

(Diary)   *September 14, 1845*

Golden days. Though sleep-deprived, Elizabeth and I love and care for baby, household, garden. Tom and Heber provide. A fool is one who is happy and does not know it.

A week after Jennifer's birth, Nell itched for the activity of her former life. Though the midwives and the family insisted that she remain bedridden for at least ten days, she knew the time had come to rise up, to be seen, to be heard, to grasp the ladle of life and stir. Having been fed on rich streams of mother's milk, the rosy child lay next to her in the ecstasy of sleep. While Nell admired its adoring little face, she planned a journey to Quincy in the spring for the purpose of melting the icy wall that separated her from her family when she left over a year ago. She understood the irresistible power of a first grandchild. For now, the autumn sun beckoned through the open door. Nell dressed. She placed a shawl about her shoulders to please Tom and stepped into the warm midday light. In this glowing moment, all seemed right with the world.

Not far from the house, Elizabeth bent over her garden, her white hair falling forward over her face and her ample hips swaying while she harvested orange pumpkins, yellow squash, red tomatoes, dark green beet tops and brown potatoes—all stacked in a pile on the grass like a bouquet of flowers. The family thrived on her delicious soups, her stews and her hot bread, topped with Old Red's yellow butter. Most of the excess vegetables, she stored in the cool cellar along with apples, pears and dried peaches. Some of it she traded for fabric, shoes, candles, pottery and the like, and a portion of it she sold at a significant price, foodstuffs being scarce due to the great influx of immigrants into Nauvoo. Elizabeth stashed her profits into a coffee can in the cupboard behind the plates. At first, Tom and Heber regarded the can as trivial, but when it grew heavy with a steady flow of cash, the men changed their tune. Nell and Elizabeth took great pleasure in this. They all laughed heartily one day after three women, straight out of Ireland, tussled over two cabbages, "the sweetest in town" and paid a quarter for one head!

"I truly believe that if Elizabeth were dropped anywhere on earth," said Tom, "she would be able to grow whatever she'd a mind to."

"That's not my doing," Elizabeth responded. "It's the rich soil and the manure you men throw there after harvest. Gardening, like life, is all about soil preparation. After that, nature does the work."

"We sure did luck out," Tom patted Heber's back. "Each hitching up to a woman of means. Why, they ought to vote. Soon, Nell will begin teaching. Then, we will kick back."

"Play cards." Heber thought he was funny. "Spit tobacco and sing along with a Jew's harp."

Beyond Elizabeth's garden, Tom and Heber called back and forth to one another over the whiz of their saws. According to their routine, they busied themselves building prairie schooners, one after another, each exactly like all the rest, and Nell, who advertised and kept records, had orders stretching into the months ahead for people who foresaw one last exodus of the Saints. On this day, however, the brothers worked for the joy of it, each building his personal dream wagon, "the strongest and most time-consuming prototype of a wagon that has ever been assembled." They used white oak, not elm, for the frame. With seasoned hardwood pins, they doweled together filed boards for a snug fit. They added six inches to the width of the wagon to prevent rollovers; they subtracted six inches from the length to decrease stress on the wheels. They built a slightly smaller wheel than they used on standard models, the felloes of black walnut because it was soft and would bear rounding. Using slightly heavier iron, they framed the rim. In the event of an unlikely failure, they bolted a spare wheel onto the underside. A lightweight storage case, which also served as a bed and a seat, fit one-third the width of the box. They added hooks, straps, railings, leather ties, ropes, toolboxes, water bags, buckets, and every possible necessity for a three-month trek. While socializing or resting on the front porch, each brother carved a nameplate for his tailgate. Heber named his wagon "Lizzy," and Tom called his "the Ark." If, or when, the Mortenson family sailed across the prairie, these were the invincible ships that would carry them.

Not wanting anyone to shoo her back into bed, Nell hurried directly to her little schoolroom, the hastily built lean-to, which Tom and Heber had attached to the home shortly after she arrived in Nauvoo. She peeped through the window at a childless room. Behind the donated pot-bellied stove, the wood and kindling waited for the spark of a fire, slates anticipated small, untrained hands, and *McGuffey's Eclectic Primer* lay in a stack ready to be read. For her first lesson, Nell had written "The Value of Thrift" on a little blackboard in front of the room. After a quick recovery, she hoped to hear, at last, little voices calling her "teacher."

Much to her surprise, the Mormon people encouraged married women to teach. "Who, if not a married woman, is better fit for the important job of educating future generations," they proclaimed. When her term became evident, "no one was better fit than a mother." Anticipating her "calling," children brought her flowers, picked along the wayside; parents sent her apples, soaps, and an occasional hen; and the Church Education Fund supplied her with paper, slates and ink. Being the children's "real teacher" was what Nell had only dreamed of in Quincy, but here among the Mormon people her dream was about to materialize.

"Good morning, Sister Mortenson," Adeline Reed greeted Nell from her carriage. "Up and about so soon? How's the baby?"

"Healthy," said Nell.

"I'll be calling soon with my apple pudding."

"Thanks," Nell answered.

These amazing Mormons! The more stressful and difficult their situation, the more they accomplished, thrived, and increased. Indeed, they were a force. No constitutional government, no state, no faction of any type could hinder or control their self-determination now. How Nell admired their industry, their craftsmanship, their diverse culture, and their tolerance. Like excellent clay, they passed through the kiln without cracking, and the mortar of their beliefs held them together through many a blast. Nell loved living among them. Despite the doctrine that separated her from them, she was of their mold.

"Nell, what are you doing in the cool morning air?" Elizabeth called from her garden. Tom rushed to his wife's side and gathered her into his arms. "Why in the world are you about?"

"Because this day is too beautiful to stay inside."

With hands that smelled of oak, Tom covered her eyes. He kissed her lightly, and turned her toward the east. "Look there, beyond our acres and over the housetops. The spire is on the temple."

"It's gorgeous," said Nell. "Oh, how I love this moment. Oh, how I love my life. Tom, do you ever have the feeling that everything is just too lovely to be true? That you dare not say so, or even think so, out of fear that some calamity awaits you?"

"Don't mention it, then," said Tom, trudging thoughtfully at her side toward the house.

9

RED REVENGE

(Diary)   *September 24, 1845*

An oppressive atmosphere hangs over the beloved Nauvoo. At the same time, the membership continues to build the temple, embellish their homes, fields and shops. Their sermons urge preparations for yet another move, this time to a far away place where they plan to worship unmolested. If we are forced to leave, I shall say goodbye to Illinois and everything I know and love.

"Tom, Heber," someone yelled outside the window. "Come, quick!" It was four o'clock in the morning three weeks after little Jennifer's birth. Tom and Nell, "tuckered out" from the baby's night feedings, slept through the raucous.

"Tom, Tom. Fire," Heber burst into the room. When Tom rolled out of bed, he fumbled for his rifle. He pointed it toward the window.

"No, Tom," cautioned Heber. "It's Brother King."

"Ya, I see him." Tom unlatched and threw open the window. "What's afoot?"

"The mob's set fire to homes down on the Warsaw road a piece. See there? The Legion's been called to meet, just south of the big bend. Get Heber. Hurry."

"He's here, Major Sir," answered Tom in military fashion. Before Nell lit a lantern, Heber and Tom, still buttoning their militia shirts, rushed out the front door. Outside, guards to the city were posted in their emergency positions, and windows flickered with dim light as far as Nell could see, all the way to the temple. Way off to the south, the sky glowed red. This wasn't the only night of violence, by any means. Since Nell had first heard of Mormons in Quincy, tension had grown between them and the "gentiles" of Hancock County. It smoldered beneath the seeming idyllic atmosphere of Nauvoo, and, at the slightest stir, roared into full, devouring flames.

"Lord, be with us." Elizabeth slid under Nell's bed quilts next to the baby. "The prophecies are true. These are the last days, Nell. I know it. The anti's have torched the whole countryside. Nauvoo is next. They'll unroof every house."

"Not with Tom and Heber and the Nauvoo Legion out there. Why would a handful of night raiders want to go up against them?" The shivering Elizabeth curled like a potato bug around the baby.

"Bear up with me," said Nell. "You're to load the spare rifles, remember? I don't know how. These house-burners are not men; they couldn't scare off an old setting hen."

"I'm so afraid, Nell. I hear they paint their faces, hideously. They've insulted and ravished our women. Why do our men leave now in our hour of need?" If horses had not thundered down the road in front of the house to further frighten Elizabeth, she might have crawled out of bed to load the guns, but she stayed. "I'll warm Jenny," she said.

"Brother Brigham has called up hundreds this time," said Nell, keeping watch at the window. "You should see all of our men, like a river streaming south. This violence is like those blazing homes. It cannot be contained. From one hateful deed to another, down through the history of mankind, it goes. Who is strong enough to resist reacting?"

"Who is strong enough to return an act of hate with one of love?"

"If I've said it once, I've said it a hundred times: people have the devil of a time stopping what they're doing."

"Oh Father, protect Tom and Heber," Elizabeth prayed. "Please, do not allow anyone to shoot them, and do not allow them to shoot someone else. Bless this home, Oh Lord. Protect this babe and us from harm."

While she prayed, Nell dressed and then, under the mending basket next to her rocker, she hid her favorite butcher knife. "I fear this business will result in further persecutions. The men mean to put a stop, once and for all, to this carnage."

Nell had not spoken truer words. Hundreds rode on that night of the red sky, but thousands would follow. A week later, Tom and Heber had been among the first to muster when Brigham Young called for two thousand men of the Nauvoo Legion to assist the Hancock County sheriff in searching out and bringing to justice the villains who had burned into cinders forty-five Mormon homes in outlying farms.

"Please don't go," Nell pleaded with Tom. "I fear for your life, and I'm asking you not to abandon me and Jenny when we need your protection."

"What I am doing is protecting you," Tom patiently explained to Nell. "You know that. Trust me. There are guards a-plenty posted all over Nauvoo. Nobody would dare to show his face around here right now. They're a set of cutthroats, robbers and assassins who need to be put out of the way, the whole lot of them. I'll be glad to avenge the Prophet's death. We will teach them what fear is."

"Abandon vengeance, for the sake of this family," Elizabeth said. "You are the older brother. Heber will do what you do." These words surprised Nell because Elizabeth had never stood in the way of what Church authorities wanted.

"I will never let it go," Tom vowed, "not until justice has been carried out. I hate the mob. God will lead us. His will be done." Tom, Heber, and hundreds of other Mormons had seethed with anger since two days after Nell's marriage when some of the elders brought Joseph and Hyrum Smith's dead bodies from the Carthage Jail to Nauvoo. Now, the flames of hatred burned anew. Their cry was "Revenge." They too would become burners. The men left on their mission. In the quiet that fills a house after the masculinity has gone out of it, the women waited and paced their clean floors.

"I hope they don't have to kill anyone," Nell said to Elizabeth, who rocked near the dim light of the fire. "How could they live with themselves?"

"I don't know," said Elizabeth. "I used to know. But, with all this hatred, I don't know anything anymore."

"What is it about men? They're a hard set. You don't see women shooting one another, or burning homes."

"No," replied Elizabeth, her voice almost inaudible. She stroked and smelled the baby's downy head. "After helping to bring a life into this world, taking life is almost impossible."

"Why do they hate us?" Nell rocked to and fro. "What is it about us?"

"You probably know the answer to that better than I do, having lived in Quincy and all. Like I said, I don't know."

"Actually, a Mormon family who had been smoked out of their home in Missouri lived with us for a few days one winter. Father sympathized with them then, but with time, he grew to despise their politics, the fact that Mormons gained control by voting together. He feared the great power of the Nauvoo Legion, but he never wanted to kill anyone over it, well, anyone except Tom."

"He disowned his own daughter over it, didn't he? I guess they fear us, maybe. Fear leads to hate and hate leads to any number of sins. They complain because we stay to ourselves, but they won't have us living among them."

"They don't want their women involved with Mormon men, I can speak for that. Oh, how I miss my family, my stubborn old mule and Ruby too."

"I know. I guess they never did answer Tom's note about Jennifer's birth."

"No," Nell said sadly. Suddenly, an idea popped into her head. "Maybe, we Sisters could make a difference. I mean, if we bartered more often with gentiles . . . On second thought, the men won't allow that, nor the Sisters either, not now they've killed the Prophet and whatever innocence we had left. It's just a matter of who has the largest militia and the truest rifles."

"God won't let them defeat us." Elizabeth rose and laid the baby in her rocker.

"Are you sure about that? Could it be that he loves them too?" Nell reached under the mending basket to touch her butcher knife.

Tears streamed down Elizabeth's cheeks. She said nothing. With her foot, she gently rocked the crib where the new baby slept. "Would you be able to kill if I loaded one of those guns?"

Nell thought about this question for so long, she almost fell asleep. "Well, if I had to," she finally answered. "If it came down to them or us, right here in this house, I suppose I'd try. If I hit anything, it would be a miracle."

Pondering their questions, they dozed in their rockers until dawn when the baby's cry pierced the night. Nell rose to change and feed the child. For some time, Elizabeth peered out the window into a darkness that was "too quiet for that red glow on the horizon." Then, she swept the floor. She served tea and hard biscuits, which neither ate. They rinsed their dishes. They listened, and when they thought they heard hoof beats, they quit whatever it was their hands were doing to listen again.

"I don't like waiting," Elizabeth said.

"Me neither. It's the hardest part," answered Nell.

"I'd rather be with them."

"Yah. But, we'd only aggravate matters. I've got to practice shooting," Nell said. "You won't, Elizabeth. We both know that. It's up to me. Nobody's going to hurt my baby, not while I'm alive."

"Wouldn't it be wonderful if everybody could live like the five of us?"

"For certain." Nell recalled how the three had supported her while she recuperated; how they carried her weight and insisted that she rest long past the time when her energy had returned; how Elizabeth had kept a fire throughout the cool September nights to warm the baby; how Tom had walked slowly with his arm supporting her around the vegetable and rose gardens and set her on a chair while he weeded; how one day Heber had scrubbed a batch of the baby's diapers until it had taken the color from his face. "Someday, I'll repay you for all you've done, Elizabeth. I swear, I will."

"I don't need to be repaid. You are the only sister I ever had."

"Everything would be perfect if my family came by, or even if they sent a note. I miss them terribly."

With their chores done, the women bundled the baby against the cool morning air of late September and carried her little basket, one on either side, up the road to Iva Lou and Minnie King's home, where it was their "calling" to assemble and seal canvas water bags for a possible exodus to "Zion." Nauvoo bustled with members preparing for a journey into Mexican territory, where they "might worship Almighty God in peace."

Neither Nell nor Elizabeth sought out the company of the King women. For one thing, they kept about them a "holier than thou" attitude, which came out of their being among the chosen few who were sufficiently devout to live the holy principle of polygamy. For another, they were waspish sorts. Elizabeth, having lived near them longer than Nell, knew their history.

Iva Lou and John King married in their youth. After giving her devout husband two sons, Sister Iva Lou announced one day that she wanted no more children, for she was a large woman and each child added to her mass. But, Brother King was bent on building up a numerous generation unto the Lord. He prayed constantly for an answer to his problem. So, when the Prophet revealed the principal of plural marriage, John considered it his own private miracle. Being one of the main carpenters during the building of the temple and a devout member of the Melchizedek Priesthood, Brother King was allowed to take a second wife, Minnie, Iva Lou's buxom fifteen-year-old cousin. A hearty appetite ran in their family. And, it was interesting that Iva Lou gladly accepted the new revelation, at first; however, as time passed, she had a terrible time trying to live it.

"I don't much like working with the King sisters," Elizabeth complained while she walked along, the fussing baby in her arms. "I'm wondering if there is a way we might leave the assembling of bags to them. Instead, why not make wagon covers at our place? Someone has to."

"I don't like working with them either, especially that Iva Lou. She's bossy as an old lead cow."

"Who's going to ask Tom and Heber?"

"It looks like that will be me," Nell said. "The two of them would weigh more than an ox," she quipped.

"Oh, Nell, your arrogance is sinful." Elizabeth laughed in spite of herself.

"Yes. We should take Iva Lou westward with us, for we could render her out and have lard for the entire journey." They both giggled at their private and familiar joke. "Polygamy isn't right," said Nell. "I fear it."

"Why? If it is God's will, we must humble ourselves and obey."

"Not I. I'm one who won't accept it," Nell quickened her step. "The Kings think they're better than the rest of us, that God loves them more."

"The authorities, I believe, know you better than you think. You won't be asked, Nell. Plural marriage is only for a special few who are worthy."

"Well, the King women don't seem all that holy to me," Nell said. "There's more to it."

"Do I hear envy?"

"Oh, you and your deadly sins. It's not envy. I just despise their uppity attitude."

"Then, is it hate?"

By the time the Mortenson women arrived, the Kings had finished the handwork on four water bags. "It's about time you're up," scolded Iva Lou. "Thrift, ladies, thrift. We must all do our part. Fetch your tools. Measure and cut that pile of canvas."

"The town is awful quiet with the men gone," remarked Elizabeth.

"Why can't people leave us alone? What started this house burning craze anyway?" asked Nell.

"It happened like this," Iva Lou said. "There was an anti meeting in Green Plains. Someone fired shots on the meeting, and the rumor spread like a grass fire through all the gentile communities that a Mormon fired the shot."

"Our people didn't do it," Minnie said, who vied for the Mortenson women's attention. "But, the gentiles testified that we did. After vowing vengeance on Nauvoo, they started burning. Tiny Mormon settlements have been torched to the ground."

"Forty-four of them," Iva Lou said.

"Forty-six," Minnie said.

"I'm telling this. You be still." Iva Lou rose and stood in front of Minnie. "Sheriff Backenstros, a friend to our cause, went to Warsaw and Carthage to raise a posse to capture the marauders. He failed to recruit a single volunteer. The way we heard it, the Carthage Greys . . . "

"That same company which was given the charge of Joseph Smith's precious life while he was jailed . . . " Minnie interrupted.

"You just sit down and stitch, young woman," Iva Lou shook her finger in Minnie's face. "You're not going to ruin my story. Where was I? Oh, I know. The Carthage Greys would have shot our Sheriff Backenstros if Orrin Porter Rockwell— "

"—bodyguard to the late Prophet—," Minnie said.

"—had not shot one of them first. I heard Rockwell's story, right out of his own mouth," Iva Lou bragged, "when John and I attended a council meeting."

"I heard it too," Minnie said, "at the same time, only Iva Lou wasn't invited to the meeting. We heard it outside the window."

Iva Lou blushed. "You go inside, right now, and tend to your nose," she hissed at Minnie. "I'm the first wife, and John said you must obey. Go on, inside." When Minnie giggled instead, Iva Lou chased her with a water bag.

"You're just jealous because John loves me the most," Minnie yelled out the window, glad to be sent into the house because the heavy work bruised her tender hands.

Embarrassed, Elizabeth and Nell hurriedly cut canvas for the water bags. More than learning what caused the fires, they were experiencing, first hand, how spiritual wifery functioned. These days, no one mentioned plural marriage in public, except in a whisper, for spies were reported to have filtered into the city. But, everyone knew that Brother King had obtained the fullness of the holy priesthood and could be equal to the Savior. Without it, the Prophet had said, "one could only attain to the position of the angels, who are servants and messengers to those who attain to the Godhead."

Presently, Iva Lou called Minnie to come back, and the two of them went on to split their story. Iva Lou began. "Rockwell and Jackson Redden, you know him, were returning to Nauvoo after helping some burned-out families move their belongings. They stopped along the Warsaw road to water their horses. Suddenly, our Sheriff Backenstros charged over a hill, straight toward them. It's a miracle Rockwell didn't shoot him because he pulled his animal to a halt just short of running them down."

"You forgot to say that Rockwell and Redden charged their arms, being wary sorts," Minnie grinned.

"What does that matter?" snapped Iva Lou.

"It matters because you always say it. It's part of the story and you forgot it."

"Quiet!" Iva Lou stretched her girth over the table and gave Minnie a slap on the face. "You've given out the best part before I got to it." She turned to Nell. "'Protect me,' Backenstros shouted."

Minnie covered her nose with her apron. Bright, red blood stained it. Still, she refused to give up. "You forgot part of it again. 'Protect me in the name of the State of Illinois, County of Hancock,' Backenstros shouted." Upon examining the apron, tears welled in her eyes.

"I mean it this time. Get out! I'm first wife. We'll have to beat you when John comes home, we will!" Iva Lou rose up like a mountain over Minnie. In attempting to avoid her sister-in-marriage, Minnie tipped her chair and rolled off onto the ground. She crawled toward the house, her face afire with blood and rage.

"She's a trial to me," explained Iva Lou. "Lazy as a slug. During the day, she doesn't lift a finger, but when John walks through the door, that woman hustles her baggage about the house with a broom. How she wiggles her tail at him! I've asked him to whip her more than once, but you know how men are. 'She's a tender, young thing,' he says. I don't know what he sees in her."

"I heard that," Minnie called from the kitchen. "I'll never forgive you."

"Don't mind her," Iva Lou said. "She'll be over it in an hour or two. She's simple enough."

Iva Lou cut rope for the bag handles, scratching her arm several times before she had sufficiently cooled to go on with her story. "Rockwell is the best with a rifle. He told the sheriff not to worry. He stood his stand. Two armed mobsters road over the hill and raced down on Rockwell, the sheriff and Redden. One horse stumbled, throwing its rider, but the other kept coming. The rider reached for his pistol, and what do you think? Before he could get it from the holster, a slug from Rockwell's rifle tore into the man's middle and blew him from his saddle." Iva Lou snickered, but Nell saw no humor in it. Elizabeth, who riveted the bags, barely missed her fingers with the hammer.

"Five more Carthage Greys arrived upon the scene with a wagon. But, not one would go up against our Samson. It is recorded in the church records, John told me, that Joseph Smith himself promised Brother Rockwell that . . . " Iva stood and cupped her hands to memorize. " 'So long as ye shall remain loyal and true to thy faith, ye need fear no enemy. Cut not thy hair and no bullet or blade can harm thee!' "

"You stood and recited didn't you, Iva Lou King?" Minnie squealed from inside the house.

"May God punish you," Iva Lou shouted. Nervously, she returned to cutting rope and presently smiled sweetly at Nell and Elizabeth. "Ours is usually a harmonious home." Little trickles of perspiration rolled from her hairline, over her cheek, down her double chin and onto the workbench. Under her breath, Nell thought she heard the good woman whisper "kill," not once, but several times. Finally, she concluded her Rockwell story. Before Iva Lou began another one, Elizabeth and Nell begged their leave.

"We're going to work at our place from now on," Nell told Iva Lou. "We've decided to stitch wagon covers."

"That so?" said Iva Lou.

"It is so," Nell said.

"I'm glad you told her," Elizabeth said walking home. "A couple of witches who need burning."

"I'd like to set fire to their skirts," Nell said. She and Elizabeth laughed harder than they ever had.

Two days later, Tom and Heber returned home, tired, disheveled and irritable. Their clothing reeked of smoke. Immediately, Heber threw his shirt into the flames of the hearth. "You needn't have burned it," Elizabeth scolded. "I could have washed it."

But, before the flames devoured it, Nell saw that she could not. Bloodstains covered the front. Heber washed and washed himself at the well. Then, at the basin in the house, he washed again. He stood silently apart. And, Tom sat beside him on the front porch, neither saying a word.

Eventually, over the days that followed, it came out that they had burned their way across Hancock County, scorching the anti-Mormons from their houses and causing them to scatter into Missouri and Iowa. Again, the skies glowed red. In the Warsaw Signal, an anti-Mormon paper, stories of their atrocities were printed; the King women learned to recite some of them from memory. "Revenge" was the key word of every article. Nauvoo was never the same.

All sorts of accusations were aimed against the Mormons. Revenge and rumors of revenge spread throughout Missouri, Iowa, and Illinois like the fires that had kindled them. It was said that the Mormons had not only torched gentile homes but had also stolen animals and goods, had spat in the face of federal laws, had counterfeited U.S. coins, had harbored criminals and had acquitted murderers. Authorities arrived to search Nauvoo for two missing men; others came to capture the Twelve Apostles.

In response, Church leaders assigned more bodyguards and organized a company called the Whittlers. When a stranger entered Nauvoo, the Whittlers followed him and circled him while whittling with large, threatening knives until the stranger left the city. Finally, Brigham Young announced to the world early in October of 1845 that the Saints had decided to abandon Illinois to the devil and migrate west "as soon as grass grows and water runs."

HIS WILL BE DONE

(Diary)   *March 15, 1846*

I curse this miserable day. My life has turned full circle, and I find myself once again in a childhood state, living with my parents. Tom has left Jenny and me, of course, to explore for yet another resting place for his precious people. A great expanse between us! I doubt if we shall ever meet again.

In December, Tom baptized Nell in the newly completed temple font, supported by twelve carved oxen representing the Twelve Apostles. Though the ceremony lacked spiritual significance to her, Nell knew that it meant a great deal to Tom; one day every week, he left work on the wagons and rode Sergeant to the temple, where he did everything from quarrying great slabs of limestone near the Mississippi to sawing lumber to building window frames. Once, he and Heber traveled all the way to the Wisconsin forests to cut timber. At great peril, they used flatboats to follow an acre of hewn lumber down the river to Nauvoo. He looked forward to the day when the magnificent structure would be complete for Nell's baptism and for covenanting thousands of Saints before they began their trek across the continent. But, Nell didn't think it made "a lick of sense" to waste their labor on perfecting the structure even while they made plans to leave it.

For Tom, the completion took on a new significance. "After we have been driven from our beautiful city," he reasoned, "it will stand as a monument to all people of the world that freedom of religion has been denied to some of the most industrious, God-fearing people on the earth. We esteem it a privilege to work on the house of the Lord.

Our blessings amply pay for our labors."

Heber added, "If we have to go, we will look backward on it as a monument to all the world of our faith, even in the most grievous times, when our own Constitution and the President of these United States forsook us entirely."

"It still doesn't seem logical to me," Nell said. "Are you sure that you haven't built up a momentum, and you just can't stop?"

"I think you've got something there," added Elizabeth. "After all, we have our pride."

"Personally speaking," Tom said, "I will be gratified when you are baptized. That has kept me going."

As the time for Nell's baptism approached, Elizabeth urged her to postpone it. "It's wrong to receive the covenants if you don't believe. Tell Tom. He'll teach you."

"I can't tell him now. I've let it go too long. He would despise me."

When Tom finally did baptize Nell "in the name of the Father, the Son and the Holy Ghost," he prayed with the most humble, inspired expression. It called up Nell's memory of their first meeting when he prayed at the dinner table in Quincy. She might have been caught up in the moment if Elizabeth's icy countenance had not chilled her even more than the baptismal waters. Now, she felt a twinge of guilt. Like a destroying angel, Elizabeth's disapproving face appeared in Nell's nightmares at night. It wasn't the face that caused her heart to race, but a most overwhelming feeling of shame that weighed upon her spirit like great blocks of temple limestone. Night after night, the dream disturbed her rest. To rid herself of her shame, Nell struggled for the courage to confess to Tom that she lacked a testimony of the gospel. But, fear and Tom's absence gave her an excuse.

In January, the nightmare changed. Nell dreamed that she and Jennifer were lost in a marvelous, glowing city. But, no people resided there as if some wizard had cast upon it a spell of complete and utter silence. No blacksmith pounded hot metal in his shop, no children played around the schoolhouse, no oxen pastured in the fields and no vegetables grew in the gardens. With the child in her arms, she ran through the streets, searching for home and calling for Tom. But, the farther she ran and the longer she searched, the more lost she became. Even more terrifying was the feeling that she had lost herself. Over and over, she called out her own name. Then, as in the dream of December,

Elizabeth's face appeared, huge and disapproving. In the loneliest hour of the night, she awoke to her own cry.

"What's the matter, beauty?" Tom's large hand slid around her belly. He snuggled close to her.

"I dreamed I was lost," Nell panted. "Never leave me, Tom."

"I'm here," he said. However, the next day he sat for hours stirring the coals of the hearth. Nell feared to ask him why. Though she did not know of the battles raging in Tom's mind, she knew that her dream and his mood had everything to do with the beginning of the exodus from Nauvoo. Whether news or rumor, she did not know, but Tom and Heber believed that President Polk was soon to order a regular army to Nauvoo to arrest leaders and prevent Mormon removal. Church trustees, who feared the building gentile rage, advertised "twenty thousand acres of good farming lands, some of which are highly improved in exchange for goods, cash, oxen, cows, sheep, wagons, etc." Some leaders, realizing that Mormon lives were in increasing peril and knowing that a token move would buy time for the majority of the Saints, crossed the frozen Mississippi in a blizzard. Many of the most dedicated members followed, fully equipped or not, well or ill, about to give birth or with young children.

Their parting had been stressful for all remaining. Bundled against the cold, Tom, Heber, Elizabeth and Nell stood at the roadside in front of their home to watch and wave goodbye. Heber's feelings were such that he could not suppress a flood of tears, but Tom's jaw tightened with anger. "It is trying that we cannot worship God according to the dictates of our own conscience, unmolested," he said. "What shall become of them in this bitter season?"

They streamed west toward the Mississippi as if ice did not crystallize on their beards, as if the cold would not nip their toes, as if their food would last and they would sit beside a cozy fire at the end of the day.

Tom pulled Nell to him. "I can never subject you and little Jennifer to this," he said, tightening her wrap. "No. You should live by a hearth. I must think."

"Think what?" asked Nell.

"Of a way to protect you." I can't let my friends freeze or starve. I need to help them, but I must also protect you and Jenny." The unresolved conflict cut deep ravines in his brow.

Heber waved to the travelers through a lacy curtain of snow. "How foolish," he said. "How brave. We will soon follow them, but not on a night like this. Which should we face, the ice or the mob?"

"When will we go?" Elizabeth asked the brothers. Tom ignored her question and trudged a distance away to brood and wave to those who had left as a signal to the mob that everyone else would follow.

"Not now," Heber said. "We have time to build more wagons and to prepare the rest. Their sacrifice means our journey may begin when the weather is less harsh."

"God go with them," Nell said.

For three months after the first group crossed the frozen Mississippi, the Mortenson family labored beyond their limits constructing an entire wagon every four days. Besides sewing and riveting covers, Nell and Elizabeth assembled supply boxes. Nell avoided the subject of leaving, for she knew Tom's thinking. Still, she treasured the slightest hope that he would not submit her and the baby to a harsh wilderness, but would, instead, break away and live happily in Quincy—or St. Louis—or anywhere in civilization.

On April 2, 1846, Heber and Elizabeth left Nauvoo with a well-equipped, robust group. Though Elizabeth was hopeful that all would go well and that they would meet again presently, Nell feared for her loved ones. Riders had come into Nauvoo from the exiles who left in January to say that they camped at the Missouri in a place they called Winter Quarters. However, they reported that dire suffering had been their daily fare. In three months they had made merely 400 miles. Now that spring had arrived, Elizabeth and Heber's journey would take about twenty days; a "pleasure excursion," the riders called it and urged the Saints to go forward when they had supplies to suffice for one year. Every time Tom opened his mouth to speak, Nell waited for the inevitable words, "It is time to go." Yet, certain signs indicated that he intended to stay.

For one thing, Tom offered Heber and Elizabeth nearly all that the four had built and "gathered unto themselves" for the trek. They left in Heber's well-equipped, custom wagon. With minor adjustments and embellishments for strength, the length was eleven feet, six inches, the breadth almost four feet, and the height, eight feet. From kiln-dried oak she was constructed with axles cut from brine-pickled hickory. She rolled on strong wooden wheels with iron support, beat out of the hot fires of the blacksmith's forge along with the chains and picks and shovels, which were strapped to her sides. Four young, grain-fed oxen, both male and female, pulled her. Inside the box, Heber stocked her according to all that Parley P. Pratt, who helped to supervise the exodus, recommended. Heber took the strong ropes he had twisted from Mississippi hemp to stake the animals. Her cover was of the heaviest canvas, which Nell and Elizabeth had double stitched; a frame of hickory bows supported it. The canvas extended beyond the bows at either end so it could be closed with drawstrings against the elements. At the front a jockey box held Heber's tools. In the side panels the women packed the precious labors of their own hands: dried squash cakes, flour, raisins, crackers, biscuits, cooked pork, ham and sausages, and "all food that was to be eaten." From riverboats, they had purchased tea, coffee, sugar and rice. Elizabeth carefully packed seeds and cloth, needles and thread, extra shoes, an iron, dishes, a mirror and *Godey's Lady's Book*, full of pictures of the latest Paris fashions. On the tailgate, Heber hung his plate with "Lizzy," carved into it.

If Tom intended to follow them, Nell wondered, why had he not saved some supplies for his family? Did she dare to dream he would stay according to her wishes? On the other hand, the handshake with which the brothers parted appeared casual and lighthearted as if they were to meet after Sacrament Meeting.

Bidding goodbye to Elizabeth, a wild beast gnawed at Nell's heart. When, or if, they would meet again, she did not know.

"We will be waiting for you at the Missouri," cried Elizabeth. "Whatever we have taken is also yours. Remember to bring some yarn, and we'll make mittens along the way."

"You know my mind," Nell wept softly. "Perhaps, this is our last goodbye."

"No," Elizabeth consoled her. "You'll be right along. I'm certain. The two of you will work this out. You'll see. You'll join us at Winter Quarters when the weather is fair. In the meantime, think on this. I have a little secret which no one but you and me will know." Elizabeth placed Nell's hand on her belly. "Our child," she whispered, her eyes aglow.

"God protect you."

"And you. I will give birth in the place God has prepared for us, where my baby will have freedom from fear and hate. You must come to help me, Nell, even as I helped you. Please. Study the gospel. Open your heart to it and you will receive your testimony. Tell him the truth. It is the only way for you and Tom."

"The only way is for him to forget Mormonism. Oh, Elizabeth, I love Illinois. It is my home and I do not want to leave it. What am I to do?"

"Follow your heart." Elizabeth left Nell in distress. She and Heber drove out of sight on a road, slippery from an April shower.

The rest of the day Tom spent in thoughtful silence. He ate nothing. He groomed Sergeant's brown coat until it gleamed with gold where his muscles rippled and his black tail and mane responded to the slightest breeze. He talked once to an outsider who wanted to buy all their land and their home for a miserly $300 and a milk cow. "I'd rather give it to the devil," Nell heard him roar at the outsider.

That night, Nell dreamed again of the empty city. She ran through its empty streets searching every house for Tom. With a start, she awakened. With another start, she realized Tom had left their bed. She arose to find him kneeling in prayer before a slow burning fire. Before dawn, he stood like a great shadow over their bed.

"I have fasted and prayed," he said. "The Holy Ghost has finally come to me." He held Nell in his arms. "I must go."

"Oh, Tom. Please let's not talk of this just now. We'll wake the baby."

"We must talk of it now."

"I don't want to go. I'm begging you, if you love me, reject this church. It will kill us."

"I can't believe what you're asking me, Nell."

"I can't believe that you would take a seven month baby out of civilization. The Rockies. Where is that? What shall we find there? How long will the journey take? Nobody knows. And, what about Indians? It's their land. They'll be more ready to kill us than a mob. There are wolves, you know. I can't expose Jennifer to the cold."

"I'm not taking Jennifer. No, nor you either, Nell. I can't. I won't."

Nell froze.

"The baby is too young; you are right. I cannot subject either of you to conditions we know nothing about. And yet, I must go. Brigham Young has asked for 150 men. I will explore with him and locate the permanent place envisioned by our beloved Prophet in Mexican territory. It will be our place, Nell. We will build it up, and no one, no one will ever drive us from our land again. Along the way, we will cut roads and build bridges and make maps. We will clear the land and tame it. Then, I will come for you."

Nell could not believe her ears. How could he leave her? Was this the extent of his love? She had prepared herself to argue about staying or leaving, but had never dreamed of parting. She tried to fathom what he had said.

"No, Tom. I want nothing to do with your plan. We could have a prosperous life here in Illinois. Renounce the religion, or pretend to renounce it, if you like. Anything to be accepted."

"Would you have me eternally damned? To forsake my calling is to forsake God."

"Forsake God, then. We are your family. We need you."

Tom asked if she had lost her mind. He described his visitation by the Holy Ghost in the night. It came to him that he must go with Brother Young to plant and build up a resting place for the thousands that would follow into the Rockies. Also, the Saints at Winter Quarters would perish, he explained, without help, thousands of them, women, children, the old and the sick. They would starve, and he had been called to raise grain in the wilderness to feed them. Thousands more must move out of Nauvoo or be slaughtered. "We are a desperate people."

"What kind of man are you?" Nell cried. "You talk of the needs of *people*, yet you would leave your own wife and child to have their heads bashed in? You are the one who has lost his mind!"

"I won't leave you to the mobs. I'm taking you home to your family. You'll be safe there until I return."

"I can't go home," Nell screamed. The baby, who had long been fussing, screamed too.

"You must go home."

"How could you do this to me? I do not exist for my parents. Would you destroy my pride?"

"Better your pride than your life."

"Then, you never loved me."

"I always loved you," he tried to hold her, but she pushed him away.

"Then, at least, take us with you!"

"Digging a grave for you or Jennifer is unthinkable for me. I cannot. I will not. He gently shook her. The baby wailed. "Listen to me. I'll come for you. I will. As our Lord went to prepare a place for us, so I go to prepare a place for you. His Will be done."

These four words Nell had heard many times before. For Tom, the discussion had ended. She lay on her bed and wept for some time. Numbed, Nell took her reaching child from Tom.

Out the window, she observed an overloaded wagon, which slipped from one side of the slushy road to the other on its way toward the Mississippi. In the driver's seat Brother King urged his oxen by cracking a whip over their lowered heads. Iva Lou and Minnie perched on either side of him, wrapped heavily against the brisk spring morning while his two sons and their collie herded, in front of them, seven head of cattle, ten head of sheep, and three goats. Nell wondered why Major King would take both his wives and two youths when Tom would not take her and the baby. Perhaps, it was because she had neglected him in the months before and after their baby's birth. Perhaps, he resented her hesitation to embrace Godliness with his zeal, or, perhaps he had known and resented all along that she had allowed herself to be baptized without believing. If that were true, perhaps he intended to take for himself a more devout wife. Perish the thought!

Nell nursed Jennifer . . . and her own wounds.

"We will make arrangements to leave tomorrow," Tom told her. The "arrangements" were bodyguards, the Ark, guns, a possibles bag, knives, bedding, the baby's necessities, and a little food. Like an automaton, Nell packed their things, hers and the baby's, into a trunk. It grieved her to use the supply box, which she had so carefully carved with the Mortenson name. Thinking of the humiliation she must undergo in returning to her childhood state caused her to weep again and again throughout the day. Finally, cried out, Nell swallowed her hurt and her pride down into her stomach, where they lay like stones.

Tom worked outside until sundown. He found Nell, not food, at the table. Before he took off his coat, she spoke. "I am begging you for the last time. Take me with you or stay with me, but don't separate us."

"Nell, believe me. I have considered both, but I can do neither. I love you. I go to build a place where you will be safe, where we can live in peace."

"What makes the decision all yours?"

Tom did not answer. The room was dark. No lamp lit the room, no fire heated the hearth.

"What a fool I have been," Nell coldly said. "I knew all along your beloved religion meant everything to you. Marrying me was just another step in your quest for the Celestial Kingdom."

The color faded from Tom's face.

"I want you to know, Tom Mortenson, I find no glory in suffering or in being tried. I never prayed for an open mind either. I prayed only that you'd love me equal to your religion. But, now I see you can't. I've lost what I never had."

"Oh, ye of little faith."

" Stop quoting those damn scriptures! This is life, not myth."

"Be still. You are not yourself. I'll not hear it."

When he drew her close to him, her legs fell from under her. "I would rather die than live without you," Nell said. "This isn't right."

"Nell, I expect you to bear up to this. Find your strength. Remember that time by the mill when we first met? You told me butterflies were strong. Remember? Please understand. This is not about *choosing* to leave; it's about *having* to. How can I explain? Would you admire a man who ran to a woman's skirts to hide from his responsibilities? I know I have the power to prevent needless suffering and death. Would you have me shrink from that?"

"Oh, no." She pulled away from him. "You go. Leave us. Only before you do, know this—if you leave me now, don't bother to return."

The road to Quincy was deeply rutted, but frozen because on this day, winter managed to get the upper hand of spring. For two days, mother and child bumped along inside the box of the covered wagon. Closely, Nell watched over Jennifer, whose bright, innocent eyes peeped from deep inside a covering of blankets like a little rabbit tucked in down. She seemed content and unaware of the fine snow that whistled through every chink between canvas and wood. On the contrary, Nell shivered uncontrollably in spite of the rocks Tom heated, wrapped in blankets and placed at her feet prior to their leaving.

Tom drove all day and all night, stopping but once to build a fire, to eat a bite, to heat the foot warmers and to exchange a few words with his bodyguards, who rode behind and before the wagon, their rifles unsheathed. Leery, they scanned the undergrowth on either side of the road, and Tom kept a pepperbox pistol in his holster and a loaded rifle in his saddle boot.

By early afternoon on their second day of travel, they pulled into Quincy. Tom's face appeared through the canvas, his nose red, his mustache frosted, his eyes circled in dark shadows. Nell yearned for his warmth, but there was no more to go on between them. She avoided his eyes.

"I'll go in first," he said, his mouth stiff from the cold. She heard his knock at the door, heard the door open, and heard her mother's voice. "Come in," she must have said. The door shut. Nell heard the heated pitch of her father's voice. Then, Tom's. Then, both, yelling at once. After an eternity, the door opened again.

It was Ruby who untied the back canvas. "My baby," she reached for Nell. "My lost lamb, come home." Nell fell into her arms and wept tears that she didn't know she had left. "Come to me. I done built de fire in yo' room, quick as I hears. Yo' mammy and yo' pappy, dey still tore up, but dey needs yo' back." Like the ewe that senses her lamb and accepts it, Ruby took little Jennifer.

Nell's shoulder brushed Tom's as she passed him on the familiar walk toward the open door of the glowing home. The little stones that had lain in her stomach rose into her throat. She swallowed them down, hard.

"I'm leaving the Ark to you," Tom murmured. "Take charge of it. Keep her out of the weather. Grease the wheels and take her for a turn once in awhile." He emptied it of her belongings and stacked them on the porch. "What really hurts is that you can't trust in the Lord. I thought I knew you, but I guess I don't."

"You're a fanatic," Nell hissed.

Tom trudged through the muck to the bodyguards, who huddled together against the wind. Before he mounted Sergeant, he raised a stiff hand and called, "I reckon I'll be back. Stay well. Be strong." They rode away into the fog.

Nell, an earth without its sun, moved to the porch. She stood near her belongings. Catching her breath in the cold air, she glanced at the Reeves' house. There, in the second story, stood Arthur, staring down upon the most painful moment of her life. Her worst nightmare had come true.

11

WHAT I WANT

(Diary)   April 13, 1849

Compromising decisions cripple me. To have one desirable element of life, namely to be with Tom, I must give up another element, namely all that I call comfortable and dear: my family, the Mississippi valley, and every familiar person and place. What parameter does one use to measure a decision? What I want? What my loved ones want? Logic? Adventure? Safety? Ethics? What? No parameter seems better than another.

All that I know is that without Tom, I am half a person. For three years and three months, I have suffered miserably without him. And, yet, what awaits this woman if she ventures into the unknown? If she does not, shall she regret it for the rest of her life? Should this woman wait for something to happen, which may never happen, or shall this woman make something happen? Shall I jump off?

"Are you feeling well, dear?" Mama asked Nell one Sunday three years after Tom left. "I wish you had gone to church with us instead of fretting away all by yourself."

"I'm not fretting, Mama. "It was a welcome change to be home with Jenny after teaching all week."

"Arthur was there," Christina chirped. "Oh, he's a beautiful man. You should see how he's changed since his stay in St. Louis. He wears a stovepipe hat and carries a cane with a brass handle."

"What for?" Nell winked. "Is he crippled?"

"An excellent catch," Mama said, who ignored her daughter's

smart remark. She took up Nell's linen sampler, partially embroidered with the ABC's, which Nell should have hung on her wall prior to her twelfth birthday to demonstrate her ability with the needle. "Why can't you sit quiet and finish this like every other girl?" She fluttered around Nell's chamber to dust and re-dust the furniture.

"I'm not a girl. Handwork makes me nervous," Nell answered. "I'd rather dig the garden or ride Blondie, or even teach than embroider."

"She likes to use her feet, not her hands," Christina said, who had made it a priority to learn the crafts of a proper wife.

"Charles says Arthur's ready to help manage the bank, after his apprenticeship in St. Louis. A real businessman, he is." Mama rushed to the window. "So, that's the culprit! That awful bird kept Charles and me awake half the night. Charles said it was a chicken, but it's a song sparrow, if you ask me. Carries on like that every year."

"It's a mockingbird," Christina said. "Papa said he's going to blow the damned thing straight to hell," she giggled.

"I'll wash out that mouth of yours," Mama said. She turned to Nell and the business at hand. "You ought to stay at home and care for Jennifer yourself, everyday. There would be no need for you to teach, if you had a proper husband."

"Don't worry about me. Like I've said a hundred times, I am married. Crumb. I need my work. It's gratifying to earn a little stash." What her mother did not know was that she had been paid mostly in coin, and, after nearly two years, she had a sizable savings, which she stuffed into two of her old porcelain dolls. They sat high on her chest of drawers and the more bulbous they grew, the broader she grinned because, when Tom came for her, they'd have plenty of cash.

"Things could change, you know, if you were open to change, that is. You disgrace our family by teaching." Mama fidgeted with the doily, which lay under a likeness of Tom.

"What is it, Mama? You seem agitated."

"Well, my dear, it's Arthur. He's paying you a visit this afternoon, and, ah . . . it could be life altering."

"Whatever do you mean? Life altering? What could he want? I've not encouraged him in any way. We've agreed to be friends."

"Sure, friends," hooted Christina. "He gets nervous whenever you're near. And, you with a child by another man! Please, Nell, I want to sit with him. I'll say you've got the ague."

"Hush, child," Mama covered Christina's mouth. "You go empty the chamber pots, like I said. Arthur doesn't want you." She turned to her disgraced daughter. "Let me be frank with you, Nell. Time's come that you face reality. You've been miserable, I know. Three full years ago that Mormon deserted . . . " Mama, who seemed very apprehensive, finally lit on the bed. "Sit here, beside me, Nell." She put her arm around her daughter. "Your father and I are getting older. We won't be here to watch after you girls forever. A woman needs a man's protection, and your child needs a father. Life can be awful harsh. Now, you might not like what I am about to say, but someone has to say it. The man you had is gone, has stranded you. The sooner you accept this, the sooner you can get on."

"Please, stop," Nell said. An unexpected sob burst from her throat. "Tom would have told me if he didn't plan to fetch me. He's honest and true. His last words were, 'I reckon I'll be back.'"

"Then, you must suspect that he is gone to his Maker. Those people have perished by the hundreds, haven't they?"

"Tom is alive. If he were not, I would know. Say no more. Please, leave me be."

"Someone needs to make you aware of the human condition, don't they dear? It falls to me, your mother, to speak right out." She pulled a handkerchief from her bosom and fanned her face while Christina listened and braided her long, brown hair. "You must grasp every opportunity to establish a comfortable life for yourself. Right? Any woman who does not can look forward to the rheumy and an early death. Look at me, stricken like my mother, bless her soul, with palpitations, and only forty-five." She coughed. "If I had suffered a difficult life, I'd be dead by now. I've told you before, and I'll tell you again: a bright, young woman must use every charm at her disposal to secure for herself a man of means, now doesn't she? I tremble to think how those novels you and Christina read have filled your heads with silly ideas of passion and falling in love, for the life of me. That will bring about your ruin, sure enough."

"I don't have your ailments, and I don't want them. I'm strong like father. I can make it on my own, if I have to."

"Sure," Christina giggled. "And, oxen fly."

"Everyone is strong at twenty-four," Mama wheezed. "Oh, you upset me so." She flew to the door. "What I want is for you to forget that Mormon, like he has forgotten you."

"Sometimes, I wish I could."

"As Ruby and I have both told you, an unprotected woman asks to be molested."

"Let's hope so," Nell quipped for Christina's benefit.

Her sister broke into a fit of laughter. "Nell would be the last to get raped." The word *rape* scandalized her mother. "Show her your garter knife."

"Garter knife? What the devil!" Mama squawked.

"Thanks, Christina. I asked you not to ruffle Mama." Though her sister appeared mature of late, she was more giddy than reliable. Nell wished she had not informed Christina of the two Mormon women who had been raped in Carthage. In the aftermath, one tried to hang herself, and the other kept to her bed, curled and wasting away, in a little ball. Nell told her sister she chose to die rather than to be such a victim. Hence, the knife.

"If you don't want Arthur, there's always Henry Hunt," Christina teased. She knew Nell despised the pot-bellied barber, who glued his little black eyes onto her whenever she walked past his shop. Three times last winter he had called to court her, and each time, after enduring his dreary babble in the parlor, Nell had to spend time talking to Blondie. Out of regard for Nell's feelings, her father told Henry to stop spending his efforts on a useless cause. "Mr. Hunt actually drools whenever he sees Nell," Christina told her mother.

"Filthy man," Mama said. "Twice her age. I know what he wants."

"Your prospects are becoming worse and worse," Christina warned.

"Few prospects are better than none at all," Nell returned with a grin. "If you mention his name again, I'll tell him you fancy him."

Mama's eyes twinkled. "Well, never you mind Mr. Hunt. I have a feeling there's an upcoming offer. At the advanced age of twenty and four, a woman must be practical. Dress pretty, dear."

"Shall I help you?" Christina asked Nell.

"Come along, dear," Mama pulled her younger daughter's hand. "Your father wants us in the buggy for an airing. But, do empty the pots first, and don't forget Jenny. Dress her warm." Not surprising to Nell, Mama failed to ask her if the baby might go for a buggy ride with them, for she treated Jenny like a child of her own. Immediately, after their return from Nauvoo, the grandparents had sheltered the curly-headed baby under their wings. Though Nell failed to see it, Father had believed that she took after him more than anyone in the family.

Christina, who easily traded her last doll for the real baby, had taken great pleasure in playing peek-a-boo and in teaching her new doll the names of animals. Ruby had happily kept her clean, well nourished, warm, and out of harm's way. Like a strong thread, the plump baby had quickly darned the hole in Nell's relationship with her family.

Unconcerned if she dressed or not, Nell stepped into the first article of clothing that met her eye. Then, she bent over her desk, correcting school papers. Outside her window, the flighty mockingbird hopped from one limb to another in the cherry tree. Stretching its neck and lifting its beak, it warbled as sweetly as a bluebird. Then, it frantically chirped to mimic a robin. After that, it flapped its wings, cocked its head from side to side in a humorous manner, and gave out an awful squawk. Darting off to another tree, it repeated the same routine. Nell closed her window. "What is that all about?" she asked nobody. "Crazy bird."

A knock sounded at the door downstairs. Nell heard Arthur's voice, and presently Ruby came to say he had come to call on her. She hoped Mama was wrong and that Arthur wanted to tell her he was engaged to an elegant woman in St. Louis, or something of that sort. However, in the shine of her mother's eyes, Nell detected a plot that was soon to unwind. She splashed cold water from the basin onto her face, pinched her cheeks and tidied her hair.

Cocky, mature and handsome, the estranged Arthur stood at the foot of her stairs. From every corner, she had heard news of his success at the St. Louis bank, of the numerous socialites he courted and of his drinking and gambling habits. His fashionable gray trousers, dark blue coat and pinstriped tie confirmed the gossip. However, he still combed his hair straight backward like her father's, and the familiar fragrance of his old shaving soap set Nell at ease.

"You look well," he said offering his hand to assist her down the last two steps. "Forgive me for arranging this meeting through Charles. He assured me you were available."

"Oh, did he?" Old irritations returned. Nell led him into the parlor and motioned for him to sit in his favorite chair; instead, he anxiously inspected his watch and paced.

"Are you in a rush?" Nell asked.

"Oh, no. Absolutely not," he feigned a chuckle. "Just a habit."

"It's pleasant to see you, Arthur."

"Yes. Well. While I was in St. Louis this past year, I came to terms with your rash mistakes and balanced them against other attributes in your favor. You were young, and I forgive you." He turned his back on her, cleared his throat and stood tall as if beginning a speech. "Your conduct has been exemplary for the past three years. In fact, you've made quite a name for yourself at the school. I, myself, admire your rise."

"Well, thank you . . . I guess," Nell stiffly returned.

Gathering his thoughts, he paused. He strutted around the room like a rooster that had lost its cock-a-doodle-doo. Then, he straightened his tie, cleared his throat and twirled his cane. Finally, he crowed. "I want you to know that the past is just that, passed. Certainly, you were an easy victim to Mormon vultures. I am partly responsible. Should have intervened. Well now, because I am Christian, forgiving is the thing to do. What Charles and I, and Harriet too, want is for you to get on with your life."

"Yes," Nell said, seething inside. "I am getting on as well as possible."

"I see. Well, as you have long known, I care very much for you. I, ah, I still want to marry you."

"What are you saying, Arthur? I never gave you cause. Have you heard a word I've said?"

"Your family is grateful. I have agreed to give Jennifer my name." He turned awkwardly and grasped Nell's cool hand. "I am fond of her and will properly educate her as my own. You may bury, once and for all, the villain who used you and cast you off."

Hands trembling, breast heaving, Nell turned toward the window. In her imagination, she hopped through it and flew away from him as fast and as far as possible. She imagined herself saying, "I don't want to marry you, not now, not ever. Tom is coming for me at this very moment." But, the words would not form themselves on her tongue.

"Don't be afraid, Nell. Most of the town didn't even know you were married to the Mormon in the first place. And, as for me, since leaving Quincy, I have become a more practical, a more worldly man."

"Christina would suit you better," Nell managed to say. "If Father suggests it, she'll answer you in the affirmative. She is very fond of you, Arthur."

"Don't be coy with me."

"Go to the devil" were the words Nell wished she had courage to say.

"Your lover has left you and will never return. You must know that by now. Let me help you. Put your life in my hands." He reached for her. "It isn't in you females to be decisive, or logical, for that matter. You're not responsible for your shame."

When his hand landed on her shoulder, she shuddered.

"That Mormon's either dead or saddled with several shoe-licking women who bear him a child every year according to their ridiculous revelations."

Out of need for support and understanding, Nell took up and held to her breast a recent novel by Charlotte Bronte called *Jane Eyre*. Only last evening she read what Jane wanted. *"For liberty I gasped; for liberty I uttered a prayer."* In Nell's head, something snapped. When she raised her hand to slap Arthur's face, he gripped her wrist so tightly she felt the bones might crack. "You snake," she cried. How I hate you. Tom Mortenson will come for me. You'll see. Then, I'll ask him to shoot you." She broke and fluttered up the stairs to her room.

"Then, marry me for Jennifer's sake," he called after her.

"Never," she screamed. "Numb skull!"

Ruby arrived with a broom, and flailed Arthur like a mother goose, all the way down the hall and out the front door. "Yo' can' see my Nell no mo'. No, sir, not over my dead body. I don' like wha's goin' on here," she hollered. "It ain' right. No, sir." The door slammed. "And don' yo' come back."

Ruby quieted Nell, persuaded her to rest on the porch swing, and brought her a warm cup of tea. They rocked in silence. "I wish that fool mockingbird would shut up," Nell finally said. "All week, it's been flitting from tree to tree from daylight to dark. Chattering, chirping, warbling, making every bird call known to man. Some creatures just can't pipe down."

"It will, soon as it find a mate."

"The mate's probably winter killed," Nell said, her head bowed. "The blamed thing doesn't even know."

"Yo' too young fo' dat talk. Arfu' don' know nofin'. But I knows. I knows Tom be livin'. He livin'." Ruby stubbornly folded her arms. "Trus' me on dat."

"What makes you so sure?"

"Trus' me."

They rocked silently together for a time. Then, Nell asked Ruby, "Why can't I stand up for myself? Why can't I speak? Every time I try, especially with a man, it's as if my brain is being crushed, my stomach too."

"I knows how yo' feels. I gets it, same as yo'. Dey be mas'ers."

"Someday, someday . . ."

A spindly stranger rode up their cobblestone driveway on an even more spindly horse. Nell assumed him to be a river bum, come to beg, but she knew he wasn't when he spoke. "Nell Mortenson, I presume. You're purdy as the picture Tom carries. I judge I found the right place." Ashamed, he examined his torn shirtsleeve. "Forgive me, ma'am. Just now, I don't look fit. See. I come a ways."

Ruby placed a strong arm in front of Nell to prevent her from running to meet the bedraggled man, but Nell threw it aside. "I'm Nell," she said. "You come off that horse. Please, Sir. Tell me about Tom. Where is he? Is he well? Has he come for me?" She tugged on his leg.

"Woo," said the spindly man to Nell, not his horse. "I come fresh out of the Valley of the Great Salt Lake, Sister Nell. I know yer Tom, purdy good." He slid from his saddle and dusted his trousers. "Man gets stiff, 'specially this bum leg." He ran a gloved finger across Nell's cheek. "Owe my life ta yer Tom."

"How's that? Do come inside. Sit and tell me everything. How is he? Ruby, run! Get cheese and chicken. Fill his water pouch."

"Tom's fair. Sick a 'taters," he grinned.

"Where is he?"

"Salt Lake, a course. Planting, 'bout now. Long about January," he began after removing his sweat-stained hat, "we was havin' an awful time of it, foodwise. Spring, that's starvin' time. Tom said to go easy on you with the peculiars." He paced back and forth in front of his horse. "Him and me was ta hunt game, see. Like some fool, I goes out alone. This old stiff, I'm a ridin' here, she breaks my leg. Slips on ice, see. She runs off, and ever time I crawls to her, the ornery devil, she wanders further off. I still feels like shootin' her, a leavin' me alone that-a-ways in the blizzard."

The worn traveler guzzled water from the pouch Ruby filled, not caring that half of it strained through his salt and pepper beard and dribbled down his shirt. He smelled like a wet dog. Over his matted hair, he poured the remainder and motioned for Ruby to fetch more. "Come evening, Sister Mortenson, the cold chews like a gaunt wolf at my fingers and toes. I'm a goner, sure, I thinks. Then, through the whiteout, I hears your Tom call, 'Will'm, Will'm!' He comes to me on Sergeant, and I shouts, 'Glory to God' cause he looks to me like the Angel Moroni did to our Prophet. He takes me home, see, through that white-out, directly to my own door, and not too soon neither. I near froze. Then, Tom, he hauls me a doctor, right to my place in that there whiteout, and near dark too. Man's got the best sense of direction I ever see."

William dug deep into his saddlebag. He drew out a bundle of odorous jerky, a string of bright Indian beads, tobacco and, finally, a worn letter. "All he ever asks me is to bring this here message ta yer hand, directly. That's what I'm a-doin'"

Nell embraced the sacred paper. Her legs weakening, she dropped onto the porch steps.

"Good luck to ya, Sister. Like to sit and chaw, but I'm hurrying on to St. Louis. Goin' to haul that family a mine over Indian country while the grass is green." He accepted the food, which Ruby had wrapped in brown paper, and he trotted away on his weary sorrel so quickly Nell barely had time to call "thank you."

Like an archeologist, Nell unfolded Tom's manuscript.

"Oh, my," Ruby said, "da's gwan be trouble." Though she couldn't read, she followed Nell's finger over the smeared words.

My dearest Beauty Nell,   *February 1849*

Like I've said in all my letters, I long for you and my sweet little Jenny! Your state remains a mystery to us since we have no word. Please, let me know what has befallen you.

I reckon we'll have the upper hand here after mid summer's harvest. Then, you will find this a fit place. I am prepared to come for you, my darling Nell, wherever you are, next spring. No benefit can come of my leaving after harvest and having to winter over in Illinois. Notwithstanding, if I do not hear otherwise, expect me a year from the time William brings this letter to your gentle hand.

Please, take heart, my dearest. Time passes quickly, and the Mormon trail will be much improved by then. Do put grease to the Ark's wheels and give her a turn once in awhile.

Forever devoted,

Tom Mortenson

Nell devoured Tom's note for a second time. Intermittently, she wept. "Oh, Ruby, I would give my life to be in his arms. I want to see his face."

"Sure 'nough, dat boy done want yo'. I knows."

"How do you know so much?" Nell suspiciously asked Ruby. "Sing out!" The slave locked her full, moist lips. "Tom needs to be told that I don't believe and that I probably never will. Then, I have to see in his eyes, if he wants me still."

"He don' want yo' livin' no lie, Honey. He jis' wants yo'." Ruby stroked Nell's hair.

"What makes you think you know so much? Holy cow. Why didn't he come for me, like I asked in my letters?"

"If Mr. Tom could come, he would. Takes time, gettin' hold on de lan'. His people hungry. 'Sides, yo' never tol' him come."

"How do you know all that?" Nell studied Ruby's troubled face. "Three years ago, I did say I'd never would go west with him—if he left me. You heard me tell him. I didn't mean it. Said it to stop him from leaving." Nell rested her head on Ruby's shoulder. The slave knew of the many letters she had sent over the years, but Tom had answered none of them. "I feel so very confused. All this talk . . . "

"Leave off what you said. He ain' goin' be rememberin' that," Ruby clucked. "He hurts, same as yo'. Swalla dat pride, honey, and do what yo' heart say." Ruby held Nell and told her of a time when she let her dreams go. She loved a young man who picked cotton alongside her on a big plantation in Georgia. Crazy for freedom, like Tom was for his religion, her young man asked her to run away north with him on the Underground Railroad. But, Ruby's experience with running crippled her. She told him to go on and save himself. He did. Ruby's master took her up the Mississippi to Illinois and sold her to Nell's family, and she never saw him again. "To begin, I cry ever' night for his lovin'. Then, I don' cry. I jus' dream. Now, I wonder how my life would-a-been. I's sho' he made it."

"I never knew that, Ruby. I never knew you loved a man. Why didn't you tell me?"

"'Cause, I don' wan' bofa yo' wif my troubles. Yo' too young."

"What shall I do? If you could live your life again, would you have gone?"

"S'pose I would. I did what I did. But, now, I wants what yo' wants. Dat be it."

"I don't want to live without him." Nell broke down again. "Oh, if only I hadn't been with child right off, I know I could have made him forget the Promised Land. Or, if he had taken me with him, we'd be back here together, right now. I could have changed him. Now, he's so close to all that hellfire he can't see anything else."

Nell read Tom's note for the third time. "Look here, Ruby. 'Like I've said in all my letters . . . ' What letters? Not one has fallen into my hands. And, it sounds as if he never got any from me. Elizabeth promised she'd write too; never did. Why? It's as if they'd dropped off the earth."

Ruby squinted one eye and glared at Nell with the other, like she always did when trying to make up her mind. Finally, she spoke. "It's not my place, but I can' see yo' suffe' no mo'. I just can'. I don' care no mo' if dey whip me or sell me eva'."

"Something's going on here. Ruby, sing out."

Ruby did. She told Nell that none of her messages to Tom had left the premises. Charles and Harriet had burned them all. She said that riders had brought letters from Tom, many of them, and some from Elizabeth too. But, Nell's parents had intercepted and burned every one. She told Nell that Arthur and Master Baker had "boiled up a plan." When the time was right, Arthur would propose again. Another part of their plan involved Tom. If he again showed his face in Illinois, he would be killed, boxed and buried. "Fo'give me, Lord." Ruby stretched her athletic arms toward heaven.

This news washed over Nell like cold water from an underground spring. Unable to grasp the gravity of it, she asked Ruby to repeat the whole story. She did. She ended by informing Nell that her parents had burned the letters out of love, to protect her and Jenny from a life of hardship and separation from them. "But dat debil, Arfu', he lus' afte' yo'. I knows what I knows."

"I don't like it. They had no right," Nell murmured in disbelief, and all the way up the stairs and into her room, she whispered, "No right." She stayed there with the door bolted, refusing conversation that night and the entire next day. After laying out the facts of her situation, she scrutinized them up one side and down the other, she measured them and pinned them to the fabric of her life, then tore them into shreds and stitched them up again. She read far into the night Bronte's "scandalous and subversive" novel. Finally, with the dawning of the next day, she emerged in the highest of spirits.

"I've made a decision," she confided in Ruby, "and you will be the first to know. What I want is to be with Tom, now." Why would she wait for an entire year? Give him opportunity to take other wives? He was capable of it because, for him, to obey without question any order of the Priesthood would constitute an act of Godliness. Why would a right-thinking wife tempt him further? "We're going to the Valley of the Great Salt Lake, Jennifer and I. What I want is to be a family again."

"Listen here, now!" Ruby answered Nell's declaration. "Yo' can' run off wif Jenny into de raw country. I won' have it." Her face looked strained from lack of sleep.

"Sorry, Ruby. I won't risk having Tom shot. I'm going! Indians, snakes, wolves be damned."

"Alone?" Ruby's eyes gleamed as large as the moon.

"No, silly, not alone. Groups leave every week for California gold. I'll hire them. There in my dolls, I've salted away my stake. Time has come to use it." After asserting her will, even if it was to her slave, Nell's soul, like Jane Eyre's *"began to expand, to exult, with the strangest sense of freedom, of triumph . . . it seemed as if an invisible bond had burst, and that I had struggled out onto unhoped for liberty."*

"And don't fret, Ruby. I won't tell anybody that I know about the burned letters. I won't. I'll not have you whipped, not the one person who has been true to me."

"Yo' a good gal, Nell," Ruby said, with the tears of a mother's loss streaming over her weary face.

"Take a look out the window, Ruby. The mockingbird's finally piped down. It's found its mate."

"Bout time."

12

MISTY GOODBYE

(Diary)   *April 14, 1849*

I am about to begin the most adventurous and daring event of my life. May gold rushers lead me to Tom!

Notice outside Henry Hunt's barbershop:

Illinois to California gold
100 days and $90 to a fortune
Departing morning of April 20, 1849
Experienced guides
Use pack animals or wagons

See Moses or Cutter — King's Boardinghouse
Sign here.

Once Nell had decided to cross the plains, she had to determine how. There were several ways to accomplish it. For one, river travel posed a possibility, one of the main advantages being avoidance of the muddy Iowa hills, which presented an extreme challenge, especially during the rainy season. A great percentage of people began their journey by steamboat, traveling the Mississippi, Des Moines and Missouri rivers to disembark on the Missouri's west bank and to cross the Great American Desert. Going by water was safe, even enjoyable, she had heard, but it was expensive. However, even if she could afford the fare, after disembarking, she may have to wait a month or more for a second rate outfit because of the stampede for California gold. News had reached Quincy that the number of people waiting to cross the prairie far outnumbered wagons and teams available. In the light of this information, Nell decided that beginning the trip with Tom's sturdy wagon, equipped with Jenny's needs in mind and pulled by a healthy, young team, seemed the best alternative.

Traveling with Mormons was another possibility. Nell read an advertisement, which announced that parties should gather at Kanesville, better known as Council Bluffs, with "teams and means sufficient to come through the three month trek without any assistance, and bread stuffs to last a few months after arrival." They would not leave until fifty adequately equipped and armed wagons assembled. Safety was the greatest advantage of travel with the religious group, who, with expert guides, had become experienced travelers, widely respected for their organization and individual sacrifice.

However, being with the Mormons also posed problems. For one, traveling 300 miles across Iowa to reach the group was a risky proposition because occasional anti-Mormon marauders continued to plague the area from the Mississippi to the Missouri even though Mormons had established several stations along the way. Being associated with the group, in any way, could mean disaster, Nell thought, and she wanted nothing to do with mobs. Another problem was that many leaving at this late date were poor, even destitute. Who wanted to plod across the continent at an ox pace in the dust of cows, sheep, goats and fifty wagons overflowing with children, old people and immigrants who had no means and spoke not a word of English? Who wanted to share the goods she brought for Jenny and herself with the starving and ailing folk from Winter Quarters? And, who wanted to attend a three-month church service? This, she could do without. A favorable alternative, she believed, was to try to join another group such as homesteaders or gold rushers.

No matter how she traveled, she felt a need to break with her family now, if at all. The burning of her beloved Tom's letters signaled an intention to hobble her, to pen her and to slay her self-determination, and the outrageous plot to kill Tom caused her much grief and hastened her decision to leave immediately. However, because they acted in the name of love, Nell decided she could forgive them, but she could not permit them to pilfer her freedom. It was not right and she did not like it. The only decision was to leave—now. And, she vowed to go bravely, like a Spartan sailing off to war.

If she felt Arthur's melancholic gaze one more time, if she watched her mother faint again, or if she heard anew her father's warnings of poisonous water, wolves, and starvation, she would not go at all. Like Ruby, she'd be left behind, a victim of her own imagination, crippled by midnight fears of being ravaged by savages or of losing Jenny to snake bite. No, the sooner the departure, the better. Outside the barbershop, Nell read about the group leaving on April 20. That imminent date afforded no time to worry or fidget, only time to pack and go. Guides, with gold fever chose not to loiter.

Henry Hunt wobbled from his shop and stood beside Nell as she copied the advertisement into her diary. "Going to live with them squirrelly Mormons again?" he asked.

"I'm going west to join my husband," she glared at him. "How the devil did you find out? I just determined to go!"

"Everybody knows, my dear," he drooled through huge, purple lips. "No need for you to leave us. Right here in Quincy this here man stands ready to make an honest woman out of you. Just say the word."

"Honest woman? *You*? Make *me* an honest woman? At least, I don't treat balding men with worthless pig grease and charge them a dollar for 'Oil de France, guaranteed to grow hair.'"

When she signed her name and began copying the list of supplies, Henry halted her writing with his fat, sweating hand. "My dear Miss Baker," he said, ignoring her marriage to Tom, "have you gone and lost your wits? You've just took and signed to travel with guides owing every merchant in town for their grubstakes. Worthless. Eyeing your money, not guiding you to the Rockies. One goes by *Cutter*," Henry shivered. "Name fits him, damn right it does. Hardest-looking scoundrel I ever took and seed."

"What about the other one?" Nell asked even though she did not value Henry's estimation of character.

"Goes by *Moses*. Huh! Moses, for Pete sakes! Let's play Egypt. You be Aaron and I'll be the pharaoh. Something sly about him."

"Well, I'll just have to judge for myself, won't I?" she responded, while wiping the hand, which he had grasped. "Goodbye, Mr. Hunt."

"You all take and come back," he winked. "Mark my words. I'll take and be here when you do. You go and hold to the iron rod, Miss Baker." He wobbled into his shop to scalp another customer.

Only minutes later, Nell did begin to judge for herself when she interviewed the guide named Moses. She put him in his early thirties, and, though he was no Tom, he seemed sufficiently strong and energetic to step forward in the event of a breakdown. Because of a shy and childlike demeanor, Nell found him to be approachable, and she easily drew out recommendations for supplies, a few details about what to wear, and an idea of her required duties. Using a crude map, he patiently described the topography and pointed out the route. Still, he lacked refinements of educated speech and manner.

Something about his shifting, indefinite colored eyes gave her pause. From her experience, honest people made honest contracts, eye-to-eye and hand-to-hand. But he wouldn't shake to seal agreements. During their discussion, he seemed to be talking, not to her, but to hands that hitched a horse to a post, to a woman's shoes as they knocked down the boardwalk or to a bed of ants. They focused on a cardinal that landed in a tree and on two boys shooting marbles from one hole in the ground to another.

A few days after, on a misty morning, Nell and Jenny began what she called "the most adventurous and daring event of my life." In Tom's tightly packed wagon, she drove to the place of departure. Her parents, Christina, Ruby and Arthur followed behind in a solemn procession. Mama wore her funeral bonnet, with a veil. She wept all the way, clasping Jennifer, kissing her and making such a general scene that it did not surprise Nell when one of the neighbor boys asked who died.

With the gray earth blending into an even grayer sky, the day seemed, indeed, fit only for a funeral. Nell's gloved hands, numb at the fingertips, stiffly held the reins of her team. In spite of two layers of clothing, the moist, cool air penetrated through to her skin and tensed every muscle, but most of her shivering came from within. If little Jenny had not smiled from under her heavy down quilt, if her mules had not pulled with such vigor, and if the Ark had not been so sturdy, she may not have been able to cast off her moorings. To avoid weeping like Mama, she concentrated on her animals. She had all confidence in a mule named Samson, for his size and strength, but Blondie was another matter. Immediately, the spoiled female had disliked the large, black mule pulling next to her and had already nipped his hide. Now, he kept a wide eye open to her. Already, she had kicked the spare mule that Nell tied to the tailgate as a backup for the main team.

When Nell pulled to a halt behind three other wagons, Moses offered his hand to help her down from her seat. "Hey, I thought you was a boy, 'til I see your—" He glanced at her breasts, but avoided her eyes. Noticing Arthur's approach, he ended the sentence with "face," and added, "I never seen a woman so bold at the reins. Where's your kid?"

"She's over there with Mama," Nell returned.

"Cutter said to watch that she don't fall out the back. He don't want no accidents slowing us up. But, don't you concern yourself, not for a second. Moses is here."

"Who are you?" Arthur wanted to know.

"Guide. Moses Goodman's my name." When Arthur and her father offered their hands, he reluctantly shook, but his eyes never met theirs. "Ladies," Moses tipped his felt hat to Christina and Mama. "Cutter's on his way. Main guide; trapped in the Rockies for . . . don't know how long. Never claimed to be a looker, but don't let that trouble you none. He knows the way like a skipper knows the sea, by the stars." Moses turned to Nell. "You about to see things you never seen before, little gal. There be a ten-mile-wide highway, level as a floor, all the way to the Pacific Ocean."

"That isn't how I hear it," Mr. Baker said. He frowned.

"The trail is hard; graves all the way," a voice directly behind Nell snarled. She did not know if she cringed because of the man's rugged clothing and coonskin cap or because of his wicked visage. A large scar ran the length of his face, splitting the eyelid and lips like a curtain opening on a lurid scene. The lips parted on the dark stage where two teeth should have been. The eyeball, a globe of milky-blue quartz, bulged from its socket. If all this had not shocked Nell enough, strands of black, shiny hair hung from his belt beside a hatchet, a huge Bowie knife, and a powder horn, filed sharp at the end. Henry Hunt's "hardest looking scoundrel" description now seemed an understatement, and Nell moved instinctively to stand between Arthur and her father.

"Indians," Cutter whispered, pointing to his scar. When he showed them six lines notched on the knife's handle, Arthur slid his arm across Nell's shoulders and pulled her to his side. She looked up at him, towering above her, his eyes grave with worry and dark from sleeplessness.

"Now, what's the situation here?" Cutter asked Moses. "Is this the woman you told me about?"

"Yonder," Moses pointed.

Nell answered all his questions and showed him the contents of her wagon, most being food in barrels and cotton sacks. She and Arthur packed twenty pounds of sugar, one hundred pounds of flour, and five pounds of tea, which she preferred to coffee, the recommended drink. There were dried apples, apricots and peaches, squash cakes, fifty pounds of potatoes, and salt pork, dried beef, crackers, honey, cheese, and more.

"Smells right good," Cutter said, sniffing at Ruby's six loaves of freshly baked bread. "What about grains?"

"Underneath. Oats, crushed wheat, beans." Nell exhibited the new Hawkin Rifle, which her father had given her, only yesterday. "I'm going to learn to fire this, Mr. Cutter," she said. She showed him the brass flask of powder and a leather possibles bag containing balls, Irish linen patches, flint, a patch knife and bee's wax. When the good side of his mouth turned upward in a grin and his whole eye sparked, Nell found enough humanity in him to trust.

"What's that?" He pointed to three tiny starts, planted in buckets and strapped to a shelf just over the wagon wheels directly next to the axle grease.

"Those are my apple trees. I'm going to plant them by my house in the Great Salt Lake Valley."

"And those?"

"I'm a teacher. I need books like a farmer needs seed."

"The trees and the books, they weigh too much, non-essentials. Get rid of them. Think light, Mrs. Mortenson. Think of yourself pulling this Ark of yours through mud a foot deep."

"That's why I brought an extra mule, Mr. Cutter. If they need my help, I'll push."

"A goat? For the child, I presume. Smart that you caged her."

Yes, it was smart, and all Ruby's doing. When she and the slave said their final goodbye at the house, Ruby surprised Nell with a parting gift: a young nanny with a full bag, having recently dropped a kid, and a snug, light cage, which attached to the sideboard. Its door dropped into a ramp. With the goat came Ruby's last word. "Yo' made yo' woman's choice. Now, go easy as de moon slippin' behin' a cloud. Protect Jenny. Be thankfo' fo' de right to go."

"The mules must have set you back," Cutter said, admiring the stud and Blondie, who flipped her nose at him.

While Cutter inspected the remainder, which consisted of personal items and bedding, Nell's father took Moses aside. She desperately tried to hear their words but could not due to Jenny's whining about the cold. Cutter studied her face with his good eye and complained loudly over the weighty silver service, the one elegant treasure she had not eliminated when deciding what to take.

"I insist on keeping it," she told him. "It's an heirloom from my grandmother. I am the image of her and wouldn't think of leaving it."

Cutter threw up his hands. "What the devil is this?" He tugged on the white fabric of her full ruffled petticoat."

"That's not a man's business," Nell said. She had worn it and the pink gingham dress beside it on that day long ago when she secretly met Tom at the mill. Though the two nearly filled her trunk, she wanted desperately to wear them again when she joined Tom in the valley.

"You don't get it. When I said the way is hard, I meant *hard*, lady. Spoons, plants, books, petticoats. It's the little vanities that take most people down. Now, do you want your family to take the silver, or do you want to dump it on some Rocky Mountain trail?"

"I'm taking it," Nell answered. A distance away, she saw her father slip Moses a small pouch, apparently a payment. Moses quickly shoved it into his pocket. She wished she knew the amount of the bribe. Then, when Cutter left to inspect the three other wagons, her father followed and conversed with him. Nell stood quietly on the opposite side of one family's wagon where she could hear, but could not be seen. She faked wiping mud off her shoe onto the wheel spokes.

"I don't like taking a lone woman and a child on the thumb," Cutter said. "I'm surprised men like you and that other fellow would let her go. What's wrong with you?"

"Let her? I don't know how to stop her. She has a mind of her own. I can't figure where she got it either; her mother certainly isn't like that. If I don't send her with my blessing, she'll go without it. It's all complicated."

"She's either very brave or very naive."

"Both. That's why I must beg of you to protect her." When Mr. Baker asked Cutter if he was an honest man, Cutter answered, "Sometimes." When he asked, "Would you protect my daughter with your life for ten twenty-dollar gold pieces?" Cutter answered, "Most likely, I'd protect her without the gold." When her father said, "Well, take it, if there's the slightest chance," Cutter accepted the pouch. With it, he marched straight to Mr. Howell, owner of the Quincy Co-op, who waited in the rain to be paid.

Nell's father found her. "I thought you'd be listening," he said because he knew her ways. "You'd be better off going with the Mormons, even if we'd have to see you to Kanesville ourselves."

"How can you suggest that, Father, hating them as you do? Holy cow. And why do you worry so much?"

"Because that's what father's do, Nell. At least, the Mormons would care for you and Jenny. I don't like this." He heaved a long sigh. They had been over it many times while outfitting the wagon. "What has gotten into you?" her father wondered. "Have you lost your mind? I tremble to contemplate the hazards that may befall you." For the hundredth time, he detailed the savagery of Indians and described all types of wild animals. "They're the least of your problems when compared to bad water. Looks clear like that from our well, but it will kill you, make no mistake." At last, he said, "How can you take little Jenny from us? How? I beg of you, for Mama's sake, don't go. Look at her. This is killing her."

Mama wailed with her arms around Jenny, unwilling to control herself and make a proper goodbye. Nell wanted to go to her, hold her, tell her how much she loved her, and explain that she must do what she must do. But her own strength, a failing dam to a monstrous lake, could not be tampered with. Also, she had resolved to never again be manipulated, not even for pity's sake.

Christina, who came along under protest, chose to ignore Nell. "You don't care about anyone's feelings," she had told her sister before they left home. "You only care about yourself. First, you run off with a Mormon, and now you just run off."

"You don't understand, Christina. I love Tom."

"Oh, I do understand. You brought Jenny to us and made us love her; now you're taking her away as if she means nothing at all to us. If you don't care how anyone else feels, at least give her a chance at life. You don't even know how to care for her. When you have to pay for this, I'll be glad." Tears had washed over Christina's angry eyes. However, at the last moment, they softened. "I'll miss you, Nell," she said. And then, "I have always envied you."

"I know," Nell hugged her. "It's not your fault. I took pleasure in tormenting you. You have a right to your feelings." Then, Nell whispered into her sister's ear. "Arthur has a weakness for women dressed in pink. Wear lilac toilet water and don't say *I love you* or kiss him until he makes promises. It's a man's nature to fight for what he wants. Otherwise, he won't value it. "

Nell turned to her father. "I won't put anyone through this again, Father. It's now or never. I have to live my life. Go on home. No sense for everyone to stand out here in the cold. Arthur can see us off."

"So be it, Nell. Since I cannot stop you and you will not permit us to take your part in this, you must be strong. You must be alert. Trust that good Baker mind of yours; foresee trouble and act to avoid it before it comes."

"I know all that, Father. We'll get there. Wasn't it Buddha who said that if you're faced in the right direction all you have to do is put one foot in front of the other?"

He paused for a moment to brace up, then, changed the topic to avoid his own emotions, as men are prone to do. "I paid the guides amply for your safety. Even so, trust neither; only, if you must trust one over the other, choose the hard-looker, the older one, Cutter. He is, at least, honest in his wretchedness."

"Father. You needn't have paid them. I already gave $90. We will be safe with all these families going along. And, by the way, I think you have misjudged that Moses fellow. He has been kind and assuring to me."

"I wish I could be as certain as you are, daughter." Into her hand, he slipped a .40 caliber derringer. "Show this garter pistol to no one, but keep it about you at all times." Caution and suspicion were typical of him, typical of him to leave her with two guns when one would do. "Be ready with a backup" was his motto. "Watch that you don't shoot yourself with it, and load it only if you expect trouble. Use about a third of the powder as for the rifle, and remember, only one ball per load. Shoot close up with this one, no more than eight, maybe ten, feet at the outside. You have to be on target. What I'm saying is that you draw this type of weapon only as a last resort because if the lead doesn't enter the heart or the brain, you might as well have thrown a rock. Do not hesitate, if you are going to use it."

"I won't. Thank you, Father. We'll get to Tom, you'll see."

As if to memorize her face, he looked at her; he held her and brushed hair from her eyes like he did before she had begun to mature. "Go on, then," he said. "Make your way." Like an old man, he shuffled back to the carriage. From the carriage, he brought little Jenny, who had to be torn from her grandmother.

"I don't want Nell," she screamed. "I want Mama." Nell held her closely while she kicked. Mama's tactics to get what she wanted were disgusting, she thought. It was as undignified as destroying your own daughter's letters. Though Nell felt relief in leaving, she blew her mama a kiss. Mama returned it and waved off her daughter with a handkerchief. Nell found it difficult to believe that her devoted family had planned to exterminate Tom.

When Arthur sauntered toward her from the haze, Nell threw the derringer into the storage box between the rice and the beans. Her father had done everything but teach her how to use it. He must have thought that in watching him target practice she had learned, but shooting was not high on her list of things to do, and she hadn't paid attention.

"I have given this much thought," Arthur said. "Though you have deeply hurt everyone, I am determined to travel with you. I'll be taking you to Tom, if that's what you want. At least, we'll know you're alive." Though he stood tall, his brown eyes aglow with yearning, an assertive man in the full bloom of his youth, he fiddled with his ear like the time when she beat him at marbles.

"Oh, God," Nell prayed, "let me hold up, like Ruby said, one more time!" She managed to smile and thank Arthur. "I can and must do this on my own. A big moose like you would eat all I've packed in the first week, and I'd have to spend my entire journey cooking instead of enjoying the scenery." Lifting Jennifer, who pulled at her Kentucky jeans, she added, "As if Jenny isn't enough." Then, she turned her back on him and drew a laced handkerchief from the pocket of her rough woolen coat. The dam had sprouted a leak. Arthur sheltered her and Jenny with his topcoat against the light rain.

"I love you, Nell," he said. "I have always loved you. If you need me, send word. Somehow. I will come to you. And, if you decide to turn around, I'll be right here."

"Turning around is what I'm doing now. I don't plan to make a full circle of it." He opened his mouth to speak, but she saved him the trouble. With her trembling hand, she covered his trembling lips. "Don't get the wrong idea, Arthur, but I love you. I will always love you and wish you well." Then, trying to say something cheerful, she told him, "I'll see you again. Tom will bring me back, someday." The mere mention of her husband's name gave her strength. "I know I can change him, make him forget Mormonism. We'll return. But, if perchance not, I shall never forget you."

"Nor I you. If that Mormon has turned polygamist, you get on home."

"Hit the trail!" Moses called as if he were leading a large train.

Arthur helped Nell wrap Jenny in her heavy quilts and settle her, with a rope tied around her waist to prevent her from falling out the back. He assisted Nell onto the driver's seat. "You needn't have dressed in boy's clothing," he said. "No one will be fooled."

When she bent toward him, he pecked her on the lips. Suddenly, he sprang up next to her. Encircling her in his arms, he kissed her with awkward passion, but Nell was unmoved by it because her attention focused on Tom's letter, which crinkled under her camisole. "My land, Arthur, why didn't you tell me you loved me before now? When you proposed?"

"Because I thought it wasn't the manly thing to say."

"Then, why now?"

"Because I don't give a damn if it's manly or not, because I'll never have a chance to tell you again. I know I won't."

"Let me hear you say it one more time."

"I love you, Nell," he said, looking quite handsome, actually. Why hadn't the fool told her long ago?

"Marry Christina, Arthur. Tell her you love her. She'll make a good wife."

"I've considered that, because I know how she feels. But, she's only enough like you to torment me." He buried his head in his coat. "Why me?"

"If you're going to compare, marry someone else, but, for heaven's sake, Arthur, marry someone. Where's the scarf I made you? This dampness will go straight to your ears."

When the other three wagons creaked forward, Arthur jumped from hers and stepped away to stand beside his horse. "Step up," Nell flipped the reins over the mules' backs. Detached of its moorings, the Ark set sail over the soaked ground and toward the vast unknown. Each time Nell turned back, she saw Arthur standing there, holding his reins with one hand, his ear with the other. She watched him grow dimmer and dimmer until he blended in with the foliage and the dreary mist. Now, the dam broke, and tears flooded over her eyelids so that she could not see, and did not care to see, more thunderheads approaching from the west.

13

THE PREDICTION

(Diary)   *April 23, 1849*

Here I am, crossing Iowa with a spoiled child who whined all day and night for her own bed, an untrained mollie, who parked her rear in the mud for an hour before I managed to coax her up, and a poor, young girl with toes crushed under a wagon wheel. My feet are icy cold, my clothing damp, and I'm starving for a hot meal. Fear of humiliation alone prevents me from turning my mules toward home.

The little wagon train traveled in single file along the main road heading north toward Nauvoo, Cutter and Moses first, riding their horses and leading pack animals, Nell's wagon second, and then three larger wagons. Nell spoke to no one, excepting Jennifer when she warned her to stay away from the tailgate. Several times, Moses trotted beside her and grinned reassuringly. Once, he tried to strike up a conversation by saying she had "done good choosing her mules" or "the weather will be clearing soon." But, she couldn't manage a smile.

Concerns for the future tormented her. How was she to wash her hair? And, when, in this cold? Where was she to bathe? Who would gather wood for a fire? Perhaps she should have left later in the year with the Mormon group that united for the benefit of one and all. Was she supposed to feed and water the mules? Milk the goat? Would Moses help her unhitch for the night? Then, Blondie. She constantly nipped at Samson, the strong black male, which Nell's father had carefully selected, and kicked the extra mule, which Nell called "The Spare." Both were very leery of Blondie, and this worried Nell because an uncooperative team was synonymous with an unsuccessful journey. Three times already, Blondie had frozen in her tracks when pulling through heavy mud became too difficult, and Nell finally forced herself to whip the ingrate on the rear, an act for which she detested herself. For a few days after that, Blondie lowered her ears each time Nell approached her.

They journeyed over a slippery road, stopping briefly to rest at midday. When the pale sun descended behind the rolling hills, the time came to set up camp. Nell made so many blunders that she had to perform most every task twice and had no time to worry. Because of the stiff northern wind, she faced the Ark westward and drew shut the strings of the back and front canvas. Though Nell chinked spaces between the cover and the box, Jennifer, who didn't seem able to stay covered, shivered from the rapidly cooling day. She dressed her chubby child in another layer of clothing and carried her into a stand of trees to search for firewood. What little she found, she stacked under the wagon to dry for future campfires. Moses did, indeed, unhitch her mules, and, for the first time in her life, Nell closely watched the process and asked if he might teach her to hitch up in the morning.

"Ah, there be no need," he told her. "I'm at your service." Removing his warped hat, he flourished a bow. With balanced features, an abundant crop of red hair, and a clear complexion, he would have been perfectly handsome if his ears had not prominently stuck out. It seemed unusual, though, that so vigorous a man possessed roving eyes. Once when they spoke, she believed he must have been talking to someone else and turned to see who it might be, but there were only the mules. She moved into his line of vision, and he covered a bashful smile with the back of his hand. "You be a fine looker," he said, his eyes upon Blondie.

"I appreciate that. You are a fine looker yourself," Nell said to set him at ease.

Before she knew it, he had all her animals, tied securely in a stand of hickories under which young grass sprouted abundantly. For Jenny, he milked the goat. Moses Goodman. The name seemed to suit him well.

Just as Nell had begun to wonder about the people in the other three wagons, a woman, who introduced herself as Mrs. Stella Suffix, appeared in a panic. "I knew we'd forget something. It's a bad sign," she predicted. "I told Ralph, I told him, we shouldn't leave home. We'll never make it, I told him. Mark my words, I said. But, he paid me no heed. I should think that after all these years together, and all these children, he'd learn."

One by one, three children gathered around their mother, each her replica: curly albino hair, little faded blue eyes with black pupils, and flat noses with crab apple knobs at the ends. While "Marm" chattered about their ill-fated journey, they pushed and shoved to be closest to her and hid their faces in her skirt like too many pups competing for the bitch's teats. They swore at one another in high-pitched voices through the largest sets of jagged buckteeth Nell had ever seen. Two must have been twins, and another could have made them triplets, only he looked a little older.

"I'm Nell Mortenson. This is Jennifer. What is it you forgot?"

"Only the most important thing. My soup kettle. I set it just outside the door, and that Ralph forgot it. Could I borrow yours? Get away!" She snapped at the children and cuffed one so viciously that he fell to the ground and crawled away yelping like a pup that had been nipped. Out of sympathy for the children, Nell unfastened her pot from where she tied it on the outside of her wagon along with other cooking utensils. She offered the woman her metal tripod as well.

"I'm going to need these in the morning, but you're welcome to use them tonight. Give it back to me clean."

"Much obliged," Stella said.

Because of the overcast sky, dark settled early upon the company. Nell lit an oil lamp for company, and she and Jennifer snuggled closely together between heavy quilts. They supped on dried peaches, Ruby's bread and hardtack. Nell, who finally gave up trying to improve their situation and to wait for a better day, couldn't help but laugh at the futile attempts of the Suffix family in starting a fire. Jennifer laughed too, the beautiful, carefree laughter of a cherished child. But, in the next breath, she complained, "I'm cold, Nell. I want my bed. I want Mama." She gathered her once white blanket, stuck the corner up her nose and sucked her thumb.

"You can't have Mama. I'm Mama now."

"No. You're Nell. Where's Ruby? I want Ruby."

"You can't have Ruby either. We're going on a long trip to find your father, and I'm all you've got."

"I want my bed," Jennifer shivered. "Baby's cold."

"Well, I want my bed too," Nell said. "You and I will just have to learn to tough it out. You've got to give up that business with your thumb. It makes people nervous, and I don't want a daughter with buck teeth."

Above the wind that whistled through every crack, Nell listened to Mrs. Suffix complain. "You can't start a fire in this wind, Ralph," and the children echoed her tones with cries for soup.

"I'll have it going real soon, Stella," Ralph assured her. After a half hour, he gave up and they finally quieted themselves. But then, Cutter and Moses cursed the wind for blowing over their tent. When the sleet and rain fell in torrents, Nell took pity and invited them into the shelter of her wagon. It was then that she learned from Moses that one wagon, owned by a middle-aged couple, turned back. They decided to try again in more clement weather.

Never had Nell spent such a night! The men fell asleep at once, of course, resting against and soaking her potatoes and flour. With heads leaning forward on their chests, they snored like the dying. Sometimes, their breathing stopped altogether. Then, Nell wondered when, or if, they would breath again. Though she made her bed upon her most pliant belongings, three sacks of corn and one of sugar, it still seemed coarse and lumpy. Her feet never warmed and little chills tingled on the back of her neck. When lightening cracked, the livestock snorted and snapped the twigs under their restless hooves. "What if they break away?" Nell worried. However, toward morning the storm ended. Beside her toasty three-year-old, Nell dreamed that Tom held her in front of a warm fireplace. Briefly, she slept.

All too soon, someone tapped on her shoulder. "You better rise up, Mrs. Mortenson. We're about to leave."

"Who are you?" Nell asked a sweet-faced girl.

"My name is Phoebe. I'm Ralph and Stella's oldest." Having soft brown hair, eyes shaped like those of a calf, not blue and not brown, and creamy skin, she appeared unrelated to Stella and the other children.

"You take after your father," Nell said.

"Sort of. He tells me I favor his mother, though. Her eyes was brindle too."

"Some say I look like my grandmother too, on my mother's side."

"She must have been a right pretty one. Here." Phoebe offered Nell a large bowl. "We used some of your wood and built a fire. While you was sleeping, Marm made mutton soup."

Nell gave a spoonful to Jennifer, but she promptly gagged and let it spill over both corners of her mouth. "She's not hungry this early," Nell explained and cautiously sipped it. Because Stella failed to skim off the fat, it accumulated on the roof of Nell's mouth where cold morning air turned it to lard. Nell shivered when she ran her tongue over it. "I'll eat it later," she told Phoebe, trying not to make a skewed expression.

"I poured mine on the ground where the horse leaked," Phoebe broke into a fit of laughter. Nell wanted to hug her. How delightful to cross the country with this pliable, light-hearted young woman!

"Our guide is a square lookin' man, don't you think?" Phoebe asked.

"Yes. You like him?"

"I like his shy smile. Ah, that red hair! He's right cute," Phoebe said. "Did you see that space between his front teeth? He winked at me this morning."

"He did? But, don't you think you're a bit young for him? He must be twenty-five or thirty."

"I'm fifteen," she said. "I look young for my age. Tell me, honest, what do you think of him."

"He's been kind to me. I suppose he'll guide us well. He'll do." He'd do better, Nell thought, if he could somehow tie back his large ears. Even with that, he wouldn't suit her, for he was one of those persons who makes a favorable first impression until he speaks.

"What about that creepy one?" Phoebe whispered.

"Scary, as far as I'm concerned. But, my father thought he was the better of the two."

"Phoebe! I don't believe this." Stella called, and Phoebe hurried away.

Because Moses had her mules hitched and ready to travel, Nell hurriedly cut slices from a brick of cheese and set them between crackers to eat while she drove the team. She prepared Jennifer for the day. Then, they drank rainwater from a large barrel that Arthur had thoughtfully secured to the wagon. He had constructed a wide funnel, which fanned over the top of the barrel so that rain drained into it. A clever man, Nell thought. Later that day, the skies cleared, the roadway hardened, and they camped early on the banks of the Mississippi River. Nell was able to build a warm fire over which she made a delicious salt pork and vegetable stew. Jennifer, who delighted in throwing rocks and debris into the fire, ate heartily and slept well beside her exhausted mother that night.

Next morning, they drove their outfits onto a giant barge, the same used by Elizabeth and Heber, and even Tom, over three years ago, Nell imagined. They crossed the Mississippi and began their trek across Iowa. After lengthening the distance between themselves and the river, they stopped to allow the animals to rest, to feed on grasses that sprouted along the roadside and to drink from a clear creek, edged by a ruffle of ice. Like fishes, last winter's dark green moss swam against its current.

"The animals are tired," Cutter said. "They're soft. But they'll toughen up. Fortunately, the road is frozen. Your team is the main concern on the trail, Mrs. Mortenson. You take care of them, and they'll take care of you."

Someone screamed. Everyone raced to the Suffix family wagon where Phoebe lay in agony on the ground, holding her foot.

"Trouble?" Moses asked.

"The wheel ran over my foot," moaned Phoebe.

"How did it happen?" Stella wanted to know. "Who's the culprit," she asked the other children.

"The twins was fightin'," the older boy said. "Spooked the horses. Phoebe, she was playin' on the tongue. She slipped."

"Damn the both of you," Stella said. Using her hand like a club, she boxed their ears. "Look what you've done to your sister. Get out! I don't want to hear from either of you brats," she called after them as they scurried away from her brutal hand. "Go after them, Ralph. Beat them and bring them back to me."

Stella cussed Phoebe with words outside of Nell's vocabulary. "How stupid can you be, standing on the tongue? This is an ill-fated journey. Oh, I knew it from the first. I told you didn't I, Ralph, when we opened our eyes this morning. 'Someone's going to be hurt today,' I said. Didn't I, Ralph? 'Everyone, be careful,' I said."

"Yes, Marm," Ralph answered. "I know what you said, but now we need to help Phoebe. She's hurt."

"'Leaving the comfort of home to lust for gold can't be any good,' I said. Didn't I? You didn't bring medical supplies, did you Ralph?" Hysterically, she circled her daughter, unaware of the mud that accumulated on her shoes and dress. "Is it broken, Phoebe?"

"Quiet, Marm," Ralph told her. "I'll have a look."

"No, Daddy. Don't fiddle with it," Phoebe cried out when he untied her shoe.

"Stop this!" Nell knelt at Phoebe's side. "You're too rough." She turned to Cutter. "Can't you do something?" Cutter seemed the proper person to handle this problem. With all his scars, surely he should know what to do.

"She'll live," he growled. "Put her in the wagon, and let's get on. Her mother can figure it out."

"Dear God, Ralph. There's blood coming out of the shoe," Stella screamed. "We need a doctor. Let's go home."

"There's no going back," Cutter said. "You women, look to her."

"Foot's still numb. You better shed that shoe, unless you want to cut it off later," Moses warned. "No sense ruining a right good boot."

"You know what to do, Moses." Nell rubbed his shoulder. "You remove the shoe." A woman could get a man to do most anything by praising his courage or by telling him *not* to try to fix the problem at hand.

"Woman's work," he said, failing to take the bait. "Come on. Ground's thawing; it's probably no more than a bruise. Heft her in the wagon. We gots some miles to cover 'fore dark."

"No, don't move her," cried Phoebe's "Marm."

"You're the guides," Nell shouted. "Aren't you prepared for this?"

"All I brought was my shovel," Cutter squinted his one good eye, "and she's not dead yet." He went to his horse. "I want you to know, here and now," he barked. "You stay away from Blue. She's a one-man horse. Try to ride her, she'll throw you. Get on her left side, she'll make you the village idiot."

"Forget the horse," Nell answered. "The trouble's over here."

Out of anger and pity for Phoebe, Nell determined to help if no one else would. "It's going to be all right, Phoebe. I'll do what I can. Your foot . . . it will heal." When Nell gently untied and slipped off the poor child's shoe and stocking, blood seeped from her crushed toes. "Get me clean cloth and whiskey," she told Stella.

"I have no cloth." Strange that this prophet of doom should be unprepared for accidents, thought Nell. Strange how she can't locate a shred of cloth for her own child. Nell asked Moses to hold Jennifer while she hurried for her whiskey. She resented using her well-planned store on these people. Though it pained her greatly, she tore a very narrow strip from the bottom of her ruffled petticoat, the one she planned to wear when she met Tom in the Great Basin. Quickly, she returned to Phoebe. Over the girl's toes, she poured the liquor. "Now, give her a swig," she told Stella. "Can you manage that?"

"Do you know what you're doing?" Stella asked.

"Yes," snapped Nell, lying. "Hurry!"

Though Phoebe screamed and though Nell doubted her skill, she straightened the big toe, which hung slightly to the side. She wrapped cloth around it and anchored it with a stick to keep it straight. The same treatment was skillfully given each of the toes, in spite of the fact that they may or may not have been damaged. A final wrap over all toes completed the job.

"Now, carry her to my wagon," Nell ordered. "*I* will watch over her. She'll rest better without the other three."

While Ralph carried Phoebe, Stella followed at his elbow. "Ralph, this wanderlust of yours will kill us all. Idiot. We'll never get to California and you'll never find your precious gold. Never. Mark my words. It isn't meant to be. Do you hear, Ralph? Ralph?"

"What you think is what you get," Nell whispered under her breath. She wished for the courage to say it aloud. Into a makeshift bed, she tucked Phoebe and gave her a large drink of rain water. "You lie there, for now," she said. A new maternal instinct surged within her, and she wanted to kiss the girl's forehead, but didn't. "Stay warm."

"You fixed her, Nell." Jennifer clapped her pudgy hands. Her eyes glowed with pride. "I'll kiss you better." She planted a juicy kiss on Phoebe's cheek.

Nell cuddled her spontaneous daughter. She hadn't realized that a child of so few years would be watching and learning from everything her mother did. "You must help me care for her. You must sit quietly so she can sleep and hold her hand. Your father will be proud when we tell him what you have done."

"I'll help her, Nell," Jennifer promised.

"You're a big girl, aren't you? Can you call me *mother*?" Without Ruby, Christina, Mama and others to care for Jennifer, Nell liked taking on the responsibility. It was good.

"Will a doctor have to saw my toe off?" Phoebe asked. The thought of it caused spots to circle in front of Nell's eyes. Jennifer scowled.

"Heavens no." Whatever made you think of such a thing? You'll be walking in a week or so."

"Heavens no," Jennifer mimicked. She patted Phoebe's cheek.

Nell cinched and tied the back canvas to prevent Jennifer from falling out. For double protection, she tied a short hemp rope around

Jennifer's waist, which prevented her from going near the back. Satisfied, she climbed upon the wagon, parked herself on the hard driver's seat, and prodded the mules to trot in order to catch up with the guides. Never mind the Suffix wagon, which strayed behind. Then, noticing Phoebe's dried blood on her hands, Nell was overcome with nausea and dizziness. She halted the mules, set the brake, climbed down from the wagon and lost what little food she had eaten. Seeing it spread over the ground, she lost more.

"Oh, how I hate this," she whispered. She wiped her mouth on a handkerchief that Christina had embroidered with yellow and pink blossoms. The colors made her sick again. When she tried to mount the wagon, she slipped and bumped her chin on her knee.

"Get up," she cracked the reins over Blondie's back. Fortunately, Blondie pulled with strength equal to Samson's, but she continually glanced back at Nell with lowered ears and with what Nell interpreted to be a scowl. "I hate doctoring," Nell called out to her.

It was all Stella's fault. With a family, the spitfire should have learned by now what to do in an emergency. She, herself, shouldn't have had to take the responsibility of mending other people's children. With any sense at all, Arthur should have followed to help her through such times, even though she told him not to. Imagine, men who left their women to fend for themselves. These incompetent, unsympathetic people! Never in her life had she doctored anyone, and she had never seen such a thing done. However, in spite of it all, she knew she had somehow, done right.

14

THE SPILL

(Diary)   April 27, 1849

Today, the Suffix wagon took a terrible spill. Brought us much grief.
Phoebe, poor girl, seems enchanted with Moses. We located a spring, my little
Jenny and I. From it, replenished our barrels. Bathed in it. Hair knotted and
dusty. If Ruby could see it! Then, dug out a hole, which the spring water filled
every hour, and the animals quenched their thirst. The tenacious little apple
trees perked up and I notice that tiny leaves have begun to sprout from all
three. Tonight, I am stiff in the joints, more than I ever was.

After crossing the Des Moines River, the sun warmed the travelers' backs and dried the muddy soil, though the air remained cool in
the daytime and water buckets crusted with ice overnight. Each evening, Nell fed corn, which she purchased from farmers along the way,
to her mules, and they quickly "toughened up" like Cutter expected.
Still, steep grades over the plush Iowa hills proved difficult for the
spunky animals.

As Stella continually predicted, her family seemed doomed. One
misfortune after another visited them, as the dawn of day meant the
dawn of some new plague, and this made the woman more witch than
fortuneteller. Nell's father, if he had been with her, would have said
they brought on their own troubles by being unprepared and by lacking
know-how, and Tom would have said that Stella had lost her faith in
God; but, to Nell's thinking, it was all of that and more. Luck, or whatever determines destiny, begins in the mind. The mind shapes that

thinking into words, which, over time, become as *real* as daffodils. "Negative," she told Phoebe after watching Stella take a whack at one of the twins. "Get your coat on. You'll catch the death of dampness. Damn! Idiots never learn."

The incident over one steep ascent continued a series of mishaps, which reinforced Nell's opinion. The bedraggled Suffix workhorses tried, but failed, to pull their heavy wagon up the grade. To aid them in their struggle, Nell suggested that her tough team be used instead. On the first try, Blondie and Samson strained and heaved and dug their hooves into the earth, but they stalled at the steepest section of the rise. Ralph backed to the bottom. On the second try, he gave the team a running start and cracked his whip over them all the way. Then, at the point where they stalled before, Moses and Cutter struggled at the spokes in an effort to keep the wheels turning. Rocks and dust shot up as human and animal flesh labored together, but, just as they gained the top, Ralph made a sharp turn. The wagon toppled. It slid down the hill as a sled slips over snow, but left most of its contents strewn in its path.

"Oh, please, God, Nell prayed, "Protect my team!" By the time she reached them, they were already on their feet. Early in the fall, they had broken away from their bindings and still had the tongue and singletree attached to them. They trembled as any human would after such a spill, and Blondie let loose a round of loud and furious whistles that would have awakened the dead. "You're all right," Nell reassured her while she stroked her nose and examined her legs. "Settle down, girl. It's nothing serious." Blondie stomped about in a panic. She shook her coarse white main, brandished her tail and snorted at Nell, as if to say, "Look what you've done to me!"

"There, now. Settle down, my girl." Nell patted her neck and inspected her injuries, which seemed superficial. "Woo. There, there." By the time little Jenny, dragging her blanket and sucking her thumb, reached the scene, Blondie had begun to breathe normally, and, as if by magic, the child had only to reiterate her mother's words, "settle down," and Blondie lowered her head to the eye level of the child. She relaxed. But, Samson flared his nostrils, pawed the ground and twitched his hide. For some time, no one dared go near him.

As for the men, Moses and Cutter had jumped out of harm's way before the wagon tipped or they might have been crushed, and Ralph bled no more than the mules. Stella braced herself sufficiently to pick tiny rocks and debris from a scrape running the length of his side.

"Oh, Ralph, these wounds are horrible," she told the shaken man. "It's a miracle you survived. Oh, what will befall us next? Trouble comes in threes, you know."

"Count yourself as one," Nell mumbled while she dabbed her precious whiskey over his scratches. Moses heard. When he slapped his knee and rolled on the ground in delight, Nell flushed. Back home, she would never have made such a comment. This wasn't home.

Luckily, Ralph brought tools, so the men began repairing the wagon, sufficient to carry them to Bloomfield, a settlement down the road a piece. Cutter knew of a blacksmith there, "fast becoming prosperous from gold rushers' misfortunes." The only benefit of the accident was that Stella's heavy oak chest was left behind because of its being badly split and scratched. She growled through her jagged buck teeth when Ralph suggested they "let it lay," and she cried when Cutter agreed. "I warned you against bringing it. You'll leave it now or later. No wonder you don't make the grades."

"I can't leave it," she screamed through teeth so large she couldn't keep her mouth shut. "It's been in my family for generations. Oh, Ralph, this is all your fault. Do something!"

"I said *sorry*," he apologized. "An earthworm could have driven that team better than I did." The woman might as well have rubbed the debris into her husband's wounds for the second time, judging from his disheartened expression.

"Toughen up, Ralph," Cutter said, his legs planted firmly on the ground. "You look like a man. Be one."

A fury rose in Nell. She wanted to tell Stella, "It's your fault for having brought the heavy chest in the first place, and it's an ugly old thing anyway, and you're ugly too." But, Aunt Emily had taught her to hold her tongue. "Never interfere in disputes between a wife and a husband," she advised. "You'll be the one who loses." Now that Nell was married, she understood why. Besides, Stella was not one to cross, being of an unpredictable ilk. So, Nell left her rage with Blondie when she and Jennifer led the upset animal to a little spring for a drink. "She blames Ralph for everything and wants him to be something he isn't. A mate who degrades the spouse will eventually be married to one without pride or self-confidence." By the time she had watered all four mules, she had begun to devise a plan for transporting the Suffix belongings to the summit. To the men, she suggested, "While two of you men work on the wagon, why don't the other two haul up their belongings?"

Moses returned with, "Good idea. You gals get after it while the men fixes the tongue. Victuals wouldn't be no bad idea neither."

"Us?" Nell asked. "Most of it is too heavy. We're not pack animals, you know." She plopped down on the slope to watch the men puzzle over the severed parts. How inept and clumsy they were! If Tom had been among them, the wagon would have been repaired by now, but it never would have toppled in the first place. She recalled his smile, much like Jennifer's. How joyous would be their reunion! By this time, he must have built a home for her, hoping that upon seeing it she would be content to remain in the Valley. He must have constructed a wide staircase leading to their sleeping quarters and a large kitchen for her slave. Well, since Tom and his Mormon friends opposed slavery—a hired servant. If only she were there now!

Simply thinking upon it gave Nell spirit. She mustered the skulking Stella and Mrs. Merrill, a nice quiet little character, from the third wagon with two half-grown girls who spiritedly pitched in. They carried sacks and boxes and bags and blankets up the hill until Nell broke out in a violent episode of perspiration. "I usually don't *glisten*," she smiled at Phoebe, who was no help at all.

As if the toppled wagon had not been sufficient trouble, Moses began taking a fancy to Phoebe. Nell watched him offer her a fistful of wild strawberry blossoms. Several times, he lifted her in and out of Nell's wagon, and he continually brought her slender strips of jerky from his saddlebag—with soiled hands. Phoebe, obviously flattered, combed her hair more than necessary after he said, "You're a fine looking gal." But, Nell didn't tell the poor wretch that he paid *her* the same compliment only a day before.

"You keep away from that man," Stella lectured Phoebe. "Suffix women are weak when they're young. Men want only one thing."

Everyone helped to upright the wagon. This time, Cutter drove. He selected a route around the steep rise and the emptied wagon creaked on, but not with Nell's mules. "They have got to see me over the Rocky Mountains," Nell told everyone. "I'm sorry, but I will not risk them anymore. I'm not responsible for what happens to you. Besides, Blondie won't play the fool a second time. The others have learned to follow her lead."

"That's a mule for you," Ralph said.

"Well, ain't that Christian." Stella kept herself in a constant boil. "You'll fit right in with them Mormons. I just hope your outfit tips over and there's no one to help you. Then, you'll know how it feels."

"My wagon isn't going to tip, not ever! It's the best built rig around."

"No, no," little Jennifer said. When she kicked dust onto Stella's shoe, everybody laughed. She tottered to her mother, who felt wretchedly satisfied that Stella must abandon her chest.

The accident cost travel time. After the tenuous repair, the Suffix family squeaked along at a snail's pace, avoiding the slightest bump. Nell overheard Moses complain to Cutter. "At this rate, we'll never make it to California. We'll be too late to claim our mine. What if we cuts out?"

"Can't," answered Cutter.

"We got to. These damned wagons moves too slow. The folks can make it their own selves. We brought them this far. They're trained. Let's beat it."

"I said, *can't*!" Cutter said again.

"Me, I ain't milking me no smelly goat, no more. Not me," Moses returned. "That spoilt gal gots to step up and do it her own self. She can wrestle her mules too. I don't want none of it."

Nell remembered her father's advice. "Trust neither. If you must trust one over the other, choose the hard looker." Though Moses had seemed genuinely caring, his words sat with Nell for some time. Then, she reasoned that he must be exhausted. People say the worst things when they're worn out, she told herself.

15

QUAGMIRE

(Diary)   *April 30, 1849*

Unbearable weather. Roads, a quagmire. Should have waited for some Mormon group.

Two days after the spill, the Suffix wagon wobbled into Bloomfield, Iowa, and just in time because directly in front of a wagon repair shop, the rear wheel rolled off. Without support, the heavily loaded box slumped on one corner, cracking several boards. They too wanted repair. The wheelwright, an indolent fellow who argued that he'd rather sleep than work, finally consented to do the entire job "for a price," which left the Suffix family nearly destitute. "You folks are coming through here so fast and furious that I never have a day to call my own," he complained. "I'm about to quit and go for gold myself." While waiting, Nell grazed her mules, purchased two fifty-pound bags of oats, and paid a nickel for her and Little Jenny to have a warm tub bath. Never had bathing felt so good! The Merrill family, which always lagged behind, now stepped forward. They drove Stella, Phoebe, and the three boys to the home of the town doctor, who had left his premises to deliver a calf; consequently, Stella asked his wife if she might "take a look-see at the toes." She did. "They look like regular broken toes," she said. "Happens all the time."

"Can you do anything more for her?" asked Stella.

"No," the wife answered. "She'll mend the way she is." With that, she charged Stella $1 for her trouble. When Stella related the story over the campfire that evening, even Cutter laughed; Nell, who had become accustomed, somewhat, to his disfigured face, felt gratified that he permitted himself some degree of amusement. "That doctor's devil of a wife invited the whole tribe of us in for a cup of hot tea," Stella said with her angry gray eyes flashing. "We accepted, naturally, the house being warm and all aglow. She didn't bother to inform us that her litter had the whooping cough until my boys and the Merrill's huddled around the hearth next to them. A doctor's wife too!" There was a long silence after she said this. Nobody laughed. Nell ran little Jenny to their wagon for the night.

Outside of Bloomfield, it began to rain and continued for four days straight, sometimes as a light mist, sometimes as gray sleet, other times as a waterfall. If the miserable dampness wasn't enough, Blondie stuck her head through the back of the wagon and inched inside as far as possible. Having been raised in Quincy with a proper roof over her head, she was now unwilling to act the part of any old beast and subject herself to inclement weather. But, because Nell took pity and allowed it one night, Blondie brayed on the next and wanted to make a habit of it.

Each day blended into the next, and Nell measured time, not by her clock, not by distance, but by the number of puddles crossed. The mules kicked up mud so high that it reached the footrest and coated her trousers. On the first day, she changed into dry clothing twice, but on the second, she simply disregarded the filth and scraped it off whenever it dried. The strict cleanliness of civilization had to be abandoned, she learned, if she were to spend her time traveling across the continent. On the third day, they arrived at a point where the road had been so completely flooded that it appeared to be a pond. To judge its depth, Moses and Cutter wallowed through, their horses knee deep in muck.

Cutter waved for Nell to follow. Instead, she pulled back on the reins. "You can make it," Moses shouted over a great roll of thunder.

"I don't like it," Nell yelled back. "It's saturated."

"You can make it," Cutter called.

Blondie, her legs as stiff as posts and the whites of her eyes enormous with fear, glared back at Nell.

"Get up," Nell called and snapped the reins over the mules' backs. When Samson surged forward with the power to pull Blondie along, Nell decided that perhaps the guides were right. Her fears were unfounded, and Blondie, must be trained to obey.

"Come on through. Come on," Cutter called. "You're holding us up."

Nell slapped the team's rears. "Step up." All stepped forward, save Blondie. Even deeper, she dug in. When her ears dropped, her rear flank quivered and her tail switched, Nell clearly knew Blondie had determined not to set foot in the sludge.

"Let me learn her," Moses said. From the roadside, he cut a long, thick willow, and Nell, being as hungry, exhausted and ornery as he, believed a little sting might be what the spoiled Blondie needed. But, she "wouldn't be learned." Moses pitched into her, hard and furious, striking her over and over again until his switch broke. Rushing for another, he cursed. "I'll make her mind if I have to kill the block-head."

Blondie turned a terrified eye upon Nell, and her usual whistle sounded more like a scream. "Oh, no you don't," Nell sprang from her wagon. She blocked Moses. "Give me that switch. If my mules need beating, I'll be the one to do it."

"Out of my way," Moses demanded. Gritting his teeth and flaring his nostrils, he shoved her aside. Nell, who lost balance, slipped into the muck. "I's tired of watching you fiddle with that worthless jackass. She gots to be learned."

"Leave it to me," Nell shouted, and Jennifer screamed from the wagon, her arms reaching out for her mother. Blondie snorted, gave out a horse's whinny following the wind-down of a donkey's bray, and ended with a high kick in Moses' direction.

Moses struck Blondie once more, with a vengeance. "Whinee . . . aw ah aw." Then, Cutter appeared. He said nothing—simply rode Blue straight toward Moses and sideswiped him. The brute hit the mud with a splat. That ended it. Insulted and dripping, Moses trudged away. "I ain't tendin' to your mules, no more," he grumbled at Nell. "I ain't milkin' no lousy goat no more neither."

Hoping he didn't mean it, Nell did not respond. "Trust your good mind," she heard her father's voice as if he were standing next to her.

"I'm backing up," she told Cutter. "This is impassable. I'll find another way."

"Suit yourself. We're not waiting on you," Cutter answered.

Since Blondie willingly obeyed, Nell backed the wagon and pulled off the trail and onto higher ground where she halted her stressed team. "He's bad," little Jenny said, pointing in Moses' direction. From this time forward, Nell intended to trust her intelligent animals, her own instincts, and those of her child over the decisions of these men, who were driven by greed. Ralph, however, had not learned from her experience. When Cutter waved him on, he drove directly into the quagmire and immediately stalled. The longer he encouraged his team, the deeper they sank until they stood mired up to their bellies. Without a word, the Merrills followed Nell's lead. Again, her team, excluding Blondie, that is, had to be doubled with Ralph's, and after long, laborious hours they inched the wagon through. Now, the new wheel began to wobble! Again, Nell overheard Moses complain to Cutter, "I tell you, we's better off without all these laggards."

"We've been paid," Cutter said. "Now, we're mired in with them up to our eyeballs. When you're in with a gang, that's trouble, but when you're alone, that's trouble too." Nell had to agree. People could be awfully complicated and troublesome. But, having to travel alone in this wilderness would be even worse. Yes, being utterly alone, that would be her greatest fear.

In the late afternoon, the company gave in to the miserable weather and camped on a level patch of ground on a rocky hillside. A wind from the northwest whistled through Nell's wagon, which was again crammed with wet folks: Moses, Cutter, Phoebe, herself and Jennifer, all shivering, muddy and ill-tempered. "Just for this once," Moses insisted. His eyes shifted from one side to the other, never quite settling on anyone. "Our tents won't stand."

"You'll owe me," Nell returned. "Why does everything have to be so hard?" When Blondie worked her nose through the canvas, Nell laughed, for it hit her that nothing was left to do about the predicament except to find humor in it. "You look like a mud ball," she told Moses.

"Same to you," he smiled broadly. The space between his two front teeth rendered him a boyish quality. "We crossed only one puddle today," he remarked. "Trouble is, it was five miles long."

"That's not funny." Nell had to smile.

Phoebe, the one person in the group who didn't resemble a mud ball, giggled. Then, suddenly, her face dropped, a cloud having drifted over her spirit. She bowed her head and covered her face with her shawl. Jennifer, who didn't care how anybody looked, mimicked her mother and laughed.

"If my husband were here . . . "

"Well, he ain't here, is he?" Moses said.

"I am," Cutter said.

"I know," Nell smiled.

With night as black as pitch, Blondie intermittently ground her teeth, but that blended in with the snoring of the men, the shuffling and blatting of the goat in her cage, and snorts from Samson and The Spare. Lying warm, but crowded, under her feather tick, Nell recalled the old saying, "Misery loves company."

In the other wagon, the Suffix family could be heard grumbling at one another about the cold. One of the twins, Hailey, got slapped for losing a shoe, and the other, Bailey, came down with the croup. All night, he coughed, and before daybreak Stella startled everyone in the camp with her high-pitched warning, "Get away from him, you idiot, or I'll break your arm! He has the death of dampness." Over an impotent breakfast campfire, Ralph complained that rheumatism of the face had kept him awake the entire night. When thunder rolled across the sky, everyone agreed to the uselessness of traveling until the storm passed.

16

FINE TURKEY SHOOT

(Diary)   *May 2, 1849*

Weather greatly improved, but feet still ache when cold. Never again will I complain of heat. Two Merrill children have contracted the whooping cough. Parents let it be known they'd turn back for Bloomfield, to locate the doctor and recuperate. A quiet lot, their leaving won't make a great splash.

Excursion, mostly boring. In distance, I see one swell, another and another as if the prairie were a vast rolling ocean. Girls make delightful shipmates. Phoebe's toes improving, but I have had to tear more off my petticoat to heal the dim-witted girl. Opened plum preserves to prevent black scurvy.

Cutter shot a turkey. Ralph shot a horse!

In the Appanoose Mountains of Iowa, the weather cleared, an unusual warm spell setting in. New growth, fresh streams and hardened roads perked downcast spirits, and the sun painted a healthy glow on everyone's face—except Bailey's. While the other boys scampered alongside the travelers, pretending to shoot Indians in the trees, and while they played wagons with toys Phoebe created from chips of wood, grass and cloth, he complained of a headache and chills. Always, he coughed.

Even though Ralph's cheek swelled and the lines in his brow deepened from much pain and little sleep, he managed to remain cheerful and frequently remarked of the beautiful scenery. Nell marveled at this strength and fortitude, for she heard his footsteps night after night as he paced about the camp, attempting to endure. The first words out of his mouth one morning were, "I need someone with strong hands. This hateful tooth is killing me. I'm not taking it anymore."

"Wait, Ralph, a day or two at least," Stella pleaded. "We're apt to find a dentist up the trail."

"Can't wait."

"I'll pull it whenever you say." Moses smiled too broadly for what he'd offered to do. "Only difference between me and a dentist is the pliers."

"I've got some," Nell said, "but I'm not pulling anybody's tooth."

"It has to be done right," Stella said.

"I don't give a damn how it's done," returned Ralph. But, Stella talked him into waiting by relating the horrible story of a sheep that had died of an ulceration after the owner pulled a few teeth, hoping for the right one, and punctured the side of its swollen jaw. When she asked for another strip of Nell's petticoat to "anchor Ralph's cheek" over the bumpy ride, Nell begrudgingly cut off still another piece. "Numbskulls," she grumbled to Blondie. "They'll strip me of all I have."

Later on, when the party passed through a thick stand of trees, Ralph spotted a wild turkey. "Woo," he shouted at his plugs. "Yip, yip," he yelled to alert Cutter and Moses. "There's meat!" He pointed to where the turkey had flown, and the men hustled to his side with their rifles and possibles bags. While loading, Cutter grumbled, spit and chastised himself for being "slow as an old porcupine." Moses poured too much powder down his barrel and had to pull everything out "or be blown sky high," as Cutter put it.

"Fresh meat, that's all Bailey needs," Ralph told Stella.

"Oh, you men," she answered. "That turkey is long gone. All you think of is hunting, Ralph. I declare." When Hailey asked her if he could go, she yelled, "Of course not, fool." The boy flinched as if he had been hit. "I've got one sick and would die myself if you got shot. Remember, trouble comes in threes."

To show the other men he was still in charge of his wife, Ralph told Stella, "Tend to Bailey, Mother."

And to your mouth, Nell thought. The men hurried off with the excitement of boys going to a swimming hole. They deserved some pleasure, after all their physical labors, and they needed tasks which separated them from women and joined them in comradeship, experiences they would boast of later in life like women bragged of a painful delivery.

Grateful for a respite from the hard, jolting wagon seat, Nell took the opportunity to scrub muddy clothing in a roadside stream and to hang it on bushes to dry. Two shots reported. "I'll gather wood," she told Stella. "Sounds like they got him."

"Not Ralph. He's not much with a gun."

Soon, the men appeared, walking three abreast, their voices animated. They had their turkey, all right. Cutter held it high by the legs so that its wings spread, making it appear three times the size that it was. "I got him," he yelled.

"Well, aren't you a dead eye," Nell called back. Realizing her ill-chosen words, she covered her mouth. Even under the most pleasant of circumstances, his abrupt manner and deformed visage caused her anxiety, so he relieved her stress by smiling from the pleasant side of his face.

"You say that again and I'll trade you off to the Indians," he ribbed.

Sometimes, when he turned away the mangled side of his face, she momentarily found him handsomely featured and wondered what made him tick. Well-proportioned and fit, he must have once been as impressive as he was now threatening. Someday, if she ever knew him better, she'd ask him about his past. Who scarred his face? How many times had he traveled west? Was he ever in love?

Ralph leaned his loaded gun against a tree. "I'll unhitch the horses, Mother," he told Stella. "We've decided to camp early and make a feast of it."

Everyone pitched in. Moses carried Phoebe to a dry, thick patch of grass, though, to Nell's thinking, she did not need carrying. His hands lingered around her waist too long, and they touched noses. Leaving her with a secretive peck on the cheek, he put up an ordinary little roasting rack, and, pointing out how clever he was, he broke two Y-shaped branches from a sapling. "It was me brought down the bird," he said. "If Cutter thinks he did, let the old man git his glory." He dug a round hole in the ground, positioned the branches upright into the dirt on either side and lay Nell's metal roasting rod across the top. Cutter hung the bird from a tree limb by one leg, and the children watched in wonder as he skinned it, "slick as a whistle." In their annoying, high-pitched voices, they screamed when he gutted the bird, but asked if they might make balloons with the entrails. Even little Bailey rose up from his bed to watch. Stella made biscuits and Nell boiled potatoes.

"That was a fine turkey shoot," Nell said. "To celebrate, I'll spread a cloth over the grass and use my silver." All their mouths watered when the turkey popped and sizzled over the flames.

Presently, Moses announced that the outside slices were cooked, and everyone lined up with a tin plate. Nell gave each a boiled potato, Stella served pan-fried biscuits, topped with a heap of Nell's plum preserves, and Cutter shaved juicy slices off the bird with his long double-edged blade. During the entire meal, Moses devoured his share with a full and drooling mouth, finally wiping the congealed grease on his sleeve. When everyone poked fun, he enjoyed the attention to such an extent that he made a mess of his shirt. But, when he smacked his lips, Cutter said what Nell wanted to. "Don't smack."

"I hate smacking," Stella said. "Cut that out." Ralph nodded in agreement.

Picking at the leftovers, everyone praised the "best spread they'd ever had" and leisurely sprawled over the grass like gorged cats, Moses next to Phoebe, Nell and Jennifer on a quilt in the shade of the wagon, and Ralph against the tree where he leaned his gun. Stella carried Bailey, bundled but shivering, to join in.

"Don't you throw out that tater water," Stella told Nell. "You drink that."

"Why?" Nell wondered aloud.

"Well, I don't know if there's any truth to it, but an old settler woman told me that half a potato, well-boiled, will absorb the poison out of bad water. Said it saved her life one time when a whole lot of people died of dysentery. If your Jenny was mine, being little like she is, I wouldn't give her no raw water. Think I'm pulling your leg, do you?"

"No. But, nobody ever told me that before," Nell said.

"Never heard of it," Moses shook his head in disbelief.

"Of course, there are many things you never heard," Cutter added. "You might want to try it, Mrs. Mortenson, once we leave the hills. These Iowa springs shouldn't harm anybody, but I've known a number of gravely sick people out there on the plains. Many perished."

"I'll keep it in mind, Stella," Nell said.

"Well, if you're going to do it, you best start now. Give her a little swalla."

Nell did and Jennifer found it acceptable.

"I'm wondering if there's fish in that stream, yonder," Moses said, smacking his lips. Fish sounds tasty for breakfast."

"Could be," Cutter answered. "Sunfish." His bulging blind eye appeared enormous in the midday sun and would have frightened Nell if she hadn't known him. How had he scarred his face? Who had cut Blue's rump, and why was she so skiddish?

Nell admired the quiet rustle of the trees, bright green with newly-sprouted leaves and the tiny white star-shaped flowers growing along the creek's edges. The trickle of water, the song of finch and the hum of bees blended into an orchestra perfect for a nap. "This is choice acreage for a house," Nell said. "I imagine the Rocky Mountains are like this."

"Not by a long shot," Cutter disagreed. "Compared to them, these are anthills." Frowning, he watched Moses push a slice of turkey into Phoebe's mouth, then lick his fingers. Cutter pierced his meat with the point of his bear knife, the one with notches in the handle. What did they mean, Nell wondered. Cutter's functioning eye flinched slightly. "The Rockies are more like the ocean."

"How's that?" Stella wondered.

"I guess you'd have to see both of them to know," he said.

"Bet they're not as perdy as Phoebe," Moses wiped his greasy fingers on the grass. He ate with his hands.

"Why don't you use my silver?" Nell asked.

"Genuine?"

"It's genuine. Grandmother gave it to me the day I was born."

"That right? I don't care 'bout eating with no silver. If it was mine, I'd trade it off for hardtack. Phoebe here'd like that. And colored ribbons." He smiled affectionately, his eyes intent on the grass, which he stroked. But, Cutter glared at him so terribly that his good eye appeared more frightening than the butchered one.

"Turkey's delicious," Nell said, giving Jenny a tender bite.

"Too tough," Stella replied. "I like hens."

Bang! Ralph's gun lay smoking on the ground. For an instant, no one moved. They locked eyes. Someone tittered, and someone else swore. Moses' horse whinnied in pain and blood streamed down its upper leg. "You stupid turkey brain, Ralph. Leaning a loaded gun against a tree. Son of a bitch."

Cussing all the way, Moses stomped to his crippled animal, lead it into the woods, and shot it.

"For shame," Stella snarled, revealing her jagged teeth. "There goes the rest of our savings. Looks like your trip is over, Father." Ralph hung his head in shame. "First time you hit anything and it had to be someone's horse."

Though Stella, a threatening woman, towered over Nell, and though Nell had been taught to keep negative thoughts to herself, "like a lady," something broke loose inside her brain, and she heard it like an autumn leaf snaps from a tree.

"If you had been born in an earlier time, Stella, you would have been burned at the stake!" The simple thought, once stated, somehow made Nell stronger. She liked it. She realized that not everyone lived by the rules of her Aunt Emily or her sensitive mother. Dealing with the open wilderness, leaving nurturing parents and civilization, meeting meanness face to face all required a different set of rules.

"Most people wrong others by mistake, an ill-chosen word or a thoughtless act," Nell continued. "Not you. You're mean on purpose. What you think is what you get!" Shock widened the matron's eyes, and she clutched the spot where her heart would have been, if she had one.

"You're a bad one," little Jenny said. She perceptively read her mother. "We hates you, me and Nell."

"Oh, oh," Stella said. "Please, not in front of the children." Red in the face, she stomped to her outfit with Bailey hanging like a sack of flour across her great hip.

"Toughening up?" Cutter asked Nell with a twinkle in his eye.

"Everybody makes mistakes," Nell told Ralph, who slumped on a log and clutched his greasy hair.

"But, shooting another man's horse is the worst," returned Ralph, "especially on the trail."

"'What's done cannot be undone.' Thank your lucky stars it wasn't one of us." Nell tried to convince Ralph that things would work out for him; unfortunately, for her it didn't. Now that Moses had no means of travel, he rode Ralph's horse or helped to drive his wagon, but, more often than not, he hitched a ride in the Ark behind which he tied his pack animal. Instead of taking the reins to reprieve Nell, he sprawled on a side panel, munched on her dried squash cakes, and mooned over Phoebe.

"Don't bother me your pa off and plugged my horse," Nell heard Moses tell her, "long as he buys me a strong, broke one, like he says."

Nell turned to watch his hand slip across Phoebe's upper leg.

"Oh, he will, if it takes everything we got," Phoebe answered.

"Ain't you a perdy little gal," he said. "You ticklish?"

"Don't," Phoebe squirmed.

"Moses!" Nell said louder than she intended. "Could you take the reins for a stretch?"

Back in the wagon, she quietly counseled Phoebe. "Don't let him touch you. Hear? He's not a boy, you know. I'm afraid he has ideas."

"No. It ain't like that with us."

"Then, how is it? Would you marry him, Phoebe?"

"He hankers for me, thinks I got a right smart head on my shoulders. Says I'm perdy, too."

"You are pretty, Phoebe. At fifteen, you're as beautiful as you'll ever be. Don't you think men are very aware of that? What it really comes down to is this: has he asked your parents if he might court you? What are his intentions? Has he asked you to be his wife?"

"Well, not right out." Phoebe hung her head. Then, her wide eyes brightened. "He says I smells like a peach."

"That's nice. But your fragrance doesn't give him the right to maul you like he does. Tell me you'll stay away from him. Tell me, now." She sat on Phoebe's level and held her hands. Little Jenny patted Phoebe's head. "It isn't wise to trust Moses," Nell whispered in her ear. "My own father warned me. I realize now what he knew immediately. Why, you could marry some young, handsome, gentle fellow, someone like yourself. That nasty thing is too old for you, and he knows it."

"He loves me, and I love him, Nell. I really do."

"My land! If he hasn't proposed marriage to you and your family, he won't stand by you. Oh, how can I explain? His love is "bestial,"" she heard her mother's voice in her words. "Life can be awfully harsh on a woman. You must grasp every opportunity to establish yourself in comfort. Understand? Listen. I saw him with his hand on your leg. Why did you give him that liberty?"

"'Cause, he loves me, I tell you. 'Sides, he'd be mad if I shoved his hand away," she sighed, her eyes sparkling with hope and innocence.

In frustration, Nell scratched her dusty hair. "I pray you will not begrudge me for what I am about to say. But, I think it's time you moved back with your parents. Try to understand. I can't have all this business on my shoulders. I have a conscience, after all. Your mother needs to know."

"Please, Nell, don't throw me out. Don't tell Ma," Phoebe pleaded. "Now I'm a growd woman, I hate being around her, doing all her chores and watching her box the twin's ears. What I dread most is that someday I'll be just like her."

"Say no more, Phoebe. You've got to go. I can't have Moses spreading himself over the one small space I own in the entire world. My responsibility is little Jenny, and I am obligated to stay safe for those who love me."

"If that's how you feel." Phoebe gathered her belongings, threw them into her blanket and slung them over her shoulder. "Stop the wagon," she called out to Moses.

Nell knew her words had crushed the girl and she despised herself for it, but she calculated that it would be for the best, in the long run. 'Foresee trouble and act to avoid it before it comes,' her father had counseled. Moses was the trouble she saw. She would not allow him near her child. She would not have him usurp her well-planned supply of goods, without invitation, and she did not want him in and out with his dirty feet. The wagon had become her home, not a place of rendezvous for a silly girl who threw her future to the wind. No. This venture was not about Phoebe. It was about building a new life for her family. It was about resting her head against Tom's chest, feeling the softness of his flannel shirt and hearing his heart beat under it. "Be strong," were Tom's last words to her. As if they were etched in gold, she planned to heed them.

17

HOME SICK

(Diary)   *May 11, 1949*

The way is long. Damned dust! Oh, to wear a clean dress, to have it stay clean the whole day. Miss eating at a table. Little Jenny—homesick.

Today, Nan bunted me after I milked her. When I dropped her rope, the wretched goat took off. Had the devil of a time catching her. It held us up, and that didn't set well with everybody else. Am handling my team. Satisfied with independence, thank you.

As Cutter and Moses led the remaining two wagons and eight people, along with their stock, which numbered ten, across Iowa, the hills became less steep, the farms poorer, and the way stations farther apart. But, Nell was amazed that even though they had traveled far from civilization, as she had known it, the roads remained in tolerable repair. She sighted many clear signs advertising the number of miles to the next landmark or settlement, most of them on painted boards, some nailed to trees, and others written on bleached animal skulls. The last read "45 mi – Garden Grove." Over streams were solid bridges; up steep grades, cleared passages; on rocky passes, boulders rolled aside, and always the wagon wheel ruts, indicated the way. It did not seem odd to Nell that the Mormon people maintained roadways for the sake of their stragglers and converts because ingrained in their nature was the drive to prepare for others and to improve, rather than destroy, everything they touched; this, she admired. Still, she entertained herself by imagining that Tom had done all of it himself, with great care, knowing she and Jennifer would cross the plains without him.

One evening at bedtime, Jennifer, overwrought from travel, refused to be comforted. "I want Ruby," she fussed. "Where's Christina?"

"I can't get them," Nell told her.

"I want my blanky," she sobbed.

Nell had hidden it with the hope that her child would give up sucking her thumb, and save herself from one day being called "horse face" or from ending up a miserable old maid. But, now her heart went out to the homesick three-year-old, who had recently lost everyone and everything familiar to her. Why also take her beloved blanket? When Nell opened the case where she had stored it, the unexpected cleanliness of scented lye soap, the fragrance of springtime, and the comfort of their Quincy home poured into her nostrils. The contrast between freshness and dirt, civilization and wilderness, the familiar and the unknown, overwhelmed her emotions and spilled down her face in a river of uncontrollable tears. She did not sob or cry out, for Little Jenny's sake. However, it seemed as if she were on a bridge, suspended between what was and what would be, with love and loss on either side, whether she went forward or backward. It was the loneliest feeling in the entire world. Under the covers all night long, Little Jennifer shared the comfort of her silk-edged "blanky" with Nell.

18

ILL-FATED JOURNEY

*Ralph Suffix and family have dropped out. That leaves the guides and me,
come what may.*

The Suffix family was a ruin, a disaster and a wreck by the time
the party reached Garden Grove, midway across Iowa and about 250
miles from Quincy. They had suffered every possible misfortune,
and nearly every prediction Stella conjured up had materialized, as
if saying a thing made it real. Most of their savings, $100, had been
spent on a saddle horse for Moses, but that amount had not been
nearly enough. Rare and precious, indeed, were horses at this remote
way station, but Ralph, luckily, found a farmer who owned a grain-
fed broomtail. "I wasn't born yesterday," he grumbled over parting
with it until Moses added to Ralph's savings a $20 gold piece and
Nell chipped in a silver serving spoon, which very much pleased his
wife's envious eye. Their wagon stood a shambles on the spot where
its wheel had finally broken away for the second time, and their son
lay in it near death from a combination of the whooping cough and
the black scurvy.

As if this had not been enough, Nell had reason to believe that
Moses had undone Phoebe. She heard her weeping alone one night.
After that, the girl sat listlessly by herself, holding her abdomen, and
if Moses chanced to pass, neither looked at the other, his interest lost
with her innocence.

Ralph, split in body and spirit, like his wagon's axletree, told Nell of an opportunity in Garden Grove to build and repair outfits for people like him who had also met with catastrophe. He had the idea to model some after Nell's, "tough little badgers with thick wheels."

"We can't go on," Ralph told Nell. "I know this puts you in an awkward position, a woman and child alone with two men. Why don't you turn around with us? Your husband ought to take you across with the Mormons. That way, you'd make it, sure. There are other considerations. Indians, for one. They're likely to harass a small group."

Indians. Oh, she did not have to be reminded of them! In the middle of many a night, they were merely one ingredient in the brew she boiled for herself. After visualizing them, she threw in equal parts of wolves, bears, snakes and buffalo along with a pinch of the new wives Tom had taken. She garnished the paralyzing potion with a dash of "what if he decides to travel to Nauvoo early and we pass one another without knowing" and a pinch of "what if Jennifer contracts the whooping cough." This toxic dish, digested too often, guaranteed the death of her dream. Nell decided that whenever negative thoughts came to mind, she would concentrate, instead, on her home in the Rockies. Stella had taught her something.

She assured Ralph that she would seriously consider his counsel. She did. All day and all night, she considered it. She assembled the facts. She punched them, rolled them and let them rise. She shaped and reshaped them. Finally, with her bread baked, she summoned Ralph.

"I can't turn back," she told him. My husband's love for me was based on a lie. My lie. It's too complicated to explain, especially with Jennifer involved. But, it wouldn't be right for him to risk his life for me, only to discover I am false. No. I must go to him, now that we've come this far. There will be problems ahead," she admitted, out of experience. "But, I must believe that all will go well for us."

"I do believe it will. The boys want to carry you to your folks all right," Ralph looked to the bright side.

Deep down, she pitied the Suffix family, but she was also relieved to be rid of them and all their tribulations. With them along, snow would cover the Rockies before she joined Tom. Without them, she, Moses and Cutter could travel at least twenty-five miles everyday on the open plains. Having invested in a fresh horse for Moses, she was not about to join with another cumbersome group. On the other hand, being with women and children had been a comfort, and they had given her a sense of security as well as a little excitement during end-less hours of bumping along and eating dust.

"I'll make it, Ralph. Don't you fret over me. You have enough troubles. Do you think, after you work awhile, you'll go on?"

"No. All I've done is lose my savings and distress my family. My boy is near death. I've wasted three weeks and have taken us far from home with no way of getting back." He held his swollen jaw. "It pains me to talk. The blacksmith says two are rotten. He'll pull them later today."

"You'll feel better, then. Maybe, next year you'll think of trying again."

"No. I should have known from the beginning it was only a dream." He gazed off at the open prairie.

"If we can't have a dream, what else is there, Ralph?" For the first time, Nell realized that Ralph was *Ralph*, not *Stella's poor husband*. She had wiped her feet on his face until everyone else treated him like an old rug. But, he was a mild-mannered, sensitive man, the type cruel women are drawn to and love to abuse. Nell wished she had understood him before now. But, she also wished he would wash his oily hair and look to his grooming because a strong odor hung about him. Some men!

Her empathy for Ralph caused her to wonder if Arthur had suf-fered a similar grief under her hands when she left him to marry Tom. On the hard wagon seat, one had too much time to think, and Nell decided she had better sing or babble with Jenny, instead. What good could come from moving westward and thinking eastward?

"Don't say you're a failure, Ralph. It hurts me. You didn't know, that's all. You're a reliable man. I'll wager you all the gold in the California Territory that if you tried again, you'd make it, knowing what you know now. You'd be better prepared, for one thing."

"That's sure."

"Your only fault was that you believed all those glorious reports that the road stretched across the country like one great highway," Nell laughed. "Don't tell anyone, but I did too."

"And, I believed Stella when she said we wouldn't make it. She never wanted us to."

"I know," Nell said shaking his hand goodbye. "You'll work that out, won't you?"

"Not today, Nell. We have to lick our wounds first."

"Tell Phoebe I'm sorry."

"About what?"

"Nothing, really. Just say I'm sorry."

19

CAMPFIRE

(Diary) May 20, 1849

We have left civilization behind. On the open plains, one feels like a baby bird that has fallen from its nest. Last night after sundown, we settled in around a campfire and briefly believed we owned a small circle on the infinite, star-capped land.

Prairie chickens, hawks, rabbits, gophers and meadowlarks show up once in awhile. Jennifer delights in chasing after Painted Lady butterflies.

Today, she called me Mama. Faring well.

"Sure is flat here," Cutter mused. "After we cross the Missouri, though, you'll learn what *flat* really is." He relaxed with the little group around a low-burning campfire after a grueling day of travel and making camp. "Now, we're on our own, pretty much."

Nell turned from the flame to distinguish nothing except darkness all around, nothing except the distant, impersonal heavens above. "All this flat down here and all that space up there sort of scares me, especially when there's no moon." Snuggling Little Jenny next to her, she covered the child's chubby, pink toes against the chill of night.

"I understand that. It's what *isn't* that terrifies most people," Cutter remarked, and he, too, pointed at the cold specks of the night sky. "But, look at what is. "With so many stars, I barely see Orion. Ah, hah, there it is, southwest." He helped Nell find the great hunter with his two dogs following behind while he did battle with the ferocious Taurus.

"Gut him, Orion. Gut Taurus," Moses mocked the indifferent still-ness.

Cutter, as was his habit, ignored the insolent fellow. "Orion's the easiest constellation to locate," he told Nell. "And, when you do, you feel kind of easy and comfortable, like those times when you've trav-eled for a long time and you finally return to your home. First, look for those three stars in a row. That's Orion's belt. Look carefully, now, and you'll find the dagger hanging from it. See? The other four promi-nent stars form his torso. By the time we drop you off to your Tom, it will have moved even farther west." In the darkness, Cutter revealed a new side to his character. The night sky, the campfire, and the quiet of the open prairie encouraged thoughts that people seldom entertained during the bustling daylight hours.

"Why?"

"Because the earth goes around the sun every year, but the constel-lations stay fixed, I guess. It appears to us that they are moving across the abyss, but you can't always trust your eyes. It's hard to figure. Earth is what moves. The rest of it might move too. I don't know. But, I do know that the North Star is always in the north. It never changes, and that's the beauty of it. It has guided sea-goers, trappers, adven-turers, every sort of traveler since the beginning of time. You would do well to become familiar with it because, then, you'll always know where you are."

"Why doesn't it move?"

"Who knows?" Moses said. "It don't, that's all. Haven't we got enough to do without talkin' nonsense?" Suddenly, he rustled off into the darkness to relieve himself.

"It has to do with the earth's pole," Cutter tried to explain. "Pay attention, now. To find it, you first locate the Big Dipper. The two stars in the lip, point directly to the North Star. See? Every night, I want you to find it before you sleep."

"What are all those stars for, anyway?"

"When you cipher that out, you tell me." For the first time in their entire adventure, Cutter had begun and sustained a conversation. Perhaps, he sensed her uneasiness. Perhaps, not. Perhaps, he felt more comfortable the deeper into the wilderness he trekked. One didn't know about Cutter, but her fear of him had subsided, over time and space, even though it troubled her that he held no illusions about life, no romantic dreams, and little empathy. Sometimes, words flew, bare and shocking, out of his mouth, like half-plucked chickens.

"No more towns?" Nell asked.

"Nope. Nothing to speak of, not until old Council Bluffs. I heard of a place called Fort Childs on the prairie, in Pawnee country, but I wouldn't count on it being much. If your pocket's full of gold pieces, you might pick up supplies or grub at Laramie, maybe Bridger, a couple of months off, or so. But, what they have won't be what you want." Cutter stirred the fire with a long stick. "Garden Grove was our jumping off place."

"Jumping off place? What's that?"

Moses sprinted into the circle of the fire's light and shuddered. "Blacker'n hell out there." The whites of his eyes and his large, well-formed teeth shone whiter than the sun-bleached bones that lay scattered around the camp.

"Why do I feel that the side of me turned away from the fire isn't safe?" Nell asked.

"Because it isn't," Cutter said. When he threw a rotting log onto the fire, it sizzled and devoured frantic and unwary critters that had not left with others when their lodge was first disturbed.

Moses tossed a strip of jerky into Nell's lap. When she jumped, he laughed. "Chaw on that a little. Helps pass off the time."

"I'm sick of it." Nell tossed it back.

"What folks mean by *jumping off*," Cutter picked up where they left off, "has a lot to do with the final decision to go west."

"It's just about as much trouble to turn back as it is to keep going," Moses said, the fire dancing in his red hair.

"Oh, I understand," Nell said. "Change is hard."

"I'll go along with that," Cutter said. "If you think about it, though, change is all there is. Out here, everything changes, except for that one star. I don't mean just the scenery, either. People change. They have to in order to survive. You might think of it as jumping off the shore into the ocean. Those are two different worlds—you walk in one, swim in the other."

"And what if you don't learn how to swim, Mr. Cutter?"

"You die, Mrs. Mortenson. Most important trait of a survivor is to make a move. I learned that the hard way." The mutilated side of his face twitched. "On the plains, you've got to feel what's happening when you don't see it; you've got to listen with a third ear for those sounds you can't regularly hear. Then, and most importantly, you've got to pay attention to your gut. Most people don't. That's why the poor, dumb critters bite the dust." Then, aware that his last statement struck a cord of fear in Nell's heart, he added, "No need to worry. You've toughened up. Why, not anybody can drive a span of mules through mud like you do!" He shook his head and smiled. "You're a natural born swimmer. No question about that!"

"Right off, a perdy gal like you is bound to want people," Moses belched. "Too much jerky." Again, he belched. "East of the jumping off place, the country's crawling with folks, like ants headed in all directions. They're bound to show up if you busts your axle or the measles gets you down. But, farther west, it's just us and the bed bugs we hauls from home."

"A week, maybe ten days off, is Council Bluffs," Cutter said. "Not much there, anymore, now most of those Mormons left. But, I'll wager that enough of them stayed behind to ferry us across the Missouri, for a hefty price, money-grubbers, begging your pardon, Mrs. Mortenson. Until the Rockies, it's a long row to hoe. Ah, well. Out here, you want to keep your distance from people, anyway."

"What for?" Nell asked. "I like people." Jenny had fallen into a peaceful, trusting rest.

"First off," Moses said, "if you's behind anybody, you's going to be swallowin' their dust. Your animals won't get nothing after theirs feeds the trails off. Their troubles rubs off on you."

"Like the Suffix family."

"You're learning," Cutter said.

"They slowed us up," Moses interjected, smacking on his jerky. "The three of us, we wants to git there." He wrung his hands like he habitually did before diving into his supper. "Gold, gold ever'where."

Nell shivered, more from the thought of being alone than from the chill of night. When she pitched several branches onto the campfire, flames leaped up to consume them. "But, what if we need the help?"

"That's different!" Moses chuckled at his own wit. When a spark from the fire smoldered on his trousers, he yelped like a wolf into the dark black night.

"Hush your mouth. The baby needs her rest," Nell scowled.

"Hush," grumbled Cutter. He went on. "We'll deal with our own scrapes. Basically, you're alone whether you're with people or not. Once you come to that, Mrs. Mortenson, you'll be a man."

"I'm a woman, Mr. Cutter. I'm not a loner."

"To be one, you must be the other," he said. "We each survive on our own, inside and out."

"That may be true for you," Nell returned. "I need people. My land! There's no pleasure in dining alone, no use preening without somebody about to admire the effort."

"You preen, gal, and I'll admire you long as you wants," Moses grinned, his eyes downcast, as if he couldn't endure to truly understand anyone, or to truly be understood.

Disgusted, Cutter shook his head, pulled his hat low over his face, and reclined using his saddle for a pillow. For security, he primed his Kentucky rifle of the muzzleloading style. After a time, Moses, holding his backside, again scampered off beyond the fire's glow. Nell worried that he might be coming down with the ague and remembered that it could lead to an agonizing death; she wanted no part in caring for him. "Dad blamed jerky," he remarked upon returning. It's givin' me the scours."

Well, I don't want to hear about it," Nell's nostrils flared. "It's time for me to turn in, anyway." After standing and lifting Jennifer, she pointed at Cutter. "Look at him, Moses. He sleeps all day in his saddle, he sleeps around the fire, he sleeps in his tent. I know nobody's on guard because both of you snore like the dying all night. How is he to protect us from Indians?"

"Blaa! Never you mind about that, gal. I seen him operate before. If Omahas or Pawnee comes within five miles of him, he knows it, asleep or not. Says he feels it on his neck when the hairs bristle up like a cat's. Don't you worry none. He might snore like he's sleepin', but he ain't."

"Dreamer," Nell yawned. "You're full of it. I'll use my own ears. Say, Moses, why don't you keep the fire for a spell." She carried Jennifer to their wagon. When Blondie poked her big head inside, Nell offered her a handful of oats.

20

CHIPS

(Diary)   *May 28, 1849*

Four days ago, we crossed the Missouri River on Mormon rafts. Fare for my outfit cost me $10, which seemed outrageous at first. But after the expe-rience, I realized that the risk to life, the expertise, the equipment, men and draft animals required were worth my gold pieces, and much more.

Recognized one of the rafters from my Nauvoo days, and upon hearing Tom was my husband, he kindly offered to deliver me across at no expense. Then, when it dawned on him that I made my journey with Moses and Cutter, he appeared anxious. After engaging in a long discussion with other fellows, he urgently advised me to hook up with a larger and "more honor-able" Mormon party, but they didn't know when one would reach the river. Declined. I know my guides' ways as they know mine. Like a matched team, we become more efficient and cooperative the farther we travel.

However, because we have pushed ourselves too far, too fast, we must pause or face dire consequences.

After crossing the Missouri River, Cutter, Moses, and Nell agreed to move westward a minimum of twenty miles a day. Considering the level passageway, the mild weather, and the overall health of the animals, this seemed entirely possible. The routine blended one day into another: up at sunrise, dress, make a meal of leftovers from the previous evening's meal, water and hitch the mules, and drive, drive, refresh the animals and themselves at noonday, then drive more and, finally stop for the night, unhitch, water and stake out the stock, milk Nan, fry and boil, care for Little Jenny, prepare for bed.

The two men, thirsty for gold, set a pace, which quickly deteriorated Blondie, The Spare, and even tough old Samson, causing them to plod along in the afternoon hours, their heads inches off the ground, in spite of the oats Nell fed them each night. Samson's coat lost its luster, and Blondie brayed half-heartedly, or not at all. Though this caused Nell much consternation, she neglected the warning signs to avoid an argument.

The world of verdant hills and streams that Nell had known all her life faded into a strange, vast land where she became keenly aware of what wasn't, rather than what was. It seemed that a gargantuan being, perhaps the mother of Colossus, had swept away trees, boiled off streams, butchered wildlife and frightened away the people. In order to cook at night, Nell halted throughout the day to gather every stick in sight. Lone elms and cottonwoods, which, in the distance, raised her expectations for a roaring campfire, a fresh spring, and some cooling shade, had been stripped up to fifteen feet by travelers who had gone before. Not a branch remained beneath them. Farther out on the prairie, trees disappeared altogether. The landscape was all sky and blowing grass, which endlessly bent and shimmered over the rolling land like an infinite green sea.

Then, even the emerald grasses vanished, having been replaced by stubble and black piles of manure. Blondie, Samson and The Spare grew cranky and listless, and the dust from Moses and Cutter's animals continually blew into Nell's face. One afternoon, the men decided to make camp early. On this day, even *they* complained of being tired and hungry for meat. "While we hunts, you gather chips and start a fire," Moses told Nell when they headed out with their powder rifles.

"Are you saying I should gather *manure?*"

"Yah, *shit!* Ever'where," Moses picked up a dried chunk to illustrate, and, after dropping it, he wiped his hand on his newly grown beard. "Get over it. Whether you calls it *manure, droppings,* or *chips,* it's all *shit.* Your wagon wheels have been slip-sliding through *shit* all day long. Buffalo grazed all the grass off and left us *this* to burn."

"It's harmless," Cutter said. "One woman I knew called it *prairie coal.* Smolders, once it catches. Makes a good bake fire."

"Just don't go for the green ones," Moses grinned at Nell's ankles, not her face.

As far as the eye could see, *it* spotted the ground, and Nell wondered why they had not sighted a single buffalo. Thinking of fresh meat, which "tasted like beef," her mouth watered. "Please, don't toy with me. I can't believe you'd expect me to cook with *this*," she said. "Even if I could, you're not going to catch me gathering it."

"Well, then, little gal, what you goin' to burn?" Moses asked.

"Why don't you search for wood while you're hunting?"

"Cause there ain't none, there's why."

"Then, you pick up the *shit*. That's not a job for women," Nell argued. "I hired you on to do that sort of thing, and Father paid you extra. I saw him."

"I do go fer a spunky gal," Moses glowed. "Put on the beans, Sugar. Papa'll be back with the meat." Moses' eyes roamed over her body in the same way they did over Phoebe's, and she shivered. Days of endless travel had eroded away his thin social veneer.

"Do your part." Cutter mounted his blue mare like he always did, on the right side. She was a beautiful, spirited animal but one you wouldn't go near if you weren't her owner.

On his way to mount The Broomtail, Moses passed Blondie, and she took a nip out of his ear. After he slugged her on the nose, she whirled to kick him, and would have, if he hadn't bolted out of the way. The ear bled profusely. "For a wooden nickel, I'd kill that jackass," he yelped.

"Oh, go on and hunt," Nell laughed. "I'll get a fire going by myself, if it kills me. I'll boil beans because I know for a fact, there'll be no meat." It angered her that the men had begun to think she should do their cooking, like some slave, and use the grub from her own store as well. "Chips," she said to herself when the boys road away. Then, she located her shawl, and holding its four corners, made a sort of carrier.

Again, Nell longed for Ruby and Mama. This sort of work rubbed against her grain. At any rate, she spread the shawl on the ground next to a dung pile and catapulted it onto the cloth with her walking stick. When little dung beetles scampered in every direction, she gasped and backed away. "Oh, no," little Jennifer hid her gleeful eyes behind her hands. When she asked, "What hell you doin', Mama?" They both giggled. At the tender age of three, she understood that animal feces were not to be handled. Finally, Nell learned to choose the excessively dry ones, full of beetle holes, but no beetles, and she simply picked them up with her hands and threw them into the shawl. "No, no, Nell,"

Jennifer scolded at first, but after watching her mother, she did the same.

Bound to be an everyday occurrence, this gathering of fuel must be accepted. Nell decided to call it *chips* like most other people of good taste. That would leech out some of its repulsiveness. People were terribly cruel, she thought, for not warning her ahead, but, when her crossing had ended, she planned never to mention it.

The hunters returned empty-handed to a tin of cornmeal spread with molasses and a spider pot full of simmering beans, flavored with salt and an onion. "Right good," Cutter remarked, but Moses chatted continually of buffalo boil. Nell, who felt the jolt of the wagon in her bones even though she stood on the firm earth, thought of nothing but bathing in clear water, of combing her "poor urchin's" tangled hair, of taking a midday nap and of changing into a clean dress. Her mouth gushed with juices in anticipation of a square meal; however, since she had not sighted one buffalo, she began to think of them as mystical beasts which people were not meant to know, first hand. In contrast, Jennifer fared well. Her eyes glowed afresh each morning, and the discrepancy between her soiled face and clothing and her natural happiness and beauty made her an object of inspiration. She had been able to nap anytime, anywhere, in any position, regardless of the gnats that bit her tender arms and face. To prevent that, Nell covered her with what remained of the bottom ruffle of her petticoat. At Fort Bridger, she planned to purchase material for replacing it.

In the morning, when Moses appeared to help Nell hitch up for another day of monotonous travel, he only looked at her and she began to cry. "What's wrong?" he asked.

"Nothing's wrong," she sneezed. "Dust in my eyes, that's all."

"Ah, you needs a little love. Well, git over here. You can lean on Old Moses' shoulder."

"No. Leave me alone. You stink." She backed out of the range of his odor. He still had the *scours*, and even after he thrashed his clothing over the scrubbing board in the Platte, he smelled like rotten eggs. "It's my squeaky wheel, that's all. My grease bucket must have fallen out of the wagon, somewhere. I'm worried. That cursed squeaking has got to stop!" She remembered Tom's words. "When people forget to grease their wheels, they're in for a heap of trouble." She remembered his showing her the indentation his ironsmith pounded in the metal around the hub for a squirt of tallow. With this innovation, the Ark's wheels did not need to be removed for greasing like other wagon wheels, and this saved Nell a great deal of trouble. Now, she felt like the worst kind of fool for losing the tallow bucket.

"Soon as I kills me a buffalo, I'll help render out fat for it," Moses offered.

"Buffalo, buffalo, that's all you talk about. What makes you think we'll even see one? Shoot anything. Birds, rabbits, badgers, anything. We need meat! You said you came across a badger. Why didn't you kill it? You got your gold. Now, carry through with your end of the bargain." She chucked the squash cake that she had planned for breakfast and stomped on it.

"I never said a damned thing about food," Moses shouted. He retrieved the cake, picked debris from it, and pitched it into his mouth.

"Need meat," Jennifer yelled. Blondie, hearing the commotion, pawed the ground, and Nan butted her cage.

"Here," Moses said, pulling a strip of jerky from his shirt pocket. "Have all you want."

"It stinks!" Nell sneezed and wiped a bead of dust from the corner of her eye. "Your pocket's filthy!" A horse fly bit into the tender skin just below her ear. When she viciously slapped it, its gorged stomach popped on her hand. "Disgusting flies!" she wailed.

Cutter rushed in upon the scene and asked, "What did you do to her?"

"Nothin'. I didn't do nothin'. She wants meat, that's all. What you growlin' at me fer?" His eyes shifted to the ground.

Cutter suspiciously leered at Moses. "What's going on?" he asked Nell. "If he hurt you, I'll kill . . . "

"Kill what?" Nell shouted into his face. "Why don't you take some of that orneriness of yours and go kill us a gopher? If these are buffalo chips, where are the buffalo?"

"You tell me," Moses grinned, his clean shirt mocking his stench.

For a time, Cutter stood in thought. Finally, he replied, "We've got to turn south, leave the Platte, temporarily. Here and now, there's too much competition for feed. If I remember right, and I'm quite certain I do, there's a pleasing ravine about five miles south of here." He ran his fingers through his greasy, long hair. "I'm about due for a soak."

"You? Look at me!" Nell exclaimed, louder than she meant to. "If we were to meet anyone, I'd have to hide. Yesterday, I rinsed my hair in the Platte, and I haven't stopped sneezing since." Again, tears filled her eyes. If her family could see her now! Oh, how she hated the muddy river, which meandered and split and twisted so often that trekking beside it necessitated extra travel and wasted valuable time. One old gal in a company they had passed on the trail a few days back had told Nell, "That river is three miles wide and six inches deep, too muddy to drink, too thin to plow, too yellow to wash in and too thin to paint with." At first, Nell had laughed at the description, but now she saw no humor in it. Even though she let the water settle in a bucket overnight, poured off the top in the morning and boiled it with potatoes for a half hour, like Stella recommended, Jennifer asked, "Can I have a drink?" after she swallowed some.

"Fill all the water barrels," Cutter scratched his neck. "Sometimes, it pays to quit chopping *before* you ax your foot." When he slapped Moses on the shoulder, the younger man jumped like a jackrabbit. "It's time we rested. Our animals are about done. He ran his hand over the black scalp hanging from his belt. "If Pawnee aren't camped there, I think you'll be pleasantly surprised, Mrs. Mortenson."

"Nothing surprises me anymore," Nell sneezed. "Why does everything have to be so hard?"

21

NO REST

(Diary)   May 31, 1849

Compared to mine, the life of a squash is paradise. I hate insects! A revitalizing pause has caused an event I am ashamed to relate, for my own reasons. Is there no rest? Among us is an evil, lecherous villain.

Rolling southward, Nell was pleasantly surprised. Grass gradually became tall and thick. Because the animals persistently strained at their bits to reach a nibble, she suggested that they pause before midday to water and graze them. Cutter liked the idea, so they pulled onto a stand of rich grass, unhitched The Spare and Samson, and tied all the animals around the wagon, for a quick refresher.

After spreading a quilt on the ground, Nell unpinned her hair, kicked off her shoes, and unfastened two buttons at her neck. Exhausted, she fell upon the quilt and drew Jennifer beside her. They gazed at the sky, which spread above them like a finely woven fabric with a blue *so* blue that no fiber matched it. Watching clouds drift across relaxed Nell, and she soon nodded off, in spite of the annoying gnats that circled over her and sometimes nipped her face and neck.

She awoke to Jenny's cries. "Face hurts," she said, covering her hands over her cheeks, where bumps blazed red. A whirlwind of insects buzzed over the child's head, and when Nell waved them off, they churned over her head as well. The air and the earth were noisy and alive with them, hopping, stinging, nipping, rasping, and clouding the vision. Gnats buzzed at Nell's ears, driving to fly inside. While a

plague of horse flies swarmed over Blondie and Samson, they stood
beside one another, head to rear, clever animals, swatting the irritated
eyes of the other with their tails. Without warning, Moses broke into
a nervous fit, cussing, scrambling about, and beating himself. After
a time, he dived under his tarp. If something had not engorged itself
on Nell's arm, she might have laughed—if a spider web had not
broken across her face or if a bronze-colored darning needle had not
circled her head. At another time, she might have been overcome with
laughter, but now the heebie-jeebies made her skin crawl.

Quickly, the group hitched up the teams and moved southward,
farther from the Platte. Creepy, crawly creatures for which Nell had
no name, critters large and small, florescent and gray, jumping and
flying, continued to follow and to pester all flesh. While Cutter drove
her team, Nell quieted Jenny by wrapping her in a blanket and cooling
her lumpy face with a damp cloth.

Gradually over the hours, the insects dissipated. Finally, in the
late afternoon, the harassed company reached the lush ravine about
which Cutter had spoken . . . "shaded with giant cottonwoods, tangled
elms, and thick patches of river birch." At its bottom, a precious pond
lay tucked away like a star sapphire set in a ring of buttercups, reeds
and cattails; a crystal spring, which fed into one end, trickled out
the other. Having smelled it long before the humans saw it, the jaded
animals quickened their pace toward it, in spite of their poor, pestered
condition. But, for some reason, Cutter's Blue acted up and balked at
the descent.

"We'll camp down there," Cutter pointed the way to the bottom.
"Keep a top eye open for Indians, though." Several times, he rubbed
the back of his neck as if a tick were drilling into it.

"Are we in danger?" Nell remembered what Moses told her about
Indians and the hairs on Cutter's neck. "Sometimes, I feel afraid," she
ran her nails through her itchy head.

"There's nothing wrong with being afraid," Cutter answered. "It's
being *unafraid* that I worry about. Can you shoot, Mrs. Mortenson?"

Before answering, Nell searched the undergrowth, all around, for
movement. Nothing. "I can load and pull the trigger, Mr. Cutter, but
I've never hit anything."

"Supposed not. Proper equalizer, a gun. A dagger won't do much for
a woman." He nodded at the leg where, she had believed, no one knew
she had hidden a knife in her garter. "If a man gets a hold on you . . ."

"Maybe you'll help me target practice."

"Maybe." When he freed Blondie of her gear, she shook off a dark cloud of dust and brayed, long and hard. "Shut up!" Cutter poked her with a stick. Before anyone could control Samson, he bolted into the fresh pond, immediately clouding it. The other animals would have followed if Cutter, Moses and Nell had not restrained them and led them to the outlet, where they drank until their bellies bulged. When released, Nan yanked on her rope, bunted Nell, and sprinted into the pond next to Samson.

"Dumb animals," Nell laughed at herself on the ground. Moses roared and dived into the pond along with them without regard to his clothing. Cutter buried his head at the water's edge.

"My kingdom for a bath," Nell shouted. "Come along, Jenny. We'll clean up."

"Let me tether the mules to the trees," Cutter suggested. "Moses and I will take a hike up the ridge and keep a lookout, if the two of you want to get in and bathe. We won't come back 'til you yell."

"Well then, if you're going to be so accommodating, I'll loan you a cake of my lavender soap." She flung it like a man, hard and directly into his hands, and dropped her hat and jacket onto the bank. As if he had a right, Moses gawked at her, up and down, pausing at her neckline where she had unfastened the buttons. As usual, he smiled shyly. His eyes avoided hers.

"Come away," Cutter plucked him by the shirt.

When the men vanished up the ravine, Nell and her child relished a most refreshing soak. For the second time since leaving home, they shed all their clothing. Though the pond's cold water sent shivers up Nell's back and prompted Jennifer to scream in delight, hot gusts of air and the bright sun quickly warmed them. Nell's feet sank into the slippery, slimy ooze on the bottom while water skimmers tread in circles around her and mosquito larvae performed their acrobatics everywhere, but she set her mind to ignore what might have caused her to panic only a few hours ago. Instead, she reveled in what was—twirling in circles with Jennifer and splashing joyfully in the reflective pool. With lye soap, she washed their hair, cleaned their nails, and scrubbed the back of their necks until the frigid water stole away their breath.

She set Jennifer upon the bank and nearly climbed out. But, something that would have glowed red, if she had really seen it, disturbed the willows. Nature missed a breath. A cricket paused its rasping song, and a dragonfly's wings skipped a beat. With the heightened senses and suspicious nature of a mother with young, Nell scrutinized the area. Nothing seemed out of the ordinary except a shiver shooting up her spine. "Silly me," her intellect debated with her instinct. "It's my foolish imagination." Still, she climbed out and quickly dressed. "Yip, yip," she called out for the men.

For two lovely days, the little group paused in the ravine to restore themselves and their belongings. Comparing the size of their bug bites, they soothed their itching skin with honey or mud. When Jennifer napped, the first thing Nell did was wash the silk-edged blanket because of its absolutely shameful condition. She scrubbed it until it was white again, except for an area at the corner where the child rubbed it across her nose while sucking her thumb. Next, Nell unloaded and reloaded the wagon. She scrubbed or aired all bedding and clothing, she brushed Jennifer's hair and her own a hundred strokes, she napped and even found time to read a few passages from Hamlet. "That one may smile, and smile, and be a villain" gave her pause.

Nell took special interest in her animals, not because she loved or trusted them, but because she depended upon them for her very life, and she valued Nan as much as anyone ever valued an aloof old goat, for the milk kept Jennifer healthy and provided many a delicious dish for the rest of them as well. How thoughtful of Ruby! Everyday, Nell felt beholding to her for the convenient little cage, with a drop door, which made climbing in and out easy for Nan. To milk her, Nell had merely to reach through the bars. Because the spotted goat always liked staying near Nell or Jennifer and came to them at call, it wasn't necessary to stake her out, but Nell did anyway, as a precaution. Each time the three mules fed off the grass around them, she led them to water and retied them to another tree. She untangled and cut burrs from their mains and tails, and dusted their coats with a curry brush.

Nell cooked. Not because she loved doing it, but because she loved to eat, she prepared meals that she only dreamed of preparing during the days of unrelenting travel. Having avoided the scours since exclusively drinking potato water, she urged Moses and Cutter to do the same. Moses, who balked at the idea but complied, had to admit he felt better after only one day. In a jar, she shook Nan's rich cream to make butter, which everyone devoured on newly-baked cornbread. Over cooked rice, cinnamon, sugar, black walnuts and dried grapes, she poured the milk, and she served it with ginger tea for Cutter's favorite meal.

The men also took time to rest and catch up on their chores. They bathed, shaved, and scrubbed their clothing. They relaxed and played poker. Like her, they refreshed and manicured their horses and donkeys. Jennifer loved helping them catch, smoke and eat small fish from the stream. Cutter, kind man, inspected and repaired the Ark. He riveted rawhide tugs that had grown thin, tightened iron bolts in the singletrees, and soaked the wheels in water to expand the fellows and create a tight fit against their iron shield. When Nell located her linseed oil and turpentine, she remembered that Tom swabbed the wheels with it to seal and lubricate them. "I admire your Tom," Cutter said, when he helped her paint it on. "He knows his wagons." With wax he stole from a wild beehive, Moses greased the hubs. He received several stings for his effort, but Nell drew out the poison with mud and soothed the bumps with ointment.

All is right, Nell thought. The wagon is repaired, cleaned and in order, every animal and person is fed and rested, and my little apple trees are watered and reviving in the shade.

Under her cleaned Lindsey-Woolsey blanket, she should have slept as contentedly as Jennifer, for the little dale, with its cool foliage and pleasant sounds, might have cradled and comforted her . . . if it had not been for the sense of something out there. In her night thoughts, she decided to ask Cutter if they might camp above on the prairie. But in the light of day, her uneasiness seemed foolish.

In the later afternoon of the second day, The Blue became restless. When she pawed the ground and tossed her head, Cutter began running his hand over the scarred side of his face. Every now and again, The Blue jumped at a sound that no one else heard, stared into the trees for a movement no one else saw, and sniffed into the wind for a scent that no one else smelled. Like a loyal dog, Cutter's Kentucky rifle stayed ready at his side.

"What is it?" Nell asked when he sighted down the long barrel.

"Nothing," he softly answered.

"Blue sure is nervous. How'd she come by that scar on her rear?"

"Tomahawk," Cutter replied, "when I got mine." He turned the scarred side of his face away from Nell. "We should finish up here and move out of the ravine before nightfall. That way, if game shows up at dawn, an antelope, or something, I may be able to plug it.

"Do I have time to wash up?" Nell wanted to know.

"While we move our pack animals to the top, you do that. When you call, we'll come back and help you drive out."

After they left, Nell removed Jennifer's clothing and bathed her with a soft cloth. Then, she removed her own, one article at a time, and did the same for herself. Looking back to Quincy, she remembered the white tub that she had always taken for granted along with the warm water that Ruby poured into it while she daydreamed. Looking forward to the Great Basin, she wondered if Tom would have a tin tub, at least, by the time they arrived in the valley; for certain, Elizabeth would. That could well be her next bath. "Memories and hope," she told Jennifer, who squealed when tossing rocks into the pond. "But, we're here now, aren't we, and this water's clean.

While drying her hair, Nell heard something rustle in the nearby foliage. For an instant Moses' face peered through the undergrowth, and his red hair flashed an alerting signal in the setting sun. Then, he disappeared. Instinctively, Nell pulled her daughter to her breast. She watched limbs of the willows shake as violently as her legs. From the bushes came thuds and groans. Then, Cutter, holding Moses by the collar of his shirt, climbed away and up over the top of the ravine.

No one spoke for the remainder of the day. The men drove Nell's team back onto the open prairie, where they camped beside a little spring running with clean, cool water. All went about their chores while living inside themselves. Cutter's good eye burned upon Moses, hotter than his steaming coffee, and when he handed Nell a tin plate piled high with ash bread, small bits of sunfish and lumpy Dick gravy made from Nan's milk and flour, he offered none to Moses. Jennifer made a fine meal of it, but Nell picked at hers. Whenever she glanced at the peeper, she saw only his flaming red hair, his head being lowered. Anger swelled inside her so overwhelmingly that there was no space left to think, or even breathe. *Why me?* she wondered. *Is there no rest?* The lecherous villain smiled. He nursed a swollen, blue lip and a superficial, red slash across his throat, which called to mind the name of its maker.

22

BUFFALO

(Diary)   *June 1, 1849*

Buffalo! The earth is black with them. How strange are these out-of-proportion beasts, with enormous heads and chests, and small hindquarters. Their eyes are lovely. As long as I live, I shall never see such a sight. Moses and Cutter killed three.

I despise Moses. If I were a man, I would kill him.

Until midnight, Nell slept from exhaustion. At that time, her anxiety being great, she stared, wide-eyed at the stars and determined to fathom, to the bottom, the problem of Moses. Why did he betray her trust in him? What kind of man was he, anyway, to spy on a helpless woman and an innocent child? It made her feel dirty. Why didn't someone stop her from making the journey alone? What if Tom or Arthur or her father had caught him? If Arthur had come along, would he have killed for her honor? What if Moses had shot him? What if she had waited another year for Tom? What if? Finally, it all came down to one golden plate of folk wisdom, which Mama had spouted a million times. "You have made your bed. Now, you must lie in it." *What if* meant as much as a bag of wind. It was *now* and *here*, and nothing else.

"I can accept *now*," Nell decided on this night when problems seemed as far-fetched and as exaggerated as boogie monsters. "Keep away from Moses," she whispered. "Ignore him, and stay close to Cutter." She decided to grapple with—*protect Jennifer at all costs*—

when her body ruled in the light of day instead of—*what if*—when her mind ran rampant at night. Come hell or high water, she'd learn to shoot.

Finally, in the early morning hours, when the night dissolved into day, she slept deeply. It is no wonder, then, that she grumbled, "Can't a person rest" when a rocking motion of the wagon shattered her peace. Apparently, Moses, ignorant fellow, jumped up and down on the wagon tongue to awaken her. Outside, Nan blatted and butted her cage, and Blondie whistled frantically "whiny-hee-haw."

"Alright, alright," Nell snarled. The rocking, which brought to mind an earthquake, rattled her into full consciousness. Nell peered over the side of the wagon. A great rug of dark-brown, curly fur met her eyes. Buffalo! To shed its ragged, winter coat, the plains giant scraped and scratched on the rear corner of the wagon. "Go away, shoo." She tried to poke the hide beyond the canvas, but when her hand stretched within an inch of the huge beast, she retracted it. "Hey," she spoke softly, "hey, you." For a split second, a brief and marvelous moment, the dark pool of the buffalo's eye mirrored her white face, her long curls, and the pink bow at the neck of her white night gown. Just as quickly, it blinked away her image to reflect a fright, which far surpassed her own.

It sprinted off to join others. Multitudes of others! Oblivious to the travelers, they snorted, mated, clashed, and grazed in the business of their lives all around the camp. Blatting, their young frolicked and sprinted after one another. Hot-tempered males, enormous and muscular, battled for sexual supremacy. Like enormous boulders, they blackened the verdant land as far as her eyes could see, in all directions. Behind them, they had stripped the earth of her luscious, green garment. They had devoured her to the root.

"Jenny, Jenny," Nell gathered her child into her arms. "Wake up. Look. Look what's out there."

Jennifer trembled from being so suddenly awakened to the awesome sight. She pursed her lips, rubbed her eyes, and pointed. "Cow," she said.

"Buffalo," Nell whispered, and she shuddered.

"Don't scared, Mama," Jennifer patted the top of her mother's head and hugged it. To communicate in words this precious moment when her child first showed empathy would be as futile as trying to know the golden sunset by hearsay rather than experiencing it first hand, for there is a great chasm between words and experience. Nell fell in love.

Howling, grunting and barking drew Nell's attention to a cloud of dust in the distance. From its mother's whirling body, a buffalo calf dropped in its membrane onto the ground. Circling the mother and waiting for the birth, stalked a pack of six wolves. They moved in on the vulnerable pair, working like an efficient machine. While two lunged to torment the female, face on, others attacked her hindquarters and the newborn. The calf cried out, like a human infant, when they clamped their jaws upon it and tried to drag it away. The confused cow turned her massive horns upon those at her head, then whirled to defend her heels, and whirled again to guard the calf. She fought valiantly, furiously.

"Cutter! Come quickly," Nell screamed. She secured Jennifer's rope around her waist and climbed out of the wagon in her nightgown.

Moses emerged from their tent in his long handles. He spat, coughed and scratched his butt. "My God," he exclaimed. "Buffalo!"

"Over there," Nell cried, pointing at the nightmarish event. "Get your rifle. Quick. Help her."

"What's that?" he squinted and shaded his eyes from the glare of the morning sun. "Oh, that. That's nothin'. Say, you's about the perdiest little rosebud Moses ever seen." Snagging a lock of her hair, he twirled it around his finger in a tight hold. His eyes roamed over her gown.

"What are you looking at?" Nell scolded. "My eyes are up here." After the pond incident, she had decided that crude people must not be permitted to take advantage of a person with manners. With them, one must learn to be blunt, perhaps even more blunt than they. Shakespeare was a genius when he said, "'Tis meet that noble minds keep ever with their likes. For, who so strong that can not be seduced." Out of nowhere, Cutter appeared on his horse, and Moses let go. "Did you ever see so many! Let's go. We'll *never* have another chance like this."

"I'm ready. You're not." Cutter's piece glowed with grease, and his possibles bag hung from his belt alongside his skinning knife. "Don't try to bring one down with a head shot," he warned. "Bullets bounce off."

In the distance, the unrelenting carnivores rapidly drained the new mother. To protect the calf that had never had a chance to stand, she lowered her horns and snagged one. Its yelp rang out when she stomped it into the ground. Desperate, Nell pleaded with Cutter for help. She widened her eyes like Jennifer did when she begged to be untied and lifted out of the wagon.

"What's the matter now?" His long Bowie knife whispered across his whetstone.

"Can't you see what's happening? Look! Those wolves are killing the newborn."

"Oh, that. Wolves have to eat, same as we do. What if they have pups?" She would have slapped his face if she had not been afraid of hurting his scar. Nevertheless, she lifted her arm. "I wouldn't try," he said.

"Then, I'll have to help her," Nell said, without any intention to help.

"I wouldn't do that either. Let nature be, unless you want a real mess. I told you to toughen up, didn't I? Go to your own calf. And, get dressed!"

"I will."

"Don't forget to load," Cutter told Moses, who whistled and talked to himself while trying to saddle his old broomtail. "Hold it down, now, so you don't stampede the herd."

At the wagon, Jennifer's little fingers worked the knot where Nell had tied her. What a nightmare if she should learn to unfasten it! "Did they hurt you, Mama?" Jennifer asked when Nell blew her nose on her sleeve. Long ago, she had given up handkerchiefs.

"No, they didn't hurt me. It's the buffalo. Mama is sad for a buffalo."

"Buf-lo," Jennifer pointed.

"Hey, you dressed yourself!"

The right shoe pointed outward on her left foot, and her pinafore hung awkwardly backwards, but Nell could not destroy the glow of pride on her child's face by redressing her. "Your father will be happy now you're grown up," she tightly held Jennifer, and, over her little shoulder, watched the losing battle. "My rifle would have to be under everything," she said.

By the time Nell went through the motion of retrieving it from under the sack of salt and unloosened the spout of her powder flask, the buffalo had lost her battle. In resignation, she looked after the wolves that dragged away her limp calf. They snapped at one another and ripped apart their kill. Nell determined that after she helped Cutter cook and preserve some meat, she'd ask him to show her how to load and shoot. Oh, why hadn't she paid attention when her father had tried to teach her? Out here in the middle of nowhere, a person ought to know; a person ought to keep a ready weapon and be prepared to protect the young.

"Can I have crackers? Baby's hungry," Jennifer said. Nell kept her daughter's back to the hunt.

"Crackers with preserves. How's that? Let's pretend Ruby is cooking bacon and eggs with fried apples and cream."

"I want Ruby."

"I do too, but I have to be the mama, now." While Jennifer munched on a butter cracker and played in the dirt, Nell watched the men press headlong into the buffalo. Moses excitedly dodged through them. He took aim, but his firearm failed to report because, in the thrill of the moment, he had forgotten to load. While Moses spilled precious charges from his horn and dropped many a bullet from his pouch, Cutter edged up on a group like a stealthy field cat stalking mice. He separated from the rest a young, fat one, which instinctively trotted away from him and grazed again. Cutter followed. Both hands on his weapon, he directed his horse without touching the reins. When he leaned right, The Blue turned right, and when he bent forward, the horse accelerated. Like a shepherd with a well-trained English sheep dog, he worked the buffalo into the perfect position for a fatal shot to the heart. The game dropped like a sack of beans, and Cutter pounced upon it to run his long hunting knife across the throat.

That was finesse. For some odd reason, the maneuver seemed artful. It brought to mind memories of her own mother's hands when she crocheted long strips of lace trim. They worked the hook so swiftly, so skillfully, that every stitch was cast with the least expenditure of effort and motion. To watch a person do something very well was a pleasure.

Now that Moses had loaded, he went after his quarry like a girl who had never held a hook or knotted a thread. Nell wanted him to fail. Why kill another animal? His rifle flashed and reports rang sharply across the open land. To reload without dismounting, Moses accidentally dropped his reins. His awkward efforts to retrieve them gave Nell a hearty laugh. Rather than finishing his wounded buffalo, however, he galloped after a herd even closer to the camp. Roaring and cheering, he unwittingly turned their thundering hooves in the direction of Nell's wagon, and the shot he fired, curse him, tore a gushing hole in her $20 water barrel. He circled in front of her, smiled with pride, and when he threw his hat over his head, he yelled, "Waaa haaa!" What was he thinking? That she admired his reckless behavior?

Crazy with buffalo fever, he slid from his saddle, reloaded, mounted and spurred toward two grazing females with calves. His shot hit one. Obviously wounded, she meandered from side to side, her young following. His next shot blew off the tip of her nose. When he stopped to reload, the pair wandered away, but not far enough. Into her gut, he fired another volley. She collapsed. Her struggle to rise proved futile, and with her calf blatting over her, she choked on her own blood. Like the wolves, Moses killed ruthlessly, but, unlike them, he butchered for pleasure and left the cow in the claws of a slow death.

It was over for Moses, though. He galloped to the wounded bull, and fired into it at close range. Nell could not discern if his lead entered, for the bull showed no sign. Instead, it whirled and rammed into Moses' horse with such force that it toppled, and Moses tumbled head-over-heals like a doll Jennifer tossed when another interest occupied her thoughts. By the time he lifted his head, the bull stood not ten yards away, its immense head lowered, and its powerful hooves hurling dirt clods over its back.

If Cutter had not raced between them to divert the bull's attention, Nell did not know what would have become of the inexperienced fool. The bull stomped heavily away, but turmoil continued. Cutter sprang from The Blue and planted a smashing blow square into Moses' face. This straightened him out on the grass and rendered him useless for a time. Then, a violent argument ensued. It ended with Moses' mounting his limping broomtail to go finish the animals he had maimed. Cutter trotted back to their camp overlooking the ravine on a wet animal, which gnashed at the bit. His keen eye surveyed the landscape and then surveyed it again.

"Savages? Did you see any?" Nell asked.

"No. Don't concern yourself with it. This is Sioux country, but, chances are, we won't come across a single Indian. If we happen to, don't panic. Reports are they've been uncommonly friendly to whites," he said, his roving eye at odds with his words of assurance. His hand sought the companionship of his knife.

"Moses deserved the beating," Nell told him. "Anyone who kills senselessly ought to be beat."

"Myself, I don't mind a man having a little pleasure. He spat down the barrel of his muzzleloader and ran a patch through it with his rod. "Killing buffalo is the best sport there is."

"If that's how you feel, Mr. Cutter, why did you hit him?"

"I said *killing* is a sport, not *maiming*. A creature ought to be left whole, or dead."

"These are God's creatures, the same as you and me. They should be killed only for survival, and quite frankly, I supposed you felt as I do."

"And I'm surprised that you mentioned God, Mrs. Mortenson. Didn't know God was in your book. Is he?"

"I don't know," Nell confessed. It felt good to be able to tell the truth.

"Be practical, Mrs. Mortenson. Look around. They strip the land so we have nothing left for our animals. Useless. Besides, there's not a man alive can resist a good shoot."

"I suppose my husband resisted."

Cutter's face softened. "Some men are different." His attention turned to some object in the distance, which Nell could not locate. He finished loading his gun.

"Is there someone out there? What would happen if the Indians caught Moses killing that way? The buffalo is their brother; their very survival depends upon it, so they make good use of every part: the hide for robes, the intestines for sewing, the horns for tools . . . "

"Where'd you get all that? Sounds like a book. You won't learn much about real Indians in those books you're weighted down with. Bucks kill buffalo like any other man. I could show you places where they've run fifty or more over bluffs, and other places where their arrows have left more than a dozen to rot. They take the skins, maybe the tongues, and crack some of the bones for marrow. The rest, they leave."

"I don't believe that, but then I've been wrong before. Moses is not the man I thought he was, either. Unprincipled fool."

"Sorry," Cutter said. Did he refer to the previous day when he caught Moses spying on her at the pool? Or was he sorry that he had not prevented the cur from maiming buffalo? Perhaps, he regretted his misjudgment in selecting a depraved traveling companion, in the first place. One never knew about this puzzling man.

"What do you know about curing meat?" Cutter asked.

"Nothing, I'm afraid," Nell answered. "Until today, I never

watched a butchering. The women in my family were not permitted, except with chickens. I've helped Ruby, that's our servant, prepare salt pork, but never jerky. We didn't eat much jerky."

"Where you're going, you'll need to know."

"Oh, we won't be eating jerky there, rest assured of that. It's civilized, like Nauvoo."

"Don't be too sure. Follow me, and bring the blanket out of my tent to cover the meat. We are about to begin a grand battle with flies."

She followed Cutter's instructions and him to his trophy. As they approached, a vulture, which drifted low over the kill, rose high into the upper air currents on powerful, finger-tipped wings. He would surrender to the more deadly predator. But, the flies would not. They buzzed tenaciously about the dulled eyes, the red wound next to the front quarter, and the sand-covered tongue. Already, a troop of beetles, armored in iridescent green, struggled valiantly over steep dirt clods in their march toward new quarters under the dead animal.

Nell helped to lift the hindquarter while Cutter's sharp knife separated pelt from muscle. One of a myriad ticks on the hide crawled on to her hand and she hurriedly shook it off.

Jennifer stamped on it.

"She's learning," Cutter smiled.

They watched with fascination while Cutter cut the leg from the body at its joint without the need of a saw. Straining under its weight, he hoisted it onto Blue's back, tied it securely and covered it with his only blanket. With Nell carrying Jennifer and Cutter leading the horse, they made their way toward camp.

"Thanks, ah, thanks for looking out for us at the pond," Nell said. She hadn't intended to mention the embarrassing moment. "I should have hung blankets on the limbs. I shouldn't have tempted him."

"Get one thing straight." Cutter frowned. "He spied on you. Would have, no matter what you did. Forget about it, quick as you can, and mind you, there's no need to tell that Mormon fellow of yours. If he doesn't shoot buffalo for sport, I don't see him able to stomach having his wife spied on. You're a woman of grit to come all this way. Must be some man."

"Some man," Nell agreed.

"I hope he deserves you, that he won't have a couple of extra wives, once you've traveled all this way."

"That's what I've worried about all along, Cutter." This time, Nell lifted her eyes without hesitation upon his face. He stopped walking and turned the bad side to her. It no longer frightened her. When she reached out to touch it, he pulled away. They walked on.

"It's easier to go to him than sit home and wonder when he's coming for me. My father and some others you don't know planned to put him away, if he showed up. That got to me." Her lip trembled. Did you ever love someone, Cutter?"

"I did. Had a wife. Gentle woman, dark hair and white skin. Two little boys."

"Really?"

"I did. But, I went off to the Black Hills, way up north of here. Thought I'd make my fortune exploring for the government, but what I got was a Black Foot's tomahawk in my face. He butchered me good, didn't he? Well, I finished him, all right, but he left me . . . left me to see my boys high tail it under their bed when I opened the door, to hear my wife scream." Cutter walked a fair distance before finishing his story, and it weighed on Nell's heart like a stone. "I listened to her cry for two hours, alone in our bedroom. Promised I'd get me a pair of wooden teeth, but she cried all the more. Well, to make a long story short, I left."

Bang! Moses appeared like a speck in the distance, but the open quiet of the land reported his shot with unusual clarity. After a time, he fired again, and then, again. "Bum shot," Cutter grumbled. "He damned well better take care of that cow."

"What about the calf?" Nell needed to hear something hopeful. She strained under the weight of her chubby three year old.

"You know as well as I do about the calf, Nell. You ought to let your little one walk."

"She's tired and hungry."

"Well now, we'll have fine cuts out of this quarter. You and the baby can eat your fill—like the wolves."

"I look forward to that, Cutter, but I'd like it more if you didn't make us out to be animals." She hoped he did not notice the fine spray of saliva, which squirted from her mouth as if she had bitten into a plump grape. The rebellious juices flowed over her chin while slicing the meat into strips, kneading salt into it and hanging it to dry on the rack Cutter built from ropes and willows. Time marches slowly as little green beetles when hunger gnaws at your backbone. While she built a chip fire, and, finally fried thick cuts in the cast iron pan, her stomach growled.

"This one is mine and Jenny's," she told the men, and she kept that cut in the section of the pan where flames licked over the edge, not minding that yellow grease spat at her hands when she turned it over and over again. Before it had cooked through, she forked it onto her plate, sliced off a bite and burned her tongue when she gnawed at it. The juices of the meat and those of her mouth mingled, and her blue muslin shirt was stained with fatty driblets. After three savory swallows, she cut and chewed tiny squares for the baby, who eagerly closed her little pink lips around it. "Chew good," Nell said.

When they had cooked and eaten another two pans full, Nell realized that anger hung heavily about the men like the flies that hovered over the drying jerky. The only words spoken between them during the feast occurred after Cutter grew more and more annoyed with Moses' lack of manners. "Don't smack," Cutter thumped him on the back of the head with his knuckles. "I hate smacking."

"Yeah," Nell agreed, "cut it out."

"Don't smack." Little Jennifer gave him a kick before Nell caught her by the hand and led her away. Moses' greasy lip snarled over his teeth, and Nell caught him staring square into Cutter's good eye. The spy slept alone in the tent that night. With Blondie grinding her teeth at the back of the wagon, with Samson stomping and snorting on the side of it, and with Cutter snoring underneath, Nell felt comforted. No wolf would dare to carry off her child in all that commotion!

23

POWDER, PATCH, AND BALL

(*Diary*)   *June 2, 1849*

No travel today. Cured meat. Fired the Hawkin.

Nell did everything to avoid learning to fire the Hawkin. She chased lizards with Jennifer. But, all the while, thoughts of the rifle raced through her mind like the illusive reptiles. What about the hard kick that bruised shoulders and the loud discharge, which damaged hearing? What of the misfire, which disfigured faces or blew out eyes, or the bullet, which accidentally killed a horse? She whiled away her time by watching Moses, who brooded by himself and swatted flies off the smoking meat, as if he were worthy of no better task. Mumbling to himself, the rogue cast sullen glances at Cutter.

"Shoot me," the rifle begged. There was excitement and adventure in taking it up. But, Nell wasn't certain she wanted the responsibility. Neither did she want to exchange her female vulnerability and coyness for male resistance and aggression, to substitute "I can't take a life, so you do it" for "I am capable of defending myself and others. I will kill." To shoot meant to take one more step outside the comfort of the civilized life she had always known.

When Cutter called for help from under her wagon, Nell didn't have to consider the pestering thought that the rifle was a great equalizer or that reason required her to learn how to shoot it. Cutter found a crack in one of the singletrees, which connected Samson to the wagon, and Nell gladly helped him cut long strips of buffalo hide to wrap and to reinforce it. "As this leather dries," Cutter told her, "it will cinch

up and that singletree will take whatever Samson gives it, for a time."
That done, she sat beside Cutter, who relaxed against his saddle while
he brushed his knife over a whetstone. Then, to stall the inevitable,
she watered each animal at the spring and picketed it in fresh grass.
She rendered buffalo fat from the meat, a chore she had previously
pretended to know nothing about, and she greased all the wheel-knobs
to bring an end to the squeak she had endured for several days.

"Do you want to shoot or don't you?" Cutter asked, out of the blue.
That he knew what occupied her mind, before she told him, annoyed
her.

"I guess not. It's too loud. Besides, I could shoot myself in the
foot."

"Suit yourself."

"I really don't want to do this. Just look at me, pants, boots, soiled
shirt, sunburned. More man than woman. Damned shame."

"I cook. That doesn't make me a lesser man."

"Yah, but you don't make lace," Nell liked bantering with him.

"No," Cutter chuckled. "You don't either."

"Not yet. I haven't even finished my sampler, but I will—if
you'll fire my rifle." Which is worse, Nell wondered, learning to
fire a weapon or standing by while wolves attacked a newly-born
calf? Then, Jennifer came to mind. What if the wolves attacked her
offspring and she had no means to try to protect her? Could she live
with herself knowing that she avoided learning because she feared a
bruised shoulder?

"Well, hell," she told Cutter. "It's time I jumped into it."

At the bottom of her storage box she came upon the new rifle,
sheathed in buckskin, and the finely-tooled shoulder bag of possibles,
which her father had given her at parting. Though merely seven weeks
had passed since she bid goodbye to her family, it seemed as if she had
left them years ago. These gifts, which she believed she'd never touch
until she handed them over to Tom, had become an invaluable necessity. Her fingers ran over the length of the octagonal barrel, down to
a brass plate above the trigger upon which "J W Hawkin" had been
inscribed, and on to the short stock where brass tacks ornamented the
walnut butt. Ah, a man's way of owning jewelry, Nell thought. When
she lifted it to sight down the barrel, it felt heavy, but appeared much
lighter and shorter than Moses' or Cutter's rifles. It was the latest, the
most dear, the best; when her father gave it to her, she hadn't cared

and she hadn't known.

Now that she had become the mother of her own child, she knew. In selecting it, he must have spent much thought and effort. How had he, who had never crossed the Missouri, the foresight to stock her with objects a woman never used in civilization? Even now, he must be thinking of her. And Mama too. 'Where in all the world, do you think they are, my Nell and Little Jenny?' her mama must be asking.

'They're out on the plains experiencing the most extraordinary adventure of their lives,' her father must be saying.

Her mother must be replying, 'If any harm should come to them, I shall never forgive you, Charles, for allowing them to go. I shall breathe my last breath and hold you responsible.'

'Calm yourself, Harriet. She's a Baker. We did not raise a fool, even if she is female.'"

If only she could thank both of them for worrying and caring. If only she might tell them that she was trying to understand why they fought to keep Tom from her and that just knowing they were concerned gave her confidence to go on. She mused upon this, but deep down, she knew that when, no *if . . . if,* she returned with Tom to Quincy, she would always be a child to her parents. It also began to dawn on her that a Mormon's life was as worthless as a hill of beans in Hancock County, Illinois, and that her own blood meant to put Tom under.

"That's a fine piece," Cutter told Nell. He squatted Indian-fashion on the blanket where she dumped the contents of the shoulder bag: a powder horn, decorated with tiny mirrors and etched with "I Powder, with Brother Ball, Hero-like Do Conquer All," a can of pre-cut and waxed patches, a pouch containing hundreds of weighty lead balls, and a large tin of many more caps. "Nothing but the best," Cutter said, his hand moving over the rifle as if it were a fine woman. He aimed through the sight. "With steady nerves and a good eye, a man should be able to pick off a rattler at a hundred yards with this little beauty. Well, maybe fifty. That keg has enough powder in it to put away every buffalo on these plains." He showed her that the spout at the top of her powder horn had been adjusted to measure 90 grains of charge.

"Powder first." He filled the spout and emptied it down the muzzle.

"A heaping teaspoon?" Nell asked.

"That's about it. Use less for close up, but not much more. Patch next. Looks like they're already greased. If that doesn't beat all! They're coming up with something new everyday in this modern age." Cutter held a patch to the sun. "Hmm, Irish linen." He set the patch over the muzzle and balanced a ball upon it. "You take the piece, now. It isn't mine, though I wish it were. If you want to learn, now's the time."

"No, you do it first."

"Go on," he set the Hawkin in her lap. "Tamp in, with that little rod under your barrel. Now, fit the cap here on the nipple, and you're ready for action."

"You shoot first," Nell handed over the gun. If it misfired, she did not want to be holding it.

Cutter walked away.

Presently, Nell took courage and aimed through the sight, down the barrel, at the pin. Lacking the heart to pull the trigger, she lowered the gun, and would have kept it lowered if Cutter's hand had not stopped sharpening his blade, and if Moses had not hesitated swatting at flies. They waited. In the distance, a prairie dog mound presented itself as a target. After Nell stuffed patches into her ears and wiped perspiration from her forehead, she again raised the shooter and fit it tightly against her shoulder. While the prairie dog mound wavered in and out of sight, her finger circled around the double-set trigger. She held her breath, shut her eyes and pulled. Boom! The hard butt kicked firmly against her shoulder, but it did not hurt, thank heaven. With a poof of smoke came the acid scent of burning powder.

"A dead eye!" yelled Cutter. His slap on her back caused her weakened legs to give way, and, if he had not reached out to support her, she would have toppled over. "Men! How quickly they forget their strength!" she exclaimed.

"Oh, sorry." Cutter chuckled with embarrassment. "Remember now, clean her barrel after a few shots, like I do. Spit on a patch. Run it through. Then, run through a dry one, and she's ready for more. Before you put her away, clean her good. A little soap and water works, good as anything. And, keep your powder dry, Mrs. Mortenson. That's a must."

When he asked Nell if she'd like to reload for herself and take another shot, she declined. Firing the weapon hadn't been the frightening experience she had imagined, but she certainly didn't like it.

So, this is the adventure I sought? she asked herself.

24

SLASH OF LIGHT

(Diary)   *June 4, 1849*

Let it be known to all that my guides Moses and Cutter (may they rest in peace) died of the cholera on the Day of Our Lord June 4, 1849. Both are buried on the open prairie south of the Platte River.

Late in the afternoon the following day, a few buffalo again appeared far off. Gradually, a few grazed near the camp, then more and still more, until the land all around was black with them. Though the two guides avoided the slightest glance at one another all day, the compulsion to hunt drove them together again. A few words passed between them. Then, with their rifles, they mounted Old Broomtail and The Blue, who jerked at their taut reins and stirred up dust with their hooves in anticipation.

"Watch your back." Cutter raised his hand to Nell. He sped away.

Sweet Jenny, who interrupted playing with her pet horny toad, stood and raised her hand, palm forward, like Cutter did.

"Spell me off," Moses yelled and galloped away. His sardonic grin sent chills up Nell's legs. She, with Jennifer in hand, took up his watch over the meat, but the sun and smoke had darkened and dried it, so the flies had lost their enthusiasm, and Nell wondered why Moses had stood there for so long swatting and cursing even after Cutter told him "bag it." She took up the chore of storing it away, for tomorrow the group planned to resume their journey.

When shot after shot popped from behind distant swells in the land, Nell dreaded to consider the numerous buffalo, left in ruin for sport. After a time, the volleys stopped. Then, a final shot rang out. Presently, Moses rode into camp with something . . . something like a dead antelope draped across the saddle of Cutter's lathered mare. It was a man . . . Cutter!

"Lord in heaven," Nell cried. "What has happened?"

"Cutter's dead."

"Dead?" she moaned and rushed to see. "It can't be. How?" As if the weather had suddenly changed from summer to winter, a chill wrapped around her.

"Don't rightly know exactly how it went," Moses said. He lifted the head by the hair to show the lifeless face. He let it drop. "He got mixed up with a bunch of buffalo. That's it. Got throwed. Ah, he got trampled." Moses smiled, his eyes shifting from her breasts to Cutter and back again. "You're a perdy color," he said stroking the stubble on his chin. "I wants you, gal." His eyes met hers for the first time since they introduced themselves in Quincy.

"What are you saying?" Nell asked. "What's wrong with you?"

"I'm gittin' me your shovel and planting him over yonder where the ground's soft. When I comes back, as soon as it's dark, you and me is goin' for a roll. Been too long. Hold onto The Blue, now."

"Idiot," Nell said under her breath. Who, but Moses, would make such asinine comments at a time like this? He hurried off, and Nell heard him picking through the supplies near their tent.

"Poor Cutter," she stroked the dusty, grizzled hair that hung from beneath the saddle blanket, which Moses had used to partially cover the body. "What will become of us now?" she sobbed. "How could you have fallen off the horse? You never lost balance before, not even when you slept."

Gradually, it dawned on Nell that being thrown was not an option in Cutter's case. The Blue never bucked. Something didn't fit. Frightened of what she might discover, she raised the blanket. What she found there, a gaping hole in Cutter's back, spoke of murder. The buffalo trampled him, sure enough, but only after Moses shot him. Hearing footsteps, Nell quickly dropped the saddle blanket. Her face burned with hatred.

"This here won't take long," Moses said. "Be right nice to have me a proper horse, for a change."

"Remember to mount from the left side," Nell said, hoping he would.

"Right side," Moses answered. As he led the mare and Cutter away, his hair glowed in the light of fading day to remind her of her shame at the pond. "See you sleeps your pup, 'less you wants her privy to it."

"What are you saying?" Nell called after him.

He strutted off, Cutter's shovel over his shoulder. "I wants you. When I gets back, you and me is going into the tent for a poke."

Poke? Surely, he did not mean what she heard him say. No man she had ever known, or read about, had used such a word; even so, she recognized its meaning and felt ashamed that she did. What a bewildering nightmare! Was it not the duty of men to protect women and children against the harshness of life? And, had not Moses, in his own crude way, done that all along? Cared for her animals? Encouraged her? Quieted her fears about wolves and Indians? Laughed with her? Moses could not carry out such a threat and count himself a man. He couldn't.

With this puzzle, Nell hurried to Jennifer, who played wagons in the sand. "Let's move the animals," she said. "Look, they've eaten their grass down to the quick."

Jennifer, who interpreted the world through her mother's reactions, studied her face. "Mama," she reached up to be held. Though the alarmed child had grown too heavy, Nell lifted her into her arms. She kissed the endearing, rounded cheek and sniffed the fragrance of it. Then, she turned her attention toward the sounds of Moses' shovel. Rhythmic as a clock's pendulum, it rose to reflect the golden glow of the setting sun, and fell again, a signal that time flees quickly when one needs it to stand still.

With difficulty, Nell dug at the long lariat pins, which Moses had pounded deeply into the ground to hold the grazing mules. "Men, they always overdo it," she complained to her daughter. Perspiration ran through her hair and down the back of her neck, and her face flushed despite the cool evening breezes. Moving the animals to thick patches of waist-high clump grass, she wondered what brought Moses to kill poor Cutter? Tension had grown between the two men since Moses began his flirtations with Phoebe, and they intensified since the spying, with silence and glaring messages of the eyes. But, never had she supposed Moses' resentment traveled to the unthinkable.

Now, a veil lifted from her eyes. As she had suspected, but chose not to voice, Moses calculatingly seduced Phoebe. Once he worked his will upon her, or worse still, once he feared she might be with child, he cast her off as one would the core of an apple. And the buffalo. Oh, the sickening sight of that much flesh falling in great heaps on the prairie to rot with Moses shouting a cry of victory after each slaughter, as if he had conquered the world. The lack of conscience, which allowed him to spy upon her, also permitted him to take the life of an honest man. He seemed not to fear, but to defy God. "Double-headed sidewinder," Nell said aloud.

"Look at me, Mama," Jennifer said. "Are we scared?"

"No, baby. Don't you be scared. I am with you." She picked Jennifer off the ground, as one would harvest a flower. After running with her and climbing inside the wagon, she drew in the canvas on both ends. Being enclosed and in semi-darkness relieved her fright, and she automatically began unwinding Jennifer's braids for the night.

Then, without much thought, she opened *Hamlet* to find folded in its pages Tom's letter and carefully, so as not to bend it, tucked it under her clothing next to her heart. How lovely it would be to hear him call "Nell," to run into his arms, to know his protection. For their first meeting, she'd wear the pale lavender dress with the purple sash trailing down the back of the skirt. She must not forget to mend the petticoat. Perhaps, Tom would be dining. She'd open his front door without a sound, tiptoe down the hall and pose at the dining room entrance before he'd see her there. When he glanced up, oh Lord, he'd think he must be dreaming. So ran Nell's thoughts, to a happy future hundreds of miles away.

The yellow light of the setting sun slashed through a crack in the canvas and pierced into Nell's eyes and into her heart. Her pulse quickened, her breathing came hard. Night was imminent.

"How I wish your grandfather were here," she told Jennifer, who pulled away from the cold wash towel on her face. "He might be older now, but he's strong. Perhaps, he'll ride up, in the nick of time, like he did a long time ago when I fell into the creek. There's a nice place between his shoulder and chest, right here," she showed Jennifer, "where your head fits just right. Remember? When you're there, all your troubles disappear."

In order to pour sand from Jennifer's shoes, Nell opened the rear canvas. The last sliver of sun sank below the horizon. In that final light of day, she observed a red-tailed hawk floating on the air currents overhead. Briefly, it balanced there, then, with incredible speed, it dived straight toward a speck of a bird. Upon impact, feathers flew in all directions like so many offspring. They drifted downward while the hawk flew out of sight with its victim. That ended it.

Like the small bird, she must fend for herself, or die. Nobody was coming to save her either. When Jennifer snuggled her warm head against her mother's pounding heart, Nell held it there with hands that trembled uncontrollably. They perspired on her daughter's fragrant locks.

"Mama? "Mama?" Jennifer asked while searching her mother's eyes. "Tummy hurt, Mama? Baby scared."

"Don't be scared. Mama's cold, that's all. Under the covers, now. Let's get some sleep." As worry faded from her child's face, Nell remembered the buffalo calf and its brutal death, and for a split second in her vivid imagination, Jennifer was the calf.

"No," she whispered, quietly as the flap of a finches' wing. "No." Moses was not going to leave her with her face in her hands for the rest of her natural life. She would die of it. And, Jenny? What was a child, alone on the prairie, without its mother? This was not about *her* freedom. It was about her child's life. She must do something. What?

A cold calm settled upon her. Nobody, nobody was going to harm Jenny. Tucking the little one's arm under the quilt, Nell improvised a lullaby:

> Go to sleep, little girl
> We will soon find your father.
> He has built us a home
> In his far distant valley.
> With his strong, loving arms
> He will shield us and keep us.
> He'll protect us from harm
> In the far away valley.

How quickly the baby drifted into her rest, how completely she trusted, as if her mother were a god.

From the silver service box, Nell retrieved the cold slip of a pistol her father had given her. She placed it at the foot of Jennifer's bed, along with the possibles bag. Like Cutter had taught her, she loaded it with powder, patch and ball. According to her father's instructions, she measured one-third the powder used for her Hawkin. "I hate this," she said, tamping the ball into the barrel. "Why me?" Partially hidden under the spoons, her favorite carving knife caught her attention. It found itself home in her hands. Because it was sharp with a seven-inch long blade, and because her boot knife was short and dull from slicing buffalo strips, she decided to exchange them and to use the carving knife as a backup for the derringer. She slipped it into her boot. Even though it irritated her ankle, she left it there.

This is not right, her soul cried out to her. Oh, may God damn this man who murdered his companion. May he burn in hell for forcing her to join him in his evil. If she did manage to kill him . . . what then? She'd find herself alone on the prairie, alone against the wolves, the snakes, the Indians and a map she couldn't read because she forgot how to locate the North Star. Alone to deal with wagon wheels stuck in drenched soil, alone with eight animals to feed, water and prepare for travel! Alone with her conscience. Moses knew that, and must be thinking he had her in a bind. If she shot him, she may be alone for a good while; she may perish. On the other hand, if she gave herself to him, the loneliness would last forever. Sure, other women had been ravaged and had lived, like the hollow-eyed victims of Illinois mobs. Phoebe lived. If this was the price to be paid for a man's protection, it was too high. Stripped of all pride, she would never be able to stand beside a man like Tom. May Moses' black heart rot in hell! Whatever the outcome, her life could never again be as it was when this day broke.

Night came on. The wretch had left her with no time to struggle with morality, no time for fear or self-pity, no time to mourn for a friend. Now, she commenced to act. As she lit her lantern's wick with a sulfur stick, she determined to put the decision in Moses' hands, to offer him a chance to ride away. If he did not, she'd have to aim straight, with her eyes wide open, and hold off pulling the trigger until he stood very close.

Nell prepared to leave Jennifer. For a watchdog, she tied Blondie to the back of the wagon, and the mule immediately stuck her great head inside and over the baby. Lantern in one hand, pistol in the other, Nell went to do what had to be done.

She did not see Moses until her lantern's light circled the entrance of his tent, where he paced back and forth. Aware of her approach, he smiled and smiled, trying not to smile.

"You buried Cutter?" she asked, keeping the derringer behind her back.

"Never you mind about Cutter. He's planted." He smacked his lips on a cud of black tobacco and spit it onto the ground by his feet. "That's it. I likes a woman doesn't play dumb." He hiked up his pants. "Get inside. You take them boy clothes off and show me. Hear?"

Nauseous, Nell hung her lantern on the tent post. The high burning flame shone brightly upon her aggressor, exactly like she had planned. "I'm not going inside your tent;" she revealed the gun. "You have no right to touch me against my will."

"What you wants to be like that for?" He spat again, this time on his own boot. "We both knows what you wants." He reached out to her. "Nobody has to put on no show for me, little gal. How long is it since you been with a man? He inched closer. Old Moses is gentle, now. There's nobody will ever know and nobody to put on no act for. We's alone, see, you and me."

"I'm a married woman."

"Oh, I don't mind that. You'll do. Come on, gal, give up that little ol' pea shooter. Don't want me to hit, do you?" He held out his hand and cautiously stepped toward her, tobacco juice edging his lips.

"Please, Moses, don't make me shoot. I don't want to kill. Please. Just leave us alone. You'll reach California faster without us. With all the gold you have and all you'll find, there'll be lots of pretty women. I release you from all obligation."

"*Release you from all obligation,*" he mimicked. "What does that mean? Leave a piece like you to them Indians? What I wants is nothin' compared to what they'd get. Think on it." He knew her weaknesses, her fears.

"Moses," she yelled. "It's loaded. I'll pull the trigger. I will."

He snarled, hunched over and stepped lightly toward her, play-acting the part of a melodrama villain. "I means to have you, easy or hard."

"I respect your decision," Nell returned, heartless as lead.

Talking was over. Now she aimed at his nose, but her trembling legs revolted against the thought of destroying another human being. One hand held the derringer while the other attempted to steady the hand that held the derringer, and Nell waited for Moses to step into the direct light of the lantern, where she considered him *close*. When he stood within six feet, her eyes shut. Her unsteady finger squeezed the trigger, the charge crashed against her eardrums, sparks stung her hand, and Moses' fist smashed into her jaw.

"Shoot at me, hellcat?" he snarled. Now, his fist slammed into her stomach with the force one man would use in a fight to the death with another. Nell dropped. Like a fish on the bank, she opened her mouth over and over again, but no air filled her lungs. Once she came to herself, she heard Moses swear and jump up and down. Blood poured from his ear, the same one Blondie nipped after he whipped her. "Now, look what you done. It just started healin'." He dragged her, kicking and slugging into his tent. With a thud, he fell upon her. His hands clawed wickedly beneath her coat and Tom's letter. Struggling frantically to push him off, she realized that his endurance and strength far exceeded her own. The harder she fought, the more he laughed, a sickening, high-pitched laugh.

By grabbing a handful of hair at the back of her head, the devil prevented her from moving and covered his sickening mouth over hers. She shoved him off with all her strength. A hard kick to the shin caused him to cry out, but she gasped from what bit into her ankle.

"Alright, alright," she panted. "You win. Have me." His breath smelled like a keg of cucumbers, gone rancid. "Kiss me." She cunningly offered him her lips. On her, he laid his heavy, muscular body. His saliva ran down her cheek as his lips sought hers. It sickened her. However, to distract him, she responded. With her left hand, she caressed his neck. With her right, she reached into her boot. Bringing the carver over his back, she gripped it with both hands, took a deep breath, and plunged it, up to the handle, into his back.

Aghast, Moses crawled off her. When he struggled to stand, she slapped him hard across the face. "Maybe now you'll quit smacking!" she hissed. "If you ripped Tom's letter, I'll kill you." To her surprise, Moses fell forward, flat and still as a flapjack onto his face, and in doing so, blood from his mouth struck her neck. She wiped it off with the back of her hand and gasped at the vivid red of it in the lamplight.

"I hate you, Moses," she panted. "You had no right to make me hurt you. Moses? Moses, do you hear?" To retrieve her carver, she placed her boot on his back, and pulled. Easily, it slipped out. To clean it, she wiped it across his gingham shirt, and to discover if he were alive, she kicked his leg. Through her boot, she felt his death.

Nell stumbled out of the tent and into the night. Her body collapsed. Now, as if she had gnawed all day on live flesh, her spirit revolted. It left her body and stood over it, a neutral observer. The spirit watched the quivering personage, saw it vomit wretchedly, and, in the vast openness of the star-studded night, heard its voice scream, "Mama!"

A distant coyote answered with its lonely cry, and darkness covered everything.

25

LIKE A DREAM

(Diary)   *June 5, 1849*

Alone. Sioux woman found me.

In the early morning hours between the time when the stars blink crisply in their spheres and a pale glow of Apollo's chariot appears in the east, Nell opened her eyes to an eerie calm. No blade of grass stirred. No meadowlark, no butterfly, no gnat was on the wing. No cloud moved across the sky. The animals stood like bronze statues tied to a bronze wagon. Surely, she must be dreaming. If this were only a dream, she might awaken to Cutter's "Good morning, Mrs. Mortenson" or to Moses' cough. If this were a story out of a book, she might turn to the next page where the heartache, the guilt, the upset stomach, the shattered nerves had all passed. But, this was not a dream and it was not a story. What happened, happened.

Nell rose to her knees, dropped her head and beat the earth with her fists. "Oh, God. What have I done?" she bitterly sobbed. "Help me." Something stirred in the grass next to her aching head. Over her, against the light of dawn, stood a personage. Was it Moses, or was it the spirit of Moses come back from purgatory to torment her? Had Cutter risen up from the grave? She tightly closed her eyes. "I didn't mean it," she cried out. "Forgive me." No voice responded. Through the strands of her hair, she espied buckskin moccasins, fringed and ornamented with miniature shells and multi-colored beads. Above them, a fringed doeskin garment covered the form of a woman, and a female voice uttered the musical cadence of a foreign tongue. A hand reached out to her.

Nell took it and was lifted up.

She stood face-to-face with an Indian woman! From what Nell could discern of her countenance and motherly manner, she must have been thirty-five or forty years of age. Her handsome, straight nose, her well-defined lips, her gentle brown eyes and high cheekbones rendered her face the dignity of a sculptured bust. A child would have found a cushioned place against her rounded body. Most striking was her long healthy hair, which flowed over her shoulders like a dark river with silver fish streaking across the surface. In short, she defied all, which Nell had heard and read, concerning the Indian peoples. Neither princess nor heathen, she appeared equal in her grooming to the most tasteful of European females. With acceptance and understanding, she greeted Nell.

"I . . . I must be a . . . a fright," Nell ran her fingers through her tangled hair. She scratched at the crusted blood on her jacket and dusted her trousers. "Sorry. I didn't . . . expect . . . "

A silhouette of some fifteen braves gathered in the morning haze some distance away. Anxious to be gone, probably to pursue buffalo, they called out and motioned to the woman, but she waved them off. Again, they called to her. But, her attention wrapped around Nell like a square knot. While the others waited, one of them approached on his albino, armed with a muzzleloading flintlock rifle and leading behind him a pony, which was apparently the woman's. In spite of Nell's miserable state, she could not help being amazed at this superb physical specimen who wore nothing but moccasins, leggings, and a narrow breastplate of porcupine quills, which exposed to view the most splendid chest she had ever laid eyes upon.

He slipped off his albino, decorated with a circle painted around its eye and feathers in its braided mane, and he urged the woman to mount. When she turned her back to him, he spun her around, pointed to the dawning day, and spoke in loud, authoritative tones. To her he made what seemed to be an elaborate argument; nevertheless, she answered him firmly and softly in the negative, meeting his stern gaze with the upturned lips and the flirting, spirited eyes of a woman who knows she is loved.

The group of hunters set up a commotion. They yelled and yipped and motioned with their spears, they pointed to the east, they made false starts across the swells and returned. Then, riding bareback with nothing except a rope around his feisty animal's neck, a boy between manhood and childhood flew toward them. To impress the braves, he whirled Nell's lard bucket over his head, barked war whoops, and made tight circles around the startled women. Then, he threw the bucket, which rolled in front of Nell. Though more than half of the grease had spilled, she was gratified to have it again. Nell wondered how he had come by it and how long these people had been with her, for she had lost the bucket three days prior.

This insolent act of the boy triggered an unexpected response in the woman's brave. First, the powerfully built man gave a sign for the hunters to be off, and they vanished as quickly as he signaled. Then, he pulled the insolent boy from his horse and held him firmly by the hair while chastising him. When the boy glared grudgingly at Nell, the brave, who must have been his father, led him to a nearby bluff, where they squatted in the shade of their horses.

The woman's eyes rested softly on her family.

"Mama," Jennifer called. Her white head leaned over the tailgate of the wagon. At once Nell went to her with the woman at her elbow. Without realizing how extremely exhausted she was, Nell attempted to lift her little one, but her arms quivered like two blades of grass in the wind. Using sign language and facial expressions, the woman asked if she might take the child. Nell nodded, amazed that so much could be communicated without the spoken word. Rather than immediately holding Jennifer, as most adults were prone to do, the woman, who was as much mother as Nell, first took the time to become acquainted. She tactfully talked to the young one, smiled, touched her hands, and showed her a tiny leather pouch, which hung on delicately braided rawhide around her neck. Pointing to her breastbone, she said "Sioux." Jennifer echoed "Sioux." Then, the woman pointed to the eastern horizon where the sun cast a reflective, yellow path over the grass.

"Rising Sun," Nell said. "Her name is Rising Sun."

"Sioux," Jennifer called her.

Nell pointed to her own breastbone. "Nell." Then, she showed the plains woman a nail pounded into the side of the Ark. "Nell."

Jennifer giggled.

Rising Sun seemed puzzled at first and curiously inspected the nail head, moving her eyes back and forth from it to her white cousin. "Nail?" A playful expression beamed across her face. She scratched her cheek and raised her brows.

When the Indian lifted Jenny into her arms, the young one tangled her fingers in a strand of her hair and called it *mule tail*. Nell was gratified that the Sioux woman did not understand the words; they did not approach an accurate description of her gorgeous long, raven black mane. Words cannot be counted on so much as gestures, Nell decided, to convey thoughts. Words didn't matter, anyway. The prairie mother's being there did. Oh, how Nell had taken for granted the lightness and warmth of femininity!

With Jennifer in arms, the Sioux motioned for Nell to follow her. Nell did until she realized they walked straight toward Cutter's grave. She stopped short. Only after a great deal of gentle urging did she continue on. Then, at the site, Rising Sun showed her a second mound, and when she motioned toward the tent, Nell knew that, out of a mystifying sort of empathy, the Indians had put Moses under. Tears of relief rolled from her already swollen eyes.

But that wasn't all. As if the woman knew a great deal about Nell's plight, her thoughtful care continued. On the far side of the wagon out of view of the braves, Rising Sun spread her horse blanket, part of a buffalo pelt. She snuggled comfortably upon one side of it and ran her hand over the other side, indicating for Nell and Jennifer to sit. In the morning breezes, long strands of hair whipped across her face. She spoke pleasantly in her own tongue, without a great deal of animation, as if Nell and her child were old friends who understood every word.

Then, she did a curious thing. Using flint, dried grass and chips, she built a little fire. Kneeling beside it, she gathered its smoke around her face and chanted, "Oh yah, oh yah, ah eee." Then, she motioned for Nell to remove her blood-streaked clothing. Stunned and disoriented from the terrifying experience of the previous night, Nell fell easily under her charge and turned over her jacket and trousers. She sat in her brief camisole and pantaloons exposed to the warm sunlight. Rising Sun threw the clothing into the flames, which instantly began to devour it. When it sizzled, she sang, "Oh yah, oh yah, oh yah, ah eee." She pushed the smoke toward the east and poured water over her brown face, arms and hands.

The beauty with which her hands spoke could not be given in words. Four times, they danced across the sky, tracing the sun's pathway during the four seasons. Swirling toward the southern horizon, they trudged through deep snow and warmed themselves beside a fire inside the tepee. They leaped into springtime. From the rushing waters, they plucked fish; from the prairie carpet, they gathered roots; they basked in the sun and frolicked like children. Then, the hands reached to the zenith and circled through the story of summertime when the people journeyed after the buffalo, killed the animals, cured meat, and made clothing. They spoke of warm nights, of the antelope, of the hawk and bushes thick with berries. They told of the peace and contentment of the fall season and fluttered like geese toward the south again. In the silent language of the plains, she seemed to connect with all living things.

With quiet composure, she returned to the pelt where Nell reclined next to Jennifer in her white undergarments. Out of the tall grass next to her, Rising Sun pulled a large gourd, embellished with eagle feathers and wrapped with long strips of rawhide, stained black and red. From it she poured water over a patch of fine leather until it was saturated. She rubbed it over Nell's neck and face and hands, as one would wash a child. The woman's touch had a most soothing effect. They all drank deeply from the gourd. When Rising Sun offered the remainder of the water, Nell eagerly retrieved a fragrant cake of lye soap from her grooming supplies and went about giving her hair a brisk wash, which immediately lifted her spirits and gave her sufficient strength to change into a calico frock for the first time since the beginning of her journey. She had brought it for everyday wear, and it did not equal the craft of the Sioux's garment. But, when Nell revealed herself, feeling like a newly-minted, five-dollar gold piece, Rising Sun sang a little chant. "Oh yah yah, oh yah yah, oh yah yah." The woman moved a distance away where she occupied Jennifer with something in the grass. She turned her back to Nell, and the braves on the knoll turned their backs.

Without knowing what to do, Nell followed the sun worshiper's lead. She poured water over her face, pushed the smoke toward the east with her two hands, and did the only thing she knew how to do. She knelt and bowed her head. "Our Father who art in heaven. I have killed," she whispered so as not to frighten Jennifer, for she felt like screaming. "I did not want to kill." She sobbed again. "I chose to defend my body. I chose to save my child." When the smoke curled around her, she pushed it toward the dawn. "If this is not sin, shine on me. Amen . . . In the name of Jesus Christ," she whispered, Mormon fashion. Amen."

Presently, Rising Sun's hand landed, delicate as a finch, on Nell's shoulder. She untied the leather strings of her pouch. Into her palm, she emptied its contents: tiny stones, each of an unusual character as if it had been gathered from distant parts over the centuries. When she held them in the sun and sprinkled water over them, they sparked with life. A black belt circled the middle of a little gray stone, white star-like markings gleamed from a black one, and a deep inner light shone from the milky white one. One was bright red. There were nine, in all. Each had been rubbed smooth by the power of water or by the motion of many hands over many years. Into the pouch, Rising Sun returned the stones. She hung it around Nell's neck. It was lovely to hold. In return, Nell retrieved and offered her prized soap and a bag of pony beads. The Sioux accepted them with quiet respect.

"Baby's hungry," Jennifer pouted and rubbed her stomach.

At that, the Sioux drew a leather bag from the grass where she found the gourd. She commenced to share a breakfast with Jennifer, who ate heartily, and Nell, who tried to eat, but could not. It consisted of delicious little sticks of wild gooseberries and cornmeal held together with honey, boiled bird eggs of a gray color flecked with brown, and smoked fish. For an extra touch, Nell drew from Nan a cup of milk for each of them and sweetened it with flaked chocolate, an exotic new flavor she had purchased for Elizabeth. With much hesitation and curiosity, Rising Sun sipped the offering, but she liked the tin cup more than the drink and was very enamored by the soap; she smelled it, rubbed it against her arm, and admired the lilacs imbedded in it.

In the shade of the wagon, they talked in two languages, revealing the secrets of their hearts and munching on the delicious fruit sticks. The tepee dweller told of the loss of a child at birth, of pottery, and of leatherwork. She showed Nell her thumbs, swollen at the knuckles and crooked from working the hides. But, mostly she spoke of the brave and the boy on the bluff. And some of the time, she smiled. Some of the time, moisture gleamed in her mild, dark eyes, and all of the time, her speech reflected the thoughtful, deliberate mind of one who could be counted as a friend.

Nell confessed the long story of how she had broken Arthur's heart, how she had lied to Tom, how she had stolen Jennifer from her family, and how she rejected Phoebe when the girl desperately needed her. "Last night, after I killed, I examined myself for the first time. It was most queer. I stood above myself. What I saw was a selfish, ego-tistical girl, who spit in the face of every person who ever loved her."

The fire of shame sizzled in her breast. Though Nell felt as if she had no tears left to spill, she wept.

At that, Rising Sun firmly wiped her cheeks with the doeskin and lifted her chin once, twice and three times, until Nell kept it lifted. There should be no more crying.

"Self-pity is the lowest state to which a woman's mind might fall," Nell spoke aloud to reassert her spirit. "For Jenny, I shall bear up. We shall resume the journey to the Valley of the Great Salt Lake, come hell or high water. One step at a time, on our own."

In the sand, the woman drew a waving line.

"Snake?" Nell asked, weaving her hand through the grass.

The Sioux shook her head in disagreement. Then, she cupped her hands as if she were scooping water and pretended to drink. "Nebraska," she said.

Nell recalled when Cutter told her that *Nebraska* was the Indian word for the Platte River. "Where is it?" she urgently wanted to know.

Rising Sun pointed to the right of Nell's wagon. "Nebraska," she again said. "Nebraska." Into the ground, she poked a short stick. She helped Nell understand how the shadow could be used to determine the direction of the river.

"Thank you," Nell said, feeling the wife's and the mother's need to join her family. "Thank you." How could she repay this rare woman who knew, without being told, that another human being needed to be touched? That her food, her ritual, her voice and her small gifts had made the difference between life and death?

"Wait," Nell told her. With gratitude in mind and Jennifer in hand, she went to the wagon to collect a setting of her silver to give as a remembrance. Before she returned with it, she heard the distant thundering of hooves and thought she heard, in the whisper of the wind, "ah yah, I am with you, ah yah, ah eee." Like a phantom, Nell's plains sister had appeared, and like a phantom, she had disappeared. As far as Nell could see out over the rolling grassland, no human form stirred. But, the sun had risen. Prairie dogs barked in their villages. The skylark warbled its presence, and blue flies plagued the animals, that stomped and swished their tails and stretched their tethers for a nibble of grass. If the pouch of stones had not hung around her neck, she would have sworn the Sioux woman's appearance had been nothing but a dream.

"Rising Sun," Nell called out. Her voice, punctuated by Blondie's whinny hee haw, mingled with the breathing of the vast earth.

"She's on her horse," Jennifer said. Around her arm, coiled a small garter snake!

"Drop it!" Nell yelled.

"No," Jennifer insisted. "My baby. Sioux gave it."

26

ONE TURN, ONE SHOT

(Diary)   *June 6, 1849*

Alone. Rolling again over the vast, open grassland. Determined to reach Platte. Jennifer afraid of wolves that howl at night. If I am not afraid to die, why am I afraid to live?

I am not afraid to die, Nell thought. *It's not so fearful as living.* Paralyzed, she slumped down onto the wagon tongue. In the weeds below her, a diminutive spider of a black variety, with a red dot on its thorax, dangled at the end of a thin, silk thread. When the thread swayed, the insect reached out for a blade of grass, but just before the hairy little fellow latched onto it, along came a wind current, blowing it and leaving it to dangle in space once more. Again and again, it made futile attempts. Why doesn't it jump off, Nell thought, hit the solid ground, and then crawl up any blade of grass it has a mind to?

Like the insect, she hung suspended in space, somewhere between regret and a dream, out in the middle of nowhere between Quincy and the Valley of the Great Salt Lake, swinging backward to the hurt voices of the past. 'If you don't care how anyone else feels, at least give Jenny a chance at life,' 'You'll pay for this,' 'From this day forward, you are no daughter of mine,' and 'An unprotected woman asks to be molested.'

Then, she swayed forward to the time when she'd tell Tom, 'I do not believe. I never believed.' She knew his predictable answer. 'His will be done. If you don't believe, you are no wife of mine.' Since her many letters had never fallen into his hands, by now, he could have

190

taken another wife. Or two? What then? Where would she go? How would she provide for Jenny? Protect her?

Taking pity on the wind-tossed insect, she pushed a blade of grass within its reach, and, instantly, as if it knew what for, the spider took it. He climbed down it, deep into its roots. "Thinking hurts," Nell said, "but doing right doesn't."

Nell scrutinized the disorder surrounding her. She too must hit solid ground and then make for the Platte. But, before that could happen, a hundred and one tasks needed doing. Water buckets stood empty, the tripod, pot and cooking utensils lay soaking near yesterday's dead campfire. Potato water needed boiling; a pot of buffalo stew must be cooked over a smoldering heap of chips, which wanted gathering. Jenny's arms and legs hadn't been coated with vinegar to discourage gnats, greenflies and mosquitoes, and liniment hadn't been rubbed over places where they had already gorged themselves. There wasn't a comfortable place in the wagon where Jennifer might play with her slithery friend, a place where she might move about in spite of the rope, which prevented her from going too far to the rear and falling out.

All this, and more, she must accomplish with her daughter walking in her shadow because, directly after Rising Sun disappeared, Jenny had wandered off into the tall grass chasing her snake. For a few minutes, which seemed like hours, Nell had experienced the most cruel and absolute terror of being a parent. Though mother and child had called back and forth to one another, the experience, which had added an additional shock to Nell's nervous system, caused a great fatigue to overcome her. "I can't turn my back on you for one minute," Nell had tightly held her child.

"Mean old snake lost me," Jennifer had explained. Both had need for a nap before anything could be done. "Mama," Jenny had awakened her mother. "I'm thirsty. Blondie's thirsty." A dry foam, which had begun to form around the mule's mouth, immediately caught Jennifer's attention because over two months of travel, she had learned that caring for the animals was an absolute priority.

"I'm thirsty too," Nell had told her endearing daughter. "Let's all go to the spring for a drink. That's where we'll start."

"Do you need Ruby?" Jennifer had wanted to know. "Where's Cutter?"

"He's gone. Both of them are gone. We'll never see them again."

That was all the explaining she meant to do for Jennifer or anyone else who wanted to know. After some things are buried, she had decided, they should stay buried.

"I'll take care of you, Mama. I'll walk in front." Jenny had taken her mother's hand.

Now, Nell watered and moved The Spare to a patch of bunch grass. She stomped the pin into the ground with three blows and vowed, "Before this day ends, the Ark's wheels will make at least one turn in the right direction, come hell or high water!"

Mother and daughter leaned over the spring and drank from cupped hands. Next came the watering and grazing of the other seven animals: Blondie, Samson, The Broomtail, The Blue, two pack burros and the goat. By the time Nell completed the chore, she felt overwhelmed, eight animals being too numerous for one person to handle. Yet, upon thinking how valuable they might be to her family or to trade in an emergency, she decided to do her best to take them along. After three days' rest, they looked healthy, energetic, and ready to work.

For the rest of the afternoon, Nell accomplished whatever came next. Rather than sorting through the baggage in her mind, she shuffled the baggage of her wagon to make room for the men's most valuable items: Cutter's map of the trail, his fishing pole, the muskets, powder and lead, as well as what remained of a small store of food which included tea, sugar, coffee, and flour, hardtack, jerky, dried fruit, and beans. As expected, the gold pieces, which her father had paid the guides as an incentive to lead her and Jennifer to Tom, were lodged deep in Moses' saddlebag. Nell wondered when he had claimed them. Though the sight of the shovel caused her anxiety, she tied that to a burros' pack; it may come in handy when she planted her apple trees in the valley. A person must be practical. All this she stored away but left behind a few duplications. She did not go near the tent and tried not to look in the direction of the graves. The sooner they all left this place, the better.

In the late afternoon, they did leave. Nell studied the lengthening shadows of the grass, and pointed her menagerie toward the north and the great river. Twice, she clicked her tongue. "Get up." She gently whipped the reins over the teams' backs and called out, "Get up." The wheels turned one rotation!

As the Ark's wheels turned a thousand times more, the camp and the tent disappeared from view. The outfit had not traversed one hour before coming upon what Nell believed to be an outlet of the Platte. Alongside it grew willows and a dead white cottonwood, which lightening had split and scorched. To Nell's mind it was a boon, a perfect camp, and a sign for their favorable future. Before dark, she chopped a huge pile of cured wood to be stored in the wagon in the morning, and lit a low-burning fire beside which mother and child savored a slow-cooked buffalo stew.

"The fire makes me think of home," Nell mused. "It's like an old friend keeping us company." She did not tell her daughter that the spooky darkness at her back kept her company as well. Even so, the daughter knew.

"Did Indians scare Moses and Cutter away?" Jennifer managed to ask, her thumb in her mouth and her blanket up her nose.

"I suppose so," Nell answered in a voice that blended with the beat of thrashing crickets. Rubbing the leather pouch hanging around her neck gave her comfort.

"We're not afraid of Indians. They don't scare us." Jennifer plunked down in her mother's lap.

"Heavens no. They're our friends. Lighting a fire changes a place into a camp," Nell mused, more to herself than to the child. "I don't know why, but every time we leave a place where we've made ourselves comfortable, a place where we've cooked and eaten and slept, I sort of regret moving on. It's like leaving home every morning."

Wolves called back and forth to one another across the distances. When Nell jumped, ever so slightly, and inched toward the fire, Jennifer instantly buried her face in her mother's breast. "We're not scared," she said. The howling grew louder and more frequent. Nell squinted at the darkness and saw, or thought she saw, the red glow of a pair of eyes. She sprang to her feet, her child in her arms, and stepped cautiously to the the Ark.

In the lantern's light, she loaded her rifle and those of her guides. Three shots should be sufficient. "Don't you worry, Baby. Mama can shoot. From now on, we'll keep these guns primed at night. You must not touch them—ever. If you do, you could be killed. Do you understand?"

"Dead, like a buffalo?"

"Yes, like a buffalo. Hold your ears, now. I'm going to take a shot to let those wolves know who owns this camp."

The loud bang momentarily quieted the howling, but the Hawkin's kick howled on Nell's shoulder. She had failed to hold it firmly but resolved to do so next time. "Ha. Did you see that? I can shoot. I can load and shoot, alright, with my eyes open, at least with this gun." She reloaded, "just in case," and promised her daughter, "At the crack of dawn, I'll practice. We won't be leaving this place until I hit something."

In the safety of the Ark, they snuggled closely together. Nell made a diary entry. She wanted to remember the day she moved, alone, across the vastness and fired a rifle with both eyes open. Then, for comfort, she read Tom's letter, at least the words that had not faded away. "I long for you and Jenny . . . state remains a mystery . . . if you . . . heart . . . to come for you . . . devoted." After folding the paper and sliding it under her camisole, she pulled the tick up to her eyeballs and concentrated, in order to avoid thoughts of wolves, upon the shadows of the fire's light dancing on the canvas. This only frightened her, however, since every flicker suggested red eyes, dripping fangs, or bristling hair. "Stop thinking," she told her mind. "Let it go." So, she turned her back to the canvas and concentrated, instead, on the deep, regular breathing of the warm child, who easily surrendered the cares of the world. Sleep finally enclosed her in its protective womb, and she awakened only twice to feel the cool triggers of the guns and the smooth handle of her silver carving knife—all lying within the reach of her outstretched hand.

27

ONE HIT

(Diary)   June 7, 1849

*Area infested with wolves. Made it to the Platte. Waved to people across
the river. Shot Father's rifle. Days long and hot. There's something sweet
about being independent and alone.*

Nell stretched and yawned with the carefree pleasure of awakening five years earlier when her whole future seemed certain, when
the most important decision of the day was which dress to wear. She
squirmed and reveled under the tick, which had become too warm, the
sun being high in the sky, until a gnat bit her forehead. Then, the world
of the present returned.

"Oh, for hell sakes," she said, thinking that it must be nearly
midday. Before pulling up camp, there were more chores to do than she
wanted to think about. The main goal of the day was to reach the Platte
and the trail where, if her wagon broke down, help might come along.
But, then, help may come and, if it did, she may not like it. People
could bring trouble because life was fragile in nature's rolling grasslands where tooth and nail, not sweetness and light, ruled. A second
goal was to target practice because that skill and a healthy horse were
great equalizers.

While fastening her belt, Nell glanced out the back of the wagon,
past Blondie. Resting like a family pet in the shade of the willows lay
what she had dreaded and feared all along the way—a wolf! When
diving for her gun, she rattled the pans and buckets tied to the wagon,
which spooked Blondie, who kicked and whistled to high heaven,

causing Nan to panic, butt open her cage and sprint away. Nell swore all the while it took to catch and maneuver her back inside. "Stupid goat!" Away slinked the wolf. "We've got to get out, right now," Nell told Blondie. "You guard the back, now, and I'll get us going." She hitched up Samson and The Spare, tied the pack animals behind the two horses and Blondie, and threw inside her cooking supplies along with the wood. Ready to leave, she flung a few slips of moldy buffalo meat onto the ground.

"There you are, old wolf, she called. "If that's what you're after, have it. It's all you're getting. Hope it gives you the bellyache."

Nell kicked rocks from behind the wagon's wheels, climbed onto the seat, released the brake, and snapped the reins. "Get up. One damned thing after another. Is there any rest? I'll be damned if I didn't see that thing last night. Get up." The whip cracked over the back of the lethargic Spare. Then, she called back to the wolf. "You stay away from us, hear? If I see you again, I'll plug you right between your little red eyes. I will. I can shoot. I'll plug you good." He looked exactly like the one pictured in *Grimm's Fairy Tales*. Though she had brought the book along for Jennifer, the sketches of wolves were too scary and the stories too violent to read now, when one had to live with them.

"I have to wet the ground," Jennifer said.

"Hold it, if you can. You come right up here and sit by Mama. Quick!"

For miles, she concentrated on putting distance between them and the wolf. Even when Jennifer cried that she was "wetting the wagon," Nell pushed on. She pushed on after Jennifer asked, "Did we eat yet" and did not stop to rest the mules, though their sides glistened with sweat and foam dribbled from their mouths. "We'll stop on some level spot, where I can see anything that comes along," she told her daughter when she complained of hunger again. "We'll stop now," she decided upon realizing that she had gone off without wearing her hat and gloves and Jennifer's cheeks flushed without her bonnet to protect them. "I've ruined our complexions, sure. Oh, my hands! They look more and more like those of a poor settler woman. Quick, Jenny, hand me my gloves." With Cutter's binocular, Nell scoped the area. There was nothing but green, buffalo grass, and the blue, blue sky with fluffy clouds circling the horizon like a ring of white horses.

Since all was clear, Nell climbed down from the wagon into a patch of wild strawberries at the peak of their ripeness! "Yah, ha," she called out. They had stained the wheels and all the animals' hooves a bright pink. They squished under her feet, causing her to lose her balance and she didn't mind the fall, for it took her closer to the delicious fruit. Little Jenny found great pleasure in the new experience. At first, they picked and ate on the spot, but later, they gathered some for breakfast, which they relished with Nan's milk, honey, and some crude pan bread, which Nell thought would come out exactly like Mrs. Suffix' delicious biscuits. "If I hadn't let her yeast die, you'd like them better," she told Jennifer, who turned up her nose at the "smelly old buffalo fat" her mother used to fry them. After eating their fill, Nell simmered the fruit with sugar and poured it in jars, which the voracious men had left empty.

Having a belly filled with fresh fruit lifted Nell's spirits, and she felt even more contented when she took the time to practice with her rifle. "You sit on your blanky, and watch those old bones, over there. Yell out if I hit one, will you? And stay back. This is dangerous. The sound will keep the wolves away."

Jennifer clapped and giggled when the first shot hit the ground a great distance behind and to the left of the bones. Just like her father! Nell reloaded and fired another charge. Dirt sprayed several feet in front of the target. Again, Jennifer delighted in the miss.

"What's so funny?"

"Your eyes and mouth," Jennifer said. "You stick your bum out like this." She mimed her mother's shooting posture.

"Mind your manners," Nell smiled. She loaded again, powder first, patch next and ball last. With the starter, she pressed the ball into the barrel, and then she threw the rod into it several times. When the rod bounced off the ball, she placed the cap on the nipple, aimed and pulled. This time, a bone flew into the air. "One hit!" Nell called out to Jennifer, and they both jumped in delight. The bead, at the end of the barrel, she concluded, must fill the u-shaped notch, totally and precisely, but the farther away the target, the higher she must aim. Now, with an abundance of ammunition, it was possible to learn the rifle and become a dead shot.

"I stood up straight that time, didn't I?"

"Yes, Mama." Jennifer's eyes sparkled and she hid a grin behind her hand. "You got it!" She threw her head back and her laughter civilized the prairie. Nell hoped to remember the beautiful sound and recorded it in her memory forever.

She also fired both of the guide's muskets. Being Revolutionary models, they felt too long and troublesome when compared to the Hawkin. But shooting them wasn't as frightening as she had imagined. "When we get to The Valley, I don't want you to tell anyone about my shooting. Hear? It's not a bit ladylike and I prefer leaving it to the menfolk." On the other hand, Nell liked the adventure in it.

"I love you, Mama," Jennifer said. "You're my baby." For the first time, she initiated the words, and Nell wondered what must have been going through her little head. Was it possible that she translated her mother's learning to fire the rifles into an expression of love? Could one so young understand this? No matter what she thought, Nell must protect her. They must move farther out of the wolf's territory as soon as possible.

Once again, Nell read the shadows on the grass and pointed her team to the north. After bumping along for a distance, her back and bottom ached, so she and Jennifer walked hand-in-hand leading the team for a time. They came upon some chicken-like birds pecking for seeds beneath a stand of sunflowers, and, to Nell's surprise, she was able to shoot one. They inspected the beautiful, but lifeless, little animal, barred in buff, white and brown. Its head, topped with tufts of feathers, looked from a distance like horns. A bright orange sac grew on each side of its head. She regretted stealing the life of so lovely a creature until she bit into its sweet, tender breast at their midday meal.

In the early afternoon, the animals quickened their pace, having smelled the Platte. It stood out from the rolling plains because willows and other growth lined its banks. Knowing that the mules sensed it more strongly than she, she gave them the reins, and presently, they halted at its bank. "Oh, my land!" On the opposite bank, stood a woman! From the look of her, she must have been fat as a roasting duck, and she seemed to teeter at the river's edge as if she might throw herself into the rushing water. "Hello. Hello over there," Nell called out. She and Jennifer nearly screamed out their lungs before the woman, dressed all in black, waved and called to them. Presently, a whole lot of men, women, and children gathered around her. Feeling like vagabonds, just returned home after a long journey, Nell and Jennifer joined hands and "stepped off a little jig."

"Hello," the people called in one universal shout, and something like, "Are you well?"

Knowing they couldn't hear over the spring rush of the river, Nell slipped off her top shirt and waved it for a distress signal. Not reading it as such, the people waved back. It was just as well because nobody could have crossed the deep torrent, at that spot, anyway.

28

WOLF

(Diary)   *June 10, 1849*

Shot antelope today. Meat tastes wild but will serve us well. Old Wolf follows us day after day. Dying from a tight rope around neck. Picked wild peas, small and bitter, but tasty in stew. Crave cherry pie and a tub bath.

I cannot explain how I miss people, an exchange of smiles, a kind word or a gentle touch. Let me never take for granted an understanding nod or a cup of tea someone has prepared for me. A woman had better avoid crossing alone if she can't stand her own company. Jenny gets into trouble.

The routine, which Nell established, was boring and repetitious on most days, but it promoted a happy and effective travel experience because it fit Nell and Jennifer's needs and every animal's as well. The first task of watering and staking the animals began at dawn. Then, came building of a campfire, eating a simple breakfast, usually of boiled cracked wheat or oats topped with Nan's milk and honey, with strawberry syrup or with molasses, biscuits and lumpy Dick gravy made from smoked buffalo or even an occasional nest of bird eggs and dry crackers, which Ruby had packaged two months earlier. While preparing the main meal of the day, usually stew, soup, boiled vegetables, beans and rice, or the catch of the day, Nell dressed Jennifer, milked Nan and greased the Ark's wheels. Sometimes, when crossing through mud or water, she gave them a long soaking so the wood did not shrink and allow the iron rim to break away. By that time, the animals having grazed, they traveled, staying abreast of the group across the river and giving Nell a sense of community, though it was a false sense. To avoid the ups and downs, the sludge, the vegetation, the outlets or meanderings of the riverside, they usually traveled approximately a half-mile south of it.

In the heat of the afternoon, Nell allowed ample time for resting, eating and drinking. Then, they rolled on until late afternoon when they turned back to the Platte for an evening of chores, reading, washing and mending clothing, target practicing, journal-writing, or singing and reciting rhymes from *Mother Goose Melody* around the campfire. Jennifer found much pleasure in hearing "Hey, Diddle, Diddle," "Baa, Baa, Black Sheep," and "Old Mother Hubbard" every night until she could repeat them. Before sunset, Nell always went to the river's edge to wave to the woman on the other side. On Sunday, they rested. Following the lead of the group on the northern side, Nell found that, in the long run, their moderate but steady pace added enjoyment to the trip and endurance to the team.

One day they overtook three wagons. The group was bound for the Oregon territory, their leader said, and asked Nell if she wanted to join them, being alone as she was. However, Nell surprised herself when she assessed the situation and refused. For one thing, oxen pulled their heavily-loaded wagons, and oxen moved at the slow pace of a person walking. For another, their children numbered fifteen, or more. Like a school of fish, they darted and dashed about so often that one could never get an accurate count. For still another reason, both humans and animals appeared gaunt and worn, especially the women. Even though the four men, who headed the group, might be of use if her wagon broke down, she opted to avoid their obvious problems.

In the decision-making, Nell realized that she treasured her privacy and the quiet beauty of the prairie. She took pride in managing on her own. If she felt tired, she rested; if Jennifer wanted food, they stopped to eat; if they bathed, nobody watched; and no one devoured their carefully planned store of food. She camped wherever she wanted to camp, and sang as loudly as she felt like singing. Besides, Fort Laramie appeared to be no more than a week or two away, and she liked the idea of joining the well-prepared Mormons for the remainder of the journey. She told the Oregon-bound group that she must move ahead and would try not to make too much dust in the passing.

Nell felt even more certain of her decision when she and Jennifer led the saddle horses to the river's edge for their nightly drink and discovered the woman in black waving from the other side. "Hello there. Hello," Nell called and waved her hat. "See. I told you. We're not alone in the world," she remarked to Jennifer. As was her habit, she rubbed the soft leather pouch around her neck.

A school of buffalo fish flipped in the slough where the horses drank. It didn't take Nell long to locate a pole and some hooks. She had merely to reach to the nearest willow for her bait. "I'm sorry I have to do this," she told a fat, greenish-brown grasshopper, which spat tobacco at her when she passed the sharp hook through his thorax. "As Mr. Darwin said, it's survival of the fittest, and we're hungry."

She lowered the insect into the muddy water where it swam furiously until a wide mouth snapped over it. "We got one, we got one," Jennifer screamed.

"Oh, it's a beauty, Jennifer." Nell held it up to show the woman across the river.

"We got one," she called, and the woman clapped her hands in exaggerated movements. To put the slippery creature out of its misery, Nell hit its head on a rock. Instantly, it perished. With Cutter's great knife, she was about to slice off the head, but the bulging and already filming eyes gave rise to visions of Moses' eyes after his death. Nell lost her breath, at the memory, and would have lost her greasy buffalo biscuits if she had not blinked away the vision and concentrated on the fish.

Then, Jennifer held the pole. Presently, her line shook. At that, Jennifer dropped the pole and scampered up the bank as fast as her fat, little legs would carry her. The woman across the river threw her hands into the air, and her light laughter carried to Nell's ears on a gust of wind like the seeds of a milkweed. Nell wondered what prompted the woman to stand at the river's edge, to separate herself from her own companions, to wear Sunday black every day of the week. Did she stand there pondering over some personal misery? Was she concerned that the two of them traveled alone or that they may be in distress? Or, did she stand there because Providence dictated that she should. Maybe, she was a result of Tom's prayers. One never knew answers to the mysteries of life or what motives drove others. Nell knew only that the woman's presence blessed her life. She also knew that night would soon overtake them and that she had not yet practiced shooting.

They waved to the woman and began their ascent up the steep riverbank with their fish.

"Wolf," Jennifer pointed ahead.

"Hell fire!" A wolf stood in full view at the brink of the bank directly in their path. His golden-brown eyes lay heavily within a white mask, etched in black. He appeared extremely thin, almost emaciated, though a wide jaw and a plentitude of grizzled hair about his head and neck rendered him the honest expression of a faithful dog.

"Come, boy," Jennifer said.

The wolf lowered his head and crouched in submission. The sound he made was neither a growl nor a howl nor any other sound one would expect from a wolf, but rather the raspy snore of labored breathing, which rattled less after he retched. Nell would have believed he was wounded or rabid if it had not been that a short length of rope dangled from his neck.

"Shoo. Go on. Get," Nell shrieked. The wolf yelped as if he had been struck and slinked out of sight. Nell pulled Jennifer behind the fragile protection of a willow. She unsheathed Cutter's dreadful knife. "Oh, the rifle, the rifle! Why didn't I bring the rifle?" Never again would she find herself more than one step away from it. How foolish could she be?

Nell waited in silence for her legs to cease quivering. Then, after what seemed like a long time, she inched her way up over the bank, holding Jennifer's hand behind her and the Bowie knife at arm's length in front. The wolf had disappeared, but she immediately made preparations for his return. "I've got to shoot him," she said, loading her Hawkin. "I'll be damned if he's going to eat our fish." With the gun and Blondie as weapons, she and Jennifer retrieved their catch. They heaped chips onto the smoldering fire to establish a right to the area and frighten the wolf away. "I have an idea," she told her child. "What would you think if we built a grass woman? She might scare off that old wolf and all the wild things at night so we can sleep without worry."

"And she can be my Ruby," Jennifer clapped.

For the core, Nell made a cross from Cutter's shovel and a walking stick. A hard cake of scorched pan bread, topped with her old misshapen sunbonnet, made a respectable head. With grass, they overstuffed a dress, which Nell had torn early on by walking through weeds and bushes and had stained in the terrible Iowa mud. She used the overcoat, which she never wore anymore, and tied a white scarf to the neck, which occasionally flapped, adding life to the figure.

When Nell stood it up, Blondie's eyes rolled back in her head. She yanked her lariat pin out of the ground and bolted so far away that Nell had to saddle and ride astride The Broomtail in order to catch her.

"Did you see that?" Nell laughed. "Ruby must be really scary. That old wolf won't come around now. Did you see a rope around his neck?"

"Will wolf hurt us?"

"We don't know what wild animals will do. He's not tame like a dog. If he hangs around again, I'll have to shoot him. Alone as we are, we can't risk anything." Nell lightly greased the rifles with beeswax and loaded them for the night. No wolf appeared, neither that night nor the next day. Now, however, wherever Nell went, whether it was to wade in the cool water of a creek, to stake out *Ruby*, or to wave to the woman standing on the opposite bank, she carried the Hawkin or kept it within arm's reach. It lay beside her plate while they ate buffalo fish, and it rested under her toe as she drove westward. She hoped never again to confront the scrawny wolf.

Three days after the wolf had blocked their path, Nell parted the canvas covering with the barrel of her rifle. Dawn was a time of feeding for all prairie animals, and one never knew what might appear near the camp; her best hope, however, was that the old prowling wolf would lurk into camp again. Having practiced shooting for days, her aim was accurate, and she would not be made to tremble now.

Instead of the canine, she spotted a small herd of prong-horned antelope. They were spectacularly marked to look, from a distance, like a band of braves painted for war. "Meat," she thought, now tired of slough fish day after day. With head held high, ears pointed forward, and front hooves stomping the ground, they curiously gazed at *Old Ruby*. Like steel to a magnet, the occasional movement of the white scarf drew them closer and closer.

Quietly, Nell capped the nipple and cocked the firing mechanism. She rested the barrel on the wagon's edge for stability and sighted between two distinctive white bars, which blazed boldly across the neck and chest of a buck. "To hit the mark," she whispered, "I must first believe I can. I must see it fall dead before I pull the trigger." Bang! The shot roared inside the confines of the wagon. The animal dropped. With wide horizontal leaps, the rest of the herd bounded away, their legs moving in a blur and their powder-puff rumps disappearing over a swell in seconds.

"I don't believe it. I got one," Nell exclaimed. She apologized to Jennifer, who cried after being startled from a deep sleep.

"Don't do that," Jennifer scolded.

Nell lay the gun aside to rock her darling and pet her silken locks. "Mama had to do it to kill that antelope. I'll try not to frighten you again. But, see out there. We have meat! If the family could see me now! Tom won't believe it, when I tell him. I know he won't. Let's go. We have to make certain it isn't suffering."

The beautifully marked animal lay where it fell.

"I got him. Look here," Nell pointed to a bleeding hole between the two white bars where she had aimed. "He's smaller than he looks at a distance, weighs less than I do."

"Are we going to eat him?" Jennifer asked with a worried expression.

"Yes. They're good. You'll see. There will be plenty of meat for this day and for days to come. We'll have a stew first. Yum." Nell cut the front and hindquarters from the animal, and, with some remorse, left the remainder for the turkey vultures, which already circled overhead.

The scavengers had very little opportunity to eat, however, because not long after Nell parted with her prized cuts, the wolf with the rope about its neck slouched from a patch of tall grass and chased them away. Nell nearly shot him; indeed, she had him in her sight, but something about him froze her finger upon the trigger. He had done nothing to them. On the brink of starvation, he merely needed food.

Though Nell went about the business of gathering wild peas, digging some of the largest prairie onions she had ever seen, and peeling potatoes in preparation for the stew, the wolf never glanced her way. Intently, he gnawed at the antelope's neck. Even at a distance, she heard his labored breathing, and when he seemed overcome by the exertion of chewing, he fell asleep in the open beside the carcass.

Nell regretted that she had no way to cut the rope. A small movement of her hand, a minute action from a fellow creature, could refill his cup of life, much as Rising Sun had revived her drained spirit. But, self-preservation prevented her. While the stew boiled, she watched him and speculated if he had been, at some time, a wild pet. Say that over a year ago someone came across a wolf's den. Say that someone stole a cub from the den to entertain their children. They fed him on cow's milk and tiny scraps of leftover meat until his little stomach bulged. They stroked him and reveled in his awkward play.

But, the wolf grew. Say that he did not like being left alone at night, tied to the wagon's wheel, so he gnawed the rope and ran away. He joined a pack of other wolves, but as he grew the rope tightened about his neck. It stifled his breathing, preventing him from running swiftly, an essential for survival. He could not devour his meat as quickly as the others and grew weak. Sensing that he was an impotent hunter, they nipped at him and drove him from the pack to fend for himself.

Say that, last week, he was drawn to Nell's campfire when she boiled buffalo meat. Seeing her and Jennifer, he remembered the days when people fed him and played with him. He ate the leftover meat she threw him and followed for more because his belly ached.

Nell wished to help him, but she chose not to compromise her goal to reach Tom. Judging from the slow and seemingly painful manner in which the pitiful creature ate, the antelope could last him a week and she believed they would leave him behind. Once and for all, they would be rid of him.

Except, they were not rid of him. Two days later, the same poor wolf appeared again. This time, Jennifer and Nell were enjoying a midday rest on the cool, hard soil near the riverbank. Sitting on a saddle blanket, Nell wrote in her diary, and Jennifer wandered through some short grass after butterflies. Suddenly, Samson whinnied and reared. Blondie and the others perked their ears, and Nell grabbed her rifle. Jennifer's outstretched hand reached in the direction of the wolf!

"No, Jenny. No," Nell called. "Quick, run to me." With her child hanging at her neck, Nell raised the rifle, caught the wolf in her sight, and would have fired to put him out of his misery . . . except that she remembered his gentle, golden eyes.

"I'll take care of you, Mama," Jenny said. "Are we scared?"

"Why, no. I can kill that wolf, whenever I want to. It's easy to kill, but we choose not to, don't we? We can make it. I can hit what I aim to hit, I can feed us and look after the animals. I know which direction to go without studying the shadows on the grass."

That night after dinner, Nell carried her primed Hawkin when she poured the leftover stew on the ground in the darkness beyond the reach of the campfire's glow. "Old wolf will like it," she told Jennifer. "It will go down easy." She rinsed their dishes and ladled water into her empty cast iron pot to soak it overnight. Then she said, "Let's count the stars."

29

FOR YOUR OWN GOOD

(Diary)   *June 24, 1849*

Being alone, I have occupied myself with every duty of trail life, and lacked the spirit to record my travels. Now, I have developed a routine, I shall take time, knowing I control the pace of this journey.

Wolf has given us aid and comfort. I had only to watch him to know when a party of Shoshone approached our camp. They filched my horses. We have begun our move into civilization, where a wolf's wild ways will not be toler-ated. Off I chased him, for his own good.

For more than a week, the wolf trailed the Ark. During the day, he kept a great distance behind, and in the night he avoided encroachment into the glow of the fire's light, which amounted to a radius of about seventy feet. However, if meat were frying, he warily inched in closer and licked his chops for any scrap, which Nell might throw his way. Surprisingly, he devoured every type of human food.

One day, however, he became extraordinarily bold, even protec-tive. Having pulled up to rest from the afternoon heat and to allow The Blue to relax, for she seemed extremely anxious, Nell heard Wolf's unearthly growl immediately outside the wagon. She sprang from her cot to scope the landscape. Nothing unusual. Still, the thick fur on his neck bristled, his black nose raised to sniff the air, and a broken howl cleared his taut throat.

"What's out there, Wolf? What is it?" He snarled. Then, he rushed forward in an attack display. Stiffly, he moved toward her in a sideward motion. The antic would have tickled Nell if she had not been frightened of him. To scare him away, she banged on a kettle with a wooden spoon; instead of running, he backed closer. "Go on, get," she told him. "Go mind your own business."

The pounding of hooves trembled on the branches of a sagebrush and in Nell's breast. Then, an instant later, a small party of Indians on horseback flooded over a hill. Nell climbed onto the tailgate and lifted the quilt where the muskets lay ready. With trembling hands, she capped them. She pulled Jenny's thumb from her mouth and shook her. "Somebody's here. Wake up." With her child in arms, she retrieved her primed Hawkin from under the driver's seat, capped it, and balanced it at her side. She waited.

"Indians," she spoke. "Why me?" To her amazement, Wolf stood at her side and remained there while braves poured toward the grass woman. They flowed around Old Ruby several times, until one of them pierced her through with his lance.

"Don't hurt my Old Ruby," Jennifer called out. "Dumb. Stupid."

The Indians galloped to where Nell, Jennifer and Wolf clustered and pooled around them. Wolf growled ferociously at the savages, an ill-kept, rowdy lot dressed partially in white folk's clothing. When they raised their weapons and cawed like crows, Wolf arched his back and tried to nip the heel of one horse. Its rider ignored the threat but examined the wagon. When he rummaged inside through Nell's belongings, she hated him for it. The disrespectful fellow tossed a sack of corn meal out of the back of the wagon and lifted it onto his pony. Thief! Apparently, he had missed the two primed and capped muskets, hidden in the rear. Searching for food and men, Nell thought.

A stout, middle-aged brave with feathers in his braided hair and mother-of-pearl buttons, like those in her sewing kit, dangling from his hare pipe breastplate, slipped from his horse and advanced. Wolf took a stance directly in front of Nell, the tip of his fluffy, short tail brushing her leg. "What is this, Wolf?" she asked. "Will you stand by me now?" When he turned to glance up at her with a pair of gorgeous golden-brown eyes edged in black, Nell thought he looked terribly innocent, for a wolf.

"Shoshone," the stout fellow slammed his fist into his breastplate. "Shoshone," he arrogantly said again. Wolf snarled, arched his back, and hopped sideways. The Shoshone nodded at him and stepped backward, which Nell interpreted as a sign of respect.

"Get. Get away from Mama," Jenny doubled her fist. Jerking her hand out of Nell's grip, she rushed toward the Indian and kicked a spray of sand onto his moccasins. The others whooped spiritedly. When the Indian reached out to touch Jenny's blonde curls, Nell forgot herself, screamed and pointed her rifle at his chest. He backed away.

"Come to me, Jenny," Nell tried to appear calm. "Stay next to me."

The spokesman, the one with button's from a lady's frock, tried to communicate with her; however, Nell could discern neither the meaning of his utterances nor the meager signs of his hands. She did understand, when he arched one hand over his brow and swept the horizon with the other, that he wanted the braves to search the area for white men. She understood their fear because two rode back to the hill, the highest point, where one posted himself as a sentinel. Others surveyed the area and searched nearby in the tall, arched grass. One quickly rummaged, once again, inside the wagon. When he jumped out with Nell's Linsey-Woolsey blanket and threw it over the back of his horse, Jenny lost all control. "Don't touch my blanky," she cried and broke into the most pitiful sobs. She held her breath so long she nearly toppled over from lack of air.

When an adolescent brave's wild eyes settled admiringly upon Cutter's Blue and The Broomtail, Nell knew she must act quickly; she must invent a way to dissuade him. In the face of savages, three carrying rifles, confrontation would prove useless. She must force them to admire her, to fear her, or something. Anything. Like Wolf, she would fake a show of strength and self-assurance. She would draw attention away from her horses, the most valuable commodity on the prairie, for the Indians appeared ready to confiscate them.

Out of desperation and nervousness, Nell was literally "shaking in her boots." She lost the ability to reason. "I have the magic of Merlin," were the first words that came out of her mouth. "Mrs. Nell Baker Mortenson of the State of Illinois." Taking the pouch of stones from around her neck, she held it toward them in her fist as if she were pointing a crucifix at a vampire. "Rising Sun, a, ah, gave me this pouch. It . . . it . . . it has the power to knock you off your mangy jades. Jackasses," she smiled. "It protects me." When she waved it at them, some of the braves ducked. "Ah yah, ah yah, ah eee," she chanted. "A pox upon you!"

Little Jenny's giggles sounded like Christina's, and when Nell frowned to quiet her, the Puckish child covered her hand over her mouth and giggled again. To imitate her Sioux friend's ritual, Nell stirred the dying campfire and pulled smoke toward her face with her two hands. Then, she pushed it toward the braves, who ducked again. She hopped and skipped around the campfire for those who had gathered to observe her awkward performance.

Jenny, with a huge grin across her chubby face, joined in the dance. "Jackasses," she said.

"Caw, caw," Nell called to a large raven which glided above them. When the bird answered, "caw," the Shoshone eyed it suspiciously. One brave, wearing an army jacket, scratched his head, another shook his in disbelief, and all appeared in a state of consternation. "Iey, yeh, yeh, yeh," Nell chanted. She poured a pair of stones into her palm and tossed them over the bare ground as if they were dice.

One group of Indians waved her off and rushed toward the horses. When they passed Blondie, she kicked her back legs high over their heads, brayed, "whinee-aw, ah aw," whistled and stomped. She bore her teeth at one man who reached out to touch her nose. "No, no! Don't touch my Blondie," Jenny called, her hands on her hips. Samson switched his tail, pawed the earth, and snorted in the sand in a display of aggression that he had never shown before. The Indians avoided him, but a barefooted pair of them stroked The Blue's neck and back on the right side. They knew a fine animal when they saw one. After they untied her and attempted to lead her away, Blue's eyes rolled back in her head, and the hide near the scar on her rump twitched. Nell believed she looked to her for help. The Blue whinnied, snorted and planted her stiff hooves in the sand. Frustrated and angry, Nell reached out to The Blue. They must not be allowed to steal this beautiful animal! Cutter would have wanted Tom, not an Indian, to have his horse.

Wolf gagged and slumped in exhaustion. No longer could he sustain his lavish show of strength. But, Jenny kept her bright eyes on her mother, her cheeks hot from a struggle to repress laughter, which welled up in the form of snorts through her nose.

Nell emptied the leather bag of its colored stones. Feeling a bead of perspiration trickle through her hair, she pretended to read each one. "A disease shall wipe out your entire tribe," she predicted. "All shall die."

Then, frowning at her daughter, she warned, "If you laugh, I will spank you."

Jenny did laugh. Then, like a teakettle long overdue to boil, the whole party exploded into laughter. Nell's cheeks burned. "Alright, that's it," she said returning the stones to their pouch and heaving a great sigh. "I give up. Why does everything have to be so hard? I am neither magician nor sun worshiper. I am not like you." She sank to her knees. "We are invaders in your land," she confessed. "All we need is a safe passage through."

This honesty quieted her nerves, somewhat. She drew the long line of their journey in sand, all the way from the campfire to the end of the wagon, showing their passage was very far. At the beginning, she sketched her home, a simple cabin with a daisy in front, located on the bank of the Mississippi River, a wide snake-like line. She crisscrossed the trek line with another winding line representing the Missouri River and showed hills with half circles. She drew cabins to represent the many towns through which they had passed and tepees to mean that they had met the "Sioux" and the "Pawnee." The fire of recognition shined in the brown eyes of the couple who had begun to watch her. "Nebraska," she said when drawing the meandering Platte.

She tried to render a buffalo, but it looked more like a sheep. When the second try looked like a dog, a youthful brave with the tender expression of a girl took her stick and drew one of the Great Plains giants. He returned the stick, motioned for her to draw more, and yipped to call his companions. Now, most of the braves circled around her. With a steady hand, she sketched an antelope, a fish and a prairie chicken, which they seemed to recognize. To show that two of the wagons had turned back, she erased them. Stick figures stood for Moses and Cutter. The sand that she poured over both meant that they had died. She stomped on the one she had killed. Two braves yelped. Many high peaks represented the Rockies. At the end of the line, she shaped a stick man standing by a house with a daisy in front. Then, she pointed to the west. Finished, Nell stood and faced the party, Jennifer at one side and the Hawkin at the other.

The Shoshone anxiously watched the horizon, probably for Nell's men. They were wise to worry about men, considering Nell's extra horses. Quickly, they retraced her journey from the beginning to end, pointing to the various images in the sand and arguing their meanings among themselves. Some nodded at Nell as if they approved of her; one offered her an animal tooth. But, the two barefooted braves barked in protest. One swung himself onto Broomtail's back and rode away.

When the other grabbed The Blue's mane to mount on the left side, she whirled and nearly kicked him in the head. Then, whirling again, she reared on her hind legs, and on the way to the ground, her pawing hooves struck his hip. He hit the ground, screaming in pain. Away Blue sprinted over the arid hill, her rope and two braves dangling after her.

Beyond the hill where she galloped, the wind had whipped up a dust cloud. Suddenly, it struck Nell that this could be her chance. "Tom!" she screamed. Lifting Jenny into her arms, she darted toward the hill. "Tom. Help. Shoshone," she bawled. It startled the sentry. He yelped. Hurriedly, two braves lifted the wounded man over the back of another brave's horse. Away they dashed in the direction opposite from the dust cloud. They took The Broomtail.

Exhausted, humiliated and relieved that they had escaped with their lives, Nell sank to the ground. "Holy cow. I don't believe it. I don't believe we're still alive." Light-headed, she listened for the thunder of hooves but heard only the grasshopper's clicking flight. She rested there to collect her breath and quiet her pounding heart.

"I don't believe it. Jackasses want my Blondie," Jenny stood over her mother, pursed her lips and breathed an exaggerated sigh of relief.

"We've got to hustle out of here, right now." Hurriedly, Nell staggered with Jenny to the wagon. She tied her into the back, prepared the team, gathered all belongings, and left the area. She kept the mules at a trot as long as they could take it. And, even when they couldn't, she prodded them on.

The more she separated herself from the raiding party, the more her resentment grew. First, she wept for herself. Then, she wept for The Blue, who desperately feared Indians but must have been captured by now. What gave them the right to pilfer the prized animal? Then, she wondered if they'd go easy on The Broomtail, who needed to rest when winded. Probably not. The cornmeal, she believed, was fair enough pay for passage through their land. Still, it was her cash, and they had not bargained for it. She despised them for thieving the blanket her mother and Ruby had so carefully made for her journey, but she despised, most of all, her own helplessness, the way the marauders had pilfered her self-determination, her right to say *no* and she could do nothing about it.

Making camp that night on the bank of the Platte, she despised them again for the ripping headache she had endured the entire day.

Target practicing for over an hour helped. Yet, the night seemed long.

The next morning, Nell spotted Wolf lying motionless on his side next to Old Ruby with her white scarf flapping. She feared that he had expired. With her child in hand, she moved toward him, and, hearing his labored snore, which assured her that he still lived, she sat on the grass far enough away to allow him space. "What fakers we are, Old Ruby, me and Wolf," she said. Wolf did not stir. How ridiculous she must have appeared to the Indians! Trying to act the part of the Sioux woman, who spent a lifetime listening to the legends and learning the rituals of her tribe. If these uncivilized people saw through her pretense, and they obviously had, how must she have appeared to the Mormons? To Tom? A raging wolf with no breath, a grass woman with no blood in her veins.

But, out here, the involved teachings of any doctrine seemed irrelevant. One simply tried to survive. She knew that she didn't believe in Tom's priesthood or his temple marriage. She believed neither in the spirit of the sun nor in the Methodist practice of speaking in tongues.

"What do I believe?' she asked herself. She believed in every individual's religion, in all their myths, and in their right to believe, if that's what enabled them to cope with pain. She believed in helping and in being helped. And, she did believe in a power beyond her own, a force that heard her private prayers and knew the secrets of her heart, that had given her the will to carry on after she had fallen into a well so dark and deep that climbing out seemed impossible. She believed this because somewhere at the base of her skull between instinct and reflex, a still, small voice had whispered . . . "I am with you." She believed it because the night sky was beautiful and because Scorpio stretched across the southern hemisphere to reassure her that west was west.

When Wolf strained for air and coughed, Nell's thoughts turned to him. "Poor Wolf," she remarked to Jenny. "Something has to be done or I will regret it for the rest of my life. This just isn't right." She remembered the brush of his tail across her leg and marveled at what he had done. It reminded her of her own relationship with Christina. As children, they continually pecked at one another; they fought over dresses, and with Mama out of hearing range, they called one another "slut" or "river scum." But, if one of their cousins kicked or pulled Christina's hair, heaven help the poor girl.

Nell fastened Jenny inside the safety of the wagon and told her

"Watch from here while Mama frees old Wolf." Moving cautiously to stand over him, she unsheathed Cutter's Bowie. The sharpness of it gleamed on both edges. To Nell's mind, Wolf had come to a crossroad between life and death. When he struggled for wind, she breathed deeply, in sympathy. He must be helped, she kept telling herself. Again, she filled her lungs with air and took a solid posture to summon courage to do what must be done. The knife's motion was quick and effective, but, with adrenaline pumping through Nell's veins, it seemed slow. Its sharp tip moved past the long, black-tipped hairs at the back of Wolf's neck, through the soft, white hairs of the undercoat, and under the cotton rope. It pierced through the tender hide. It lifted and sliced through the rope. Wolf yelped in pain and scrambled awkwardly to his feet, his fangs bared and sharp, even as the blade. Like a wet dog, he shook, and the blood-stained rope slipped from his neck.

"Hold on, Wolf. Hold on," Nell said while backing slowly away. "You're free."

"Hold on, old Wolf," called Little Jenny, who peeped under the wagon's canvas. Nell turned and high-tailed it to her daughter. "He's free!" she laughed. "I did it. I set him free!" It was right.

Nell thought that after the rope was removed, Wolf would leave them. Not a chance! He followed them to the end of the Platte Valley, past the magnificent Chimney Rock and into an even more arid region where decayed, castle-like formations jutted up from the level earth, where the air was so dry that Nell used her bees' wax more on her cracked lips and Jenny's nose than on the rifles. Wolf continued to follow, seeking scraps of meat or even vegetables, and steadily gaining strength. Though she and Jenny dared not go near him when he voraciously devoured his share of another antelope, he had closed the distance he kept from them to around ten feet. At night, he took to sleeping under their wagon like a guard dog with sharp ears. Though he seemed comfortable with them, he despised strangers and growled at the approach of the first white man they had seen in weeks.

"Where are you headed for, ma'am?" asked the white man disguised in the buckskin clothing of an Indian. His mule carried various animal pelts, so Nell assumed he was a trapper, left over from a bygone day.

"The Salt Lake Valley," she had to yell because Wolf barred him from approaching.

"Laramie's up this trail, a two days' ride. Where's your menfolk?"

"We got none," Nell said. If she had wanted, she might have lied . . . but she held the loaded Hawkin.

"Well, for land's sakes. You'll be needing help, I suppose." Wolf edged sideways toward him, the fur from his ears to the tip of his tail bristling. He displayed to appear larger than he was.

"Call your wolf off."

"He doesn't call." Wolf nipped at the leg of the trapper's spooked horse. It bucked and nearly threw him.

"Want me to plug him for you?" The man gained control of his horse.

"No, no. He's mine."

"Just being neighborly, ma'am," he shook his head but kept a keen eye on Wolf when he rode away. "Laramie's that-a-ways. You better kill that animal or someone will do it for you. It's dangerous."

"Hey, wait up," Nell called out. She needed to exchange a few more words with him, with anyone, but he was on his way, singing, "Oh, the biscuits and gravy my ma used to make."

They bumped along and bumped some more over the horse trail, which the man pointed out. All the while, Nell considered what he had said about Wolf's being dangerous. Before she decided what must be done, the path became increasingly more defined, turned into a wagon trail, and could finally be called a road.

When they stopped to make camp, Wolf was given his share of boiled beans and a bit of jerky, which had gone to mold. It would be the last time she served him. At dusk, when other wolves began their howling, Nell told him "Get!" She hit him on the rump with a dirt clod. Yelping and crouching, he folded his tail under his body. "Go on," she called chasing him with a long stick. "You go on, for your own good. Wolf trailed eastward on the road. In the middle of it, he lay down and the golden eyes that Nell had grown to love, flickered in the light of the setting sun. Though Jenny protested, Nell shot near him several times. "Get." Finally, after watching her for a time, he loped southward to the crest of a nearby hill. He stopped, glanced back, and then sprinted until he dropped over a ridge. Nell hoped he would be all right. Every time a wolf howled in the night, she would remember him.

30

AT LAST, PEOPLE

                                                        June 27, 1849

At last, we have come into civilization, which means that I finally bathed in a barrel, with heated water! Fort Laramie is a large structure with adobe brick walls, tall and thick. Inside are some twenty buildings—blacksmith shops, supply stores, dwellings, and even an apothecary. A person might purchase most any essential—for a price. Calico is $1 a yard! Flour $.25 a pound, a gallon of whiskey $35. Saw a horse no better than The Broomtail for $50.

Though the fort is a rough place filled with homesick soldiers, half-breeds, French and Indians, some drunken, most grizzled, and all haggling over prices, it suits me very well after being alone for so long. Oh joy, I have met the woman who waved to me evening after evening from the north side of the Platte. A Mormon. The fellowship of others pleasures me.

Driving her team up the trough of the North Platte, Nell scrutinized the numerous groups she met for a delicate face, without whiskers. Though a great variety of male characters appeared on the road, Nell saw no women. After the trapper, who wanted to shoot Old Wolf, came a few mountain men "returning to civilization" and some settlers bound for the East to gather their families and guide them to homesteads in the Oregon Territory. After them, three Crow Indians made things hot for Nell. In warpath paint and at full speed, they came in on the yell. To Nell's thinking, they coveted her mule team, burros and even her until she raised the Hawkin, that is, and pretended to converse with someone in her wagon. That and numerous companies of soldiers scouting around the entire region deterred them.

A day outside of Fort Laramie, she passed traders returning to St. Louis, after emptying their supply wagons, the largest she had seen. Six to eight mules pulled each of them. To avoid the thick clouds of dust their wheels kicked up, Nell pulled off the road and to the south a good quarter mile. There, she and Jenny counted over a hundred wagons, and would have counted more if the wagonmaster had not ridden toward her with buckskin sleeves flapping like wings on either side, looking for all the world like a heaven-sent messenger. When she told him she crossed the Platte Valley by herself, he removed his hat and saluted her with a bowed head of tangled hair. Judging from the line that separated a starkly white brow from a sweaty, weather-beaten face, removing the hat must have been a rare gesture for him. "How do, miss," he said. "Never know'd a female with so much guts."

"Did what I had to. You should have seen the antelope we shot. You should have seen . . . "

"You ain't lookin' out fer one of my men to carry ya along to Laramie, er ya?" he interrupted. "I aim to spare you one."

Nell smiled. "The rest of the way is easy. What day is this?"

"I don't rightly know, miss. "We're into June pretty good. How's the feed ahead?"

"Just ahead, adequate. Poor, a few days out. Prairie fire. You wouldn't believe it if I told you . . . "

"Need grub?" he interrupted before she was able to describe the fire, which had blown across the landscape faster than a horse could gallop. "I got cider. Now, that goes down mighty good, if yer askin' me."

"No, but thank you, just the same. What's the fort like?"

"Reg'lar. But, full of truck now, even lookin' glasses."

"How far is it?"

"A day, as the crow flies. Can't miss it."

"Are there ladies at Laramie?"

"Naw. Well, there's two big washerwomen, that be all."

"Got any in your group?"

"Shucks no. No women. None a'tall. Strikes me as mighty queer. They's a comin', though, a powerful lot of 'em in one of them there emigrant trains. Near time. Yes, near time."

He twirled his warped hat and set it home on his head. "You be one of the first this year, miss. And all by your own self, too."

"Do the emigrant trains stop at the fort?"

"Why, certain. Most want the lowdown on trails ahead. They be buyin' breadstuff, coffee, and such. Shucks, soldier boys say a bunch with females are workin' this way. Mormons, that is. Up yonder, down from t'other side. Well, if you're set on goin' it alone, ya best git at it. So long." He galloped away, never to know that his skimpy visit made her cry for joy.

She pushed her team up a bottleneck with the North and South Platte on either side. The road, like the main trail out of an anthill, crawled with increasing traffic as they approached their destination. Being more numerous now, the people never stopped to touch antennae, but merely waved their hats and yelled, their white teeth standing out on dusty, sun-baked faces.

Nell marveled at one ascent where wagon wheels had chewed two feet into the limestone. If this signaled the traffic to come, she understood why Cutter had wanted to start in the rains of late April; they would have their pick of grasses, campsites, game and firewood. The trip would be harder for latecomers who would be forced to drink one another's dust rather than the cool springs of the early season. Poor old, good old, Cutter. Life had taught him to avoid involvement, but involvement with her was his last mistake.

The next day, Jenny and Nell passed a large tent encampment of federal troops. Loudly joking and conversing, a group of soldiers congregated near the roadside. They were young, clean-shaven and handsome and wore dark blue uniforms with brass buttons and polished boots. As she drew near, four of them waved and threw their hats. They whistled and shouted, "Good day," "How do?" and "Wait up."

However, Nell paid them no regard because a distance beyond their horse corral was, wonder of all wonders, Blue. With Jenny in hand, Nell ran to her side. Her rope, which had shredded at the knot, had burned a circle completely around her neck. One side would need doctoring. Nell led her to the Ark, bridled her, and hitched her in her place at the back of the wagon.

"She yours?" asked one of the soldiers. Warily, they watched Nell recover her rifle from under her buckboard.

"We're not arguing with you," another young man said. "Nobody here can touch her."

"Who hurt her neck?"

"Not us. She was that way when she came in."

"Thieving Shoshone! I'm glad to have her back. Indians ran her off. Say, I haven't had a proper bath in months," she apologized. "Do you know where I might find one?"

"I'd sneak you one," said one fellow wearing a sword, "but it's against regulations. Are you married?"

Nell ignored his question. "Do I have to cross the river before Fort Laramie?"

"No. You're on the Oregon Trail. It's the trains on the north side that have to cross. We haul them over on our ferry for $.50 a wagon."

"How far to the fort?"

"You're lookin' at her," one pointed.

Upon approaching Fort Laramie, the subtle and melodic sounds of the prairie gave way to the discordant, clamor of people. Nell's sensitive ears heard the blast of a bugle and the clang of metal on metal, not the whisper of wind under the hawk's wing or the ripple of water at the riverbank; the barking orders of a commander and the pounding from the blacksmith shop, not the rustle of one clump of last year's yellow grass against another; three strikes of a bell denoting the hour, not the cry of a far-off coyote just before dawn; the pounding hooves and constant bellows of corralled animals, not a stomp from Samson's hoof and his comforting snort. She regretted leaving the quiet behind at the same time she anticipated the activity to come.

At the entrance of the fort, two Sioux women conversed while roasting strips of meat on sticks over a fire. Nell waved to them from her wagon, "Hello, there, hello," but they scowled and brushed her off their shoulders.

"For hell sakes," Nell grumbled. "We must be a sight for sore eyes." She tried to dust a smudge off Jenny's torn dress, and she removed her own sweat-stained hat. Her matted hair tumbled all around her face and over her shoulders when she scratched her scalp and shook it. "Greasy as a wheel hub," she grumbled. Nothing made her more cross than a dirty head. She was thinking how embarrassing it would be to meet anyone she knew when a feminine voice called, "Hello, you there!" The woman across the river! There she was, dressed in black and walking at the center of a group of women in bright skirts like the dark seed pod of a sunflower.

With Jenny in arms, Nell rushed to stand face to face with the woman, who appeared to be in her early thirties and wobbled ahead of the others to greet Nell with outstretched arms. By the time Nell joined hands with her, laughter had overcome both of them.

"I thought y . . . you . . . you were a boy," the woman stuttered, her voice small and high like that of a child. "Until just now, I . . . I believed you were a boy, alone with his little sister."

"And, I thought you were . . . " Nell did not want to say *fat as a Christmas goose* for the woman in black was actually tall and willowy as a blade of grass, a trifle thin and delicate, but great with child. The tight gathering of her garment draped over her from the yoke down like a dark tent.

"I'm Sister G . . . Gl . . . Glady Chatterley," she stuttered. She sported blue eyes lined with thick lashes under brows to envy. Her lips curved upward whether she smiled or not, and she spoke with an educated English accent which suggested a recent convert. Nell liked her immediately.

"Just us," Nell answered.

"Ah" was all Mrs. Chatterley could say, and after placing long, artistic fingers over her heart, "ah" again. "You alone with a . . . a . . . all these animals?" she gasped. The other women, who stood in a ring about her, acknowledged Nell, but did not shake hands. Because of her rag-tag appearance, Nell did not blame them. Enthusiastic to see the fort after plodding over the treeless, hot prairie, the women left with their men. However, Glady stayed. When she discovered that Jenny and Nell were also traveling to the Valley, she shrieked with elation. "Splendid! You must join us . . . us for the remainder of your crossing, if you would like. Come. I'll ride with you to our camp for a visit with Bishop Brown. Devout, I . . . I . . . assure you, and an ex . . . exp . . . experienced wagon master." Though Glady's voice reflected carefree childhood, the dark circles under her eyes and the worry lines between them indicated that she was, indeed, an adult, who had traveled far.

A mile from the fort, on the bank of the Laramie River, the Mormon encampment appeared like a tranquil village. Fifty or sixty wagons circled around a herd of grazing oxen, horses, mules, goats and milk cows. Guards with rifles stood watch, and everything appeared uncluttered and orderly.

Immediately, Glady located Bishop Moot Brown, a man of fifty or so with the furrowed brow of one who takes on the worries of others. "These are the p . . . pair we located across the river," Glady said.

"Remember, I p . . . p . . . point . . . pointed them out to you weeks ago . . . Mormons. She'd like to travel with us to the Great Basin."

He offered his hand, but Nell did not take it, just then. She remembered her embarrassing pretense with the Shoshone and her vow never again to be untrue to herself or others. "I am not Mormon." There, she said it, come what may. She shook his hand.

"Oh, I see. Well, I'll declare," he said as if he had come upon a poor urchin, dying of thirst. "I hope someone can teach you the gospel."

"Already been taught. I lived in Nauvoo with my husband for more than a year. Aside from that, if you wouldn't mind, I'd like to join your group."

"Where is your man? I want a word with him." The bishop ran a knotted hand over his perspiring forehead.

"She's alone, p . . . p . . . poor girl. Her husband's in the Valley." Glady rubbed a tender hand across Nell's shoulders, which caused Nell's lip to tremble under the strain of self-pity.

"Don't tell me that you, u-hum, acting on your own behalf, wheeled your wagon across the plains alone!" the Bishop said in alarm.

"Well, not all alone. For some time, we traveled with others. Then, for three weeks, give or take a few days, it was just us . . . and a . . . wolf."

"What are you saying, sister? I've no time for, u-hum, joshing."

"I'm not joshing," Nell answered, her hand resting on her bear knife. "When I say *wolf*, I mean *wolf*."

"I reckon you do, begging your pardon, sister. Can you shoot that rifle?"

"I can," Nell said.

"She can," Jenny frowned. "We kill cantaloupe."

"You say your husband's already in the Valley? Then, I reckon, I'll know him. I wintered over there this past year. Who is he?"

"Tom Mortenson."

"Land a Goshen, sister," he smiled and again shook her hand, this time longer and harder, with the respect he would give to another man. "God bless you, sister. You're welcome. I'll look after you myself, u-hum, if you need looking after. Why, I'd carry you in my arms right to his front door, if that's what you had in mind. Tom's wife! If that don't beat all! Didn't know he had a wife." Then, seeing her face drop, he added, "A-hum. One man doesn't learn much about another man's private life when a loaf of bread is all that stands between him and the wolf, so to speak. That first year, we acted with precious few words. And, the second, too. But, praise the Lord, Brother Mortenson kept the lot of us from starvation, he being one of a handful to harvest grain. Some of us boys didn't irrigate. Most of us planted too early and got froze out. You know how it is; when your bellybutton's gnawing away at your backbone, you plant, early or not." He yelled to a guard, "Come, get this wagon. Pull her in between the Chatterley's and mine. Tend to the animals, if you would. This is Brother Tom Mortenson's wife. Praise the Lord." Rushing to follow the order, the men said "How do?" and "Good day, Sister Mortenson." They tipped their hats as if they had known her for years.

Nell, overcome by the sudden realization that she was no longer alone, felt light as a soap bubble and brushed away a tear, which she hoped no one saw.

"I can't thank you enough," she said.

Moot Brown gave her Hawkin the once over and grinned. "It appears that Brother Mortenson has got his work cut out for him, so to speak. We're glad to have you with us, though. The Lord works in mysterious ways, he does." He shook his head and turned to shout, "Over there, boys. Grab that goat." Nan, being unlocked from her cage, broke and ran. "Goats! They're more trouble than they're worth," Brother Brown said. "I always hated goats." Since no one chased after the animal, he turned to the task himself. "Quite a woman," he said, hastening away. Then, he halted in his tracks. "What became of your group? What made you decide to go it alone?" Without waiting for an answer, he chased after Nell's little, spotted nanny. The next time someone asked these questions, she must be prepared to answer.

It had been difficult to admit that she was not a true believer, but to confess to killing a man—to tell it all as it was and be completely straightforward, that was another matter. Orrin Rockwell, Moses, and Cutter were types who took life, not her. Mothers were not supposed to destroy life; they created and nurtured it. Revealing the truth could be a real problem for Tom, being the straight arrow that he was. And, Jenny? She must never have to explain to anyone why her mother had killed. No, anyone who truly wanted to keep a secret, especially one that invited gossip, should bury the key to locked lips. It was enough that Rising Sun would tell her children and they would tell their grand-children.

"Come with me, my d . . . dear," Glady placed her petite arm through Nell's. Ever so slightly, the woman's nostrils flared, and Nell sniffed the sleeve of her torn, soiled blouse. "You'll have your bath, Sister Nell, but first let me show you my wagon. There's ample room for three, if you and Jenny would like to r . . . r . . . ride with me. Or, I can ride with you, if you p . . . pre . . . prefer, but you simply must tell me of your adventures. Elder Brown's boy can drive one of our outfits. He's exceptional with draft animals."

"I'd like to drive my own mules, if it's all the same with you. Ride with us. It's been a long time since I had a proper conversation."

"I suppose so. What happened . . . happened to your wagon train?"

"It's a long story, too long to go over now. Suddenly, I'm weary." Oh, how she longed to tell Glady. She needed to hear a friend say that she had done right to kill Moses, that she had no other choice, that any woman would have pushed the knife into his back. But, for the rest of her life, she also needed to bear the burden of her own guilt.

"We have p . . . plent . . . plenty . . . plenty of time to reveal everything while we're bumping along in the month ahead," Glady said. Like Moot Brown, she was curious and would not let Nell rest until the unfinished story of the missing group had been revealed.

Glady owned a large and well-equipped wagon, literally bulging with quality provisions and equipment. Nell first noticed a cast iron pot-bellied stove.

"My husband and I, God rest his soul, planned to install this in our chamber to keep warm in the winter."

"My sister-in-law carried one to the valley just like it. I hope it made the trip."

"L . . . look here," Glady said, lifting the lid of one leather-covered trunk. "I've got seeds enough to grow vegetables for every Mormon in Zion. I've got lanterns, spices, gunpowder, calico and a scrub board. See that churn? Before I married, I won a blue ribbon for churning butter f . . . faster than any woman in Lancashire. And, notice where I've wrapped my flo-blue China inside our clothing, a setting for ten, all the way from jolly old England. So far, m . . . m . . . merely one piece has cracked. You can't imagine what I've been through to p . . . p . . . protect . . . protect it. Each time we move, I p . . . p . . . pared down most of my cherished treasures to give p . . . place to more necessary articles, but these go where I go, no matter what. Oh, forgive me, I must raise my feet for a bit." Glady closed the trunk and reclined upon it, her belly curving gracefully above her like one of the hills to the west.

"You say you're not Mormon. How do you p . . . pl . . . pl . . . plan to live with all of us in the Valley? I mean, won't you feel a bit out of place?"

"I don't plan to live there for more than a year, maybe two. The reason I've come all this way is to talk some sense into my husband's head. Pardon me. I don't mean to offend you, but you have to admit that Mormon theology is as pompous as that of any other denomination."

Nell was a bit blunt, but, after all she had been through, she did not feel a need to mince words. "I have a hard time believing that yours is the only true church on the planet, considering that Catholics and a whole lot of others profess the same thing. Considering that most churches follow the Golden Rule . . . A steady diet of golden plates and priesthood keys is harder to digest than jerky, begging your pardon."

"I don't m . . . mind," Glady smiled.

"I'll get Tom to take me back to Quincy, where I came from, and he'll work in my father's bank. Two years from now, after the mobs have broken up, we'll be home. You'll see." Nell repeated the old words she had spoken to her family last April and to Cutter along the way; but now, they sounded as hollow as an old burned out tree stump. What rang true was, *I do love this people* and *this journey is too damned long to do twice.*

"Your Tom m . . . , pardon me, m . . . must be devout. How do you manage?"

"Oh, he loves his religion, but he loves me too. I'll change him." The words seemed naive and foreign, as if she had memorized them from a play. "He'll leave behind his fanatical ways, and it won't matter to him if I believe or not." She scowled and rethought the lines she had memorized from a former life.

Now, she understood that trying to change nature was a useless craft. Nan was Nan and no one could stop her from sprinting away if she believed it was time to travel in the confines of her cage. Blondie could be counted on to nip Samson if he pulled beyond her ability, a meadowlark's warble never changed, and a wolf could never be a dog. Why, after sacrificing to build the new Zion, would Tom suddenly change and return to a state that robbed him of his religious freedom? And, why, if she loved him for who he was, would she want him to return? "Oh, Glady," she exclaimed, "I'd give my life to have him hold me again." Now, this was exaggerated, but true, just the same.

"Elder Brown t . . . t . . . told me we'll spend less than a month more on these miserable, jarring byways, and then, glory be to God, we'll be home. Your Tom will hold, hold you again."

"And, you'll have your baby."

"Yes . . . yes. I'm miserable, and more so everyday. Will this child ever come?"

"If I know Tom, and he's a builder, you know, he'll have a house all ready for us. A bustle oven will blaze at the rear of the house in our main room to heat, boil and bake. Our parlor will be in front of that with two bedrooms on the side. I'll have a very large one with a dressing table and a closet with doors for clothing. Neither he nor I brought a chest of drawers, though," she said, and remembered when Mrs. Suffix' drawers tumbled down the hill. "But, Tom can build one, maybe he already has, to surprise me. First thing, I'll plant my apple trees in the back of the lot. Tom will have to fence out all these animals. Then, I'll get me a big yellow cat that will lie at my feet while I sip tea beside the fire. And Tom will be there in a rocker with Jenny asleep in his arms. A home, at last! Oh, how I dream of it."

"Hum," Glady looked puzzled. "Your cot . . . cot . . . cottage sounds too adorable to leave."

A man's boots stood on the floor of the wagon beside a flintlock. "Where's your husband," Nell asked but wished her mouth had not gotten ahead of her brain, for she recalled Glady's saying, 'God rest his soul.'

"Willard . . . he drowned in the Platte shortly b . . . b . . . before I first saw the two of you. It all happened after the elders decided we should cross the Platte. When the men took the last wagon, on the Cutter, that's the company's flatboat, Willard, he and his horse slipped overboard and went under in the swollen torrent. His horse was washed onto the bank a mile or two downstream, b . . . b . . . but I never saw my dear husband again."

"I'm sorry."

"That's why I stood by the river at every opportunity . . . to d . . . dis . . . discover, discover his body for a proper burial, but we never found him. My Will, he was an . . . honest man, Sister Nell, a master barrelmaker." Glady said all this matter-of-factly, as if Willard had been another woman's husband. This puzzled Nell nearly as much as her own comments about changing Tom and wanting a lovely home even though she planned to return to the Mississippi Valley.

"A barrelmaker, was he? Now I know how you afford the mahogany clock and that dress from Paris. One barrel cost me twenty-five dollars at Winter Quarters!"

"That's reasonable, Nell. Did you know that Willard spent m . . . m . . . m . . . more time in his apprenticeship than a doctor has to? I was proud to be his wife."

"Yes. And the craft pays more, with all the demand for a fast one."

"Will's were as fast as any. The process to build one takes days. Even a tight one will leak, though, if you don't k . . . keep it wet."

"Yah, I know about wet," Nell said. Their talk turned to less personal matters, and Glady took Nell and Jenny for a real tub bath. Within a stand of cottonwoods, the Mormons had hung blankets for privacy and had built fires under large pots to heat water. Wooden barrels and buckets cluttered the area.

Nell bathed Jenny first; then, she indulged herself. While she washed her hair and scrubbed her back with a lathered sponge, her newfound friend poured small amounts of boiling water into the tub, for comfort. "You can't imagine how it feels to be treated like a woman again, having men to take charge of the animals and repair of the wagon, being in company at night. I almost forgot." Nell rewarded herself by trading her Kentucky jeans for her green cotton dress, the one she wore when Tom preached to her for the first time. She felt modest, held her hands in her lap and kept her legs together at the campfire that evening when all the folks lounged about singing:

> "Come, come ye Saints,
> No toil nor labor fear;
> But with joy, wend your way.
> Though hard to you this journey may appear,
> Grace shall be as your day."

Elder Brown's wife motioned for Nell, Jenny and Glady to sit beside her on a patched quilt, which was bright as autumn leaves strewn under a tree. She asked them to sit there even though the blanket was already crowded. "The more, the merrier," Sister Brown told Nell, clearing a space. At her breast, a baby girl with raven-black hair, like her own, suckled. The strong arm of her husband hung upon her shoulder, and the half-grown boy called Jacob nestled his head against her back. He was gangly with a gentle face like his father's. Clearly, they all adored Lily Brown, the archetype Mother. She smiled at Nell several times as if wanting to strike up a conversation.

"How old is the baby?" Nell finally asked.

"Six months." She licked a finger and twirled a fine curl on top of the tiny head. How old is your Jenny?"

"Three," the toddler held up three fingers.

"My husband, here, I'm Lily May, but they call me Lily, tells me you have been going it alone. How in the world did you manage?" Though middle age had robbed her of a slender waist and had given her a wide, strong back, she kept a complexion unequaled by any of the younger women. She might have been one of the dark ladies in Edgar Allan Poe's works, her faultless skin rivaling the purest ivory. Her eyes suggested cracked, blue glass.

"How did you manage, u-hum, to wend your way alone?" the bishop entreated. "What in the devil became of your fellow travelers? Your guides, so to speak?"

Nell found herself relating the story of the Suffix family and the storms that pelted them and created impassable muck across Iowa. Then, she told how, one by one, the wagons dropped off and how she went on with Cutter and Moses. She described the great herds of buffalo and how she learned to camp on the open land, how she cared for her animals and how she found Jenny who got lost in the high grass. There, she stopped. Blinding tears boiled from under the lids of her eyes, and she found herself remembering the details of what she had been too busy and too tired to think on, until now . . . Her own hand lifted the blanket under which Cutter lay, draped over his horse like a dead antelope. The wound in his back spoke of murder. Sunset glowed on the shovel that Moses lifted upwards, over and over again, to dig the grave. Then, with the derringer, she aimed at Moses' face, and he was on top of her in the tent. The pungent odor of his male perspiration caused her to gasp. A bird landed on her shoulder. But, it was not a bird. It was a helping hand.

"Now, now," Lily May said, against whose breast Nell found herself. "We should have known your trials were painful. We should have allowed you time to restore yourself. How thoughtless of us. Moot, do something. She's cold."

"I'm alright," Nell sniffled.

Jenny sniffled next to her. "Don't scared, Mama," she said.

"I'm sorry," Nell explained. "My guides died . . . of bad water, cholera . . . I guess. Thinking of their suffering . . . I don't want to talk anymore . . . I . . ."

"Dead like a buffalo," Jenny told everyone. She patted her mother's head. "Don't sad, Mama."

"We understand," Lily May said. Nell felt comforted in the folds of her mothering arms.

"Would you like a blessing?" asked the bishop.

"No. Thank you, all the same. But, do remember me in your private prayers."

"She's all worn down," Lily said. "Help her to her wagon, Rass."

"Here, allow me to carry you," said a very deep and mellow male voice. Some tall drink of water with a strong back and full muscles, a person by the name of Rass, lifted her into his arms and carried her. Feeling pampered, Nell let him do it, even though she was more physically fit than she had ever been in her life. The spirit, though, hungered for the lifting—and was fed. Passing by one wagon, Nell thought she heard someone say "hello" with a voice that reminded her of a talking magpie she had watched once in a sideshow, but she could not see who it was in the dark. On her pillow, she discovered a little pocket, woven from bunch grass and filled with three chestnuts.

31

THE TRUTH

(Diary)   *July 2, 1849*

"Onward Christian Soldiers." In high spirits. Continuing on the last leg of my journey with the Mormon people. We left Fort Laramie and the Great Plains behind to continue over a more varied and adventurous terrain. Though we come upon monoliths in an array of colors amazing to behold, this territory taxes our equipment and us far beyond that of any rolling grasslands. Still, I am comfortable with Mormons, a people of conscience, skill and ingenuity.

Rass Stiles replaced my cracked singletree, in the nick of time, for the raw-hide straps had fallen away. Sister Brown's Jacob, who is sweet as a girl but strong and handy as any man, drives Glady Chatterley's team. Being far gone in pregnancy, she rides with me. In spite of being tossed to and fro, she insists on keeping pace with the group.

We talk freely. At first, Glady was just a woman across the river, but up close she's very complicated. She thinks highly of me, though I try not to be duplicitous. During rest periods, the wee ones gather around me to learn their alphabet from my Eclectic Primer. Hot and dry.

After a pause of two days at Laramie, the move began toward the Cumberland Gap of the West. Nell drove her team while Glady occasionally wobbled alongside the wagon to stretch or sometimes jostled beside her on the seat, but, most often, she tried to relax in the box while entertaining Jenny by sewing rag dolls from scraps of discarded clothing, yarn, shell beads and buttons. No matter the mode of travel, she appeared uncomfortable, tired and hot, but refused to complain. With a traveling companion, the days flowed by quickly, and Nell's spirit brightened daily with the anticipation of being with Tom.

One afternoon the train stopped for their midday rest on a high meadow with a magnificent alpine view. In the shade of pines, the lighthearted travelers surveyed the surrounding Rocky Mountains of various shapes, sizes and hues. From near to far, their colors graduated from green to dark blue, to medium blue, and, finally, to dusty blue. Though the midsummer sun beat down upon the travelers' backs, crisp air currents refreshed and cooled them. They filled their lungs with the fragrance of pine and played hide and seek under the dense forest. However, when Nell peered back into its depths, her heart skipped a beat at the thought that bears may be hidden behind the bows. Then, she looked to the west and wondered how the devil the Ark was to make it over those high peaks. Compared to them, a bear was nothing.

Traveling up one grade and down another, the women talked. "You'll like Tom," Nell told Glady. "His voice is very deep. Sometimes, especially in conversation with men, it's booming loud, authoritative. But, when he prays, it goes all soft and low-like. His face calms, innocent as a pup's. I can't resist him then." She told her companion about her life with Tom, how they met and courted, how she ran away with him to Nauvoo and parted in anger. "I'm so ashamed, Glady," she confessed. "And I wonder if Tom still loves me."

"Why wouldn't h . . . he? You're as honest as the trail is long."

"You don't know me."

"O, don't I? I . . . I . . . heard you tell Bishop Brown, up front, that you didn't believe. I heard you say it, plain and direct. I admired you so v . . . very . . . very much. Only yesterday every woman in the train wished they had your . . . sp . . . spunk. And, I actually think the Bishop admires you for it."

Glady referred to Bishop Brown's lecture before the evening prayer. First, he chastised the men for cussing the oxen and for playing cards. Then, he told the women they ought to be ashamed of themselves for rolling up their sleeves, lifting their skirts, and unfastening their neck buttons. When the scolding became repetitious and drawn out, Nell raised her hand to say, "Would you excuse me Bishop? I need to get on to bed."

"I'll vote for that," the Browns' sweet-faced son seconded." A light laughter rippled through the congregation.

"That was honest, to be sure," Nell answered, "but it bordered on *ornery*. And Moot Brown is not my husband. I never pretended to him that I had a testimony. You should have known me four years ago. I acted the part of a true believer. From the time Tom first preached to me until he left with Brigham Young, I didn't listen to a word he said. My thoughts centered on . . . his, well . . . his body. When he prayed, I watched those down-turned eyes that seemed to see past the earthly veil and into heaven's gates. I watched his lips, full and moist, his broad shoulders, his heavy neck, and the curly hairs on his arms. That's what attracted my attention, not the gospel. When he asked me if I believed that Joseph Smith was the true and living Prophet, I said 'yes, oh, yes.' Who wouldn't? When he lowered me into the baptismal waters at the temple font, I believed that Tom would raise me up, not Jesus."

"Good grief!"

"Then, after we married, I had to keep pretending. A lie calls for more lies, and each of those lies require a set. I got so mixed up that I didn't know who I was anymore. I was afraid that if I told him I didn't believe, he'd grow to despise me. 'Thy will be done.' That's his motto and creed. He is totally and unquestionably devoted to Latter-day Revelation and the Priesthood. So, I sat through every service nodding *yes* while my stomach growled *no*. Tom doesn't even know me. But, now, you do."

"Well . . . maybe, in that respect, y . . . y . . . you might improve. But, you love him. That's powerful. What woman would have the grit to travel so far for her man?"

"Yes. Love. But, if I had known what I know now, I'm not certain I would have left," Nell laughed. "A person just as well drive to the moon."

"I hear that," Glady agreed. "Ah, Nell, you're lov . . . l . . . lovely. Every man's dream. The kind of woman the rest of us love to hate. Vivacious. Petite, yet full. You're not scrawny or l . . . lan . . . lanky or all burned out. Why, if Jenny weren't right here beside you, I'd never believe you bore a child. Flat stomach. Eyes like a pond. Hair to envy."

"Wait a minute! Take a gander at this. Nell pulled a face. "Cracked lips, red eyes and forearms hard as a milkmaid's. I'm sunburned and scratched and windblown. My nails are ragged and my hands are brown like an outside slave's. The reins have built calluses so thick on my forefingers that I can't feel anything there."

She wouldn't want Tom to see her now. After she had cast aside her trousers for a frock, she continued to wear a vest and a belt at her waist, with Cutter's threatening knife, a powder flask, and a possibles bag hanging from it. Though men surrounded her on all sides, the Hawkin always lay under her seat . . . loaded, but not primed, and out of Jenny's reach.

"Don't be so hard on yourself," Glady tried to assure her. "Your own h . . . hus . . . husband will go beyond the superficial. How . . . how you make me laugh."

"I try to do right by Jenny."

"There you go. A n . . . n . . . nurturing mother," Glady sighed.

"A fierce mother," Nell added.

"You wouldn't hurt . . . hurt a fly."

A short distance away a prairie chicken ducked behind a brush. "Supper," Nell whispered and halted her team. Taking the Hawkin, she aimed and fired. Feathers flew in all directions. She re-loaded and plugged a second before any of the men riding alongside them had primed their rifles.

"Got 'em," Jenny shrieked. "Dead, like a buffalo." She congratulated her mother with a hug, and they both dodged through tumbleweeds to retrieve the meat they had savored over any other on the journey.

Glady's eyes enlarged, and for more than an hour she didn't speak. When she had ciphered it all through, she addressed Nell.

"Forget what I said about your b . . . b . . . beauty and your gentle nature. What I . . . I . . . I *can* say is you're a dead shot." Glady grasped her stomach, threw back her head, and hooted.

After gaining composure, Glady went on. "Speaking honestly, because I do, somehow, care . . . care for you, in spite of yourself, Sister Mortenson, what I can't understand is this: If you loathe yourself when you are not yourself, what makes you say you can unstitch Tom and make him over to suit you better? A person shouldn't give up their passion, not for anyone."

Glady's words rolled off her tongue and hit Nell like a rock. Neither spoke in the space of crossing a ravine. Then, the delicate woman went on.

"Listen carefully to what I'm about to say. Judge me for it, or not. I lied to you when I said I went to the river to find William's body.

What I really went for was to dupe others into believing I grieved for the man. I told them . . . them like I told you, that I wanted a proper burial for him. Truth was, I didn't care. He wouldn't I . . . I . . . I . . . let me be who I was. See. See what comes of it, Nell? When he drowned, the weight of an ox yoke fell from my shoulders." Glady, her back to Nell, folded her arms. "Now, you know the truth."

She sniffled until all the wagons pulled into circles for a midday rest. Then, because her face had swollen, the other women cooed to her, "poor thing," and "little mother." "He's at peace with God," one said, and another sobbed, "What a shame, and her about to have his child." They brought her soup, cooled her forehead with a wet cloth, and elevated her legs. "I'll assist, my darling, when your time comes," Lily May Brown promised.

Glady smiled weakly at the women. "Y . . . you . . . you are so very kind." From the corner of one tear-filled eye, she glanced at Nell, who thought that her lips turned slightly upward at one corner. But, she wouldn't lay a bet on it. Nell wondered, but did not ask, why someone so lovely as Sister Glady Chatterly felt relief, not grief, when her young husband drowned. And the stuttering? What was that all about? It had begun to wear on Nell's nerves.

32

LAST CROSSING FERRY

(Diary)   July 6, 1849

At Fort Casper, a Mormon ferry carried the Ark to the north side of the Platte for the first time. But, not without delay, for the flooding river is unforgiving and treacherous in deep mountain canyons.

With trepidation, Glady, Jenny and I left the southern bank along with nearly a hundred fifty others, their animals and fifty-one wagons. Never more will we follow our old waterhole, our guide and sometime friend, for we have taken a route to the north which, Moot Brown says, will lead us to a canyon trail along the pristine and drinkable Sweetwater River, over the South Pass and into the promised valley.

"How much farther is it?" somebody asks Bishop Brown, most everyday. Asking is a fool's game, for the answer always has something to do with "Too far."

For two days, it rained, steadily but gently. Nell, at first, reveled in the fresh, light air. It cooled her scorching flesh. It promoted a peaceful sleep and the removal of the stuffy kerchief, which she had worn against the choking dust of the trail. However, every blessing carried along with it a downside. The rain slowed travel to less than ten miles a day. It delayed the greatly anticipated last crossing of the Platte River, and quickened Glady's tender heart. Standing on its bank in awe at the roaring torrent, which she likened to the stampede of a thousand buffalo, she announced to Nell, "Hell will freeze over before I cross it."

When the Brown Company first approached the site, several ferrymen rode out to greet them in spite of the rain. Many rejoiced at finding their old friends from Nauvoo, Winter Quarters or the Great Basin in excellent health, even though some were in desperate need of supplies. After the usual protective circle was formed, after animals grazed and people ate, after the chores were done, the ferrymen built a large bonfire. They sang in praise of the Lord. They prayed and they listened to instructions concerning the delay in crossing and upcoming route from Thomas Grover, Superintendent of the Last Crossing Mission.

Grover, a slight man whose oversized hat rested on his ears, told the gathering that President Young had sent his team of experienced ferrymen to aid all Mormon companies in their last crossing of the North Platte, but they also earned money and supplies for the valley settlement and for the arriving Saints by operating the ferry service for "gentiles." Only a week prior, he and "the boys" had arrived. At once, they set out to build two very solid ferryboats by digging out three huge cottonwood trees for each base; across these, they laid and solidly anchored, thick planks of white pine. Each carried one wagon, so another must be built to accommodate the rush of emigrants.

"Even before we completed one of the rafts," Grover told them, "a group of Missourians arrived asking for a lift, and we haven't had a decent break since." The business continued with one small company after another, some bound for the Oregon territory, but many more rushing for California gold. Besides currency, supplies such as bacon, flour, cornmeal, coffee, beans, soap and animals were among goods they accepted as fare. "We expect to earn more, a-plenty, from even bigger trains soon to arrive from eastern parts, so you folks are right welcome to divide all we have among you."

"Glory be to God," a woman shouted. "Glory be to God," Nell thought, because she had been forced to dip into her beans and flour to help several families feed their starving children. "The Lord will provide," called the couple that had polished off a pot of the jerky stew she cooked to last for two days. Someone else praised the Lord "for sending manna to this people lost in the black hills," and a family broke into song, their sweet, harmonizing voices competing with the violent roar of the flooding Platte.

"Then all that was promised the saints will be given.
And none will molest them from morn until ev'n.
And earth will appear as the Garden of Eden
And Jesus will say to all Israel, "Come home."

"I'm not going to come home," Glady said in Nell's ear. "I can't cross the river."

Out of politeness, Nell might have asked her why. "You'll go," was all Nell said. She understood Glady's dampened courage. Hadn't her husband recently drowned? Wouldn't her first instinct be to preserve the life of her unborn child?

Eagerly, Bishop Brown summoned every man, woman and child for a prayer of thanksgiving, which lasted longer than any prayer Nell had heard. With head bowed and eyes partially closed, she listened while the prayer turned into a lecture against swearing, card playing and gossiping. Nell diverted her attention behind the bishop where the small figure of a woman scurried about among the wagons. In her apron, she carried something, which she distributed here and there. When she tossed an article into the Ark, Nell rose in alarm and would have left the gathering to discover what the small personage was about if the bishop had not finally said "amen" and people opened their eyes. Then, with the prayer concluded, he called for a renewed spirit. "I have been this way twice before," he added. "The easy portion of our journey is over." Stretching his hand toward the river, he continued, "Oh Lord, we, thy children, ask thee, in the name of Jesus Christ, to aid us in our exodus. Deliver us safely across these waters and beyond, over the Mighty Rocky Mountains. Deliver us from our enemies that we might go unto the land of thy promise and build up unto thee a new nation."

In spite of the "girding up of loins," the experienced ferrymen, and Elder Brown's prayer, there were complications. The once quiet, shallow, and meandering Platte ran not only swift but sixteen feet deep and icy cold. To make matters worse, a stiff wind whipped up the current. After a day's delay, the river settled, somewhat, and the ferryman attempted to test it. Nell, Jenny and Glady watched from the bank. With a few supplies lashed onto the flatboat and six strong swimmers on board, they pushed it into the river. Though they fought with oars and poles to guide them across, the river tossed the ferry to and fro and down the river's main current as if it had been a slip of paper manned by ants. Men and raft were carried out of sight. On the verge of tears, Glady declared, "I shall not step onto a raft." She wobbled to her wagon where she wept profusely until Nell diverted her attention by helping her with final preparations for the birth of her child. Meanwhile, the struggle continued, and Sister Lily, who stood beside her husband to avert him from leaving the shore, informed the women later.

Lily told how Brother Grover feared a loss of life and equipment, how he sent Moot, in spite of Lily's protests, Rass Stiles and four other men on horseback to retrieve the stranded test crew. She explained how the rescue group returned hours later to report that the raft had reached the opposite bank, "praise the Lord," some two miles downstream; however, they questioned the condition of the crew, who lay drenched and exhausted for some time before one finally stood to wave a white handkerchief. Any attempt to rescue them would prove foolish. The stranded men would have to find a way to keep warm on the other bank until the river settled.

Upon retiring to her wagon for the night, Nell found upon her pillow a small pouch of roasted chestnuts. They tasted delicious, and reminded her of the warmth and comfort of her Quincy home at Christmas time. During favorable circumstances, Nell might have given in to tears, but the uncertainty of fording the river caused her to bear up and take her sleep while she could.

The following morning, the Platte having quieted, somewhat, fifty men with a small raft, ropes, horses and oxen headed down river to rescue the test crew and pull the equipment back upstream to the landing site. Nell and other women waited with hot soup, a bonfire, and blankets. And, return they did, shivering, hungry and bruised, but alive. In the process of saving the crew, one good horse drowned because a rescue rope entangled around its front legs. An old ox perished from the exhaustion of straining to pull the stranded raft across the hundred foot, swollen river, and so many men were tired or shaken that the order of the day was to recuperate, to wait for the torrent to subside, and to praise the Lord that not a man had been lost.

Late, the next afternoon, the river having quieted, the company attempted and completed the crossing of four wagons, and two days after that the entire company, except for a few reluctant individuals, had attained the northern bank.

"Jump off." Nell held out a hand to Glady.

"I'm . . . not stepping onto that, that . . . er . . . raft," Glady balked on the bank.

"Your china's already over there. What do you plan to do, grow old and die over here without it?"

"I'm not afraid . . . t . . . t . . . to die," Glady said. "I'm not afraid."

"Well, then," Nell impatiently motioned for her hand. "If you're not afraid to die, why are you afraid to live?"

"I . . . I . . . I'm not."

"Jacob and I will sit beside you," the fair-faced Lily assured her. "Come along. Lift your skirts. It's only a step."

"Walk on," said a ferryman. "Are you going, or not?"

"Not." Glady leaned away from the raft. She leaned against Rass, who stood solid as a post behind her.

"May I hold you, and the ropes, and not let go, while we cross?" he offered.

Glady gazed gratefully into his eyes. She accepted! For some reason, Nell envied her for it. It was not because of his tall and manly stature, not because of his thick and wavy brown hair or his heavy mustache and distinct brows, and certainly not that he seemed the antithesis of Tom. It was not because Rass had once carried her and not because she had found him strong enough to be gentle. It was because he helped a lady in distress. After all, she *was* a married woman. The crossing of the final, timid handful occurred without incident.

With everyone safe on the other side and poised at the base of the Rockies, nobody asked, "Are we almost there," for in the distance loomed the tallest, blue mountains, one behind the other, that anyone, except the guides, had ever seen.

33

TALK ABOUT GIFTED

(Diary)   *July 10, 1849*

At a narrow ravine called Prospect Hill, all marveled at some distinctive red buttes. A tiny roadside grave reminded us of our mortality, of our present fortune and of the sacrifices endured by those who have gone before.

In the same day, we came to a great, rounded mountain called Independence Rock. On the southwest corner, hundreds of names have been chiseled or painted: Ella Bullock, Mary Matthews, and Alice Hansen, all women I knew in Nauvoo. Searched in vain for Tom's. Many of us ascended to its top. From that vantage point, we felt as if we had reached the heavens, for the country stretched boundlessly around us. I envied an eagle for its wings. With them, my flight to Tom, Heber and Elizabeth would be swift. Meanwhile, we push on, like ants over clods toward another river, the Sweetwater.

Having time to fill the pages of my diary is a luxury. In the evening hours, I have also been reading to the children Horatio Alger's Ragged Dick and Struggling Upward. Instructive. About a boy, who is a poor orphan on the first page and prosperous on the last because he shuns "noxious tobacco" and embraces hard work, honesty and cheerfulness in adversity. The children have developed the habit of gathering around me whenever I sit. I like that, especially when their mothers prepare my meals in exchange, for they believe their children's behavior has improved. But, to my thinking, most of them are still naughty.

Glady continues to ride with us and makes a pleasant companion. She's a gifted artist, unlike anyone I have known. Still, she brings with her a trunk full of dark and troublesome baggage like someone else I know.

Odd. Whenever I pass by the Urie wagon, a magpie, or parrot, or something, says 'hello.'

Glady slept poorly. To turn over required her to rise into a sitting position, and then she shook the wagon like the buffalo that needed a back scratch. Habitually, in the predawn hours, she left her bed and lingered apart until after the blare of the bugle at dawn. Upon her return one morning, Nell discovered that she had been sketching the scenery, and that her art was more than an accurate depiction. It conveyed an attitude, a story, or an idea, which inspired one's soul.

"Why do you rise in the darkness? Is it the baby?" Nell asked her.

"Yes, my . . . my back hurts, and my side numbs. Whether I recline, sit or stand, something aches. The baby pushes against my lungs so I can't breath properly. But, it isn't that, exactly. I . . . I'm ashamed of wasting time painting. I'm afraid people will think b . . . ba . . . badly of me." Glady's hopeful spirit suddenly turned dark, as was her habit when her thoughts turned to her late husband.

"What do you mean, waste time? This journey needs recording. Someday, folks will talk of it like we speak of the Mayflower or the Revolution. We're part of a great migration."

"I'm ashamed of p . . . p . . . p . . . painting. Yet, I paint. And, I'm ashamed I didn't shed a tear when poor Willard drowned. Indeed, I tried to, but couldn't. So, I faked a cry for the sake of the others. Heaven, forgive me . . . me, but when the river swallowed him, I watched, cold as a stone."

"What could you have done?"

Nell's question was the sulfur stick that sparked a cured kindling; nothing could smother the blaze that would follow. "When w . . . we lived in Lancashire, England, I . . . I worked in a clothing factory to earn passage to America. Willard, he converted and we saved every last farthing for a move to the Zion of our Lord. You can't imagine how I hated sewing," Glady chattered. "An artist ought to paint. I . . . Isn't . . . isn't that right? But, Willard, he wouldn't have it. When he left for the cobbler's shop, where he . . . he . . . he apprenticed, I'd paint. After he went off and drowned, I felt like he'd finally gone to work, for good. Now, I . . . I'm . . . I'm trying to paint again beee . . . because I must. Whether it's worthwhile or not, I can't say. My m . . . mama sketched thrushes and turtledoves in her spare time, and when my papa hung her works on the wall, he'd say, 'You're a real person, Margaret. You're s . . . s . . . somebody.'"

"Painting was her passion, and yours," Nell said. "Teaching may be mine. When the community wouldn't allow me to teach in Quincy because I married a Mormon, I felt I'd lost part of myself."

"That's it. Though my late husband wouldn't allow me to draw in England, I frequently prayed h . . . he . . . he'd come around, being a convert and all. This newfound religion, I believed, had softened his heart, so I asked him if I might draw the scenery along the way. But, no, he wouldn't hear of it. 'God will punish you,' he repeatedly told me. For sloth a . . . a . . . a . . . and for underhanded pr . . . rrr . . . pr . . . practices, you shall rot in hell.' I strove to carry out my wifely duties, but nothing would do. I was termed 'sullen,' 'devious,' and 'useless thing.' But, mostly 'toad.' Even so, I brought supplies," Glady breathed a great sigh, stretched her back, and continued with the doleful story of her life. "One day, when h . . . h . . . h . . . "

"*He*? Do you mean to say *he*?"

"Yes, he. One day when h . . . h . . . he and some of the brothers left to scout the trail, I drew a buffalo herd at their wallow pond. You should have seen how I captured their size and strength, their activity. I had it . . . it, I tell you. Well, when he caught me with my charcoal, he tore the sketch from under my hands and r . . . rip . . . ripped it into shreds. Shreds. After all that work! 'Put up that nonsense, you toad. Draw, indeed! A man needs to eat.' Those were his very words. But, it wasn't about the food."

"What was it?"

"I . . . I don't know, exactly. Looking back, I first noticed his ornery nature on our wedding day. He told me, 'Pin, pin, pin your hair up before the missionaries arrive to marry us.' So, I did. Mother, Aunt Tilley, and I worked all morning to wave my hair and iron the wrinkles from my dress. My dear friends said . . . said I was the most beautiful bride in Lancashire. Everyone sort of fussed over me, like I was some du . . . duch . . . duchess. Never felt like one before, or since. Do you know what Willard said when we met prior to the ceremony?"

"I couldn't guess in a million years," Nell said. "Go on."

"He said, in front of everyone, 'What happened to you? We had an understanding this wedding would be humble, and you're all gussied up. If you th . . . think, think this marriage is going to be one big holiday, you've got another think coming. I'm a plain man. I want a plain wife.'"

"He didn't!"

"He d . . . d . . . d . . . did." She drew a deep breath and rested for a time. "My so-called husband said, 'I desire you to drop your hair before the elders arrive. No man wants a trollop.' Accusing me of being a trollop, and on my wedding day! All he had done was to wash his trousers and grease his hair. So, I tr . . . tr . . . tr . . . "

"Tried," Nell blurted out.

"Tried," Glady went on. "I tried to understand his embarrassment, my being in white and all." Now, Glady blazed on, her face hot with resentment. "To set it right, I dropped my hair and changed into a common housewife's dress—worn and scrubbed several times . . . several times. That pleased William. Me? I smiled, yes smiled, the whole day, but deep, deep inside, I m . . . mourned . . . mourned. Wouldn't any bride?

"In the moments before our vows, I knew quite well that I was about to make an irreversible mistake. But, one cannot back ou . . . ou . . . ou . . . out at the last moment, can one? I prepared, he being my said husband, to forgive and forget. But, that very night, before we consummated our vows, he dropped a slice of cake on the floor. He called me, he did, from my bed to sweep it up. This small act would portend my future. Can you imagine it?"

"No," Nell said. A man's got to pick up after himself and learn to wipe his big feet at the threshold. If he goes from mother to wife, he never grows up around a house."

"Indeed. Still, I might have learned to live with that if it hadn't been for the other . . . "

"What's that?" Nell added fuel to the fire. "Relax now and take your time."

"You know. My drawing. He wouldn't let me draw. In primer school, I was known for it. Before I married, a few pieces sold. 'Thames in Winter' fetched an outlandish price from a rather wealthy London family. A real person, I was . . . was. But, Willard, he couldn't tolerate it, not him. No. It was my place to be humble, to serve, to obey. Consequently, I learned to paint . . . paint in the moonlight after he slept, or in a shadowed grove near our cottage. You can't possibly imagine the intricate plans I devised to conceal my supplies. One day, h . . . h . . . Willard discovered several papers under the bed. Then, I really found in him a tyrant. 'Toad,' he called me. He called me 'toad.' His eyes literally glowed with hate. I . . . I ran from him into the street. When he caught me by the hair, he struck and struck me, strongly and suddenly, across the face."

"O, Glady! How cruel. Didn't anyone help?"

"Definitely not. P . . . pe . . . peo . . . ple won't interfere when a man disciplines his ungrateful wife, will they? He must keep, keep her in her place. I might have revealed it to my sweet old mama, but only to break her tender heart. I didn't. After that, he bullied and struck, not every week, and not every day, but constantly." Glady paused to hide her face in her hands. "God for . . . forgive me, Nell. When the river swallowed Willard, I felt like a wild finch set free from its cage."

In the predawn hours the following day, Glady quit the wagon. Nell, who became concerned about her being alone, considering the darkness and her condition, was relieved at her return. Under a full moon, she showed Nell a painting of Chimney Rock. "To properly see this . . . this, you must hold it under the glow of the moon," she said. The majestic, inverted funnel stood before Nell like she had seen it for the first time one evening, velvety and black against a multicolored horizon. Goose bumps rose on her arms because of its strange and lustrous beauty.

"You're a real person!" Nell exclaimed.

"When everyone sleeps, I . . . I work on it," Glady smiled. "It's horribly drastic in the light of day. You'll see, in the m . . . m . . . morning. I couldn't believe my eyes when the Chimney first came into view. What a strange sight, after weeks of traveling the flatlands! I remember think . . . thinking it was only a mile or two ahead of us, but we had to travel four days before we approached it." The artist stepped backward to display her art at the proper distance. "Is it worthy? Would someone actually pay for it, do . . . do . . . do you think? The proof is in the pudding."

"How much do you want?" Nell asked.

When Glady hesitated, Nell reached down her neck for her money pouch. "Will you take two dollars?"

Smiling openly, Glady accepted. After vowing to free Glady's hands from her everyday labors, Nell convinced her that, in the future, she ought to sketch during the day and shed her black shawl of shame for one of a bright hue, worthy of her talent.

"Do an oil of each drawing after you settle in the Valley," she advised. "You'll make a living from it." The artist in her agreed to try.

With each passing day, Glady's weariness increased. Still, each evening she could be seen at her easel, frantically depicting favorite scenes of the day as if she hadn't life left to accomplish the desire of her heart. First, she recreated the herd of buffalo, which Willard had ripped into shreds. It fetched a promissory note of five dollars. Then, she drew a prairie dog village, so realistically portrayed that one elder said, "Makes me want to target practice whenever I see it." On the spot, he traded it for his wife's Sunday shoes. Antelopes, hawks, snakes, buffalo grass, sunflowers, lone trees, meadows, and anything the creative soul admired filled the pages of her sketchbook.

The artist became especially obsessed, however, with one solitary and desolate scene. West of Fort Casper, the teams plowed through four miles of the most forlorn regions in all the world. Leaning to the side of the trail, a sign called it Red Valley, and that described the whole of it. Slabs of rock, ranging in size from a hundred foot precipice to a pebble, formed the topography, in shades that ranged from deep red to salmon to soft pink, all stained by dark ores. Already bloodshot and itching from fine clouds of red dust that hung over the entire train day after day, the travelers' eyes blurred in the dazzling glare of color. All were prompted to hesitate and admire the stamina of one green juniper. It flourished in a rocky crevice with nary a teaspoon of sand or soil in sight.

At a very meager stream of pink-tinted water, the company paused in order that the horses might drink, they having less stamina than the mules and oxen in this scorching region. "What's that?" asked the mother-to-be. She pointed to a mound of dirt near the side of the trail. Heaped with red rocks to keep out scavengers and marked with a red sandstone slab, a tiny grave spoke of tragedy. Someone had rudely inscribed it.

Leigh baby, 1848

"I'll wager you the baby died at birth," Glady said. She held her stomach.

"No. Not that," Nell argued. "Babies die for hundreds of reasons. Typhus fever, measles, cholera. Maybe, the mother lost track of it or it fell out of the wagon. It could have crawled under a horse. Who knows?"

"With so slight a grave, the b . . . b . . . baby had to be newly born. 'O God, I pray every night, give me a healthy child. Let me have it and let it thrive.'" She displayed her hips. "Too narrow?"

"I had Jenny, didn't I? I barely have hips." Nell protected Glady by failing to tell how long the labor had lasted with Jenny, how she screamed, and how she insulted the midwives. She didn't repeat the gossip of her old aunts who said they despised "those Amazonian women, so endowed that they merely had to squat and push once or twice."

"It's the smallest grave I've ever seen," Glady lamented.

"Come away," Lily put a loving arm around her shoulder. "We don't have to stand here, all depressed, over some old grave. You must be used to seeing them by now."

"I'll never become accustomed to it," Glady hung her head. "Seems like there are so many little mou . . . mou . . . mounds. Sometimes, the mother lies beside them, doesn't she. This trip is no bloody holiday! It's hardest on the women."

"Come away," Nell hooked her vigorous arm through the slight arm of her friend. "You're tired, that's all. You need to nap."

But, Glady shook off their arms and slumped down next to the deserted little heap. "What bothers me is that the b . . . baby didn't live long enough to receive a name. Isn't that right? It's so sad, Nell," she cried. "There's . . . there's no flower in sight. You'd think, wouldn't you, that someone might have carried it on a little way out of this scorched region."

"You mustn't linger here," scolded Nell. "Get up. The mother had to leave it, for some reason that we'll never know."

"The mother was young like me, and couldn't push it out fast enough. The baby never had a chance, did it? They buried it here because—the sand makes for quick digging."

"The trek was too long," Nell admitted.

"Too damned long," Glady agreed.

"Let's not dwell on it. The way I see it is this: I don't care how I'm buried or where. If there is a God, I'll be in heaven. I'll be too busy with my new life up there to concern myself about where I'm buried down here. If there's not a God and is no heaven, then, it won't matter either. Nothing will matter."

"Don't sad," Jenny said. "Get up." She patted Glady's head, as was her habit whenever anyone suffered in her presence. Her liquid blue eyes, her golden curls, and her sweet complexion made her appear, in that particular light, as if she were a painting. Nell held the adoring imp. "Did bee sting Glady's finger?" she asked her mother.

"No. She's just tired," Nell said. She thought Jenny hadn't understood what was said, but the three-year-old had quickly absorbed and readily accepted the realities of trail life with an ease lost on most adults. Jenny told Glady that she saw lots of dead animals and she never cried. "They don't get up," she said. "Buffalo gots dirt on his eyes. Gots dirt on his tongue. We make meat out of him," she smacked her lips. Then she grew serious. "Does baby have dirt in eyes?" She blinked and rubbed her face.

"No. Baby's wrapped in a blanket." Nell led her daughter away and left Sister Brown to deal with the mother-to-be.

For three days Glady ignored her art. Lying in the wagon each evening, she napped or listened while Nell read to the children. The mother-in-waiting spoke rarely, and only then in regard to the necessities of camp life. On the third day, Nell heard her moan. But, it wasn't from her labor. "Heaven help the mother," she murmured, "to have to remember leaving her freshly-born offspring in that barren, lonely, Godforsaken place."

"Let it go," Nell sternly called back to her. "You're hurting Jenny. Ah, for hell sakes, toughen up. What's done cannot be undone. When you're doing something important, like recording this journey, fancy yourself as a big old work plug and plow away." Nell told Glady about Mrs. Suffix, who predicted the worst for herself and her family. "Like a prophecy, her words materialized," Nell said. "I learned from her that you get what you think."

The remark, the passage of time, the friendly encouragement, or whatever steeped in Glady's mind, allowed her to gradually revive and to continue her pictorial history. They pushed up the Sweetwater River Valley. With great detail, she recorded their struggles down one of the worst descents of the entire crossing. At the center of her drawing, her own wagon, the teams being doubled, slid sideways down a steep grade. Its locked wheels and a broken spring left deep tracks in the ground. Tied to the back of the wagon was a long rope; clinging to it, women, men and older children, their heels dug into the rocky soil, strained to keep the wagon from toppling. Two boys, who had lost their grip, lay laughing on the ground, but a woman at the end of the rope, who refused to lose hers, was being dragged along on her belly. Below this center scene, men struggled with pickaxes, bars and spades to level a road washed out by spring floods. Above it and far off, reigned the majestic Rockies.

When three families vied for this black and white sketch, Bishop Brown broke in with a tongue lashing, but Glady was delighted and told Nell, "No one shall ever brutalize me again, not ever."

"Good," was all Nell answered, but her friend's resolution gave her enormous satisfaction.

The group gradually ascended into the South Pass and some of the most stunning country any of them had encountered. Nell marveled at the thick timber, rich grasslands and rushing streams, where many women knelt to wash their hair. On Sunday, they rested in a verdant meadow called Deer Creek. Some of the men caught thirty half-pound catfish with the camp net. Others shot mule deer, whose white tails easily flagged them, and everyone savored all the meat they could eat. "I adore this place," Glady smiled. "The air is so clean you can bathe in it. I adore the sound of the breezes whistling through the pines like some distant river, and I adore that shy little chipmunk. It sits upright and holds biscuits in its tiny paws while it munches." The beauty, the food, the rest, the music from a fiddle and the companionship of the camp lifted the red curtain, which hung over Glady's heart.

This place reminds me of England," she mused. "The pines and aspens, how glorious." She took up her charcoal. Struck with an idea, she worked. Her shame and self-consciousness disappeared, and she completed a piece in oil. The reality of it astonished everyone. Glady had captured the loneliness of the tiny grave of red sand, had heaped it with red rocks to keep scavengers out, and marked it with a sandstone slab. Rudely scratched upon the face was:

Leigh baby, 1848

In admiring it, Nell felt the sweltering, dry atmosphere, she tasted the fine sand, and, once again, her eyes blinked from the sun's blinding reflection off the red rocks. Bishop Brown and others wept at the pitiful scene, which, they thought, they had left behind.

"This is all I could do for the baby," Glady explained. "Now, whoever looks upon this rendering, shall remember it, at least. They will ask, 'Which of the Leigh women gave birth coming over?' 'How did it die?' 'Why was it buried in that arid place?' Mothers, who have been through Red Valley, will know that the woman traveled all the way across the prairie with the baby kicking inside of her, only to have it perish here. They'll ponder upon her hopes and dreams for the child. Then, they'll know the heartache."

Nell gazed upon the grave, made more sacred by the barren loneliness of Glady's art. She could not move and could not take her eyes from it. But, she did not wish to own it.

"Wouldn't you want your child remembered, even if you hadn't given it a name?" Glady asked.

"I would," Nell answered. "In a way, it's a gravestone for all babies buried on the trail. Do you know how gifted you are?"

"Yes," Glady said. "But, it isn't me. It's God in me."

"I wouldn't deny it," Nell said, who realized that her companion hadn't stuttered all day.

34

HARDEST ON THE WOMEN

(Diary)   *July 14, 1849*

Let it be known to all that on this day, Robert Chatterly Mortenson was born somewhere on a high mountain pathway called the Great South Pass. The wind here never stops.

Glady began her labor. The company had ceased travel for the day. Nell had pulled her outfit into the protective circle and Glady had pronounced the area "a broad and empty landscape" when her pains began. Immediately, a dozen or more women had fluttered around Glady's wagon to offer a helping hand. Lily May Brown, who had attended other deliveries but would not call herself "midwife," had already been set aside to supervise. "Stay near," Lily had told Nell. "I need you to calm her and talk her through this, it being her first. Since the water broke so soon, the delivery may be hard."

Before climbing into Glady's schooner, Nell gripped the pouch of stones, which Rising Sun had gifted to her way back on the plains. She poured them into her hand. One, she gave to Lily, another to Glady. "These are stones rubbed silky smooth by many Indian mothers. A dear Shoshone woman gave them to me out of love. I am doing the same. Rub them if you need to."

"Superstitious," Lily said, but she slipped hers into her pocket.

"I'll rub mine," Glady said. "I'll keep it always." Earlier in the day, she must have suspected that her time had come, for she had laid out a tiny baby's gown, a miniature bonnet, wetting cloths, and a soft blanket as well as some worn cotton cloths. "It hurts awfully," she groaned. "I didn't know it was supposed to hurt like this. How long do you suppose this will take?"

"A few hours, at least," Nell said. "It will be over before you know it, though. When you hold the little darling in your arms, you'll forget all about the pain. Let's try to think of something pleasant to pass the time. You relax. When a pain comes, squeeze my hand."

On Nell's hand, Glady's grip increasingly tightened during each push. After a couple of hours, she gripped it so hard that the white imprint of her fingers remained long after the pain subsided. Hours later, there was barely time for the color to return when Glady squeezed again. When the hand prickled from insufficient circulation, the little patient's moans and groans turned to wails and muffled screams. "Oh, Nell. I can't take this anymore. Is there something wrong? Why doesn't the baby come?"

"It is coming," Lily said. "You have to be patient." A hand reached over the wagon's backboard with a square of buckskin, which had been soaked in the cold river. Lily took it and pressed it over Glady's forehead.

"Have to be patient?" Glady whimpered. "It was Willard did this to me." The next pain came, and she screamed, the scream that a mortally shot jackrabbit makes when its enemy approaches with a club.

The faces of mortified women appeared under the canvas cover. "What can we do?" they asked. "Is it coming?"

"I'll call if we need something," Lily snapped. "Shut the flap. We cannot have her chilled." Chilled? All three women perspired in the stagnant air of the wagon's tight interior. Oil fumes from two brightly burning lanterns and camphor, which Lily constantly rubbed over her hands, blended into one noxious odor. Still, Lily insisted that none of the fresh mountain air invade the tight quarters.

The next time Nell opened the rear flap, she saw that most of the women had left, and the four who remained slept with their mouths wide open under one large quilt. Jacob came to tell his mother that his baby sister fussed for her mid-night feeding, so Lily hurried away to care for her infant and to rest. "I'll call if anything happens," Nell assured her. But nothing happened. Another pain. And, still another. Glady, worn from the torture of it, begged, "Let me die. Oh, God, let me have it, or die. Help me. Can't you help me, Nell?"

Sister Brown returned saying she had tried to sleep but with no success. She brought an antelope steak for Nell.

"Today's kill," she said. "Will you eat?"

"I'm not hungry. Can Glady have it?"

"Not hungry," Glady moaned.

Nell left to wander around the wagons and stretch her neck in the cool, refreshing night air. She nibbled on the antelope, but in her dry mouth it lacked flavor. She drank from the water bucket, and then poured a full ladle over her face. Back in the wagon, she raised the quilt while Lily peered under to determine if the baby's head had appeared. With her hand over her mouth, she rose. "A foot," she whispered in Nell's ear. They stared at one another, trying, with their eyes, to decide what to do. "If it doesn't come quickly, this could be bad. It could drown, if it breathes too soon. The only one I delivered breech—died." Lily rubbed the stone in her apron pocket.

"Oh no," Glady screamed.

Nell's heart beat at her temples, and a wave of heat spread over her from head to foot. "Must she suffer so?" she cried on Lily's shoulder. "Whiskey?"

"Yes."

Nell opened the flap and said "whiskey" to the women, who sat up straight under their quilt, their eyes wide, their faces pale and drawn. Like a flock of frightened birds, they flew away. Moments later, a gentle hand reached through the canvas and set two small flasks and a large jug on the floorboards.

"Drink," Nell told her tortured friend.

"Something's wrong, isn't it?" Glady found strength to say. "What are you whispering about?"

"Nothing," Lily answered, stroking the clutched fist of the suffering sister.

"Don't lie to me, Lily May. I have to know."

"It's breech," Nell confessed. "When the body slips out, we may have to help with the shoulders and head."

"We may have to pull some," Lily added.

"Pull then!" Glady gulped a spoonful of liquor. Nell guzzled at the bottle.

"Precious Jesus," Lily said. She tore the jug from Nell's hands and cast it, hard upon the floorboards. When it shattered, the women outside gasped.

"I need you," Lily told Nell. Now, the reeking whiskey blended with the other odors. Nell's ears rang and her vision blurred. She imagined herself in a coffin. Without warning, circles appeared before her eyes. She toppled over the backboard, through the canvas and into the arms of two women, who had been at their peeping holes.

"What are you trying to do, frighten us to death?" one asked when Nell came to.

"Air, precious air," Nell gasped. Inside, she heard Glady's labored breathing. Determined to stick by her friend, she climbed back, where the three waited for another pain. Lily threw aside the quilt. Glady pushed, Nell tugged gently on the tiny red legs, and Lily reached inside the birth canal to work the shoulders through. Then, Glady stopped pushing. Her face turned to the color of ashes, and her eyes rolled back.

"It's coming, my dear. Push." Lily bawled.

"She's out cold." Nell felt lightheaded again.

"For crying out loud." Lily sobbed because the labor had stopped with the head still inside. "We've got to pull it through. It's probably dead." She shook uncontrollably. "I can't take it if this one dies. What shall we do? It's turning blue."

"Move." Nell nudged Lily May aside. She slid her hand through the birth canal. Locating the mouth, she hooked her thumb over the infant's lower jaw and pulled the chin down onto its chest. With that, the head slipped clear. Holding the tiny blue thing upside down by its legs, Nell slapped it on the rear like her midwives had done with Jenny. Lily wiped fluid from its nose, mouth and face. Then, because it hadn't breathed, Nell slapped it again and she pinched it, for good measure.

"Oh, no," the voices outside moaned like the wind before the first snowfall. "Please, God."

"Let it breathe, Lord. Let it breathe," someone pleaded.

"In the name of the Father, the Son and the Holy Spirit . . . " a male voice prayed.

The baby coughed, gasped, sputtered and sneezed. Finally, it squeaked. Nell slapped it once again to ensure that it did not stop. With trembling hands, Lily tied and cut the cord. Nell wrapped the fussing child, which looked very much like a little, old man, and placed it into the hands, eagerly reaching for it. Lily waited with a pan for the afterbirth.

"What is it?" Glady murmured, her eyes sunken and rimmed in blue.

"A boy," Nell said. "He's perfect. Nice work, dear girl."

"Can I hold him?"

"The ladies have him. They'll clean him and wrap him in my wagon. You'll soon have him."

"We need more cloth," Lily May whispered again. The lines between her eyes deepened. She pulled Nell aside. "We've got trouble. I don't have all the afterbirth. It came out in fragments. She's bleeding awful bad."

"Fetch my petticoat," Nell cried to the women outside. "It's inside my trunk." Nell had carefully mended it after she used a few strips to wrap Phoebe's toes, Ralph's jaw and Jenny's cut finger. She had washed it with the last of her soap and tucked it away so it would be fresh when she met Tom. Now, she must use more of it; strangely, that was of no consequence. Saving it didn't matter anymore.

Through dry, cracked lips, Glady tried to say something, but it wasn't loud enough to hear. Nell and Lily exchanged grave, fleeting glances.

"Please, don't push my stomach. I've had enough." Because Glady had difficulty sipping water while on her back, Nell lifted her head and tried again. She drank, but little.

"Beeswax," Nell said, and a hand reached through with a tin of wax. Nell rubbed it over her friend's lips. Another hand gave them the petticoat, and Nell ripped it in half. When Lily pushed aside the saturated birthing cloth to replace it with the petticoat, a stream of red blood gushed forth. Instantly, it spread through the white material.

"I'm so cold, Nell. Cover me," Glady shivered.

"Quilt," Nell loudly said, and a pair of hands offered one. Nell slipped the second cover over her trembling friend and held her close. The new mother rested, for a time, but woke with a start when Lily kneaded her stomach again.

"Stop. Make her stop, Nell."

"She has to do it." Nell kissed her cheek. Where she pressed her lips, the skin remained white and indented.

"I'm so tired," Glady sighed.

"Try to sleep," Lily May said. In the pan where the afterbirth lay, she wrung blood from Nell's petticoat. It needed emptying for the third time.

"I'm dying, Nell."

"No, you are not. Hold on."

"I am . . . I'm numb . . . The baby . . . "

"Beautiful. He has your hands," Nell sniffed.

"Raise him for me. Promise."

A hard lump grew in Nell's throat, which she could not swallow. She tightly closed her hot, red eyes, but that did not prevent tears from boiling over them.

"I'm not worthy to raise your son," she managed to say.

"Everything . . . I have . . . is . . . Nell's," Glady told Lily.

Lily nodded. Because she seemed to sense that the two women needed privacy, she left, her hands full of the bright red cloth. "Quick, bring the baby," she told the women outside. They flurried away.

"Raise my son," Glady whispered.

"I killed a man," Nell confessed. She rubbed the mother's slender hands. "He tried to rape me and I killed him."

"Some men . . . need . . . killing," her sweet friend said. Her arms felt cold. She tried to say more, but Nell could not hear. She placed her ear close to Glady's mouth. "Promise. You're strong . . . "

"Yes," Nell said, and that small word, she knew, would change her life and the lives of generations down through time. "I promise. I'll love him like my own, and he'll grow to be a fine person, like his mother. I'll protect . . . "

Lily came with the baby. She placed it under the covers between Glady's beating heart and Nell's. When its mother smelled it and pressed her blue lips upon its cheek, it rooted and purred there like a kitten.

"What shall I call him?" Nell asked.

"Robert" was her final word. The worry stone rolled off her slender fingers and hit the floorboard with a thud.

35

WHY?

(Diary)   *July 16, 1849*

Let it be known that Glady Chatterley is buried a small distance from Deer Creek under a pine. Her grave is marked.

In the quiet hours directly before the world begins to tangle 'round itself like a fishing line, Robert cried. With Jenny and a lantern in hand, Nell carried him, through a blustering wind, directly to the Brown wagon. There, she found Lily, nursing her chubby, creamy-skinned daughter. Lily May motioned for Nell to climb inside. "Cute little thing," Jenny said several times while she twirled the baby's silky, black hair into a point at the top of its head.

"Do you like Lily's baby?" Nell asked. "Would you like us to have one?"

"I want one," Jenny answered and moved to see what her mama carried in a bundle.

Nell uncovered Robert's face. He blinked from deep inside his blanket like a baby rabbit peeping out from its dark hole for the first time. "What do you think?" Nell asked Jenny. They examined his miniature toes, hands and ears. They saw that he was red, wrinkled, and thoroughly helpless.

"Beautiful," Lily cooed to him. "He has Glady's eyes."

"I always loved them. Her long hands too. Look." Nell showed Jenny the tiny fingers curled around hers. "I wonder if he'll be an artist."

"Can I have him?" Jenny asked. "Can he play wagons?"

"He can't play yet, but, if you like him, I guess we can keep him."
Nell motioned for Jennifer to sit, and she placed the baby on her lap.
At once, Robert fussed and rooted at his blanket, his mouth wide open
like that of a newly-hatched sparrow. "He's hungry. What am I to do?"
Nell asked Lily, whose left breast soaked her dress while she nursed
her child on the right.

"There's only one thing we can do," smiled Lily. "You know it."
She pulled her child from her nipple. Into the crook of her arm she took
Robert. "I guess, in a way, he's partly mine," she said. When she bared
her engorged breast, milk squirted onto Robert's face. He took to the
nipple, chocked a little, and suckled.

Jenny rubbed her little brother's head. "You can feed him, but he's
not yours."

Lily's weary eyes moistened. "I understand." She reached out for
Nell's hand. "I'll never do another birthing," she said.

"You'll have to, Lily. You're the only one. And, I must help. Sister
Hall is due." Nell wiped a stray tear from her eye. "It goes against
reason." She yawned. "Why? Why was she taken when she had just
begun to live?" Nell tried hard not to break down, but, without permis-
sion, a stream of tears rolled over her face.

"No man, nor woman understands the mysteries of God." Lily
rubbed her swollen, red eyes. Her mouth looked dry. She pulled Nell's
head to her shoulder. "I know how you feel. But, we must tuck away
our sorrow, for now. There will be plenty of time for it later. Right now,
a long journey lies ahead."

"I know all about tucking away," Nell sobbed. A sudden and powerful gust of wind rushed from bow to stern of the wagon. Lily covered
the babies' faces, and Nell rushed to pull the drawstrings.

"Do you think you'll have enough for both of them?"

"I'll try. But, I can't be up all night with two babies. That and the
travel would dry me up, sure." Lily was the picture of rounded and
motherly beauty with baby Robert suckling at her breast; he purred in
ecstasy.

"Do you think he'll tolerate my goat's milk at night?" Nell asked.
"Nan's a real milker."

"He must," Lily said. "You better take care of that snake-eyed
goat."

"I do," Nell said. "Isn't Jenny the picture of health? She hasn't
suffered one day from the ague, or anything else. We drink boiled

potato water."

Nell explained to Lily what Stella had told her, but Lily seemed skeptical.

"I don't give Sarah water, not yet. Only breast milk," Lily said. "She's thriving, thank God."

"That she is," Nell agreed. "Your boy Jacob. I don't know what I'd do if he hadn't been driving Glady's ox team. At first, I thought he'd disregard the animals and show off, like some of the others. I thought he'd turn Glady's flo-blue china into chips, but not one piece is cracked. Do you think he's old enough to have Willard's buckskin?"

"That would mean the world to the boy, Nell."

"Then, it's settled. You nurse and Jacob gets a mare. She's a young animal, sure-footed and well-trained. There'll be milk for your gravy too. Nan's a pain, but her milk glorifies flapjacks and cooked wheat too. I pour it over rice and raisins."

"Done," Lily said. Her flecked blue eyes rested affectionately upon Nell. "You are a good little woman," she said. "My kind. When the others come to know you, they will love you, even as I do. They need to learn that not everyone in their world is going to be Mormon. Friendships are not formed overnight, but many respect you. I know that."

"It doesn't bother me if they can't warm up," Nell pretended not to care.

A tiny burlap pouch came flying into the wagon. Knotted with a hemp string, it contained three chestnuts. "What the heck?" Nell exclaimed. Outside, the brown blur of a woman's skirt whizzed by.

"Why, that's Effie, Uriah's wife. Around forty. Childless." Lily caressed Robert's cheek with her finger. "She doesn't talk, never has."

"If that doesn't beat all. She speaks to me whenever I pass the Urie wagon. Says 'hello' like some magpie. I say hello back, but there's never an answer. What's going on?"

She's a riddle," Lily explained. "I've seen her out of her wagon but once or twice. Then, she kept at Uriah's back as if she were attached to him." Lily kissed the newborn, enveloped in the elegant sleep of an infant, and then she handed him over to Nell. "The most I know about her is that she's adept at weaving and handiwork. Once, she hung one of her tiny, brown dresses over a bush to dry. Several of us admired it, up close. Something to envy! While the rest of us wash and pick through our harvested cotton and flax to remove imperfections, she leaves them in, as if she loves the seed husks, the stained fibers and little bits of debris. Beside the dress was a shawl, un-dyed and of the most fine flax, woven with an intended mix of loose and tight threads to form a checked pattern. Most natural. Fringed with the pale color of dried shafts.

"Oh, she must be the one who left me a little bundle of chestnuts a while back. Another time, wild onions. I've never seen her, except in shadows, maybe."

"Yes. She's the one," Lily said. "Odd little creature. Never talks."

"People talk in different ways."

Jacob's face appeared at the back of the wagon. "Can I use your shovel?" he asked Nell.

"I'll come," Nell said, who didn't have to ask "what for." Neither did Lily have to be asked "will you mind the children." She nodded. Nell left to retrieve the shovel, which she had hidden behind foodstuffs, to avoid the death that was on it. Under a lodge pole pine, the men had already begun to dig. Passing by, Nell heard the solemn, and all too familiar, sounds of opening a grave: the light grunts of workers, the rasp of shovels pushing over rocks, and the thud of dirt on dirt. Taking deep breaths inside her wagon, she located the shovel and placed it into Jacob's hands. What was to come, Nell could not bear to think upon. To preoccupy herself, she led each animal to water. She milked Nan. Then, in preparation for the day's travel, she hitched up Blondie and Samson , and Glady's oxen as well. She asked the men to lift the yoke onto Glady's team. She cleaned her wagon . . . and Glady's. When she came upon the polished stone that Glady had dropped, she pocketed it. All too soon Jacob returned the shovel. "Time," was all he said.

Nell reluctantly moved to the graveside. The sight of Glady's body, wrapped in her quilt next to the hole, stunned and then numbed her. After that, she heard very little except the final words of a male voice reading from Genesis. "'Unto the woman he said, I will greatly multiply thy sorrow and thy conception; in sorrow thou shalt bring forth children; and thy desire shall be to thy husband, and he shall rule over thee.'"

Several men gently lowered Glady into the earth. Nell dropped in the worry stone. After the shovels had done their work, Rass staked a marker at the head of the mound that read "Glady Chatterley – 1849." That ended it.

If Nell had followed her emotions, she would have thrown herself upon the grave; she would have wept her heart out. She might have died there. But, with everyone pining about, some weeping, some holding one another, others moving on to prepare for the day's travel and with Jenny standing on one side and little Robert in Lily's arms on the other, she couldn't. Instead, she rose onto the seat of her wagon and told the team, "Get up." Leaving her friend behind was a terrible thing. In vain, she tried to reason with an utterly broken heart.

36

GETTING ON

(Diary) *July 16, 1849*

Now, I know why the mountains to the north of South Pass are called the Wind Rivers, a seemingly odd name, until early this morning. A terrific wind kicked up, and it rushed through the pass like a storm at sea. Sudden and frightening gusts lifted our schooners, the sturdy Ark included, off their wheels on the leeward side. It blew our gear from aft to stern, and some of it went overboard.

One wagon toppled where it stood. A gust tore away its canvas. Buckets, tin plates, pots clanged over the rocks, and horse blankets took to the air like magic carpets. After the storm, anything left uncovered or untethered, might be found wrapped around a sage or entangled in a pine bow.

I suffered like everyone else. Blondie bawled. Nan broke out of her cage and, finally, after a desperate search, Jacob found her, shaken, but well, in a shallow cave. Before I remembered my apple trees, the squall tore them from their moorings and sent them rolling. My Illinois soil broke away from their roots and was lost. If the trees survive, I shall be fortunate.

Exposure to the frightening element has given little Robert the colic, but we are claiming him, just the same.

How I long for the spacious safety of my parents' solid home. How I wish for Ruby's helping hands and sound advice. How I yearn to fall into the strong arms of my husband and to greet my darling Elizabeth and Heber. Does anyone know what she has, when she has it? Or, must we all find out the hard way?

Because there were plenty of arms to snuggle Robert during the day, Nell was able to perform all her ordinary tasks, but she soon discovered that at night he was definitely hers. After she fed him Nan's milk, through a flask with cloth knotted at the end for a nipple, he writhed and squeaked and squirmed. All night the lantern glowed in her wagon, for Robert rarely slept for more than three hours at a time. Nell tried to rest between feedings, but anticipation of his next cry kept her from actually sleeping. Between dozes, she fed him. She laid him across her legs and rubbed his back to comfort him. Still, he cried. She burped him, patted him, and rocked him to and fro. He squirmed and blatted and squawked and wept. Some nights, she wept too. Once, she found herself cursing Glady for leaving Robert, and when she did wrestle a few winks, she dreamed that he really belonged to Lily . . . really. Nell even resorted to praying. She asked God, out loud, to deliver Robert from his misery and to allow her, at the very least, one full night's sleep.

One evening, after an especially bumpy day of travel, Jacob offered to spell Nell off for one night. But, a few hours into it, he pounded at the door of her first sound sleep in days. "Me and this gull dern baby doesn't get along," he whined. "Tomorrow, I got my work cut out for me." He told her that he was willing to do most anything to pay for his horse, but not that.

And, Jacob wasn't the only one that Robert irritated. Some nights, his wails aggravated Jenny. In her dreams, she cried out, "Shut up, Baby." And, she had to be trained not to pinch him when he fussed. People in the wagons on both sides of Nell's could be heard grumbling in the wee morning hours, and drivers scrambled to avoid parking next to them when the wagons circled for the night. If Robert had not begun to smile, if he had not smelled so beautiful, and if he were not so adoringly helpless, Nell (and a few others) might have . . . developed a strong aversion to him. But, he was new to life, and his job was to strengthen his lungs. He ran the show.

However, all was not lost. A week later, exhausted and frustrated in the dim light before dawn, when people are known to surrender to their deepest sleep, Nell walked Robert round and round the periphery of the wagons. "Hello," a quiet voice murmured when she passed the Urie wagon. Nell returned the greeting. A face as round as an apple appeared. It's eyes, the ones that had watched her from under the canvas, bulged in their sockets like those of some nocturnal creature.

When they blinked, it appeared as if a curtain had dropped over the moon. Effie. So, this must be Effie.

"Hello," Nell said again, this time with enthusiasm. "I'm Nell Mortenson. I'm so pleased to meet you."

Effie curtsied, cocked her head, and blinked. She smiled. Or, Nell thought she might have smiled. *Seemed pleased* might better describe her expression. Like a chipmunk nibbling on a crust of bread, her short, stubby hands played at her mouth. "Hello," she clearly said. She leaned toward the fussing baby for a quick look. Showing two prominent and endearing front teeth, she grinned.

"Here," Nell said. "Do you want to hold him?"

Gently, Effie took the child. Resting Robert's little head at her shoulder, she rocked him to and fro, she rubbed his little back and patted his bottom. Robert burped. When he let out a squeal, she put her mouth to his ear to make secret sounds. As if she had taken Robert into her nest, somewhere deep inside the earth where he was totally protected from human plights, he fell asleep, and stayed asleep for hours.

Regular as a timepiece, the affectionate little night person appeared after every voice had quieted and after the campfire's light had died. Nell fed Robert Nan's milk, changed him, and handed the "Little Mouse" to Effie's eager arms. At last, she slept.

"I am with you," sang a clear, small voice in the back of her dreams. "Oh yah, oh yah, ah eee."

37

GOIN' FISHIN'

(Diary)   *July 20, 1849*

*Nothing I have ever seen or heard of parallels the awful beauty of the
Rocky Mountains. Words cannot describe my urge to seek out their wild and
virgin places; yet, I fear what I might find. Goin' fishin' tomorrow at Black's
Fork.*

The stalwart company inched their way into the Rocky Mountains.
Like the lovely, yet dangerous Circe, who enchanted Odysseus' men
with her beauty and turned them into swine, they beckoned, one
behind the other as far as Nell could see. The nearest range clothed
herself in one of those delicate and dazzling fabrics that goddesses
love to weave: blue-green sage, pale yellow foxtail, green bunchgrass
and gray-brown soil. Beyond this seemingly simple temptress, lay a
second range, robed under heavy folds of dark purple like a queen;
the third rival draped herself with soft blue, up the long slope of her
legs to the curve of her ample hips and over the round fullness of her
torso; and the fourth, veiled in pale lavender, appeared untouchable,
cool and aloof.

Nell stood before them, intimidated by their awful beauty and
would have drunk their magic potion if she had not dreaded a dangerous and intimate knowledge of them. She knew she must step forward and cross their fearful peaks in order to complete her journey;
she also knew that she could, and would, with this crew of toughened,
experienced Mormons. In order to bear up, she tricked herself into
believing that only four obstacles lay ahead, but, in reality, she did not

know how many she must outstrip before she too might recline.

To cross the first mountain, all fifty-one wagons wound their way through a gap with perpendicular cliffs on both sides, its narrowness barely allowing for a single file passage. Cool and moist as a cave, the gap offered a brief reprieve from the fierce summer sun. There, ferns hung from seeping walls, and between the wagon wheels, a trickling stream caused the mules' hooves to slide this way and that off its moss-coated rocks. Nell, drugged by the brief refreshing passage, stayed her team, basked in its moist serenity, and momentarily forgot the cares of the world. Yet, there was trouble in it. When Uriah Urie, who proceeded behind her through the fissure, yelled "huh, huh, get up" and cracked his whip over his slow-moving oxen, the gap roared and flung loose rocks headlong at them. Swiftly, Nell drove forward again into the scorching sun.

The following day, the Brown Company crossed a high summit with sparkling patches of snow in its crevices. They made of it a refreshing dessert by scooping it into bowls and pouring molasses over the top. When Jacob and his two sidekicks initiated a snowball fight with other young men, the rest of the company quickly joined in. Rass Stiles hit Nell in the back of the head with a handful of loose snow and hurried forward to brush it off. A handsome man, that Mr. Stiles! Of an age when manhood is at its peak, he sported a fine pair of gentle, brown eyes, thick lashes and a short heavy beard, which sent arrows through the hearts of many a woman in the company . . . but not through Nell's, for, of course, her desire was for her beloved Tom, who prepared a home for her in the great valley. When he approached Nell, her hand spread directly over Tom's letter, which stuck to her breast under her bodice.

In that same day, they came upon a steep grade adorned with countless types of alpine flowers. It took their breath away. Most halted their teams, and, for the sheer delight of it, bounded down the hill to have a closer look, the ladies being especially charmed. Even Effie Urie, who caged herself inside her wagon during the day, ventured out. The bodice of her dress had been decorated with the most rare and intricate handiwork Nell had ever seen. A threaded needle, near the neck, suggested that the work was hers. Nell held Effie's short, square hand and pulled her uphill.

Feeling a presence behind her, she stopped. It was Rass. Nell flushed. He suggested that they all have a contest to see who could gather the greatest variety of "posies." Many light hearts took part. Nell picked slender, star-shaped columbines, bright orange Indian paintbrushes, violet blue-bells, goldeneyes, and white yarrow with minute blossoms clustered in the shape of a parasol. In all, she found twelve species on that one glorious hill. Rass discovered one flower that she did not. "Add this to your collection," he said. "The only way to keep a beautiful flower is to give it to someone of equal beauty." He gave her a cluster of wild roses. Though the soft innocence of yellow petals lured her hand into grasping the bouquet, it pricked her fingers. Plucking one of the blossoms, Rass pushed its stem into her hair. "Devastating," he said. Briefly, the rope of his desire drew her to him, and they stood closer to one another than was wise. Then, frightened of her own yearning, Nell turned from him to fake a search for more flowers.

She might have found some if Effie had not plucked a stinging nettle and ran squealing for her husband. "Watch out for the nettle," Uriah called out. He lectured his alarmed and whimpering wife in a loud voice that caused her to hang her head, she being uncommonly private. "Gad. I told you, Effie, to watch for the nettle, didn't I? I told you two days back. It's vicious. I'm the one who knows. If you would listen to me, my pet." With soap, he led her to a stream where he scrubbed her little hands. "Wash it off, right good, now," everyone heard him say. "Now, it feels like a dozen hornets stung you, doesn't it? There, there, the bumps will come down in a couple of days. You should have had me with you, Effie. I can spot nettle a mile off."

Down this flower-strewn grade, the company struggled. They unhitched each team, locked their wagon's rear wheels and restrained them with long ropes to prevent them from running out of control and shattering like toys on the rocks below. After that, the trail took them through some fairly level country, made pleasing to the eye with thick blue-green sage. When they bumped over it, however, their wheels broke down, and many in the company complained of severe headaches caused by the jolting. The angry hands of the sage reached out and tore the hems of many a sister's skirt, above their ankles and Mormon standards, and the men grew cantankerous with one another and impatient with their wives and children.

After fighting the sage for ten miles, Blondie quit. She plunked down for the first time since Iowa. Even though the obedient Samson dragged her for a few yards, she refused to stand. Before doing so,

Nell had to bring forward The Spare and unhitch her. Then, she shook herself and walked to the back of the wagon without being led.

So, at the end of the day, when they camped alongside the banks of the Black's Fork, Nell rejoiced and thanked God with the others. Tomorrow, Sunday, would be "a day of rest." That meant, rest from travel, but no rest from washing, animal tending, wood gathering, food preparing or clothes mending. Although the mountains ahead blocked her sight, Nell whistled to herself each time she remembered that the river would soon lead them to Fort Bridger, and approximately two weeks after that the wearisome trail would lead her home.

That evening after the routine chores, at least half of the company relaxed around the fire. The group fiddler played his favorite tune, and those who had learned the song raised their voices to the mountain peaks.

The sky with clouds was overcast,
The rain began to fall.
My wife she whipped the children, who raised a pretty squall.
She bade me with a frowning look to get out of her way.
Oh, the deuce, no bit of comfort's there, upon a washing day.

My Kate she is a bonny wife,
There's none more free from evil.
Except upon a washing day, and then she is the devil.
The very kittens on the hearth, they dare not even play.
Away they sump with many a thump, upon a washing day.

A friend of mine once asked me,
How long's poor Kate been dead;
Lamenting the good creature, and sorry I was wed
To such a scolding vixen whilst he had been at sea.
The truth it was, he chanced to come upon a washing day.

I asked him to stay and dine, "Come, come," said I "old buds."
I'll no denial take. You shall, tho Kate is in the suds.
But what he had to dine upon, in faith I shall not say.
I'll wager he'll not come again upon a washing day.

For it's thump, thump, thump and scrub, scrub, scrub
And scold and scold away.
Oh the deuce,
No bit of comfort's there upon a washing day.

When the fiddler played "The Old Grape Arbor," Nell danced with some of the women, but Mr. Stiles, whom most of the unmarried girls claimed as their beau, could not take his eyes off her. Like the refined lady that she was, Nell pretended not to notice. Still, while he watched, she twirled faster than before. She pointed her toe with more grace, stepped lighter, and flipped her long mane into the fire's light, all for his benefit.

Side aching, she rested beside the boy Jacob, who sprawled on the grass beside Rass and Brother Urie. While Effie crouched behind a wagon wheel, camouflaged in brown, Uriah craved nothing more than being the center of attention. "There's plenty of fish around here," he said. This was his third crossing and he knew. "Over there a piece, in that little inlet, I took a beautiful mess in '47, when President Young crossed with me. I set my hook with grasshoppers."

"Which inlet?" Jacob was curious to know.

"You keep quiet," Uriah retorted.

"Let the boy speak," Brother Stiles said. "I too would like to know. "Why be selfish?"

"Maybe I don't want it known," Uriah said, grinding his teeth in anger. "The mite ought to keep quiet instead of making trouble. If the boy would listen, he might learn a thing or two. I listened when I was a young fellow, or I wouldn't be the tanner that I am today. A man's got to have a trade, and how I got to this point was by listening."

Uriah, who seemed all head because of his great mass of curly, grizzled hair, told about how he caught fish in '47. Relating his story in such a long-winded and roundabout manner, saying little about his topic but everything about himself, he allowed no other person to slip in a word edgewise. One by one, people slipped off to bed, but behind the wagon wheel, Effie listened intently to her husband, her large, round eyes reflecting the red of the campfire.

Nell pulled Jacob aside. "What would you say if we took those nice poles that Glady left me and went fishing in the morning, before Uriah gets up? What would you say to that?" She winked.

"Good. We'll show him." Jacob's voice cracked when he attempted to whisper. "I'll wake you before dawn. I'll dig worms." Tickled, he rubbed his hands together.

Nell agreed to bring all the gear, and she asked Lily May, who would be up anyway, to watch over her Robert. "You be careful," Lily warned. "I heard Moot talking about bear. A day back, someone saw a trail, clearly worn with tracks, big tracks too. Down the trail, two . . . three days, is the Bear River Valley, and they don't call it Bear River for nothing."

"I'll take the rifle."

"That's good. But, listen, you watch over my Jacob. I have to let him go, I know, or he'll never grow into a man, but you watch him. Hear?"

"I'll watch."

"You're one person I never worry about, Nell. I nearly broke my sides laughing when you won that sharp-shooting contest with the men last week. Oh, my land! I'll wager you missed Moot's expression when you out-shot him!" Lily threw up her hands. "And Brother Urie, his bottom lip nearly touched the ground on your first hit."

"He's an old bagpipe," Nell confided in her trusty friend. "He wants the best fishing for himself; that's why he warned us of bear."

"He might be ornery as an old wolverine and he might have a big mouth, but Uriah's been here before. Remember that. He says the bear out here aren't shy like our black bears back East."

"I'm the one who knows!" Nell mocked Uriah. She left to string the poles with line and to tie on hooks so everything would be ready for morning.

And, a splendid morning it was! Her line rolling up and down with the current, Nell sat next to Jenny on the carpeted bank of a pristine stream with dark green moss flowing over rounded boulders at the bottom and water of such clarity that large trout might be seen leisurely waving in its depths. Nearby, Jacob fished, and Jenny delighted in a flock of yellow-breasted finches, which flew out from the willows in tight circles to catch the flies that hung over the stream. Because the gushing waters drowned out all sounds that might have come from the camp, Nell gave herself over to the place. She slapped away a few bees that had begun to swarm over the purple clover upon which they relaxed.

Her line jerked! Nell jerked back with equal force. If the tip of her pole had not wiggled violently, she would have thought she had hooked a log. "Jacob, come quick," she called. "It's a monster."

Jacob reminded his excited companion to wind in. "Don't lose him. Keep it tight. I'm coming." Down the bank he ran, laughing all the way.

"Hurry, Jacob," she called again. A silvery body flashed above the current and nearly wrenched the pole from her hands.

"Don't let him take you," cried Jenny. She clung to her mother's pant leg.

When Jacob reached her side, Nell offered to give him the pleasure of bringing in the fish, but he would have nothing to do with that. "You have to do it. He's yours," Jacob squeaked. Nell wound the line around her spool. While raising and lowering the tip of her pole, she wound and wound some more until her arms ached. Finally, the great trout splashed near shore. This was no catfish and no eddy fish! Nell, trembling at his great size, his hooked jaw and pulsating gills, lost her wits and scurried up the bank to drag him in. Only then did Jacob help. He pounced upon her trophy, clutched its slippery body in both hands, and threw it away from the water. Steel-gray on its back and pearly white on its underside with crimson slashes at its throat, it flippity-flopped in the clover.

"Nell," Jacob said, who had forgotten himself. "You got him. A cutthroat. Look at the red! Two pounds, three pounds, maybe." By the line, Jacob held high the flopping trout. With another flip, the hook released from its jaw, and it fell on the ground. "Oh, my heck," Jacob said. "Good thing you kept the tension. You might have lost this beauty." While Nell and Jenny watched in the tender, cool clover, Jacob whacked the trout on the head with his pocketknife. He ran his sharp blade the length of its belly and stripped out the entrails with his thumb. Then, he tied it through the mouth and out the gills with a thin rope; the other end, he attached to a riverside willow, and, at last, he dropped the fish back into the stream for cooling. "This will feed a family," Jacob beamed.

"You're a fine young man," Nell told Jacob and patted his shoulder. "How did you learn all that?"

"From Pa. In Palmyra, we fished a lot, but I never saw a cutthroat and I never saw a trout this big. He was a real fighter. How did you snag him?"

"I don't know. I used your worm. Cast out as hard as I could, into the middle and let the current carry my bait. Then, I just waited. Beginner's luck, I guess. Where'd you leave your pole?" Nell squinted to see that Jacob had anchored it under a heavy rock. The tip bounced up and down. Nell pointed at it, Jenny screamed in delight, and Jacob, his silken hair alive with morning's silver light, sprinted away to bring in another fine fish.

"That will fill *your* pan," Nell cried. She and Jenny hurried to gloat over his catch. Then, they all moved upstream and discovered several deep, dark holes under the bank where the roots of willows tangled around themselves. Into one of these Nell dropped her line. She basked on a patch of cool grass with Jenny's curly head in her lap while Jacob worked his way upstream, dropping his line into holes as he went.

From where Nell rested, the early glow of dawn touched every-thing with silver. A silvery spider crawled along his translucent thread attached to a cattail on one side and a wild current bush on the other. Light shimmered back and forth across the thread as air currents swayed it like a tiny drawbridge. Through the bows of a pine, shafts of silver touched each needle with a magic glow, and behind the pine and high above it, the leaves of aspens shook like silver coins. A lumines-cent star played here and there upon the stream and in the curls of her napping child. Even the hairs on Nell's arms gleamed in silver. This was a scene to commit to memory.

Nell heard, or thought she heard, a low groan. Perhaps, she only felt it. Downstream, nothing stirred out of the ordinary. Upstream, Jacob worked his line. In the dark undergrowth to the side, nothing moved, save the ever-quaking aspen leaves. Nell listened, her hand curled around the butt of her rifle. Nothing.

Then, she told herself that sometimes a dead tree, which has fallen against another, scrapes across it to make a most unearthly sound. She told herself that the boulders of the river will roll over one another and that the imagination is a trickster. She willed her body to relax. *Stay lost in the beauty of morning*, she told herself. *Don't panic, foolish, foolish woman.* But, the groan grew inside of her. It gnawed in the pit of her stomach, it ran down her spine, it tickled her back between the shoulder blades. It rushed into her legs, telling them, "Get up. Run." Again, she turned to the undergrowth. Nothing moved, neither the tall grass, nor the wild rosebush, neither the willows, nor the thick pines.

Gently, Nell nudged Jennifer. "It's time to go. Wake up, baby." Urgently, she wound her line, untied the rope that held her great trout, and, all the while, kept her eyes on the forest shadows. Afraid to yell, she found her way to Jacob. "We better go now," she half-whispered.

"They're still biting," Jacob protested. "I've caught six. Did you see?" He pulled his trophies from the water to show her.

"We have to go now," Nell whispered again.

For a moment, Jacob chewed upon her words. He fed on her eyes and must have found the meaning there, for he gathered his gear, slipped on his shoes and lifted the mess of trout over his shoulder. He followed Nell through the thick grass toward camp.

Presently, they heard the voices of men ahead; Rass Stiles and Uriah Urie appeared with their poles balanced over their shoulders and rifles at their sides. Remembering Rass's grin the previous day among the flowers, Nell's heart thumped harder than usual. Quickly, she erased the vision of his engaging demeanor and shunned a brief yearning for his moist, full lips. She loved Tom. Even so, Rass was going to make a fine catch for some fortunate female. A carpenter, he specialized in the making of furniture. In his spare time along the way, he carved a set of chair backs with intricate designs, which told the story of his journey, the story of river crossings, of buffalo, of ox teams, and of campfires. Everybody greatly admired them, and they often amused themselves by observing him at his craft.

"I don't like that Brother Uriah," Jacob confessed. "He'll be sore when he sees we got to the holes before he did. Did you hear how he kept the whole camp awake last night braggin' 'bout all the buffalo fish he snagged on the plains? One by one, the folks snuck off, smack in the middle of his story, until he sat there rattling on to himself. And, him, he kept right on braggin' and actin' out his old tale with only the dying fire left to hear. Me and the boys like to died a-laughin'. Old coot. Crazy for fishin'. Even when we had fresh buffalo, he went to the shoals of the Platte for them muddy old trash fish."

"Shhh, he'll hear you," Nell warned. Because of Effie's help with Robert, she needed no trouble with Uriah. "Good morning for fishing," she said as the men approached.

"Why are you packing your piece?" Uriah asked. "It ain't no woman's place to pack no piece. I'll get to the point, here and now. There's been talk. If you want to fit in, you got to shut your eyes during prayer. You got to wear a frock like the rest of the sisters—all of the time. You got to put down that piece. No, sir," he shook his hoary head. "It don't seem normal, a woman not trusting to the men."

Nell opened her mouth to give him what for, but didn't after Rass winked to suggest that Uriah's words should be taken lightly. "Splendid morning," Rass said. He brushed his tongue over his straight teeth. Like the trout stream, his thick brown hair rippled with silver light and finished with an upturned wave at his neck.

"Yes," Nell answered. "Splendid."

"Nice fish. Where'd you catch them?" Rass asked.

"Follow our trail," Jacob said. "They're in some of the holes under the bank. She got hers in the middle of the stream."

"I told you there'd be trout, didn't I?" Uriah broke in. "I know'd. I'm not only a tanner. See here, I'm a gamesman, too. Remind me to tell you about the prairie hens I got, boy. Fed the whole camp in '47, I did. Did you catch all of them fish, boy?"

"No. Nell caught the big one her own self."

"Gad. I wouldn't be showing it around, if I was a woman, that is," Uriah said, his buckshot pupils hard upon her. "It isn't seemly. I'm telling you this for your own good. Gad. I wouldn't be bragging about no fish, if I wanted to fit in. I see'd this kind of thing a'fore. It don't work."

"I don't give a damn," Nell said. She winked and smiled good-naturedly at Rass. "And, nobody's about to stop me from protecting myself with this rifle. It stays with me." Nell was about to say more, but decided against it because of Brother Stiles' presence. She smiled, and met his gaze, knowing he would admire her rich, blue eyes.

"Looks like you got your piece primed," Uriah observed. "That right?"

"That's right." To assert herself, Nell spoke louder than was her custom. "No flint on it yet."

Jenny, who had frowned at Uriah during the entire conversation, gave him a swift kick to the shin. "You're a mean one!" She would have kicked again, but Nell prevented her.

"Better tend to your young one," Uriah pointed at Jenny. "If I had her, I'd learn her, right good. You'd never see a girl of mine kick, no ma'am."

"Come along, Brother Urie." Rass nudged him forward. "Leave them be." Because he had forgotten to fasten the top button of his shirt, Nell's attention moved straight to the exotic, curly hair on his chest. She remembered that Tom, being of a light complexion, grew a few stragglers on his.

"We ought to be off, if we're going to catch anything," Rass said. "Sun's up."

Uriah continued. "You're apt to shoot your own toe off. Or, worse, you're apt to plug some young'n in the back. I seen it before. I could tell you, if we had time. I . . . "

"Let's go," Rass said, his voice deep and his eyes flashing with anger. His hand gripped Uriah's arm.

"I told you there'd be trout in that stream, didn't I?" Uriah looked up at Rass.

"One word, before you go," Nell said, on impulse. "I thought I heard something in the pines."

"What was it?" Rass wondered. "What sort of sound?"

"I don't know. I didn't see anything," Nell answered, embarrassed to have mentioned it. How could she tell these men that the tickle in her back and the hollow spaces in her windpipe were what caused her to peer backward, to gather her gear and to rush away? How could she explain a sound that she felt more than heard?

"Woman troubles," Uriah shook his heavy head. "They worry. Effie does that all of the time." A fat, green grasshopper, spitting tobacco juice, crawled out of his shirt pocket. "Now they've taken all the big ones, we'll be lucky . . . " Uriah talked on, as the men tramped over Nell, Jenny, and Jacob's faint path. His voice died away as the distance lengthened between them. Once, when Nell turned to look after the men, she saw that Rass had also turned. He waved. It would be so easy to love Rass, Nell thought. But, that was the trouble. It would be easy.

"That old jealous Uriah!" Jacob said. "He's mean and I don't like him."

"I don't like him too," Jenny said.

"You shouldn't kick," Nell scolded her daughter.

"I kick him hard. He's mean." Jenny agreed with Jacob, who was charmed. "Can I have pancakes, Mama? I'm hungry."

"Fish," Nell held up her prize.

"I hate fish," Jenny pouted.

"You'll have to eat it and be grateful." Nell turned to Jacob. "Maybe he's right, Jacob. Maybe I should wear a skirt, especially if trousers turn people against me."

"I ain't heard nobody say nothin' 'bout that. He's just waggin' his old tongue. What I think is really burrin' him is that you miss Sunday meetings. Word is goin' 'round you denied the gospel."

"I never did believe all of it, not really," Nell confided in the boy. "All my life I was taught from the Bible. Nothing else."

"Ma said you got your reasons, for that and for packin' a weapon."

"I do," Nell said.

"Well, don't bother me none. My heck, who cares if you believe Joseph Smith was a true prophet or not?"

"I see it this way, Jacob: if you don't believe in a God who favors one people and in the Book of Mormon, it might bother most who do, but you can't base your life on a lie, no matter what."

"Yep. And, if I had me a shooter, I'd keep her on me."

"You would? I'm not saying you should carry one around in the civilized world, mind you, but out here, it's different. You can save yourself with a rifle when nobody else can, or will. Nobody's going to make me put my Hawkin down, not after what I know. If you want fish for breakfast, you're the one who's got to get up early and go. Do for yourself, or do without, I say."

"I don't want fish for breakfast," Jenny fussed. She had been awakened too early.

"It don't bother Brother Stiles, your packin' a shooter," Jacob squeaked when he giggled. "Anybody can see that."

Nell heard a commotion. She turned to see Rass and Uriah sprinting toward them. A great, brown grizzly charged at their heels with a half-grown cub following behind.

"Hell fire," yelled Nell. She dropped everything, except her rifle, and lifted Jenny into the dumbfounded Jacob's arms. "Run," she screamed. "Run like hell. Don't stop." Jacob galloped over the undergrowth like a colt, but Nell could not have run if she had wanted to. Something inside her gut prevented her. She crawled through the grass and under the protective bow of a pine. There, on her stomach, she fumbled in her possibles bag for a cap, placed it on the lip and steadied her aim by balancing the rifle on a rock. She took a deep breath and waited for a shot, clear of the men.

What happened next, Uriah told those who gathered around a bonfire that night. All day, Nell had been bombarded with questions about her heroic efforts and had told her story so many times it seemed stale. To avoid the onslaught, Jacob and even little Jenny took naps. But, an army of eager listeners waited to hear it again, officially.

"Well, she goes this way," Uriah began.

The camp recorder wrote, officially.

"Me and Brother Stiles was goin' fishin', see. I told Rass that fishing Black's Fork was like setting your line into a bathtub full of hungry trout, so he wanted to get to it pretty bad. We locate ourselves some of your big, green-like grasshoppers and away we go. I know, by the way the ground cover is bent over, somebody's up before us, and I inform Rass. I do. Sure enough, we meet up with the little lady. She's got the baby and Brother Brown's boy. Gad, does my mouth water when I see that three pound cutthroat the woman's packing." From the corner of Uriah's mouth, saliva collected. It spilled over onto his dense, dark beard.

"Gad, I'm ready to get fishing. But, I see the Sister here has her piece. It's primed, boys, and I'm afraid she's going to shoot somebody. I seen it before. She's asking for trouble, I said to myself. It's up to us menfolk to . . . "

"Get on with it, Brother," someone called out.

"Let's hear about Rass and the bear," someone else said. "Let Sister Mortenson tell it."

"Quiet now," Uriah said. "I'll get to that. Let's see. So, I warned her about the gun. Write that," Uriah told the recorder with his nimble tongue. "Say Uriah Urie warned Nell Mortenson against packing a primed piece." He turned again to the eager listeners. "Later, I knew I misjudged, I'll admit to that. But, generally speaking, I'm right. Gad, I still can't make out how she fires that gun, let alone hefts it, it being a regular man's piece and her being right tender-like."

Nell stood, her Hawkin at her side. "Let's get one thing straight. I'll not hand over my weapon."

"It's loaded, but not primed," added Lily. "Nell knows her gun."

"We haven't got all night," Bishop Brown said officially. "Women are stronger than you might think." He threw wood onto the blazing fire. Lily, who cradled little Sarah in one arm, circled the other around her husband's shoulder and gazed admiringly into his face. She glanced around for her Jacob, who listened with friends and mimicked Uriah's expressions.

"The woman, here, tells me flat outright her packing a piece ain't none of my concern."

"I suppose you agree, now, that it wasn't," Lily May said.

"I do, now. Yes, ma'am, I do. You don't expect a man to know everything, right up front, do you, like some gypsy? But, if you'll let me finish, I'll get to the part about the bear. 'Wait up,' says the little lady."

Nell was compelled to interrupt. "For your information, Brother Urie, my name is Nell, Tom Mortenson's wife. I don't like being called *little lady*, right to my face. Write that down," she told the recorder. Say, 'Sister Mortenson wants to be called *Nell*.'"

"Alright, then, whatever you say. Just let me get on with it. There's people waiting. Ah, ah, Nell, here, tells us she done heard something in the boonies. But, she can't make it out. Naturally . . . her never having seen nor heard no bear. Now, if it had been me hearing it, boys, I could have told you exactly what it was. I know bear."

To Nell's thinking, he wouldn't have heard anything.

"We paid her no mind. Well, I didn't, knowing how women lean to fearing the woods and caves and all. We go on a couple hundred yards and get pert near the bank when, gad, out of nowheres comes the grizz with a cub behind, bigger than me. Before I turn around to beat it, she's on her hind legs, roaring and waving them long claws over my head. Gad, I'll wager she be seven foot, or better. And me, I see the blood in them little mean eyes. She's whipping her head from this side to that, like she wants to rip me apart. Put that in the log," he told the recorder. "Whipping her head from side to side. Next thing I know'd I'm out of there like a jackrabbit. I pass poor ole Rass, beating it, same as me. I hear him scream like a woman when I pass him cause he knows there ain't nobody, now, between him and that grizz."

"Shouted," Nell said. "He didn't scream. He gave a shout when you caught up with him. You latched onto his shirt, and nearly crawled up his back to get in front of him. That caused Rass to trip. I saw it."

Disregarding the truth with a wave of his hand, Uriah described how the sow flinched when Nell plugged her. Enraged, she took out her wrath on Rass. At the moment he stood, she slapped him down. Mauled him. Nell saw her four-inch claws slash across his back and her terrible jaws close around his leg. Nothing at all could be done about it.

"Gad. Was I scared," Uriah explained.

"Watch your language," the bishop said.

"If I put all the times I been scared into one bundle, it wouldn't equal this once. I'll guarantee that. Ahead of me, I see Jacob, beating it with the baby. I see Nell, here, in the grass with her sight on us. 'Shoot, shoot,' I said. But, she must have been too nervous to the pull the trigger."

"Oh, I was afraid, plenty," Nell said. "But, that's not why I didn't shoot, right then. Rass, you see, blocked my line of fire." Nell tried to think why she had not taken flight when the bear petrified her out of her wits, so much so that she wet all over herself. She remembered a curiosity, and an excitement, that compelled her to stay and take part in the drama. It was the same force that prompted her to cross the plains and the same force that, at that moment, caused a moth to flutter slightly above the grasping flames of the bonfire. When the blaze seemed to have the moth in its clutches, it darted upward—and then drifted down again to sport with death.

"Finally, she fired off," Nell heard Uriah say. "Gad, that lead whizzed by my own ear. I don't know which I was more afraid of, that eight-foot grizz or the woman with the piece." He chuckled, but no one else did.

"Write that," Nell told the recorder. "Uriah Urie was more afraid of Nell Mortenson than the eight-foot grizz." Jacob and his friends, who screwed their faces behind Uriah's back, dropped to their knees and slapped their hands over their mouths to muffle their glee. "I ran all the way to camp and never turned my head, not 'til I got here. That's when I see Rass is not behind me. He's being knocked around like some rag doll. I hear another blast. Down drops the sow. The cub's long gone. That grizz, she nearly fell on top of poor ole Rass, all 500 pounds of her. Gad. My heart ain't never beat so fast."

Nell remembered the thud of her own heart. She remembered the offensive smell of her own perspiration while she tried to reload. Desperately, she struggled to steady a bead on the ferocious animal, but her vision blurred; perhaps, if it had not and if her arms had not weakened, she might have stopped the bear before it got to Rass. Perhaps, not.

"A man don't hardly know how he's going to react when he's scared spitless," Uriah admitted. He met the stare of the eyes that watched. "I reckon I should of stopped to help Sister Nell do the shooting. But, I'll tell you, I was in the thick of it. I just beat it to save my own hide. Gad, I ain't never been in a position where I couldn't think straight. Can't even recall dropping my pole or my rifle, but, as you saw, they fell near the place where the bear came out." Remembering, Uriah paused for some time. Then, he lowered his hoary head between his knees. His audience remained nervously silent for so long that an uncomfortable air settled, like the wings of an enormous black bird, over the whole assemblage.

Finally, Nell broke the silence. For some reason, which she did not comprehend, she needed Uriah to remain his old cantankerous self. To see him down hurt her heart. "If I hadn't had my Hawkin loaded and ready, I would have run too. There isn't any shame in trying to survive. And, if that ol' 600-pound grizz had come for me, I don't know what I would have done."

"You would have re-loaded," Uriah spoke again. "You knowed what you was doing. I didn't. You saved my life, and Rass's too, if he lives, that is."

"What happened," asked one frustrated elder who couldn't put together Uriah's story.

"Two shots, two hits," answered Nell.

Sober and tired, people sat before the fire, their gaze turned toward the tent where Rass fought against the pain of his wounds. Effie, having been coaxed from her wagon because of her expertise as a seamstress, had done her best to patch him, but she said he lost a great amount of blood. Now, she cautiously crawled from under the wagon and rested her head on Uriah's shoulder.

"How is he?" Nell asked.

Effie hid her large eyes in the folds of her husband's shirt. "He'll make it. Sipped tea."

These words were the most she had spoken to anyone, as far as Nell knew, and they were difficult to understand, her fingers playing in her mouth. Some had been wondering if she might be dumb. "Hello," she said to Nell. Then, proud that she had spoken, face-to-face, she smiled, faintly. "Back full of cuts," Effie's eyes moistened. "Leg bad. Not sew." Effie pulled Nell aside. "Scalped. One side." Momentarily, she forgot herself. "All off skin. Stretch. Fill in. Sew. Rass pieced." After Effie curtsied, she scurried back to her wagon.

One by one, the people left the fire. Some filed by Nell to give her back a friendly pat, to say "Good eye, Sister," or to simply tip a hat or smile. Uriah stayed to douse the coals.

"Your Tom would be proud, Sister Nell. He ought to been here to see you shoot that 800-pound grizz."

"By the time we enter the Valley, that bear will weigh a thousand pounds," Nell said. They both chuckled.

"You're an uncommon woman, and I'd be downright favored to

live right next to you in the valley. It don't bother me none, you denying the gospel. I figure you'll come back to it, if your man gives you a right good talking." He kicked dirt over the coals. "Listen, I'll tan that bear's hide, if you want. Make a right nice rug."

"Thanks, Uriah." Nell rested an elbow on his shoulder. "You're a forgiving man." Their laughter mingled and echoed up a nearby draw. "I don't much want to remember that old bear—but, I will—without the hide."

38

BROTHER RASS

(Diary)   July 21, 1849

Yesterday, an enormous grizzly mauled Brother Rass Stiles. I shot the bear. Never in my life do I expect to be so unnerved. All night, bears chased Jenny and me in one of those "I can't run" nightmares! This morning, Lily and I coaxed Effie Urie out of her wagon to inspect the ferocious animal: 600-pounds, four-inch claws, three-inch fangs. Out of concern for Stiles, for some lame horses, and for two broken axles, Bishop Brown canceled travel on Monday.

In the meantime, I shall care for my own children and teach those of others to read. Jacob Brown reads more skillfully everyday, and Effie, who approached me about being illiterate, is learning her alphabet along with Jenny.

For five hours at a time, little Robert sleeps. All he knows is the rough ride of wagon life. He smiles in his sleep and coos when Jenny and I talk to him. Because Lily, Effie and I are all mothering him, I am concerned that he may be confused once we go our separate ways. Visited Rass. He'll make it.

"Nell. You've got to go to Rass," Lily May said the day after the mauling. "I took my turn with him after baby Sarah woke me, early until now, and he's been mumbling about you, saying the wildest things! I can't figure. Now he's conscious, he's asking everyone outright, 'Where is Nell' and 'Won't you please find Nell for me?'"

"No. He can't do that," Nell answered. "What's wrong with him?

Doesn't he know I'm married?"

"He knows. I told him. But, he thinks he might be dying and he doesn't care. I'm tired of trying to explain to everybody that he merely wants to thank you. Huh! The way they look at me! What are you going to do?"

"Listen, Lily, between you and me, woman to woman, I can't go to him."

"Why not?"

Nell considered. Only to herself did she honestly answer Lily's question. Rass was a dashing, vigorous man, well-spoken and gifted in his craft. He had attracted her, attracted her more than she wanted.

"I don't know why," was Nell's response to Lily's question. "I just can't. If I feel sorry for him, I'll want to help him out, on account of my saving his life and all. Then, I'll be doctoring him. There's no time for that, not with my two children and the livestock."

"Tell Rass, not me," Lily said, her face close to Nell's. You can't have people talking when you get to the valley. You'll want to go to Tom, spotless as a saint. I think the man's in love with you. It has the makings of some right meaty gossip, you know."

Nell agreed to go to Rass, but not immediately. "I've got chores first," she said. "Tell Rass to hold tight. I'll come presently."

"We've run out of cloth for his leg. Might you have anything?" Lily asked.

"Half a petticoat," Nell smiled in her heart. "As you know, Lily, 'The best-laid schemes o' mice an' men gang aft agley, and lea'e us naught but grief an' pain for promised joy.'"

"What did you say? What?"

"Oh, nothing," Nell answered. "Robert Burns, about my petticoat. It doesn't matter anymore." She tore off a small ruffle, the only one trimmed in lace, and dropped it in her trunk for a memento. After Lily left, Nell sponged with lilac soap, her favorite. She pinned her hair on top of her head, and changed into a clean, calico dress—pink—the color that flattered her skin, all out of respect to a dying man. Carrying a bucket of cool water, a strip of her petticoat, a small jug of whiskey and some ginger root, she left the napping babies with Effie to go and heal the suffering.

"Nell," Rass moaned when she threw up the tent flap. "At last you've come." Lying on his side, he exposed a back, which looked like a darned and bloody sock.

"Wow, it's hot as a smithy in here," Nell said. Feeling faint, she slumped to her knees. "I don't do well with wounds," she said. "This heat! No wonder you're uncomfortable."

"Uncomfortable isn't the word. My leg . . . can it be saved? I hate pain."

Nell knelt beside Rass, whose pasty face glistened with sweat, and into his cup she poured half water and half whiskey. "Drink. Nothing is better to brace the nerves than a cup of diluted spirits, two or three cups being even better. After inspecting the leg, which appeared like a slab of meat tied for the oven, she again lapsed into a state of light-headedness. "You can have the whole jug, if it helps," she said, "but make it last for two days, at least. It's all I have left."

Rass drank the liquor. He took the cup and gladly swallowed more, then more. "Don't guzzle," Nell said. "Sip." Knowing from the experience of childbirth that a gentle touch, contrasted with the pain, provides a wealth of relief, she swabbed cool water over his forehead, neck and lips with the last ruffle of the petticoat she had planned to wear when she met Tom.

Rass sighed. "They say you saved my life."

"I shot the bear, if that's what you mean. I saved my own hide, too."

"Thanks, Nell. Thanks. I want you to know . . . "

"Save your strength, Rass. Let me do the talking." She unbuttoned his shirt. "They've kept you too hot, haven't they? You'd think people wanted the sick to die of suffocation."

"Nell, you're the only woman I've . . . "

She slipped a slice of ginger root between his teeth. "Chew, Rass. This should help you heal." She touched her finger to his down-turned lips. "Hush. Not another word. You don't want to say something in your weaker moments that you will regret later. Another drink. It will take the edge off."

"I can't endure it," Rass said.

"You have to, Rass, one throb at a time." She held his hand. "I'm sorry, my friend. I know it hurts, but you've got to fight it for a couple of days. Then, gradually, the pain will fade. Before you know it, you'll be whole again. Young, strong men like you, heal fast." What she didn't say was that gangrene could set in.

Rass shut his eyes, and when he opened them again, they glowed with anger. "It was Uriah!" Clutching Nell's upper arm, he drew her close. "He pulled me down. Didn't he?"

"Pulled you down?"

"Yes! He did. He tripped me. I remember. I felt his hand on my shoulder."

"Hush," Nell said. "Relax. Don't waste your strength on anger. Tuck it away, for now. You need all you've got to heal."

He rested for a time, then wanted to know, "Am I dying?"

"No. If you have to ask, you're not."

"I wish I were. They prayed, the elders. They blessed my leg. It didn't work worth a plug nickel." Nell dipped the ruffle and laid it, softly, gently across his forehead, marked deeply by the lines of agony. "You're the only one who helps me," he sighed. "Don't leave me, Nell. Please, don't leave."

"Hush, Rass. It won't be long now until we reach the valley, in civilization again—and no more bears. Tom, that's my husband, isn't expecting me. He planned to come for me next spring."

"Why did he leave you? A man who loves a woman doesn't leave. I would never have . . . "

"Oh, he had to," Nell explained, but she feared Rass spoke the truth. The church meant more to him than his own family. Trying to conceal her disappointment and uncertainty, Nell told Rass how Tom left with Brigham Young to pave the way for her and Jenny. She described the house that he would have built, by now, with a garden and a well in back, a flowered path to the front porch, and a big cottonwood on the side with a swing hanging from one branch.

Rass winced.

"Breathe deep and long. Relax your forehead. You don't want the lines of an old man when you come out of this, do you. Now, tell me about something you dream of, the most beautiful thing you've ever seen."

Rass lay quiet for a time. "It's a woman," he finally said. "Spirited. Willful. Kind. Intelligent, blue eyes with a ring of darker blue around the iris. They see right through a man, into his soul." Holding Nell's chin, he turned her face from side to side. "A straight and noble nose, but not too large, and a little milky way of freckles across it."

"Rass" was all Nell could say. Wanting him to continue, she feared what he might say next, the liquor having taken effect.

He pulled a pin from her hair. "When the sun shines on her hair, it's all afire with red and gold, but in the shadows, it's dark blonde. A man could get lost in it." He pulled another pin, and her hair fell on one side.

Nell pinned it up again. "For my sake, dear Rass, if not for your own, say no more. I will not, I can not, call on you again." She collected her things and her composure. "But, remember this: you were spared for a reason. 'There are more things in heaven and earth, Horatio, than are dreamt of in your philosophy.'"

"I won't tell anyone that you quoted from the Book of Mormon," Rass said.

"I didn't. That's Shakespeare!" Nell laughed. "What a flirt you are, Rass. Your mission is to heal yourself and live. We are all depending on you." What she wanted to say, but didn't, was "if I were free to be courted, you are the man I would choose to court me." But, it wasn't right. It wasn't right because she had journeyed most of the way across a continent. For what? For Tom, for family and for home. She chose not to pursue Rass, and not to allow him to pursue her. And, that choice would make all the difference. Yesterday's experience brought home to her an important lesson that she had learned over the twenty-four years of her life. If you flutter above a flame, you might get burned. And, Rass was, indeed, a flame.

He moaned.

Nell lifted the cloth from the leg. Because circles appeared before her eyes, she quickly soaked the cloth in whiskey, returned it and slumped down to clear her vision.

"Will I be lame?"

"I don't know much about doctoring, Rass. Thank God it wasn't your face." Nell didn't want to frighten him, but, in her opinion, he'd be fortunate to keep the leg and, if he kept it, he may limp. "I never ceased to marvel at the body's power to heal itself." What a pity it was that this statue of a man had been disfigured. Silently, Nell wept. "How I wish I could suffer instead of you—for a little while, at least."

"I wish you could too," Rass faked a smile. "Friends?"

"Friends."

39

HOME?

July 31, 1849

Tomorrow, God willing, we will enter the Valley of the Great Salt Lake.
So say scouts from the settlement who joined us two days ago to aid and
encourage us over the worst terrain of the entire trek, the Wasatch Range.
Even though the elders have improved our pathway, we've broken more
axles in the last week than we did in all times past. Zigzagging up one steep
summit, the Brown's wheels collapsed inward, all at once.

Willows. I've seen enough of them to last a lifetime. They block the trail
and tear our wagon covers. Even the stumps, where travelers have chopped
them to the quick, are severe on the wagons. Because of them and some very
steep banks, we crossed one creek at least a dozen times.

With Lily and Jacob, I rolled boulders off the top of one steep mountain to
watch the velocity of their descent. How they rumbled and echoed! How they
smashed to pieces! These V-shaped canyons grow lush with pine, scrub oak,
birch, vines and wild wheat. Along the way, Jenny and I have eaten elderber-
ries, currents and gooseberries too.

Oh, happy day! I can hardly describe my feelings on reaching the place
so long desired to see. With the end in view, my feet are heavy, but my heart
is light. My babies need a solid bed to rest their little heads, and my apple
trees need planting before they wilt away. Soon, I shall beach the Ark at the
door of my beloved Tom. My only hope is that he is alive and well, that he
has rejected any and all widows and that he will open his arms to this weary
gentile.

"There it is!" One of the scouts galloped past Nell's wagon. "See through the V? Zion." The valley appeared faint and far away, so Nell strained Blondie and Samson with a willow across their rears. The scout sped on to point out the view to Rass, who sat up in a shallow, uncovered wagon, which moved forward in front of Nell's. After Nell had tutored Effie, she had begun to speak in broken English. However, Lily informed Nell of the full details of his recovery. Effie's patchwork on his head had taken. His back, though it would always have the appearance of being darned, was also healing well. But, the bite in his thigh, no stitching could mend; only the man's body could do that. Traveling hurt Rass. Still, he refused to stay behind.

Late in the afternoon, the company pulled onto the foothills overlooking the full expanse of the valley. Shaped like a serving bowl, mountains surrounded it all around. Nell's first impression of the settlement itself was that the whole thrust had been spent on planning and basic survival, on food, meager shelters, and protection. With a large fort at the center, wide roads clearly followed the plan of a grid, like those in Nauvoo. Living quarters consisted of a few finished homes, but mostly people lived in makeshift cabins, tents, and wagons, which clustered close to the fort. Fewer dwellings dotted the outer landscape where fences surrounded meadows and animals grazed, where creeks, glowing in the evening sunlight had been diverted for irrigation, and where fields of yellow grains promised a heavy harvest and gardens backed every lodge.

Suddenly, the company gave up a general shout. They threw their hats high into the pink atmosphere and yelled, "Glory to God. Glory to God in the highest! We are home." Many in the train gathered around Brother Brown like children who wondered what to do next, and he offered a prayer of thanksgiving.

"Our kind Heavenly Father. We, thy children, give thanks unto Thee for delivering us from bondage into the land of Zion. According to Thy promise, great suffering brings great rewards. Never again shall we be molested or driven from our homes. Thy road has been rough, oh Lord, but we are willing and shall become a mighty people in thy sight. Now, we pray that Thou wilt continue as our Shepherd as we go our separate ways to mingle with Thy greater flock. May we be a blessing unto them and unto Thy Kingdom. Home at last. Glory be to God! In the name of Jesus Christ, Amen."

A welcoming committee arrived on horseback to escort the newly arrived to a resting place where they and their stock would receive care. "You are not to worry for your futures ever again," one of them proclaimed. "Pastures await your animals, and land awaits the work of your hands. We have spaces for the shops of craftsman. Here, at last, we are all brothers and sisters. Your need is our own."

Nell, with a pang of regret and confusion, bade farewell to her friends. For so long, the trail had been her life and these people had been her fast companions through such intense hardships, that leaving them hurt. She hugged Lily May and Jacob and shook Moot's strong hand. They promised to visit one another soon. "If church is the only place where I shall find you, I will be forced to go," Nell told Lily. They all laughed. She found Effie in her wagon, crouching low. "There you are, Effie," Nell said. "We must see one another soon. The baby will need you, probably for the rest of his life. You and Uriah may want to live close to us."

"Nell Effie love," Effie said, chewing on her collar.

"You are my Effie, Nell said. "When we're all settled, I'll have a school. Will you attend?"

"She will," Uriah said in a booming voice. "Depend on it. But, for now, we've got to get going."

Nell hugged or shook hands with many of the others, especially the children she had schooled. Rass had turned to wave goodbye to her at intervals throughout the day. Now, he wished her well. Then, not knowing where to go, she asked one of the welcoming committee if he knew where the Mortensons lived. The man offered to drive her second wagon so Jacob could ride Friendship to the immigrant staging-place with his family. Another man, volunteered to come along and help with all of the animals and equipment. "You Elizabeth's sister?" he asked.

"No. I'm Tom Mortenson's wife."

"Well, if that don't beat all," he removed his hat. "Uncanny how a man can work and pray side-by-side with another man for two years and never be told about his wife. Uncanny. I guess this is Tom's little girl. She's his image." He bent to shake Jenny's small hand. Then, his eyes fell on Robert, bundled in Nell's arms and less than a month old. He scratched his brow and frowned.

"How'd you come to bring the two wagons, sister?" the other man asked. "And all the livestock?"

"It's a very long story," Nell said. Having crossed also, the men accepted that it was. One led the way while the other tied his horse to the back of Glady's wagon and went about the business of driving the ox team into the valley floor. Far off, Rass waved to Nell. She thought she heard him yell something like, "Remember what I didn't say to you." Darn Rass, paying no attention to what people might think. He needed a good wife to look after him.

"Will I go to Father now?" Jenny asked.

"Yes. But, not tonight. We don't want him to see us for the first time in three years when we're dirtier than front porch rugs. Do we? We're going to your Auntie Elizabeth's house. You'll like her. She's light-hearted and young and very pretty."

"Are there bears at her house?"

"None. No more bears."

"Good," Jenny said, trying not to suck her thumb. "We don't like bears."

Evening came on. Nell pulled up to admire a view of spectacular color. Like a ball of fire, the sun balanced on the western horizon. In front of it, the Great Salt Lake shimmered like a white satin ribbon, and over it a few wispy clouds blushed pink on their undersides. Behind it all, the sky changed gradually from brilliant gold at the horizon to soft lavender behind the clouds and, finally, to the truest blue at the zenith; the east flushed with pink. The very air hung thick with pink; it glowed on the wagon covers, on the horses' hides, and on Jenny's soft cheeks.

They passed acres upon acres of crops: corn six feet tall, yellow wheat almost ripe for harvest, barley and oats, one patch already cut and standing in bunches. Oxen, cattle, sheep and horses grazed in fenced fields. They passed several log cabins so small that Nell wondered if the Mormon people had already bought themselves slaves. To her surprise, four white children played in front of them and a woman sat nearby under a lone tree. She waved and called "yah ho" to Nell. Then, stretching her back as if it were out of joint, she hastened to a thriving garden at the side of the road and bent over a row of carrots. After pulling one, she held it high for Nell to see.

The closer they drove, the more obvious it became that most shelters housed many people. When one stately log house with an upstairs and windows all aglow came into view, Nell cherished the thought that it must be the home that Tom had built for her. Not so. When she asked her guide if it were the Mortenson place, he replied in the negative. A little way up a dusty lane, however, he pulled up in front of a tiny log cabin sealed with adobe. "This is it, sister," the guide told her. "Looks like your folks are home, so we'll be going along now." Nell thanked the men, who galloped away.

At an uncurtained, unglassed window, a face appeared. A halo of fine, white hair suggested an angel. Then, Elizabeth exploded out of the doorway. "Nell," she screamed. "It's you. You've come." She was far gone with child, and a two-year-old reached after her. Except for her stomach, she was nothing but skin and bones, and her once rosy cheeks had sunken inward to a degree, which added ten years to her life. She fell into Nell's arms. They kissed, and each gazed long and lovingly into the other's face.

"Elizabeth, what has become of you? Are you well?"

"Yes," Elizabeth replied. "Some." One of her once beautiful teeth had begun to rot. "I am feeling a bit better now, I think." She leaned heavily on Nell's arm. "But, look at you, Miss Nell, brown as an old cotton picker. And trousers, too! What's this?" she asked, her hand on the long knife at Nell's waist. "I can't believe my eyes."

"Who is it?" Heber called from the house, his voice like Tom's.

"It's Nell," cried Elizabeth. "She's home."

Heber, who wore suspenders over his long handles to hold up his oversized and tattered britches, hurried to Nell. He picked her off the ground and twirled her round and round, all the while kissing her neck.

"Where's Tom?" Nell asked.

"Gone. There's a party up the canyon, having trouble making it in. Tom left yesterday to help."

"We don't know when he'll be back," Elizabeth added.

"Oh," Nell's voice faltered. "He must have passed me on the way. How could I not know it?"

"Tom takes shortcuts."

Elizabeth frowned at Nell's dirty clothing. "You'll want time to clean up anyway, won't you?"

"We make no pretenses here, Nell," Heber said. "Those days are long gone. You go to him as you are."

"Oh, I will. But, not with sunblisters and tangled hair. I've got to wash. You must promise me, Heber, that you won't mention my name to him until I am prepared."

"You haven't changed a peck, Nell," Heber chuckled. His face looked gaunt and drawn. "The crossing hasn't touched you, thank God."

"It touched me, Heber. Believe it."

"Only to make you even more beautiful," Elizabeth longingly said.

"Robert's fussing, Mama," Jenny called from the wagon. Nell turned to her children.

All of them crowded into the two-room cabin to show off their babies and to become reacquainted around a table made of crates. Nell told them about Glady, how her husband drowned in the Platte, and how, after giving Robert and all her earthly possessions to Nell, she died. Night darkened the house, so Elizabeth lit a short candle. While it burned, Nell, speaking matter-of-factly, told them that her guides had been stricken with cholera and had died "in spite of my desperate efforts to keep them alive." Again, she lied. But, this time, it was for the love of her family. She would live by it.

"Tom won't want to hear that," the astonished Heber declared. "Do you mean to tell us that you crossed the plains with two men?"

"No, not to begin. People dropped off."

Heber grimaced.

Nell didn't dwell on an explanation, but told them that after the men had died, she acquired their two pack burros and saddle horses along with food, mining tools, rifles, and the gold her father had paid them to deliver her to the valley. Out of a leather pouch, Nell spilled over a hundred and fifty dollars in gold pieces.

"Lord be praised," whispered Elizabeth, not wanting to awaken Little Nell, who had fallen asleep in her arms.

"I have waited a long time to show you," Nell cupped Elizabeth's bony hand in hers. "Where's your money can? Whatever I have is yours." She started to tell them about Rising Sun when the candle flickered, spit and died away.

"Shall we light another?" Heber asked Elizabeth.

"Can't. That was our last. You know that." She turned to Nell. "We've been saving it for a special occasion."

Elizabeth and Heber offered their only bed to Nell and her babies. Nell thanked them, but refused saying that the wagon had become their home and both she and the children slept comfortably in it. "But, tell me one thing more. Where is Tom's place?"

"Just on the other side of that corn patch," Heber told her. "Don't expect too much, my dear." He left to unharness Nell's teams and to turn the animals into his pasture for the night.

"Let me move that Blue mare, Nell called. "Don't go near her. Leave the goat in her cage." She turned to Elizabeth. "These babies sleep better on full stomachs."

"I'm not a baby," Jenny said.

"No, you're not," Nell agreed. "You've crossed the plains."

When Elizabeth suggested that they take a walk to see Tom's place, for an enormous full moon had risen over the peak of what everyone called Mount Olympus, Nell unhesitatingly agreed. With their babies, the two women sauntered up a lane.

"Is he well?" Nell asked.

"He's well. He's got ten acres into wheat and ten more in corn. Nice crops. Like the rest of us, he's had two very lean years; planted too late the first, too early the second. Those of us who stayed at Winter Quarters nearly froze to death, you know. Nearly starved. The journey about killed us. Little Nell, here, has never been well."

"She's not Nell," Jenny said. "Mama's Nell."

"I named her after your mama," Elizabeth explained.

"Thank you," Nell said.

Elizabeth went on to explain that after this year's harvest, the animal misery would be history. "Now, the farmers know about the growing season and irrigation. Coming in, did you see the gristmills all over the valley? Waiting to grind all this wheat. We're proud of our new water driven sawmill. It can cut up to a thousand feet of lumber in a day!"

"Answer me one question, Elizabeth. Why didn't Tom come for me when Heber came to Winter Quarters for you?"

"To have you live like a gopher? Look at me, Nell. I'm a skeleton. Can't you see what I've been through? I lost my first child. Stillborn, in the starving time."

"Starving time?"

"Spring. But, you, you're the picture of health, you and fat little Jenny."

"I'm not fat," Jenny sniffled. She wanted "up." Holding Nell's leg, she asked, "Is this my Auntie Elizabeth? You said she played. You said she caught butterflies."

"Not hardly," sighed Elizabeth.

Jenny squinted in disgust. "I'll play with your girl."

"She's tired and a little rough around the edges," Nell explained. "Watch out she doesn't kick you. There will be time now to teach her

manners." Nell stopped walking and turned to Elizabeth. "Are there
other women? You know, polygamy."

Elizabeth smiled, but covered her hand over her teeth. "Whatever
do you mean? Tom? Heavens, no! He's too busy raising crops and sacrificing for others. It's not the women you're up against."

"Thank heaven!" Nell sobbed from relief. "What does he say about
me?"

"Not much. I stopped mentioning you a long time ago when I realized how it injured him. I did hear him talk, just lately, about fetching
you from Quincy next spring. Why didn't you send him a message
in these three years? One small word would have meant the world to
him."

Nell tried to explain her bitterness about Tom's leaving her and a
newly-born child with the parents who had disowned her.

"They intercepted his messages to me, and after Ruby brought
herself to reveal everything, I left. It hasn't been all tea and cakes for
me either, you know."

"I suppose not."

As they strolled up the lane, Nell reveled in the soft sounds of
night: the rhythmic chirping of crickets, the rustle of the breeze over
heads of wheat, the croaking of far-off frogs. Smelling the irrigation
water running through young alfalfa made her think of the Mississippi
River and home.

"If I know you, Nell, you're dreaming of a home like we had in
Nauvoo. Well, let me tell you, here and now, it isn't. In fact, it's rather
rough, not quite . . . ah . . . well, how shall I describe it? You'll have to
fetch water from the ditch, for one thing. For another, Tom built it . . .
temporarily . . . for himself. What I'm saying is that you could go there
with cracked lips and tangled hair. But, look, there it is!"

Elizabeth could never have prepared Nell for Tom's shelter. A hut!
No wider than two privies, but not as tall as a man, with no windows
and not even a step at the doorway. Compared to it, her two wagons
were castles. "Hell fire," cried Nell. "That's where he lives? Dirt floor
and all. Shit! I knew it."

"It's more than I had when I got here," Elizabeth scolded. "You be
thankful that the roof doesn't leak, that you have a roof, for that matter.
There's a little hearth in it to keep your hands and feet warm in the
winter and a dugout underneath where water never freezes. Behind, is
a maturing garden . . . a cellar to store your carrots and potatoes. He

shoveled that out last week. It will be chuck full by fall." She wiped Nell's face with her tattered handkerchief. "Stop feeling sorry for yourself. You've got nothing to whine about. In the morning, you'll see the extent of Tom's work. From here on, everything is gravy."

"It's not that, Elizabeth. I just thought . . . " Nell sobbed for herself. "I'm all tuckered out, that's all. I still feel the bumping of the wagon in my bones."

"You don't know how it's been, living here on the fence between life and death. Tom continually thought of himself last. It consoled him, knowing you and little Jenny were comfortable."

"I would rather have been here, Elizabeth. I could have helped."

"How long have you gone without food?" Elizabeth asked. "Have you ever spent every hour of the day dreaming of biscuits and gravy . . . or just biscuits?"

"I don't particularly like biscuits, nor gravy either, but I have given many a thought to Ruby's apple dumplings."

"Land of Goshen! Try surviving an entire winter on twenty pounds of potatoes and a pound of tea!"

"Who ever did that?" Nell asked.

"I did . . . at Winter Quarters!" In the light of the moon, Elizabeth's resentment hideously flowered on her face.

"I'm sorry," Nell said holding her. "I'm awfully sorry."

With her dreams shattered, Nell tucked her children under their covers in the Ark for still another night. Then, one-by-one, she tossed away each fragment from a chest full of dreams: the large house with a winding staircase like the one Arthur had built for her, the summer-house stocked with hams and pans of milk floating with yellow cream, a slave woman to help with the children and household duties, a stone-faced bustle oven in the dining area, a feather bed and a room for the babies to nap in, all day if they wanted. She discarded the dream of the one-horse carriage she would use to drive to town. To town? What town? The town was a fort! Out went the idea of an orchard behind the house, tea parties with friends, and the big maple tree with a swing. Had she asked for too much? She thought not. In Quincy, the morning before she met Tom, she had all this and more . . . but not love.

All night the words she had told Jacob at Black's Fork came back to her, "If you want fish for breakfast, you've got to get up early and go fishing." Nobody was going to fish for her, not then and not now. She realized, on this night, what Tom must have understood when he first arrived in Nauvoo and in the valley. With the journey over, the building must begin. In the end, she promised herself, and God, that if Tom could love her for herself, she was willing and able to help these Mormons build up another community. After all, hadn't she killed a bear?

40

HOME, AT LAST

I have crossed the great American prairie. Home, at last!

Early the next morning, Nell awoke to the flapping of her gingham dress against the canvas. She opened her eyes to it, and recalled that it had flattered the pink tones in her complexion more than any dress she had ever owned. With intricate tucks at the bodice, lace trim on the sleeves, and tiny covered buttons down the front, it was certain to please Tom the same as it had the first time she wore it to meet him at the Old Mill in Quincy. That was a lifetime ago. She had better hurry inside and iron it. She had better make herself look presentable, while she had a chance. Nell knew, from experience on the trail, that after the day started, she'd have no time for herself. None at all. If a woman had written Genesis, "no time for herself" would have been mentioned, right next to childbirth. That was a woman's plight.

Should Tom return and go to the far side of the house, where she had pulled the Ark with Blondie tied to the back, he'd rush to Elizabeth's. He'd ask why the unfamiliar oxen, the burros, Samson and Blue were in his pasture. That would certainly spoil her plans. No. Tom must see her before anything.

Way off, toward the head of it, plodded what appeared to be a shabbily dressed, old beggar. With a shovel over his shoulder, he stumbled, perhaps on a clod, but quickly caught himself, and moved up the furrows. Nell thought nothing of him until she turned to deliver the milk to the children. Something in the man's gait gave her pause.

Once again, she watched him. He removed his warped hat to wipe his forehead with his sleeve. Tom! Her beloved Tom! How long she stood there, she did not know. She did not know that her mouth fell agape or that her heart beat double. She did not feel the milk that spilled over the side of her pan and soaked her trousers. When Tom disappeared into the tall corn, she hurried to feed Robert, who had begun to fuss.

After Robert had his fill, Jennifer said, "Little Jenny's hungry, Mama," and Elizabeth called, "Breakfast." Until she set a tin plate in front of Nell, with the same flourish she used to serve a fat, roasted hen in Nauvoo, Nell failed to comprehend the severity of the family's need. Thistle roots, camas bulbs, and a two-inch carrot lay in the bottom of her dish.

"When the wheat ripens, the Mormon people will never go hungry again," Heber apologized.

"We've had spinach," Elizabeth said, holding her stomach. "I bit into an ear of corn yesterday, but there wasn't much to it. It's hard to wait."

"I saw Tom," Nell said. "I must go to him."

"Another week, and we scythe the wheat," Heber said, smiling at Nell's comment. "After that, we pick corn. We'll trade with gold rushers for sugar." He massaged his wife's shoulders. "Then, you women can make us cakes, all we can eat. Lord, how I dream of sweet cakes!"

"Don't mention it," Elizabeth whined. Her face turned pale when the two-year-old tugged at her sagging breast. "I hate it that I can't feed her. She never gets enough."

"Oh, my darling Lizzy. Forgive me," Nell begged, feeling almost ill at comprehending their dire hunger. "I was too busy thinking of myself to realize. My old nanny is dripping with milk this morning. Have all you want, for yourself and the babies. Robert and Jenny thrive on it."

"Truly? Praise the Lord," cried Elizabeth.

"I've got flour, over two hundred pounds of it." She combed her hair in the reflection of a piece of window glass on the wall. "Cracked wheat too, all you'd want. Beans, salt, jerky, tea, crackers, cornmeal, molasses, even a little dried fruit, and a few old squash cakes. Have it all. You're hungry."

"We make do," Heber said.

When Elizabeth collapsed onto their only chair, Nell sent Heber to milk Nan. She scurried for a bag of fruit and the makings for flap-jacks with honey. Returning, she knelt beside Elizabeth. "I'll watch over you and Little Nell and the one to come the same as you watched over me when I had Jenny." Quickly, Nell tried on the gingham dress. "Use flour, sugar, and a little dab of that yeast," she told Heber. Beat it gently. Place that can of honey by the fire. It's hard." She cupped her old friend's face in her rough hands. "Morning sickness?"

"I need food, that's all."

"It's over, Elizabeth. Right now. I have sugar, enough to last for months. Jenny and I slept on it all the way. And, we can stretch the honey with water. *The Frontier Guardian* said I should bring enough to sustain us on the trek and for six months after. A cock-eyed idea, I thought, but I brought it anyway. I did. With my grub and that in my second wagon, we have plenty. Plenty of livestock as well."

Heber was ready to fry the batter, but he had no lard for the pan. "Oh, I forgot," Nell told him. "The lard's on the left side right next to that sack of rice."

Cleaning her teeth, Nell once again caught a glimpse of Tom moving in and out of view while irrigating the corn. Even from the top of the field, she recognized his heavy shoulders; hunger and spirit-breaking work had not changed them. She remembered him at his plow in Nauvoo, straight-backed, thick-necked and filled with male energy. She remembered carrying his lunch and water to the field and sitting with him under a maple tree while he heartily ate. Though she lacked culinary skills—and still did—he never failed to say he liked her cooking. Then, they lay together in the shade. What kisses they shared! His mouth was so much like hers that she sensed nothing except the feel of it, warm, innocent and bold.

Nell brushed her hair and tried to pin it up, but it wouldn't stay, so she tied it back with her strip of leather. She couldn't help but be aware of the feeding family. Elizabeth, Heber and Little Nell devoured the flapjacks. They reminded her of old Wolf when she threw him scraps for the first time. She watched Heber drink half a cup of honey—straight. While the incident broke her heart now, she thought that, one day, they would laugh together about it. It helped her to understand Tom's urgent need to advance the people past the survival stage because, in this, she was now one with him. "Is there any meat for my beans?" she asked. "I should set some to boil for Tom, when he comes in. For the life of me, I *will not* have him starving."

Elizabeth said they had none, and never did have much, since Tom and Heber used the last of the gunpowder last February. She gulped down a cup of Nan's warm milk and shut her eyes to the pleasure of it. "Once or twice, Tom snagged a cottontail by poking a long stick down its hole. But, these two, they're too proud to ask anybody for anything."

"It's time they learned." Nell recalled a line from Shakespeare. 'The firmest friendships have been formed in mutual adversity, as iron is most strongly welded by the fiercest fire.' Gad, Lizzy," she said, also remembering Uriah's favorite word, "there must be three kegs of powder in the wagons: balls, patches, primer, four rifles, and even fishing poles. My land, I want to go hunting. Coming in, we saw mountain goats on the foothills, and antelope, too. It was all I could do, not to shoot them."

"You, shoot?" Heber made an inquiring, fixed glance into Nell's face.

"Well, yes." Nell pretended to take aim.

"Oh, Nell! I'll believe it when I see it. In the wheat, we sight an occasional jackrabbit and deer too, if we had the means to come by them."

"We do now," Nell said, going to the window to look for Tom. He was midway down the field now. When he dug his shovel into the earth and came up with a heavy load of mud, which he easily flung to dam a furrow, she flushed with the same heat, which warms the blood after drinking a cup of hot tea. She remembered her love of watching him work. Behind the corn, he disappeared again.

At the "mirror," Nell pinched her cheeks. With a trembling hand, she pushed some stray hair behind her ears. If the sun had not baked her skin, if Elizabeth had not wasted her hoop, which Nell had asked her to carry west, to build a corral gate, and if her petticoat had not been used to heal her friends, she would have looked somewhat like she did when she first met Tom—if it had not been for her cracked lips. She smeared a dab of honey over them.

"How beautiful you are!" Elizabeth said. But, her voice had in it a yearning for the old days and the sadness of what was not.

Nell swept Elizabeth's words over the floor of her mind. "How ridiculous I look," she finally said. "I want you to have this dress, Elizabeth, for later, after the baby. There's a deal of manual labor here, and it doesn't suit me anymore." But, what she thought was that wearing it, in these hard times, with these beloved people would not be right. Against the tattered and faded clothing of her family, she'd stand out like her blistered lips. Embarrass them? No. She didn't like it.

Along with other supplies from Quincy, she had packed her self-ishness, but somewhere along the way, she had thrown it overboard. The used-up petticoat didn't matter anymore. She pulled off the dress which Elizabeth accepted with much gratitude. As if Indians were swooping down on her, she slipped on her Kentucky jeans and muslin shirt; she fastened her belt and adjusted her heavy knife at her left hip. Around her neck she hung her powder horn and possibles bag—in case she spotted a deer. Only, the button shoes remained on her feet, for the warped, hard boots, which had seen her from the Mississippi to the Great Salt Lake, were done.

Ready to go to Tom, Nell glanced out the window. He was closer now. Suddenly, he threw the handle of the shovel high into the air. The blade had broken off. He stomped around. If Nell had not known better, she would have thought he was cussing. Helpless, she watched him kneel to clear a furrow with his hands. This was not right!

Nell dropped the ribbon she was about to knot around her hair, and flew to her wagon. The shovel lay hidden where she had left it, behind the rice. She pulled it out. Now, it did not matter where it had been or what it had done. Tom needed it. That was all she knew.

"Watch my babies," she called out, sprinting past the cabin and up the road toward Tom's property.

A work plug trotted up the lane in front of Tom's shack. Astride it sat two women. "What now?" Nell said aloud to herself. From their spry manner in sliding off, Nell judged them to be very young. They dressed like twins, in long and thickly gathered skirts—as if they owned all the fabric in the world. Seeing Nell, they froze with their arms around one another and waited for her approach. One of them carried a basket. With a curtsy, she uncovered it to display a batch of sweet breads.

"What's your need?" Nell asked.

"We're the Gardner sisters," said one. "We're the ones that brings bread to Tom." Between each sentence, she stuck out her tongue and took a couple of short pants. "We watch out for him," the other panted too. "He helped our brother put up a cabin after planting time, last spring. A man like that has an appetite." Connecting bonnets, they giggled, the way little sisters do.

"Our father was killed," said one.

"At the Haun's Mill Massacre," panted the other.

"We brought turnips last week," said one.

"Swiss chard," said the other.

They both panted.

"It's us that has first pick," they announced in one voice.

"First pick of what?" Nell asked. She set the shovel down and pushed the sharp blade deep into the crusted road. She capped and cocked her rifle. Girls like that wouldn't know it wasn't loaded. "Well, I hate to be the one to bring you sad news," she glared into their bright, naive eyes. "But, I'm Nell Mortenson. I'm Tom's wife." She nodded at the basket of bread. "He won't be needing that. Clear out."

She had to help them mount their plug. As they trotted away, their dust settled on Nell.

Behind Tom's shack, Nell passed a peeping chick that had slipped through its cage. The frantic hen beat her wings and clucked to attract it, even though she sheltered a half dozen others under her wing. To the side of the pen was the fruit cellar Elizabeth had described. Next to that, a wooden stake had been driven recently into the baked ground with other stakes around it like a constellation of stars. Did she dare to dream that Tom was about to build a home . . . for their family?

Then, she saw him in the wheat field checking the heads. She called his name. He turned, and turned full around. He studied her . . . and she him. Blood pounded in her neck, the midday sun pounded on her head, and her button shoes pounded toward him on a worn pathway through the wheat.

"Nell?" she heard him call. "Is that you?" The sound of his voice paralyzed her. He closed the gap between them, slowly at first; then, he stopped short. Rooted like a pine, he stood while the wind of recognition whispered through his bows. "My beauty?" he shouted. He ran. She ran. With a broad grin across his sun-baked face, he opened his arms to her. Though a strong, natural impulse urged her to fall upon the shoulder that she had yearned for and to kiss the face for which she had, so desperately, pined to see, she stopped short. Her outreached arm, palm forward, signaled to him that something stood between them.

"Why didn't you . . . ? Britches? Whose knife? How did you get here?" He asked everything at once.

"I never believed," she blurted out. "I was baptized falsely, because

I wanted you, not the Church." She let it rain on him and, somehow, finished that which she had planned, for months, to say. "Most likely, I'll never believe, exactly."

"I know that," Tom said softly. His lips turned white with desire. "You knew it all along?"

"From the first. Still, I had to have you," he reached out his familiar broad palm.

Dumbfounded, Nell chuckled inside her soul. Though her path of guilt had spanned a continent, she had deceived no one, not Tom, not God, and not the Mormon people. Only she had believed the lie.

"Can you accept that I *do* believe?" Tom asked her.

"I've always accepted it, haven't I? I love you as you are. Your people are my people."

"Well, then, is it settled?" Tom realized that she needed to clear the past. Face-to-face, each memorized the subtle, and not so subtle, changes in the other, the deepened lines, the shadows, the loss of weight and luster, and the clothing, his worn and soiled, hers, those of a backwoods boy. Each smiled.

"One thing more," Nell said. "I have a baby." Tom's smile and the tenderness around his eyes faded away. Before her statement hurt him, she added, "My dear friend died giving him life. She asked me to raise him. I said yes."

"Well . . . " Tom stood silent. He picked and began to shell a grain of wheat. "Almost ripe," he said and pushed it into her mouth. At last he said his final word. "His Will be done. A man needs a son. Is there anything else?"

"Not now. And you?"

"Nothing that won't wait."

Like a sparrow, Nell's freckled hand went to nest in his. Though she tried to blink them back, tears of relief welled under her eyelids like water when it fills a cup slightly over the brim. She blinked, and they spilled over her cheeks. Gently, she set her rifle down.

"Well, then?" he said. "You've come a long way, Miss Nell Mortenson. Take the last step." He pulled her to him. They held one another long and close, and each wept on the other's shoulder for the lonely, vulnerable spaces where they had walked apart and for the fact that no amount of talk could ever fill them in. Each uttered the soft sounds that people make when knowing they are loved. Each kissed the other, on the eyes, the neck, the hands, and on the lips. Nell reached between her breasts to retrieve a scrap of paper, with a faint *Tom* printed on the outside. "Your letter," she said placing it in his hand. He pulled the leather tie from her hair and unbuckled her belt where the long knife hung. Nell removed the gear around her neck. Freely, his hands roamed over her waist and hips. He lifted her off the ground. When she slid down against his hard body, he nestled his face between her breasts. Each melted into the other. Home at last, they dropped into the wheat and barely noticed when the irrigation water began to seep under them.

41

TAKING ROOT

(Diary)   *October 10, 1849*

Tonight, I sit before a roaring fire sipping tea with the man I love. The cellar is stocked with smoked venison, pumpkins, carrots, potatoes, onions, squash and sundries. Grains overflow the bins in Tom's old hovel, our livestock huddle together against the wind in fenced fields, and our children sleep in their own beds. Gracious friends are building all around.

We are able to entertain occasionally because of a long table and six elegantly crafted chairs. How shall we ever repay Rass? I have written to my family.

One Sunday in October Nell composed a letter to her loved ones in Quincy. A neighbor, about to leave for Hannibal and return with his family in the spring, had offered to deliver her letter to her parents by his own hand. So, Nell wrote under the shade of her own newly constructed front porch, which she considered not only a luxury, but also an expression of Tom's love. He built it to suggest the one at her parent's home in Illinois, where his first utterance to her had been *beautiful*. In doing so, he put her in touch, a little, with her past and the dear people she would, most likely, never again hold. It was odd, she thought, that she now pined for those with whom she had so easily parted.

Perhaps it was best that her parents could not see her now. Lye water had roughened her hands, exposure to the elements had weathered her once fair face, and hours of tromping over clods and clearing her garden area of rocks had spoiled her button shoes. No amount of gold could purchase a new pair, for the cobblers in the settlement, inundated with orders, did not promise her any until December. Every now and again, it became necessary to secure them with another strip of rawhide. But, never mind the shoes. Few had new ones, and the old had developed into a symbol of pride for having made the trek or for being willing to toil for the right to worship unmolested and build a prosperous community.

"*Jennifer and I have made it safely to the Valley of the Great Salt Lake,*" she began her letter. "*Entering it was one of the brightest moments of my life. I could hardly believe the long journey was accomplished and I had found my home. A dear friend died along the trek, leaving us a perfect, thriving baby named Robert. Fortunately for him, I brought the spotted goat. Thank Ruby.*" Due to a scarcity of paper, Nell composed with small inscription and cut her information to a minimum. Ordinarily, she might have begun with a description of the amazing mountains, which towered to the east and blazed like fire with red oak and yellow aspen. Looming above, they grounded her, filled her with the sense of knowing who she was and where she belonged.

"*I found Tom well and whole,*" Nell wrote. For emphasis, she underlined it. She recalled the first day they met after her crossing. While she walked by his side, he finished watering the wheat field. How gratefully he accepted her shovel! When she said, "Thank goodness it will be used to grow food, instead of planting people," Tom wanted to know what she meant. As Nell had planned, she did not mention her guides, but she wept when she described how she helped to deliver Robert. When Tom dammed a watter furrow, he told her he had to kill two Indians, but he wouldn't say how or why.

"We rested our livestock and bathed in a lush ravine," Nell said; she didn't mention Moses.

He said, "The crops failed in '48," but wouldn't discuss the starving time. Neither did he seem anxious to give detail to "we paid a heavy price building the trails." And he would not explain the long, white scar on his leg. "Some things are better left unsaid." He hung his head over the shovel.

"I know." Nell planned to never again mention the scar.

Walking across the top of the field, they laughed together about the mud in Iowa, about using chips for fuel, and about the time Nell fooled the Shoshone. Incredulously, Tom listened to her stories about learning to shoot and killing antelope, prairie chickens and the bear. When she told him about cutting the rope from Wolf's neck, the wrinkle between his eyes deepened.

"You shouldn't have gone near a wolf," he scolded. "Why the devil didn't you wait for me? I said I would come!"

After Nell explained why she chose not to wait, he finally admitted that he admired her judgment. At the end of the day, after the wheat patch had been watered and Tom had devoured a huge helping of beans, they sat silently holding one another on Elizabeth's frontstep.

"Unbelievable," Tom shook his head. "All that way just for me. I'll do right by you, Nell Mortenson."

"And I by you."

As the days passed, they talked their talk. Old memories washed away; new ones grew, and the shovel became just another shovel.

"A clear stream runs year-round, nearby," she went on with her letter, thinking that Christina would giggle if she read about the irrigation ditch between her home and Elizabeth's. It did, indeed, run year-round, but, because it flooded in the spring, Tom and Heber dared not divert it too close to their homes. Nell was forced to use a horse-drawn cart to carry the occasionally muddy water for Elizabeth and herself. In the spring, when the ground thawed, she hoped they'd have a well. This, she chose not to write.

But she did proudly reveal several details concerning overall prosperity. *"The Mormon people live freely, beneath the security of self-government and the protective barrier of mountains, which few outsiders desire to cross. After the harvesting began in August, life quickly improved for everyone,"* she wrote.

And, it was so.

"Sturdy homes, similar to our own, have sprung up all around." She chose not to say that her "lovely home" lacked window panes; instead, little hinged doors which could be tightly locked against the winter's cold and fall's insects and vermin, covered the openings. The prospect of being shut up inside a dark cabin all winter drove her to the porch now, in spite of an October chill; however, she preferred dark, closed rooms to the blistering cold that Elizabeth described with cougars, coyotes and wolverine prowling about in deep snow. With or without glass, Nell wished that Ruby and Christina and all of them, including Arthur, might see for themselves.

Even while her place took shape, the men started adding two rooms to Elizabeth's. Nearby they put up the Urie cabin and, to Nell's complete and joyous surprise, the Browns'. The gristmill ran day and night to grind their wheat and corn, and smoke rose from every chimney, a sign that the women had again begun to bake pies, pies overflowing with pumpkin and squash from the gardens and crab apples and serviceberries from the canyons, pies topped with rich, thick cream, and venison pies, too.

She wrote, *"I am content to live among these admirable people. An infinitude of cordial generosity exists among the Mormon women."* Lily May, and dozens of other ladies, rode sidesaddle back and forth from one cabin to another sharing their bounty, exchanging recipes, assisting with childbirth and curing bilious fevers. Effie, who lived near enough to walk, often spent the night to care for Robert and sometimes carried him home for a day or two. Clearly, the child had two sets of parents. The words "let me know," "see you on Sunday," and "I'll help this afternoon" were more often used than "farewell" or "good luck." Nell was happy to report, *"Even my fragile little apple trees took root and sprouted leaves."* The number of leaves that sprouted was only three, but they turned yellow two months after and dropped to the ground like those of indigenous trees, and Nell knew they had survived.

She wrote briefly of an increase in personal belongings. *"Great numbers of emigrants, limping toward California gold mines, passed through our valley this summer. We have traded our foodstuffs and fresh animals for their stressed livestock and some of their most prized possessions."* By the time the gold rushers had hauled items over the Rockies, they seemed glad to be rid of anything but the bare necessities, especially after hearing vivid and ominous descriptions of the western desert and the Sierra Nevada Mountains. One day, when a young couple from Missouri stepped onto her property, Nell felt uncharitable, especially after Elizabeth whispered in her ear to remind her of earlier persecutions and the resulting trek that followed.

"What do they want, Nell?" Elizabeth scowled. "All patches and shreds," she whispered to Nell. You better go for your rifle."

"Indeed," Nell said and she scurried toward the house. Near and ready for any eventuality, it hung above the hearth next to Tom's and the powder, patches and balls. Indians, not altogether friendly, wild animals, and misfits lured by dreams of instant wealth in the California Territory, were known to pass through the area. This was Mormon country, and she meant to support the effort to keep it that way.

"What's your need?" Nell called out to the curious pair. The husband said they had abandoned their wagon before crossing the last of the Rockies "on account of it falling to pieces before our very eyes." He was as tall as his wife was short, one of those husbands who takes one step while she takes two, a pacing, on-the-go type, who runs on nerves, not bread. By a rope, he led one of his horses; by the braid, he led his winded wife. Advancing, the rag-tag man asked if the Mortenson women would be interested in trading breadstuffs for a few articles. "We'd like to unburden one of these plugs and ride it," he said.

"Ran out of flour way back," the redheaded, diminutive woman hung her head. Her nose was as small as her ears, but neither was so small as her lips that looked like a straight line, drawn on paper. She grew uncommonly thick hair in her braids and on her arms, and it was red and shiny, the kind of hair one might like to pet. Both were all patches and shreds.

They reminded Nell of her lonely desperation on the open prairie. They reminded her of the small leather pouch full of hand-polished stones, the water gourd, the sun ritual and the kind, exotic face of one who might have been hostile. "I may be able to make a swap with you," she told them with her eye on the mahogany dressing table, strapped to a huge horse. A dressing table! Three drawers with rounded edges and shiny brass knobs, perfect places for her mother-of-pearl brush and comb and three cherished handkerchiefs, edged by her mother's hands!

"What do you have?" Nell asked.

"Well, this here . . . " the woman-child sighed. Though she smelled very much like her horse, Nell placed an arm around her shoulder. "This here table," said the girl and rubbed the surface with a dirty, but loving hand. "Josiah says I'm never gittin' it over the Sierras. It was gived me on our weddin' day. Pa gived it. He maked it." She wiped her nose on her shredded shawl and then covered her hairy arms with it. "Dead, now. I mothered it this long way from St. Louis, this long way, and him wantin' to switch it for scraps." When she yanked her braid from Josiah, he didn't know what to do with his anxious hand.

"We got to eat," Josiah gruffly told her through his long, untrimmed beard. "She's bone tired, that's all," he explained.

"What will you take for it?" Nell asked as Elizabeth munched on a turnip.

"Flour, cornmeal, coffee, whatever it is you got," Josiah said.

Elizabeth pulled Nell aside. "I wouldn't be trading to any low-down Missourian," she warned her. "Tom won't condone it, I know that.

You don't want to run short with the kind of winters we have around here."

"I like it," Nell said. "It's the right thing to do." She turned to the girl, having made her decision. "I'll care for it as you would. A brief spark of light shone in the girl's eyes. "I'll fill your flour sack, ten pounds, ten pounds of corn meal, a squash, five carrots and all the salt you want. Bargain?"

"Bargain," the miniature woman agreed, but her bottom lip quivered.

"You won't think bargain when we're all famished," grumbled Elizabeth. In spite of recent prosperity, she fretted continually over food storage, as if spring would not come again. She hung sacks of flour on every wall in her chamber room, and with all the sacks full, she double-stitched the hem and sleeves of a good dress and filled it to the neck with crushed wheat, for mush. Under her bed and in a washtub, she hoarded cornmeal and even oats for a milk cow. "Learn from the squirrels," she kept telling Nell. "I, for one, will be prepared for a crop failure. Never again will I watch oxen grow fat in the fields while my babies starve in the house."

"I think you're wise to give it up," Nell told the heavy-eyed girl, whose skirt had shredded to the knees. "It will only slow you down, if you're going on, that is. But, if you want my advice, it's too late for travel. I'd winter over here." Reluctantly, the girl who was not quite a woman nodded for her husband to give the table over to Nell, but she turned away from it and wept as if she were parting with a child.

"Latch onto that flour and be grateful," Elizabeth told them. "We remember Missouri." She probed in her pocket for a slice of raw potato, which she craved lately. "God only knows how hard we've toiled for our flour. Better to trade that piece now for something you can bite than to leave it on the desert for lizards to hide in."

"One more thing," Josiah said.

"Not that," the wife said when he began to unleash a small leather trunk. She restrained his hands. "Not my sacred treasures!"

"Hush, Henrietta." Josiah shoved her aside.

But, he should not have, for that was the end of young Henrietta's tether. Like claws, her hands shook an inch from his eyes. "Take me home," she screamed. "I need Ma. I never asked to come!" Then, she scratched her way up his back and nearly toppled him. When he dropped the trunk, she pounced upon it and covered her body over it like a cat protecting her kitten. "I hates you," she howled. "It's ain't yourn to swap."

"Tired?" Elizabeth asked, finally trading bitterness for pity. Holding her stomach, she reached out to touch Henrietta, but reconsidered. Instead, she turned to Josiah. "What's wrong with you? A man ought not push a woman as far as *he* can go. Get it?" She paced around Henrietta. "Wait here. I'll bring bread and a cucumber."

When Tom and Heber came in from the fields, they sympathized with the rejected and downcast Josiah, in spite of his being Missourian, because he said he'd never heard of Mormons until a few weeks back. They offered the pair a square meal, which Nell ended up cooking and a comfortable straw bed for the night, which Nell ended up making in the woodshed. Elizabeth bent over her washboard to scrub their clothes and directed the exhausted girl toward the ditch where she might groom, but she told Nell, in private, "I'm not heating water for that wildcat."

When the Mortensons waved them off the following morning, Henrietta marched north toward the fort with the little leather trunk on her hip, and Josiah rode south on one plug, his foodstuffs strapped to the other, toward the California territory. "If she hadn't looked at you as if you were a duck, coming out of the oven, I might have helped her," Nell told Tom. "There was trouble in that brash glance." Tom laughed like he used to when they were first married. Henrietta's story was much too complicated for the letter, so Nell moved on to write, "*We've acquired a cow and a calf.*"

That came about because a surprisingly large number of travelers foolishly neglected their draft animals, even to the point of death. Nell knew the attitude. Instead of being a way of life, the trail was, for them, an urgent journey toward a goal. Not two weeks after she arrived, a family that had abused their animals and killed a mule out of neglect traded their cow and a newly-born calf for Moses' and Cutter's burros. They went with Nell's blessing. She never liked seeing them there in the field. The cow looked so gaunt that Tom doubted she would make it through the night; nevertheless, she did, and a daily ration of oats, plenty of running water and free roaming in the harvested pastures quickly revived her and filled out her sagging flesh. The new mother eventually gave excess milk.

Her ink and paper nearly depleted, Nell longed to be able to converse with her family face-to-face in order to explain in detail how she came to meet Rass, how she shot the ferocious bear, and how he surprised her, only yesterday, with a most extravagant gift.

"I am much ingratiated to a very generous friend who has given us six intricately carved chairs," she wrote. *"I can not tell how dear they are to me."* From that one sentence, she could have written a book. Oh, how Ruby would have loved such a story! Even if Nell had more paper, she didn't want to say that until now, she, Tom, and Jenny had supped at their table sitting on tree stumps, which weighed so much Nell could not move them when she scrubbed the floor. She didn't want to say that on the morning when Rass knocked on her door, she had been sitting on one of those backless, uncomfortable stumps, reading Bronte's *Jane Eyre* and yearning for her comfortable rocker, left for thieves in their sweet Nauvoo home.

One day, when she opened the door, Rass stood before her, whole and more fine-looking and straight standing than ever. Having driven in a stiff October wind, his face glowed with robust health and his dark hair hung in thick waves over his broad forehead and at the nape of his neck.

"Rass," Nell flung open her door. Before she thought, she jumped into his arms. He smelled like pine, sage and snow all-in-one.

"Nell Mortenson," he exclaimed, hiding a secret behind a half smile. "I see that he did indeed have a home ready and waiting for you. Too bad! I hoped to find you destitute and weary for a place to rest your lovely head."

Nell smiled. "Rass, you'll never change. Come in before the wind carries both of us away. Shall you take a cup of tea?"

"I shall, gladly. But, first, come. Have a look at what I've brought."

In his open wagon, Nell found chairs! "For me? Oh, Rass, what a dear friend you are." He set three of them around her long table, their backs being those he had carved during the journey. On one, a buffalo grazed, its shaggy coat standing out in relief. On another, an alert antelope stared out from the polished wood, frozen there in the act of stomping a foot. "The Ark!" Nell said while seating herself on a third chair.

"The very one," Rass said. "Good eye, as usual." He knelt beside her, as if to propose, and took her hand. "Is he good to you?"

"Yes. He's a gentle, upright man."

"Shall I mention polygamy?"

"No," Nell said. She dreaded hearing, or saying, the word . . . but bore it in the back of her mind like a throbbing sliver under her nail.

"And, do you love him . . . still?"

"I do."

Rass left and came back with the other chairs.

"These I carved after I set up shop near the fort. You should visit me, sometime, to see it. Thriving business. No payments in money, yet, but plenty of grub, clothing and services. I've got a tight cabin," he said, placing the fourth chair where the setting sun hit it. A campfire glowed there on a pale swirl in the wood. The Rocky Mountains towered over a tree-lined creek on one, and, on the last, a grizzly bear stood on its hind legs, its fangs as ferocious as in real life. Nell admired each while Rass rolled the stumps away from the table and against the wall. He limped.

"Never have I seen such beautiful chairs, Rass!" Nell exclaimed. "How will we dare to sit on them?"

When Jenny crawled onto each to try it out for size, Rass took her into his arms and kissed her cheek. "I miss you," he said. "Someday soon, I'll bring a chair for you."

"How will I be able to pay you for these treasures?" Nell asked.

"Nobody could pay for them. I did it out of . . . "

"Oh, here's Tom. Hear Sergeant's hoof beats on the lane? Papa's home," Nell told Jennifer, who rushed to open the door.

"Who's here?" Tom burst inside and a rush of cold weather followed him. In his heavy winter coat, he looked solid and virile. Eye-to-eye, the men froze stiff, like one male elk confronting another.

"This is Rass Stiles." Nell, noticing the tension between them, cleared her throat. "Remember? The man I told you about, the one who was mauled?"

"Yes, ah yes. How do?" Tom offered to shake. "I recall, now, seeing you at the fort." The broad and the narrow hands shook. They gripped too hard and too long for congeniality.

"Rass has made me—us—some chairs." Nell pulled them out from the table.

"I see that," Tom said. Taking his position close to Nell, his leg pressing against hers, he slid his arm around her shoulder. He looked, not at the chairs, but at his stumps, set aside against the far wall. "We can pay you in wheat, I reckon. I've stored plenty to do that."

"Nell has already paid," Rass told Tom, whose eyes narrowed.

Nell, her legs weak, sank onto one of the chairs.

"She saved my life. For that, I can't repay her, but I hope that these, being my best work, show my gratitude." Rass nodded and gave Nell a half-smile.

For too long, nobody spoke.

"Well, I should be off before the storm blows in," Rass sighed.

"There's one more piece. I suppose you could fetch it, Tom."

From the doorway, Nell followed the two men with her eyes. Never had she seen so striking and so capable a pair as they strode abreast in their heavy boots. They shook hands again, and Rass climbed into his wagon to deliver the last item, a rocker, the finishing touch that makes a house a home. Down the length of its back stood a woman with a rifle in hand and a child clinging to her skirt; she gazed toward some far-off mountain peaks. Upon close inspection, Nell found the woman's skirt was slightly raised. Curled about her leg was a vine of wild roses. Nell could have wept.

"I told him I'd bring him all the flour and venison he needs for the winter," Tom said. "That may cut us short, but the man deserves his pay. I'll get the stumps outside." With ease, Tom carried the logs that Rass had rolled across the floor, one under each arm.

Nell heard the front door open and close. Tom's voice called out, "We're home. If it's alright with you, I invited President Brigham Young and two of his counselors to supper day after tomorrow."

Nell dropped her pen. Hurriedly, she wrote, *"Brigham Young, President of the Latter-day Saints, is coming to supper, and I must shine Grandmother's silver."* Since returning the silver blade to the case that one time on the plains, she hadn't touched it. Why hadn't she buried it on the spot, she wondered, and, in the same thought, decided to ignore, if possible, the emotions that clung with the knife like blood. She needed its length for making a clean slice on the venison roast, she reasoned, and that's all. After polishing the silver, Ruby's pumpkin pie recipe must be located, the floor must be swept, the table set, the potatoes peeled, and she had to remind Lily May to bring the bread hot. If only Ruby had come with me, Nell thought; she's deft at preparing supper, and, besides, there's so much I haven't told her. *"I long each day for the sweet bosom of my family,"* she concluded. *"Fervently, I pray that all is well with you. Ever yours, Nell."*

In the last bit of the space, she wrote, *"Tell Ruby I did right."*

42

WHEN BRIGHAM CAME TO SUPPER

(Diary)   *October 12, 1849*

Today President Brigham Young, Wilford Woodruff and Jedediah Grant came for supper. We were highly honored. Oh, joy. Young has promised me a schoolroom of my own. Also, he approached the dreaded subject. Shall I write the word? Polygamy! I must say, it had no effect on me, not in the least.

"How many pine hens did you kill?" Nell asked Tom.

"Two cocks and a hen." He dropped an armful of wood beside the hearth.

"We can't go short, not on President Young. He's used to the best. Are you sure that's enough?"

"It has to be," Tom said. "I'm not killing our laying chickens, not for anybody." From behind, he held her. When he nibbled on her ear, her first impulse was to slide around in his arms and kiss him, but she had to keep busy kneading the bread; this afternoon, in fact, she would meet the Lion of the Lord for the first time. "Don't fret," Tom whispered, his hands moving firmly over her hips. "Pine hens are almost all breast . . . like you." When his new beard scraped across her neck, she turned, grabbed both of his ears with her floured hands and gave him a juicy smack on the mouth.

"Go on, now, set Jennifer at the table. It's venison stew from the deer I shot. After you eat, take our babies to Effie. She's going to mother them for us. And, don't forget to fetch Lily May's pies. Then, check in the cellar if the cream has risen so I can skim it off. I've got to churn the butter and sweep the floors and . . . "

"You already swept twice." Tom dusted little clouds of flour off his ears. While Nell planned aloud, his attention was drawn to a crude sketch of Brigham Young that hung on the wall below his rifle. He had won it in an arm wrestling contest. Knowing it would please Tom, and President Young, as well, Nell had taken down her rifle to replace it with the likeness.

"Gracious touch," Tom said. "You must not lather yourself up over this, Nell. I think the Prophet is more interested in counseling us than in gorging himself. He said he needed to discuss something or another with me."

"Did he say what?"

"No."

"I can guess. There's talk of sending people to colonize south of here. If that's it, we're not going, Tom. You tell him that."

"His will be done," Tom said. "If the Lord asks us to extend his Kingdom here on earth, who are we to refuse, being instruments, as we are, in his hands?"

"Where have I heard that before? I suppose you must decide whose hands you are in, but I can tell you this, for certain: my trees are establishing themselves and stand an even chance of bearing an apple or two next fall. They won't bear moving."

When Nell plopped a serving of scorched stew onto Tom's plate, he grinned and pulled her onto his lap. He tried to rub berry juice off her cheeks. "If you must paint up, please use a little less," he teased. "What kind of example do you think you're setting for our daughter?"

"Why, I have nothing on today," Nell merrily sassed. She slapped his hand away. "My cheeks are naturally rosy."

"It's syrup," Jennifer laughed. "She did it, and so did I."

"Painted ladies, both of you." Tom growled and bit Jennifer's sweet neck.

"Eat, Tom. Then, shoo. I've got to scrub dishes and rub tarnish off the silver, if possible. It hasn't been polished since Quincy, you know. The butter! I forgot to churn it."

"Ah, forget it. Use the old brick. Sit down here beside us and eat. Then, we'll all walk together in the warm sun, up to the big willow tree at the head of our field. It won't take long. I've got a surprise for you."

"I can't, I tell you. Not today. Everything has to be *celestial*, don't you see? He's accustomed to . . . " To save her legs, Nell churned from her rocking chair. How she loved it! Now that the days had grown shorter and colder, she relaxed on it each evening with her feet propped near the blazing hearth. Wrapped in a quilt, which dear Lily May had brought one day, and reading from the *Rubaiyat of Omar Khayyam*, which most Christian leaders frowned upon as blasphemous, she sipped her tea, concocted from joint weed and wild peppermint. After a few sips, she usually dozed in the chair that curved to fit her body like an old slipper.

"Shoo, Papa." With the miniature broom Tom had made for Jennifer, she swept under the table around his feet. Tom gathered the straw that fell away.

"You're the image of your mother," Tom rubbed his daughter's cheek. "But, you've painted only one side and it's so close to your mouth that it looks like a spill, not a blush." He turned to Nell. "Brother Stiles thinks much of you, I see. The other day when I took him a load of breadstuffs, he said he would accept no payment from me. Said it's between him and you. What does that mean?"

"A bear. That's what's between us. Rass needs to give. But, we need to go beyond that, I think, to accept the giving, gratefully. Accepting is the harder of the two, especially if you're proud." She side-glanced at Tom.

"You're a good person," he said savoring his scorched stew. "With all my religion, I sometimes wonder if I can measure up to you."

"I love you, Tom Mortenson."

"I love you too, Beauty. Can't live without you."

For a time, their love filled the kitchen to the brim, leaving no space for thoughts of jealousy, betrayal, or anger or petty misunderstanding. It muffled the scratching of Tom's knife across the everyday tin plate and softened the swish of Nell's churning cream. Tom, his expression as peaceful as when he said he loved her, averted his attention to the likeness of Brigham Young.

"What did Governor Young talk about in meeting yesterday?" Nell wanted to know.

"Plural marriage, mostly. He said, 'God never introduced the patriarchal order of marriage with a view to please man in his carnal desires, nor to punish females for anything which they had done.'"

"Then, why does it punish?"

"Oh, Nell. You know there are blessings. The greater the sacrifice, the higher the glory. Those Saints who live their religion will be exalted."

"In what way can a man be exalted with three bickering wives and twenty screaming children? Answer me that."

"You should have come to meeting. As close as I recall, Brother Young stated, 'If I be made the king and lawgiver to my family, and if I have many sons, I shall become the father of many fathers—or the king of many kings.'"

"Ridiculous! How can a woman find satisfaction in that? It's man-talk. While Tom stroked the beard he had begun to grow for the winter, Nell pushed her churn aside. "And, don't delude yourself for one moment into thinking that this territory will ever become a state while its people practice plural marriage! The rest of the country won't have it. We will be singled out and molested, all over again. We will again be plagued. I tell you, I don't like it. It isn't right."

"It's in the Bible, Nell. In this latter day, it's God's commandment to his people. God's laws override man's laws."

"In heaven, maybe. But, we have to try to live on the earth." Nell poured liquid off her butter. She salted it. Into her "all the way from Nauvoo mold," she pressed it, and then rushed it to the cellar to cool for Brigham. "This is going to be a long day," she told Tom as he left to take Robert and Jenny to Effie.

It was long, indeed. Nell carried endless buckets of water from the ditch and heated endless pans of it over the fire. In the water, she washed the white napkins, cut and hemmed from Jenny's cast-off blanky; she was a big girl now. In it, she scrubbed breadboards and cleaned her cupboard doors, thankful that she had doors. She washed the pine hens before setting them into the Bustle Oven, thank God for it, to bake. And, in it she set to boil the bounty of their garden: crisp potatoes, bright carrots, large onions and beets. By the time the sun had begun to slide toward the distant western mountains, her hands had wrinkled like last year's turnips, but she hoped they might appear normal before the Prophet arrived. "I'll be damned," she said when the gravy boiled over the pan.

"Beauty, you must promise you won't cuss while he's here," Tom said, who had retrieved Lily May's warm pumpkin pies.

"I thought you said he'd have to accept us for what we are." She carefully set the table with her "carried across the continent without one breaking" plates. Glady's painting of Chimney Rock embellished the wall near the table. As moonlight had softened it on the prairie, candlelight would soften it now.

"Don't do it. It's important to me."

"I shall not swear, Tom. I promise. I even promise to be pleasant and silent, unless I am spoken to . . . if you'll take me to your swing tomorrow."

"Who said I had a swing?"

"You did."

"I said I had a surprise for you."

"Oh, I thought . . . " Like a wife of twenty years, Nell knew what Tom was about to say before he spoke.

"Well, I will take you to the swing," he said, carrying inside an armful of wood. "If you're willing, I'll push you as high as you've ever been." He grinned widely.

Flirting with her eyes, Nell hurried outside to grab a few stems of copper tobacco weed and yellow-topped sagebrush to use for a centerpiece. She smoothed footprints off the bear rug that Uriah had tanned for her.

When Tom said he heard the church leaders drawing up the lane in their carriage, Nell removed her apron, rushed to her cracked face mirror, rubbed bees wax over her lips, and straightened her eyebrows. The mirror reflected Tom, preparing himself for his patriarchal role. Tucking his shirt into his trousers and adjusting his topcoat, he stood straight and cleared his throat. At that last moment, Nell lit two tallow candles, which she and Elizabeth molded and decorated with lace, the last evidence of Nell's beautiful petticoat. "It looks like Christmas in here," Tom said.

When Brigham Young, Wilford Woodruff and Jedediah Grant pulled up to the hitching post in their buggy, Tom greeted them while Nell set the table with the three pine hens, whipped potatoes, gravy, watercress, boiled vegetables and balsam root, which Heber called "Mormon biscuits." Nell graciously seated the men, who admired her silver and her flo-blue dishware.

"Napkins," Woodruff said. "This reminds me of the old days. Special."

"You'll never know," Nell told the kind man, who lowered thoughtful eyes as if he understood.

"Fine chairs," Young told Tom in a low and resonant voice. Then, identifying them as "dear works of art," he asked who crafted them. He noted that such chairs would embellish his parlor. After a lengthy prayer by Brother Woodruff, President Young noticed his likeness on the wall and expressed his gratitude. When he complimented Tom for his fine vegetables, Tom said proudly that the garden grew only after his wife began to care for it. "She has apple trees too, in the back. Brought them by herself across the prairie this past summer." Brigham made no further comment, but he praised Tom for his ability to raise corn, barley and wheat; he said that if Tom couldn't make the land prosper, no one could.

"Thousands of Saints will gather in from the nations of the earth in the years to come. This will become the great highway of nations," Brigham prophesied, eyes fixed on the mounds of steaming potatoes. He called Tom in the name of God to continue his production of wheat for the gathering of Israel in the great state of Deseret.

"His will be done," Tom replied with respect.

A kind of reverence hung about the men, which sent chills through Nell's body. When President Young looked thoughtfully into her face, she held her breath. Since he was known to be an excellent judge of character and a prophet, Nell wondered, in spite of herself, if he were aware of her imperfections, her swearing, her rejection of the doctrine and that one unmentionable sin. But, to her relief, he said nothing about that.

"I have heard that sister Mortenson is a teacher," he said. "We must look to the education of our children, and I think it wise that she begin her work as soon as possible." Before Nell as much as nodded in the affirmative, he instructed Brother Grant. "See to it that a schoolhouse is built near here with a proper heater for the winter." Tom smiled with a sort of tension in his jaw, and Nell had to turn away to avoid appearing excessively pleased.

"For when the elders are called upon missions or must devote their time and attention to the growth of the kingdom, the wives must be industrious and provide."

"His will be done," Nell said.

Tom rolled his eyes at Nell's capricious remark while the self-proclaimed governor asked if they had offspring.

"We have two very fine children," Tom proudly told the leaders, "a girl and a boy. Nell's midwife in Nauvoo recommended that she have no more children." This comment amused Nell because Tom had misinterpreted her midwife's remark of more than three years ago. "She's the worst woman I've ever seen for having babies" was what the woman said, and Elizabeth had agreed. Nell smiled.

When Young told the couple they should consider plural marriage, Nell dropped the spoon from the gravy dish, and her hand faltered when she bent to pick it off the floor. There it was! Polygamy. Attempting to freeze her facial expression, for she feared the Lion of the Lord and hesitated to come between Tom and his conscience in the presence of his leaders, she wiped the gravy off the floor and served a second helping of hot bread. The counselors praised the sweet flavor of her yeast and asked if they might have a start.

"It hurts my feelings," Tom's prophet continued, "when I see good men, men who love correct principles and cling to the counsels of the Church, who have lived near to God for years and have always been faithful, with not a child to bear up their names to future generations, and I grieve to reflect that their names must go into the grave with them."

Nell shut her eyes and prayed for God to be with her. She knew what was next. "His will be done," Tom would say, while he stood surrounded by the Gardner sisters, their mother, and the twenty children of her most dreaded dreams. She envisioned herself packing the Ark and waving goodbye to all her friends as she and her children began a long journey back to Illinois. At the same time that she envisioned it, she knew there was no going back. She could, however, support herself and the children by teaching in the schoolhouse Brigham promised her.

Thick and heavy as a winter quilt, a tense atmosphere spread over the room, but Brigham Young's voice droned on as if he were simply telling them to obey the Word of Wisdom or to love one another. "Under this law, I and my brethren are preparing tabernacles for those spirits which have been preserved to enter into bodies of honor, and be taught the pure principles of life and salvation, and those tabernacles will grow and become mighty in the Kingdom of God."

Before Nell's eyes, the room swirled, the butter melted, and a trickle of perspiration made its way through her hair at the temple.

"It would please me to see good men and women have families; I would like to have righteous men, such as yourself, Brother Mortenson, take more wives and raise up many holy children."

"More bread, your honor?" Nell coolly asked. Her blood boiled.

The robust leader paid tribute to the Gardner sisters whose father had been massacred at Haun's Mill in Missouri, and Nell remembered the two silly girls, the ones who brought Tom a basket of food last summer, a day after she arrived in the valley. Young said their mother was a hard worker, an agreeable woman and that the daughters were also of childbearing age. Wouldn't the three of them glorify his sturdy home? "The people of this Church owe much to these women for their sacrifice," Young added.

"We expect you'll support the Prophet's request, Sister Mortenson," Elder Grant said.

Clearing the plates and reaching for an answer, Nell avoided Tom's eyes. "Ask my husband, Sir. He is both a servant of the Church *and* a principled man." That would satisfy the elders. But, Nell wanted her say. She wasn't about to allow anyone to ruin her family, not after coming this far. Their weapon was words. "But, because you asked me, I am forced to be forthright with you. Polygamy is a shortsighted proposition." She looked square in the eyes of each man. "I'll not have it," she might have added, but that was between Tom and her. Elder Grant's back stiffened in his chair, Woodruff's spoon clanged on his plate, and Young quizzically arched his brows at Tom.

"I know quite a number of men in the Church who will not take any more women because they do not wish to care for them." The Governor lowered his eyes at Nell while the other two nodded agreement. "A contracted spirit causes that feeling. I have also known some in my past life who have said that they did not desire to have their wives bear any children, and some even take measures to prevent it; there are a few such persons in this Church."

Tom frowned.

"When I see a man in this Church with those feelings and hear him say, 'I do not wish to enlarge my family, because it will bring care upon me,' I conclude that he has more or less of the old sectarian leaven about him, and that he does not understand the glory of the Celestial Kingdom."

"How is the pie?" Nell asked.

Jedediah Grant said it was the best he had ever eaten, and they all complimented Nell upon her ability to satisfy the palate with what .could have been a monotonous meal. Wilford Woodruff found especially palatable the pine hen, calling it "a most succulent delicacy." Tom licked the pumpkin and cream off his lips while the other three men wiped theirs with the white "borne all the way from Illinois" blanky. Nell knew she would be boiling off the stains directly after they left.

Brigham told Tom to think upon what he had said and to remember, "Saints who live their religion will be exalted, for they never will deny a revelation which the Lord has given or may give." At the door, he shook Nell's hand and told her to keep an open mind.

"I always do," she said.

"I know you'll do what's right," he told Tom.

With the President's hand resting on his shoulder, Tom escorted the elders to their buggy. When their voices faded, Nell cursed aloud the revelation of Joseph Smith. Then, she flung open the boarded window, and the crisp October air rushed over her perspiring brow. She unpinned her hair and wiped her hot neck with her apron.

Through the door across the room, she scrutinized Tom and the elders while they talked and gestured in a congenial, vigorous manner. Then, there was a moment when Tom stood eye-to-eye with President Young. While placing a firm hand on Young's shoulder, he shook with the other. Surely, he was saying, "If it be His will." They parted, and Tom raised a hand, Indian fashion, after the departing carriage.

Briskly, he entered the cabin, rubbing his beard and murmuring to himself. Nell turned her back on him to brood upon the steep, snow-tipped mountains that she had grown to love, the mountains that gave her a sense of permanency, a sense of always knowing where home was.

Behind her, Tom stomped about the room. She heard him open one of her drawers. He dropped something inside and shut it. What was he doing? Stalling? Avoiding his inevitable decision? Again, he paced, the sound of his boots pounding in her chest. Soon, his firm hands gripped her shoulders, and when he turned her around to face him his eyes told her a long story about love.

"Shall we fetch our babies?" he asked. "I want them home."

In his arms, Nell saw that Tom had removed from the wall the likeness of Brigham Young. He had returned her rifle to its former place on the wall.

"I feel more comfortable when that's within your reach," he said with that one-sided smile.

"His will be done?" she asked.

"My will be done," he answered. His moustache twitched. "No other wife."

"You're damned right," Nell almost blurted out. But she didn't. Overcome with the joy of having completed a long and perilous journey, she rested her head on Tom's shoulder, the place she had so desperately struggled to be.

"We both did right," Nell said. "Thank God we're home."

ABOUT THE AUTHOR

Laura Stratton Friel is a lifelong resident of Utah, where she has a deep historical heritage. Raised on a farm in Cedar City, she attended Southern Utah State College. In English, she earned a BA from Brigham Young University and an MA from the University of Utah. She published short stories and won a national award for a feature article, now in the Utah history text, *A World We Thought We Knew*, McCormick and Sillito.

Laura spent most of her adult years in Salt Lake where she and her husband of forty years raised three sons, Strat, Aaron, and Jared, and she worked as an English instructor. Though she has "retired" in Ivins, she writes, travels, gardens, enjoys outdoor recreation, and teaches English at Dixie College. She loves her family and friends.